A Fitzwilliam Legacy:
(Volume II)
New Year Resolutions

Tess Quinn

A FITZWILLIAM LEGACY

A Novel in Two Volumes

❖❖❖❖❖

Volume I: Seasonal Disorder
Volume II: New Year Resolutions

.

Cover Design 2013 by Garland R. Travis

Cover Art from original photograph by the author

ISBN-10: 1484864616
ISBN: 978-1484864616

DEDICATION

For my girls: Annika, Jessica, Abigail and Megan

*In the hope that they too will someday appreciate the wit,
humour, and romance of Jane Austen*

And for 'Nugget',

In the hope that he will grow up to be someone's very own Mr Darcy

ADDITIONAL TITLES BY TESS QUINN

The Road to Pemberley (Ulysses Press, 2011) – contributor
short story: "A Good Vintage Whine"
Pride Revisited – collection of short stories, CreateSpace Press, 2013

COMING in 2014

A Tale of Two Darcys (working title) – a novel of
Fitzwilliam and Georgiana Darcy

ACKNOWLEDGMENTS

Releasing fiction to the public can be a daunting enterprise for an introvert, but made infinitely less risky and more pleasant with a support network. Fortunately, mine has been extensive. To all the *Pinkers*, my thanks for furthering my love (and comprehension) of Jane Austen, and especially for encouraging me from my first efforts at writing Austen-based fiction. Moreover, my gratitude to you for friendships that carry me through every challenge is illimitable. A special extra thank you is added for Sandra Platt, who graciously hosted my stories on her website, where this novel also debuted in altered form in its first iteration.

Many thanks as well to Kate Warren, Regina Silvia and Suzanne Boden for their sage observations and advice on plot points, language, narrative clarity, and grammar and punctuation. Any remaining shortfall in readability belongs squarely to me – as I gratefully accepted most of their enhancements even as I wilfully disregarded certain of them for my own purposes.

A huge thank you to Garland Travis, for sticking with me on cover designs even through the desertion along the way of not one, but two, illustrators. I appreciate your attitude, your encouragement – and your graphic talents! I must also thank Janet Taylor for her help in converting my photos to workable art on short notice and during a crazy-busy time.

I lost a colleague and good friend this spring, quite unexpectedly. Carol Maslowski expressed an interest in reading my fiction, and would devour each draft chapter as soon as it was written. Her enthusiasms proved a welcome cure for writer's block on too many occasions to count! We used to discuss my characters and their stories as though they were our friends, rather than words on a page. For that, I thank you, Carol – and I miss you! And thanks to Maria Maldonado, the enthusiastic third partner in our monthly 'dinner and period film club' where so many of these discussions occurred! The laughter we shared at each gathering was balm to my soul.

Lastly, loving thanks to my family – none of whom fully comprehend this penchant of mine for Jane Austen but who never miss an opportunity to make sport of me for it, to my delight.

CHAPTER ONE

Tuesday, 1 January 1799 (New Year's Day)
Pemberley, Derbyshire

❖❖❖❖❖

"NO! ELIZABETH," Darcy's voice took on a tone to brook no argument, "I will not have it!"

Lizzy glared at her husband but to little effect. She was at something of a disadvantage for a fair argument – she was still abed only a few moments after awakening, lying comfortably back against soft pillows, the linens pulled up to her neck against the chill of the room. Darcy, on the other hand, not only had risen, but was fully kitted out in his shooting attire; he stood rigidly with bright daylight from behind giving his large frame a dark, hulking presence. Though not angry in the least, his expression as he towered over her was well set in formidable obduracy to lend credence to his words.

Lizzy was not a woman to tolerate being dictated to, but to be fair she could count only three instances in their marriage, in their whole acquaintance – this occasion to be included – when her husband had lain down such commands. And if she moved past her very natural resentment at the liberty, she would have to admit that in each prior instance, he had been completely in the right in his judgments, blast him.

He was right this morning as well. Moreover, she knew what compelled his urging; not only could she excuse it but she must admire him for it. She would not argue the point long, only enough to establish that she could. Then she would capitulate as a dutiful wife, having made her point, and lie back again in blissful submission. For the command Darcy had the temerity to issue was that his wife remain in bed for much of the morning.

"Darcy, I am not debilitated, I can get on perfectly well."

1

"You are exhausted, Lizzy, and little wonder. We are all fatigued, but you... and Jane... you want rest. I will not have you, either of you, taking ill for overtiring yourself with social formalities."

And therein lay his anxiety. How could Lizzy resent that he feared for his wife and child? *She* knew that the babe was healthy, as a woman in her condition well might – despite her acknowledged fatigue – but he could not be certain, could not control what served as a complete mystery to him. He wished to err on the side of caution. And he had been remarkably tolerant this month gone that Lizzy had not altered her routines in any way. She could only love him for his concern, even as she played with him a moment before giving in.

"Now you decree my sister's habits as well? Does Bingley approve yet of your meddling in their lives in such degree?" Lizzy tried to maintain a defiant air but could not control the smile that began in her eyes and now forced her resisting, quivering lips to turn up at the ends. It did not escape Darcy's notice.

He relaxed his rigid bearing, sat down on the bed and lightly traced her smile with his fingertip. "You teaze me over this, my love, but I will not rise to it. Will it be so much a torment to languish in bed a few hours more?"

It was time to submit. She kissed the finger that caressed her lip and said, "A perfect torture! – if only from your absence to keep me warm. Can you not take your own counsel?"

He laughed. "I am sorely tempted but have, as you see," he said as he indicated his attire, "an engagement I cannot delay much longer."

"Pity," she said, and stretched provocatively such that her bosom just began to peek out from the covers.

"Minx!" Chuckling, he rose to go stir the fire and add coals.

"Thank you," she purred when he'd finished and returned. "But the fire is a poor substitute."

"Well, Mrs Darcy, if you will insist on lying about scandalously clad in nothing, I had best ensure the room is warm enough to keep you from an injurious chill."

"*Now* who acts the teaze? Need I remind you, Mr Darcy, that I should not *be* lying about scandalously clad in nothing if *you* Sir had not taken your pleasure in divesting me of my attire in the night?"

Smiling at the memory, he duly accepted responsibility with complete absence of regret even as he casually leaned down to retrieve her night shift from the floor. "You raised no objection at the time," he countered. "But you might desire a less provocative appearance when Alice arrives with your breakfast shortly."

The mention of breakfast brought Lizzy back to practical matters. She allowed Darcy to slide her night shift back over her head and then draw the top in and tie the ribbon as she slipped her arms into the sleeves. His fingers hovered for an instant at the neck edge, until he opted for his damnable self control. "Darcy, perhaps I should rise after all. What of breakfast for our guests? I should not abandon them."

"No need to do so. The gentlemen finish theirs as we speak so that we may leave presently. As for the ladies, at my direction *all* of the maids are instructed to provide a repast to their mistresses in bed with the express good wishes of the gentlemen that they enjoy their leisure while we fools brave the weather to bring their dinner back to them."

"You are a thorough man, Fitzwilliam Darcy, and thoroughly wonderful." She had the grace to blush a bit as she said, "I confess it *will* be nice to lounge a bit longer than custom."

"Good. Then I shall leave you to it." He bent to kiss her, but before he could accomplish his intent, she asked if he could spare a moment more. "Of course, what is it?"

"I wonder at your converse yester eve with your aunt. My curiosity was quite pronounced, but somehow it flew out of my head when we retired last night."

"Mmmm. It quite flew from mine as well." He fingered the lace at her neck once more before proceeding to tell Lizzy that Lady Catherine had owned to her heart ailment and the driving force to see Anne settled. He had once again made a plea for her to consider Retched as a custodian on their cousin's behalf regardless of his decision to marry, though Darcy could not feel he had gained any advancement.

"Ah, was that what tested your composure when you returned to the parlour then?"

"No." He shook his head in disgust. "No, I rather expected her to turn a deaf ear. But she did begin to speak of what she fears for Anne – I thought she was to tell me finally the monstrous reason she cannot trust her daughter to look after herself, but she no sooner swore me not to speak further of it than she stopped yet again and would not go on."

"So you are none the wiser?"

"Indeed I am not. I tell you Lizzy, it is enough for me to throw my hands up and renounce them all."

"You would be hard pressed to do so, Mr Darcy. I know you too well."

"There are still the Americas," he said with a grin of supplication.

"Too late, my love. I do not fancy having my lying-in attended by a merchant sailor in a ship's hold. By the by, did you speak with Sir James last night?"

"Only briefly. Why do you ask?"

"He appeared... pensive. I could not work out if his arrival in the midst of our varied calamities accounted for it, or if perhaps he regrets his hasty decision to sell Albion Park. I should hate Jane to suffer the disappointment of it."

"Or yours, I warrant, at having her settle so near." He laughed at her look of contriteness. "He said nothing at breakfast; we settled to meet this evening to review his solicitor's papers. But I shall drop a hint in Mr Gardiner's ear to try to draw him out, shall I?"

Lizzy agreed. Uncle Gardiner had an affable way of cajoling people into revealing all sorts of things to him. Darcy glanced at the mantle clock and exclaimed that he had best gather his shooting party to get things underway. "I want your promise, Lizzy, that you will rest today while we are engaged."

She gave it him, and he kissed her and rose again to leave. "Mr Folsom returns, but not before half one he says – so you have no obligations for some hours yet. Oh! and he has agreed to examine Mrs Hewitt as well if she so desires."

She nodded, more and more liking the idea of a leisurely morning as she thought on it. But even so, before he reached the door, she asked: "As I am precluded from rising, will you be so good then to ask Mrs Reynolds to attend me in my chamber, say at half ten?"

He raised his brow and Lizzy said, "Darcy, I shall rest, I promise you. But we have a ball on Saturday! I must make some arrangement for it. I shall not move from here, upon my word." Shaking his head in resignation, he said, "Very well. I shall send her to you. Thank you... for indulging me."

Lizzy was quite surprised to find that, following Darcy's leave taking, she promptly dropped back to sleep again, waking only when her maid Alice appeared with tea and toast more than an hour following.

❖❖❖❖❖

The men of their party had many of them been grumbling at the early hour when they appeared for breakfast, but now as he joined them again, Darcy found most fortified and ready to depart, only Edmund Hewitt still hurriedly finishing his coffee and toast. He had come down later than the others; indeed Darcy was a little surprised to see the man at all. He had half expected Hewitt to be obliged to forego the event to sit by his wife.

But when questioned on the subject, Hewitt laughed. "I thought I should be obliged as well! But when I told Susanna of my intentions, she raised a fuss over it and ejected me from her chamber, insisting I fulfil my duty as your guest."

"A considerate gesture," offered Mr Gardiner who, despite not taking part in the shooting today, had risen at his customary hour and joined the men for their early breakfast.

"I confess to some surprise, my friend," said Henry Wentworth. "I would not have credited Mrs Hewitt with such a selfless display."

Her husband took no offence – Wentworth knew his wife's temperament too well. "Nor *can* you, I think. She pronounced herself too steeped in pain to put herself to entertaining me all the day. And then, she can more easily procure laudanum from her maid without my regulating the doses, though I had a word with the girl and she promises she will take care." He turned now to his host. "As to that, Darcy, I spoke with Susanna and she does indeed wish for Mr Folsom to visit her today – says she cannot be trusting of Mr Grimes's diagnosis and insists that Lady Catherine's town specialist refute his conclusions."

"Yes, of course. I shall leave instructions with my housekeeper."

"I am terribly sorry for all this kerfuffle, my friend," offered Hewitt. "I would spare you all and take Susanna home could she ride in the carriage."

"Do not think on it. The inconvenience is all on yourself and your wife."

With that, the men ventured out, all but Edward Gardiner and Sir James, who remained in the breakfast room for further discourse over a final cup of coffee. Darcy had managed to take aside Lizzy's uncle and charge him with drawing out Sir James, and this Mr Gardiner did now with diligence. But though he learned a great deal of interest about the man, he could glean nothing of a troubling nature concerning Jane and Bingley's purchase of Albion Park.

❖❖❖❖❖

The maid had only just removed her breakfast tray and Jane Bingley contemplated whether she wished to rise or linger in bed a while longer when a knock surprised her. An instant later, with a creak, the door inched open until Kitty's head came into view.

"Oh, good!" she cried, entering with a little hop and a giggle. "I did hope you were not asleep."

"No, I am not. Kitty, did you come from your chamber like this?" Jane showed amused alarum, for Kitty wore only her night shift with a light shawl over her shoulders, and she was bare of foot. Her hair was still tied in strips. "What if you should have met with someone?"

"Oh, la! I did." At Jane's dismay, Kitty quickly defended herself. "It was only our Aunt Gardiner; she was going to Lizzy's rooms. In any event, I know the men are all out shooting!"

"My uncle and Sir James did not go shooting, they could well be about. And what of the servants? Truly, Kitty, for Lizzy's sake, I should hope –" She stopped her lecture as she noted her sister was shivering. Sighing with indulgence, she moved her coverlet back a little and patted the bed next to her. An instant later, her sister was tucked up with Jane, hugging her on one side.

"Ach!" cried Jane when a cold foot connected with her leg. "Kitty, you are freezing!"

"Sorry."

"To what do I owe the pleasure of this visit, sister?"

"Nothing," replied Kitty.

Jane wondered briefly if her sister might miss sharing a bed as she had done for much of her life. But it was a year and half again since she had shared a room with Lydia, and there had been no further need after *three* of her sisters had married and left home.

"I am bored, I suppose," offered Kitty now, but with little conviction.

Jane would have asked her sister if something was amiss, but a knock sounded again. When Jane called out for the visitor to enter, Margaret Gardiner appeared carrying an over-robe and leg warmers for her niece.

"Catherine Bennet," she said, but despite the formality of the greeting, she conveyed no anger, only patient correction. "What are you thinking, child, coming out so scantily clad?"

Kitty made her excuses again as she happily accepted the leg warmers and put them on under the covers. Mrs Gardiner laid the robe on the end of the bed and she and Jane exchanged smiles of tolerant resignation. Mrs Gardiner was in morning dress already, but despite this, within minutes she had joined the others under the coverlet, the three of them ensconced quite cosily with Kitty warming up nicely in the middle.

"You have been to Lizzy?" asked Jane of her aunt.

"Yes," she laughed. "She was ordered by her husband, as were we all, to remain abed today; but however, she may be along soon," continued Mrs Gardiner. "She is expecting Mrs Reynolds at any time on some business, but will join us after."

"I think it sweet," said Jane, "the men have our welfare only in mind."

"As though we are so fragile," her aunt added with an amused shake of her head. "I should like to see them give birth to just *one* child!"

"But I do not see why we could not join the shooting for their noon break at least," whined Kitty.

"I for one am perfectly happy not to do so," said Aunt Gardiner. "We have had enough activity of late; a day of leisure does not come amiss."

"But it is so tedious!" Kitty said. "I confess if I must sew one more shirt for the parish, I shall not be answerable for my actions."

"Kitty—" Her sister admonished her.

"As you speak of the parish," began Aunt Gardiner, a twinkle in her eye as she smiled innocently and directed her gaze over Kitty's head to her eldest niece, "what think you of that young vicar, Jane? I find him most charming."

"Mr Reavley? I like him very much."

As one they looked at Kitty between them and she began to cough.

"And how nice for you, dear," added Mrs Gardiner, "to have young and unattached friends to find society with during this fortnight!"

"I suppose." Kitty looked from aunt to sister and back, and said, "I am not so stupid as you believe. I do know what you get on about."

"Why, my dear, whatever can you mean?" Margaret Gardiner adopted a wide eyed expression from which Jane looked away as not to laugh.

"I am not interested in Mr Reavley!" protested Kitty.

"Of course not," said her aunt. There was a lull in their conversation a moment. "Why?"

"What do you mean?"

"I mean, why is it that you profess not to like Mr Reavley? I find him most amiable, do not you, Jane dear? There is something about his mouth when he speaks--"

"Indeed, he is a delight." She looked at her sister now, all humour set aside. "He does seem to like *you* a great deal, Kitty."

"Well, he may like me all he wishes; it will not change my opinion!"

"Why ever not?"

Even as the question came gently from Jane, Aunt Gardiner exclaimed, "Then you are foolish, my girl! An eligible young man, with a fair living, and easy amiability – what can you find about him to possibly dislike? *And* what is more, he finds *you* of particular interest!"

Kitty waffled, beginning to speak a few times and then stopping to reconsider. Finally, she said, "I simply do not find him an attractive prospect."

Mrs Gardiner was astonished. "I cannot believe you! Kitty, you have chased after much plainer men, yes and stupider!" She held her tongue a moment, but her niece stared straight ahead, neither looking nor replying to her inquisitors.

Jane began, "Do you know, Mr Reavley is that kind of man who will grow into himself and only improve with age. He looks very young now, but with good features that will make him quite handsome in a few years time."

"Oh, I must agree with you," replied her aunt. "He will age with grace, much like your uncle has done... only perhaps without the fullness of stomach that speaks of Edward's fondness for food." She laughed.

"Perhaps," said Kitty, thrusting her lower lip out into a pout. "But still I am not interested."

"What more would you ask?" said Jane.

"A fortune, for one!" replied her sister. "Or barring a fortune, at least a uniform! I do have my heart set on an officer."

"Ah, I see," said her aunt, coming around to the very point she intended to address all along. "So Mr Reavley is not an officer!" Kitty shook her head slightly in acknowledgment, but her aunt had not done with her. "Are you certain this is your objection?"

When Kitty looked to her peculiarly, Mrs Gardiner asked, "Is not your objection more that he *is* a vicar than that he is not a soldier?"

Kitty only shrugged, but the answer was in her eyes and finally, under the scrutiny of both her bed mates, she said, "And what if it is? Why should I wish to waste away in a parsonage with a stodgy, doddering old man for the rest of my life?"

"Catherine!" Mrs Gardiner exclaimed. "A doddering old man indeed. He is not but six or seven years your senior and I have seen nothing in his demeanour to suggest he is anything but a gentleman with varied interests. How can you proclaim him stodgy?"

Kitty did not reply. Jane nudged her slightly in the side and said, "If you were to be introduced to Mr Reavley at an assembly and knew nothing of his profession, dear, would not you find him amiable?"

"I suppose so." The reply was grudging. "But he *is* a vicar, Jane! And I *do* know it! Can you imagine how my sister would teaze me to end up stuck away in a country parsonage while she enjoys all the pleasures of the regiment?"

"Is that what this concerns? What Lydia would think?"

Kitty blushed, but made no reply.

Aunt Gardiner decided the moment had come to be serious. "Catherine. Putting aside what I think, or Jane, or even Lydia – do you *like* Mr Reavley?" She looked so pointedly at her niece that, fidgeting under the gaze, Kitty replied in a small voice, "I suppose I do."

"And yet you would allow Lydia's opinion – or your presumption of it – to keep you from better acquainting with the gentleman?"

"No... er, not entirely. It is not my only reason for lacking interest."

After several minutes of converse in this manner, Jane finally managed to get Kitty to confess that, though she liked Mr Reavley after all, she had been afraid to encourage him, precisely *because* he had seemed to return the affection with decided intent. In the end, the young woman had often entertained flirtations, but they had been just that – no question of any continuance beyond a few dances and a bit of a lark. The idea that a gentleman actually had singled her out; that there was an expectation of moving beyond idle frivolity; that she might be faced with a prospect of settling down to a life she most assuredly would be ill suited to – he was, after all, a vicar, and she was no mousy Charlotte Lucas – well, the idea quite frightened her.

"Good! My dear, you *should* be frightened!" said Aunt Gardiner, and both her nieces looked to her in surprise. She smiled then, softening the declaration. "Or at any rate, take some care in the matter. Kitty, courtship and marriage are serious occupations, not to be undertaken lightly no matter how entertaining the ways we engage to secure them. The man you accept one day should be someone whose company you can envision for your lifetime, and if you do not choose wisely, it can be a very long and miserable life indeed. For in the way of things you will pass much more time with him than ever you will with your sisters *and* be dependent upon him even so. And I will tell you now that whether he wears the colours of a regiment or the collar of a vicar is of far less significance than whether he is kind and good and will care for you as well as for himself."

Kitty's eyes widened in anxiety and she coughed again, Jane patting her on the back lightly to help her still it. When she had quieted, her aunt went on in an earnest manner. "I urge you look at your elder sisters and the marriages they have made. Mr Bingley and Mr Darcy are the finest of gentlemen, good men who are devoted to Jane and Lizzy and to providing for their families."

Kitty interrupted her. "Yes, but they are rich and can do so easily!"

"There is that, I grant you; no doubt it eases the struggle." Mrs Gardiner looked to Jane. "But Jane, would you care less for Mr Bingley if he earned five hundred a year rather than five thousand?"

The answer was clear to see in her soft look. "No, of course I should not. I love Charles for his gentleness, his easy manner, his earnest heart and steadfast loyalty. He is everything that a man ought to be."

"There, you see?" asked her aunt. Kitty looked less than convinced, not of Charles Bingley's attributes, but of his fortune being secondary. "And I daresay Lizzy would say the same. Why, did not she refuse Mr Darcy once, with all his wealth, before she came to understand that she loved him?" Kitty was clearly surprised upon hearing this.

Changing direction, Mrs Gardiner said, "But consider Lydia, whose approbation you are so eager to seek! Is her judgment so to be admired? Do you believe her to be happy with Mr Wickham?"

"Her letters are always full of excited news of the regiment and –"

"But is she *happy* with Wickham?" Unable to reply, Kitty sat with her mouth hanging down as she considered.

"I daresay if you read what is not contained in her letters, you will see that she is not happy much of the time; she is in fact quite miserable. Excitement there may be in the regiment on occasion, but it does not often carry into her marriage where she passes most of her days. Yes, to you she writes of dances and of the officers with whom she takes her turn on the floor, for of course she wishes to impress you! But how often is her own husband one of her partners any more? He no doubt makes straightaway for the gaming tables." Kitty grudgingly nodded.

"And does he stay at home with Lydia and the child of an evening? No, he takes to his club and drinks and gambles while she waits at home upon his return, or must find companionship in other neglected wives." Mrs Gardiner hesitated a moment, but felt then that she had gone so far, she may as well not mince words. "Wickham makes his way with apparent ease to bawdy houses, yet finds the path to his own door less direct. He takes Lydia to task on the slovenliness of their quarters, yet they had to let go their housemaid when he lost three months' wages at dice, and the day-cook will follow soon. Were it not for the principle settled on Lydia herself by—"

Mrs Gardiner caught herself before speaking further, and adjusted her speech. "Well, they might be very hard pressed indeed." Kitty ignored the gaffe, assuming her own uncle paid Lydia's annuity, but the picture her aunt had painted was grim and she thought of it now with alarum.

"You did not know these things, did you? I assure you, it is the truth. You see, she must confess to us this unseemly side to her husband when she appeals to Jane and Lizzy, and even me on occasion, for housekeeping funds—which she is no better at managing than Wickham."

Kitty looked to her sister for verification, and Jane nodded solemnly. "Yes, it is true, Kitty. Perhaps our sister exaggerates now and again to persuade us, but clearly Wickham has little thought but for his own gratification, though it pains me to believe it. I had hoped he would change when little Harriet was born, but..."

"And is this what you wish upon yourself?" asked her aunt. Kitty shook her head violently side to side.

"No, I thought not." Aunt Gardiner softened her expression now, and raised her hand to caress Kitty's cheek tenderly. "Do not emulate Lydia, my dear – it pained me greatly when we were obliged to marry her to Wickham, that she could not comprehend as we did the future she faced. But I should hate to see you too fall into such a life as she bought for herself. Rely on your own sense, what your own feelings tell you. And if you must follow after someone's example, look closely at how Mr Bingley and Mr Darcy treat their wives.

"Or dear Uncle Gardiner still after these years," added Jane.

"Is this not what you would rather find for yourself, Kitty? For I will tell you, uniforms fade with time, but good men only grow better. I do not tell you that you must encourage Mr Reavley. If you truly do not like him, then indeed you must *not* encourage him. But listen to your own heart, Catherine. Lydia's hasty and capricious actions purchased her misery, poor child, no matter the rousing picture she paints for herself and for you."

Kitty was quiet a moment, deep in thought and, while she was considering, a light knock upon the door heralded the arrival of Lizzy. She was dressed for the morning and on her way to check on Mrs Hewitt and the others.

"Lizzy, is it true," Kitty asked her without preamble, "that you refused Mr Darcy once?"

Lizzy closed the door behind her and crossed to the bed, looking first to Jane and then to their aunt for some explanation behind her younger sister's inquiry. Jane only smiled and Aunt Gardiner nodded and shrugged apologetically.

"Yes, Kitty, I did. But I would ask you, please, for his sake, never to mention it either in my husband's presence or to any other person." Kitty nodded idly. "I mean it, Kitty," Lizzy pressed her. "He is never to know this is commonly acknowledged, nor is anyone else! Not anyone!"

"Yes, I promise." Glancing at her sister's fierce countenance, Kitty repeated herself with greater intensity.

"It was before I knew him well enough to be certain I loved him."

"But he is rich!"

Lizzy chuckled. "Yes, he is. But wealth alone does not define the character of a man, either the possession or lack of it. I am only grateful that Mr Darcy's strength of character allowed him to offer to me again when once I knew my own heart. Many men would not be so forgiving." She looked again at Jane. "Do I take it this has something to do with a certain vicar?"

Kitty smacked her lips in exasperation. "Is there no one who does not have an opinion of Mr Reavley?"

Lizzy laughed. "I dare say there are enough among us who have noted his interest in you. But Kitty, it is *your* opinion that matters."

"So I am told." She bit her lip in consternation: "a vicar." She looked at Lizzy again and said, "*You* refused a vicar! You refused Mr Collins!"

"Yes, so I did! But it was not to do at all with his being a vicar!" She screwed her face up in distaste as they all laughed.

"I *do* like him," said Kitty finally. "Thomas Reavley, that is, not the odious cousin. But I think it may be too late."

"Why do you say this?" asked Jane.

"I believe he has given me up," Kitty replied with a glum expression. "Last night he barely spoke to me at supper and, later, when I asked if he looked forward to the ball on Saturday, he only shrugged – he made no renewal or reminder of his requests to dance – and soon after spied his musician friend and walked off. Then later, I asked if we should see him today and he only said he supposed not. It did not signify in the least to him. I think perhaps I have passed any chance of his liking me."

Lizzy smiled to herself, causing Jane, who noticed it, to silently question her sister. Lizzy winked at Jane, but replied to Kitty.

"If you have determined that you like Mr Reavley, Kitty dear, and this is not just idle flirtation – for I would not have you trifle with a man's genuine affections – then I suggest perhaps you try again in earnest."

"Do you?"

"I do. You should persevere; do not give up. And if he is indifferent, then try once more. If the first two approaches do not work, try for a third! It seems about the right number. Two is too few, four perhaps too many, one cannot quite be certain. But a woman should not make any judgments without at least trying thrice for the object of her desire! You see it all the time in popular novels, do you not? The heroine facing some peril and only on the third attempt is she saved?" She laughed now at the perplexed faces that met her rambles and became more serious. "Kitty, from what I have noted of your Mr Reavley, I believe an earnest approach from you may restore his good opinion."

Kitty appeared somewhat mollified if not wholly convinced.

"Now," said Lizzy. "What say you run off and dress for the day, and give Jane liberty to do the same, while my aunt and I see to our invalids? And knock up Georgiana as well, see if she is still abed!"

"Oh, I did that before I came here. She is writing a letter to her companion."

Kitty started to leave, then stopped and came back to give hugs to her aunt and both sisters, before grabbing her robe and bounding out of the room. Without waiting for the questions to come, Lizzy related the circumstance of her advice to Mr Reavley the night prior. "I think perhaps our vicar took counsel too well," she laughed, "but between us perhaps we have done them both a service!"

"I do hope, however," said Mrs Gardiner, "that Kitty might employ some discretion in her renewed interest."

"Oh, I do not know," replied Lizzy with a smile. "I believe you hope for too much. But in any event she has led him a merry dance for some days now, I think he deserves a bit of outright flattery."

❖❖❖❖❖

Lady Catherine deBourgh made her way downstairs and into the conservatory. She wished a change of scene and to escape the nervous ministrations of Dalton. There was nothing wrong with her; she needed no one to hover over her – what she most desired was to be alone with her thoughts. Elizabeth and her aunt had called earlier, a duty call no doubt, though their concern seemed real enough. Lady Catherine tolerated it even as she assured them she only wanted solitude. She had, she said, a great deal to occupy her mind.

They had not remained long, and Elizabeth had in the end proved useful. She confirmed that the men were shooting today, upon which intelligence Lady Catherine announced her intention to pass the morning in the conservatory. Elizabeth agreed to send Mr Folsom to her there upon his arrival, but otherwise leave her ladyship undisturbed per her desire.

As she settled herself comfortably upon a chair, she took a deep breath and looked about her. Darcy had a fine conservatory, she mused, much finer than her own at Rosings, although it galled her to admit of it. Perhaps she would set about having hers reconstructed in the spring; she would ask her nephew who his father had commissioned for this one – surely Darcy knew. She thus employed herself for some while with designing in her mind the room she desired, when at one moment she heard footsteps signalling someone's approach. It would be the physician as expected.

"Mr Folsom? Are you so convinced to find me upon my death bed that you call so soon?" she asked with little humour. But the gentleman who appeared from around the corner and faced her now was not, indeed, the physician; and Lady Catherine's next words stuck in her throat as he greeted her.

"Hello, Cat."

CHAPTER TWO

LADY CATHERINE SAT, staring fixedly at the countenance of her caller. She had known somehow that this meeting would occur, that it must; but it was too soon – she was yet unprepared, had not expected him to be about the house at this hour.

"Forgive me. I should not have disturbed you," the visitor now offered. "I will leave."

As he turned to go, she came to herself again. "No! Wait, James."

Sir James Thornton faced her again and made her a bow from the neck, but said nothing and remained in a stance of readiness to depart.

They studied each other warily, looking past the alterations of so many years to seek the youths they had been. Beyond a suggestion in a tilt of the head or lift of the chin there was little of the familiar immediately to see. A lifetime had re-formed even the sparkle in an eye or the set of a mouth that might have been recognised beneath the creases time had bestowed. The corporal shell was there to identify, certainly, though aged – mutual recognition had been instantaneous when Lady Catherine had entered the drawing room yesterday – but the people they had once been? If they existed still, they were deeply buried; there was no trace.

"Why are you here?" asked Lady Catherine finally.

Sir James knew she did not refer to this moment in the conservatory. "I am here to transact a sale of my property. But no, there is more to it; because I was invited by my new acquaintance to usher in the new year amongst young and amiable people who make me feel younger in return." When Lady Catherine offered no reply, he added: "I knew Mr Darcy to be your nephew, of course, but I had no idea you passed Christmastide with him here. Indeed, we neither of us spoke of you; but I believed I had heard that you were estranged. I would not have accepted his invitation to cause you discomfiture, Cat. I was nearly as amazed as you, I dare say, to find myself being introduced to your daughter even as you entered the room yesterday."

Lady Catherine averted her eyes a moment and, when she returned them to Sir James, she only said, "No one calls me by that name."

A sad smile found its way to Sir James as he dipped his head in acknowledgment. "Lady Catherine." Now a look of puzzlement replaced the smile. "But what of you? Did no one alert you to my expected arrival, make mention of me?"

"Not within my hearing; or if I heard '*Sir* James' spoken of in passing, I would not associate it with you."

"No, you would not, of course."

"Nor did I recognise 'Albion Park' when Mr Bingley talked of it."

"A little considered property, of no favour in the family then; I myself never visited until I owned and discovered an appreciation of it."

Another silence ensued, whether from a surfeit of things to say or nothing at all. They looked about them at the conservatory, occasionally darting glances at each other, glances that flitted away again without taking hold. Finally, Sir James gestured at a chair near to hers and asked, "May I?" Lady Catherine assented.

"I can leave tomorrow, Ca... Lady Catherine — when my business is concluded with Mr Bingley. I have no wish to be entertained at your cost."

Lady Catherine considered this but a moment before saying, "No, stay. I dare say we can tolerate the situation now the shock has passed. It is of little consequence to me, but would be all the more noticeable for you to depart so abruptly."

Sir James acquiesced, then added: "I have told no one of our former attachment; I will follow your desires."

"Good. I see no purpose for any to know of our... acquaintance."

"As you wish," he replied softly. After a pause he added, "I am happy to have met Miss deBourgh. Your daughter possesses many of your features. She is perhaps more delicate in constitution; and yet I would know the connection at once."

"Anne did not, alas, inherit the vigour of the Fitzwilliams. She has suffered ill health from her infancy."

"I am grieved to hear it — a cause of worry and pain for you all, I fear."

Lady Catherine was decidedly uncomfortable with this discourse and looked to turn it from herself. "How comes it that you are titled now?"

Sir James glanced down at his hands and did not reply immediately. "My brother died."

"Without issue?"

"Yes. It was not yet two years, I believe, after you married Lewis deBourgh. Of course I inherited—returned to reside at Mickle Shearing."

"I did not know," she murmured.

"No. I married soon after – the sister of my brother's widow, in fact. We lived quietly."

"Children?"

"One only—Emma; but I lost her two years past and, not long after, her mother. It will be for my nephew to inherit from me, Eleanor's boy, a good enough sort. He has been in residence some years already at Mickle Shearing – since I found a preference for this country over Gloucestershire and made Albion Park my home."

Lady Catherine looked at Sir James now, an inscrutable expression on her face. At last, she asked, "Were you happy?"

"Yes." Only after this perfunctory reply hastily offered did he close his eyes to actually consider the question. When he opened them again, his gaze was clear and direct. "Yes, I was. I am."

"Hmmph." Though his glance asked the same of her, she offered no other reply.

"Your Ladyship?"

Lady Catherine and Sir James both looked towards the source of the voice.

"I am here, Mr Folsom," she called out.

Within seconds the physician had appeared. "Oh! Do forgive me, you are engaged. I can return."

"No, no," replied Sir James affably as he stood. "I have only been conversing with Lady Catherine while she awaited you. Please, Sir," he said as he waved Mr Folsom forward. He made his courtesies to the gentleman and then again to the lady, and left them to their business. They had said all that was required.

❖❖❖❖❖

Frances Jenkinson rose late, having stayed with Anne deBourgh for much of the night prior. Anne had slept under the effects of the strong sedative which Mr Folsom had administered, but although she had remained insensate all those hours, her slumber could not be considered uniformly restful. Quiet interludes had been interspersed with periods of agitated movement and low murmurings.

And through it all, Mrs Jenkinson had attended her charge. She had stilled the hands when they twitched, bathed Anne's brow with damp cloths, whispered reassurances to the woman – and when Anne would slip again into deep sleep, her companion had contemplated what she must do.

This episode of Lady Catherine's had frightened her daughter; there was no doubt of it. But it had also shown Frances just how wrong she had been to withhold her employer's illness from her friend.

Some part of her had known all along that Anne had the right to know of her mother's condition, that the shock of first learning of it when it took her mother's life would be worse than hearing of it from the start and having time to come to terms with its possible consequence. And to make matters worse, this secret that stood between them was colouring their friendship. Perhaps Anne sensed in Frances that she held something back, causing her to do the same – for it was assured that of late, the ease with which they had always talked was altered, Anne herself seeming to shut away her feelings.

It could not continue. Frances must confess to Anne what she knew of her mother's condition and hope that, since the onset of this late episode, Lady Catherine would not see it as a betrayal and summarily dismiss her. To continue to withhold the knowledge would only continue to eat away at the easy relationship Frances and Anne had enjoyed for years, and that was not to be accepted.

Once having determined to speak with Anne in the morning, Frances had finally retired, and now, somewhat rested and revived by a wash, she returned to Anne's room to find her awake and dressed for the day, taking tea and toast in the armchair near the window.

"Good morning," said Anne with a shy smile meant to hide a troubled countenance. "Did you sleep well?"

"Tolerably," replied Mrs Jenkinson, and joined her companion.

They made idle conversation while she herself ate breakfast, and when the maid had cleared the tray, Frances took a deep breath to still the flutters in her stomach, and said, "Anne, there is something I would speak with you of, if you feel well enough."

Anne lowered her eyes a moment and replied softly, "I am perfectly well." She looked up again and said, "Indeed, there is something of consequence of which I must speak also."

As they gazed awkwardly upon each other a moment, the maid re-entered to say that Mrs Darcy and Mrs Gardiner were without. An instant later, the ladies were shown in. They remained only a short time, long enough to be assured that Anne had suffered no acute repercussions from her distress the day before. Lizzy was able to confirm that Lady Catherine also appeared no worse for her spell, was in fact quite back in form and planning to remove to the conservatory for her leisure. Against feeble protestations that it was unnecessary, Lizzy offered the services of Mr Folsom to Anne when he returned that afternoon.

Mrs Jenkinson walked Lizzy and her aunt to the door when they finished their call, giving a smile and tiny shake of the head in reply to the question Lizzy posed. And as she took hold of the door to close it after them, she offered in a low voice, "I will tell her."

When the companion returned, she noted that Anne sat straight and stiff with a resolute expression on her face, and before Frances could even settle in to her chair again, Anne began to speak in a rush.

"Frances, I must talk with you, I cannot maintain my own counsel any longer!"

The alarum her friend felt was only surpassed by amazement when Anne went on to speak, not of her fear for Lady Catherine's health, but of her own secret with which she had been tormented for days. She spoke of the marriage offer her mother had made of her to Colonel Fitzwilliam and the turmoil it had engendered. Little by little, with careful questioning once the surprise of the situation had faded, Frances learnt of the events of the past days as Anne understood them – that the issue of how Colonel Fitzwilliam would turn was yet unknown, perhaps yet undecided; but if he should accept his aunt's proposition, Anne could not settle on what to do.

When Frances would censure the Colonel for not seeking his cousin's opinion from the start, Anne defended him—explaining the roundabout way in which she knew of the offer and that her cousin had been forbidden to speak with her, had been made to promise. He could not. And indeed, Anne had been grateful to be thought ignorant of it. She had hoped Fitzwilliam's interest in Mrs Chaney would dictate his reply, leaving Anne free of the necessity to choose.

She did not resent her cousin for entertaining the idea, and therein lay her dilemma. She could not wish to marry Richard Fitzwilliam any more than another man, but she knew his want of funds, knew the deBourgh fortune would advance him; certainly they would offer more good to him than to her. She did not begrudge him that assistance. In addition, she feared that if he offered for her and she did not accept him, her mother might retaliate with an alternative match, one less palatable. At least she liked her cousin! They had always got on well.

Frances argued the point with her carefully so as not to further agitate her charge but, though Anne listened she could not be persuaded to a firm position. After some discourse, she said, "I can only wonder if my mother's attack yesterday was the consequence of this unresolved event. If that is the case, I hope my cousin will offer his reply today and have it done." She appeared to have finished, but then added, "But then I should not know how to proceed! If he accepts, how could I further disquiet her with a refusal, or deny him? Oh, Frances, how if I should lose *you* by marrying?"

She began to cry now, and Mrs Jenkinson knelt by her and embraced her friend. "Shh-shh," she cooed. "Do not distress yourself with that notion."

She knew better than to add to her friend's suffering by continuing to argue, but could offer her succour of one kind. "You listen to me," she said, drawing back from Anne and looking her directly in the eye. "You know my hope, but whatever you feel you must do, I will stand with you. You have said more than once that your cousin is a good man. If you cannot refuse him, as we would both wish, know that I will not leave you, dear Anne. I promise you so much. The Colonel will just have to accept us together. It is little enough to allow you for what he gains, is it not?"

Anne nodded as she wiped tears away with the handkerchief Frances had slipped into her hand. "Thank you, dearest friend. I am better for having unburdened my fears to you."

"Of course you are," Frances replied with false heartiness as they embraced again, all the while wondering at this turn of events. Could she now tell Anne what she knew of her mother's illness? Could it possibly give Anne the courage to refuse to marry? Or would it instead drive the woman into her cousin's arms, driven by unwarranted guilt?

"Anne, if you give me leave, I will speak with your mother, I will tell her your feelings in this matter and that you should not be put to such a choice."

"No. I cannot ask such a thing of you."

"Yet I offer it."

"No. I beg you do not – dear Frances. It gives me untold comfort to think you would take this burden from me, but I must undertake my own fate in the event."

"But what will you choose? That is, if your cousin should ask for your hand after all." She had little doubt of his acceptance, but offered Anne the false comfort of uncertainty.

"I do not know. Perhaps it will not come to it, I may be spared such choice still. But if I must... I do not know. I suppose if he were to agree to your continuing on, I might accept. But then..." her voice trailed off; she could no longer give her thoughts to the other horror that quite naturally went along with marriage. To change the subject, she looked back at her companion. "But, you had something you wished to tell me, did not you? What is it?"

Mrs Jenkinson hesitated only a second before replying. "It was nothing, I am sure; in fact, it has gone clean from my head in light of your news." She closed her eyes upon the lie as she embraced Anne once more. A little longer, to consider this intelligence in light of Anne's revelation, that was all. Just a little longer.

❖❖❖❖❖

Most of the ladies, augmented by Uncle Gardiner and Sir James, were gathered in the drawing room when the gentlemen returned from their shooting. Only Lady Catherine and Mrs Hewitt remained sequestered, the former returning to her chambers following her conference with Mr Folsom and the latter never having left hers. Indeed, *she* quite seemed to enjoy her invalid status: Elizabeth, Jane, Amelia, and Margaret Gardiner had agreed to take it in turns in the morning to keep the lady's company and Susanna Hewitt made the most of such attentions.

Even Georgiana had taken a brief turn out of a sense of obligation, accompanied by Kitty; but both young women were delighted to have their good deed cut short by the arrival of Mr Folsom to attend the lady – and following his examination, Susanna was again well dosed and resting with only her maid required in attendance. Elizabeth, upon the men's return, was able to inform Mr Hewitt that the town physician had confirmed Mr Grimes's diagnosis and treatment in every particular, a judgment, however, which had not found favour with his wife at all.

Anne had succumbed to Mr Folsom's examination again and had been given good report; indeed, she had seemed stronger and in better spirits when she and Mrs Jenkinson joined the ladies in the drawing room in the afternoon. It seemed she had fared the best of the gentleman's patients – for despite her mother's claim to be in fine fettle, the physician had found Lady Catherine's heart beat still to be quite elevated when first he attended her in the conservatory; he insisted that she humour him by resting at least one additional day as she herself could not provide satisfactory explanation for the anomaly.

The physician's report now having been summarised, the gentlemen were asked to account for their day; and an amusing hour was spent as they each tried to top the others as to shooting prowess. In the end, the only certainty was that the game larder was full, the men cold enough to welcome the fire that blazed in the hearth, and the ladies well entertained.

When they retired to dress for dinner, Lizzy asked Darcy how the day had gone. "Very well in all. A bit sluggish of a start, but the chill in the air soon inspired activity, and you saw with what delight Bingley of all people claimed the honour of first success." Darcy had been pleasantly surprised at young Mr Hewitt's easy demeanour with his elders as well as his eye and proficient handling of a gun; the young man had given Fitzwilliam some good competition.

"How did Retched appear today?" asked Lizzy.

"In quite good spirits, I must remark. I believe he laid aside his troubles for a few hours." As Lizzy smiled to hear it, Darcy added: "It may interest you to know that Retched and Wentworth found much common ground in the field."

"I am surprised!"

"Are you? I am not. In truth, they possess a number of qualities to commend friendship; outside of this contention over Mrs Chaney, they have genuine regard one for the other."

"I dare say I cannot in general fathom men." Lizzy shook her head as her husband regarded her quizzically. "Your ability with such ease to separate and place into compartments in your minds circumstances such that they do not touch one upon another. You loathe the idea that Nathaniel Hewitt finds your sister to his liking, yet you admire him for an easy manner and good aim. At one moment Retched is a fierce rival of Wentworth for Amelia's affections and the very next he is clasping him by the arm and offering him brandy for being a good fellow."

"Precisely."

"And you see no inconsistency there?"

"Not really, no," Darcy replied, as Lizzy just shook her head.

He smiled back with complicity. "There was one brief moment of tension, however, if that better meets your sense of regularity – when we took our break at mid-day."

"What happened?"

"Nothing, I suppose. But we had stopped and were talking as one does while warming ourselves with drink, when in passing Hewitt – Edmund, that is – remarked upon Wentworth's interest in Mrs Chaney. I looked immediately to Retched and he took the remark well enough, though his countenance was perhaps set with too determined a dispassion. I confess I was concerned. I thought perhaps it would put my cousin out of sorts for the afternoon, but the moment appeared to pass when Wentworth replied with no particular enthusiasm and then changed the discourse. Wentworth's gaze, however, centred upon Fitzwilliam for a long moment before moving to meet mine."

❖❖❖❖❖

Amelia Chaney came down the stairs slowly, keen for the chance to make some amends but also nervous over doing so. She had dressed with particular care for the evening; the maid had restyled her hair three times before she could be satisfied with her image in the glass. How silly she was being – but the critical attention to her appearance offered welcome distraction from the greater anxiety of the challenge she faced: to redress the untenable situation her foolish judgment had wrought.

She reached the first floor and turned her steps towards the drawing room, but hearing her name spoken from behind caused her to stop and turn.

Henry Wentworth stepped out from a shadowed alcove. Amelia's stomach lurched as he came towards her and she concentrated on steadying her voice. "Mr Wentworth. Do you come this way to join the others?"

"Yes. No." He chuckled. "I shall presently; but I confess I have been waiting in the hope of waylaying *you* before you entered. I would have a moment of speech if you will oblige me."

"Speech with me, Sir?" Instantly she was on guard, fearful of what motive the gentleman might have for a private meeting even as she dismissed the absurd notion that their acquaintance had progressed enough for any kind of intimate declaration.

Mr Wentworth sensed her anxiety. "Do not concern yourself, Mrs Chaney. I shall not, I think, place any burdens upon you. I only wish to attain clarity on a point which puzzles me sorely."

Despite her unease, Amelia allowed herself to be shepherded out of the main thoroughfare into the little-noticed alcove in the hall.

"I must beg your indulgence, Madam, for what is to come," he said. "I am afraid I have never learnt the virtuous art of holding my tongue when I have a strong opinion. I have a tendency to overstep myself even with my friends," he chuckled, "a meddlesome fault I am certain Darcy and Hewitt would confirm in a heartbeat."

Amelia had no notion of the opinion Mr Wentworth was about to share, but even as she assured him she believed no such thing, his preamble gave her pause. She looked into the gentleman's eyes, indeed was held by them with his candour, even as she began to wonder at the wisdom of hearing him out.

"If I overstep propriety, it is only from an earnest desire to see my friends well served. And so, I must be forthright with you; perhaps abruptly so. For I do hope in our brief association I may consider you a friend."

Despite growing misgivings, Amelia nodded. Mr Wentworth smiled then. "I have startled you, I think, but as I have begun, I will do my worst. Mrs Chaney, it cannot be unknown to you that I have taken much pleasure in our short acquaintance. Indeed, I cannot say in this year past when I have more enjoyed the company of a lady."

Good Lord, thought Amelia; *it cannot be he intends a declaration! I must stop him —*

"But I am discomfited to believe I do so at the cost of my friends' happiness and, what is more, I wonder it is not counterfeit as well."

"I —" Amelia's intended words were arrested as his found place in her hearing. She could only gape at him in confusion. She stammered at last: "I... I do not know how to understand you, Sir."

"When first I arrived at Pemberley some days past, Madam, you were introduced to me in the company of Colonel Fitzwilliam, and I believed then that there must exist between you some understanding, if only by the quality of attentions you afforded to one another." Amelia became deeply flushed as he spoke. "Such notion was dispelled for a short time by subsequent events; yet from careful observation this last day, I believe my first impression was correct, was not it?"

"Indeed, Sir, there is at present *no* understanding between Colonel Fitzwilliam and myself."

"At present perhaps – no, not formally. My dear lady, I have not the right, nor insight into the Colonel's mind to speak to you of that gentleman's regard or intentions, though I see them quite to my persuasion; but I beg your indulgence to ascertain yours. I have seen the manner in which you gaze at him in unguarded moments; I have concluded that, for reasons known only to yourself, you mask your affections for him... and from him... to your own unhappiness. As such action appears to distress you as well as our mutual friend, I cannot but wonder at the deception."

Amelia fumbled for words, unsure how to reply. She owed this man an explanation, since she had wronged him in nearly as great a degree as she had the Colonel, yet how could she admit in such a forthright manner what had driven her actions. She had used Mr Wentworth abominably.

But as tears collected in her eyes, she noted in his only undeserved compassion; and before she knew what she was about, she was confessing everything to him – or nearly everything. She would not further injure Colonel Fitzwilliam by recounting his personal affairs, but only intimated that circumstance and malicious counsel had led her to a foolish belief only recently controverted that the good Colonel's welfare was best served by hiding her preference.

Some moments later, when she came to the end of her recital and the forgiveness she begged for her callous misuse of Mr Wentworth had been conferred with excellent humour, he assured her of his continued friendship—but at a cost.

"A cost, sir?"

"Yes. For the maintenance of my good opinion, I require you grant me the first dance at the ball on Saturday. And after, I shall relinquish you to your gentleman with all good will towards you both and the sincere wish that you will find your selves in concert. I do not count it such a high price between friends, do you – one dance?"

"Indeed I do not," she replied with a smile of relief that brought them both to laughter.

"He is a fortunate man, your Colonel Fitzwilliam." He held out to her a handkerchief, as he said, "Well? Will you?"

"I will, Sir, with glad heart!" Her reply was enthusiastic and, in a spontaneous gesture on both their sides, they embraced quickly and then parted with some embarrassment.

"Now, then," said Mr Wentworth, "we will speak no more of it and hereafter will count each other a friend. Shall we join the others?"

❖❖❖❖❖

Fitzwilliam came down the steps quickly, aware that likely he would be the last to arrive for the dinner hour. He had much enjoyed the shooting earlier, the activity always gave his spirits a boost – and the company had been especially buoyant. Young Nathaniel Hewitt had given him a run for best on the day, but in the end Richard had turned in a superior performance. He had been so thoroughly chilled upon their return, however – for a second day – that he had lingered contentedly over his bath. Tipton, the wonderful man, had kept him continually supplied with steaming hot water and Fitzwilliam had found it difficult to rouse himself for some while. But now, refreshed and realizing how ravenous he was, he would join the party and hope that dinner was announced very soon after.

As he came to the main hallway, he fancied he heard his name spoken from the direction of an alcove off the stairs. Believing himself summoned, he ambled over to oblige. What he saw on his approach, however, was Henry Wentworth and Amelia Chaney in close discourse.

"*Well? Will you?*" *asked Wentworth with an affectionate encouraging smile, while Amelia dabbed at her eyes with a handkerchief.*

"*I will, Sir, with glad heart!*" *Her reply was enthusiastic and following, they embraced.*

Fitzwilliam lost his appetite in an instant. Without conscious thought, somehow he realised that only one circumstance could worsen for him what he was now witnessing: to be discovered doing so. With haste, he withdrew before either of the party noticed him and to spare his own senses further evidence of the couple's intimacy.

CHAPTER THREE

FOLLOWING DINNER, Darcy excused himself after a hastily consumed Port, encouraging the remaining gentlemen to linger over their discourse. He had not attended his aunt all day and, given her continued order to rest, should ask after her. Fitzwilliam thought to accompany him but then reconsidered, not wishing their present unreconciled matter to be raised to the detriment of her recovery. Instead, Darcy walked up with Edmund Hewitt who was to attend his wife.

Half expecting to be turned away by Dalton, Darcy was surprised when Lady Catherine invited an interview. He found her not in bed as might be anticipated, but fully dressed and sitting in the small adjoining parlour. She collected various papers she had been reviewing into a pile and set them beside her as Darcy took a chair nearby. She waved aside his inquiries to her health, insisting she was fully recovered and only humoured her physician with her continued retirement. "I shall resume my usual habits in the morning. Until such time, I dare say you have more than sufficient residents with whom to find entertainment."

Darcy remarked that they would welcome her return in health, to which she replied, "Hmmph. You have no need to flatter me, Nephew; I am as aware of my repute as I am unconcerned with it."

There being little to say in reply, Darcy remained silent.

"My solicitor has brought me certificates relative to my assets," she said as she laid her hand possessively upon the papers to her side, "and at present he awaits my direction to prepare documents pertaining to my daughter. They cannot be further delayed – indeed, I am impatient to have them settled. Atherton, as it is, has interrupted his usual business to travel to Derbyshire–"

"At *your* direction, Aunt," said Darcy.

She stopped momentarily, but then overlooked the remark. "— as your cousin does not see fit to apprise me of his intentions in the matter, I must press you for an answer on assuming custody of Anne's fortune on her behalf. Will you not affirm it so that I may direct finally my man's efforts? I have no wish to visit this more than once."

Darcy expelled his breath in exasperation. "Madam, I am tempted to tell you I have done with the whole of it and let that be an end for all the disquiet this has wrought – if I do not, it is only out of concern for the welfare of *both* my cousins. A concern, incidentally, little related to your fortune!"

"Darcy, this is tiresome. I require an answer, not further edification. I am anxious for the former and too old for the rest."

"It may interest you to know that my cousin has, in fact, made a decision, Aunt; one that he withholds now only because of your incapacity – he awaits your improved strength."

"My recovery will be complete to have this settled. What has he decided?"

"I cannot tell you, nor would I were I privy to it. I know only that he is resolved."

Her Ladyship glared at Darcy a moment before saying, "Then advise him to speak to me in the morning, before breakfast. I will receive him at nine. I will brook no further delays, I warn you all. I have been far too accommodating and look where it has found us."

Darcy rose to leave. "I will relate your message to Richard."

She stopped him. "There is yet the matter of *your* answer. I have little confidence in Fitzwilliam to choose wisely and must move alternately with haste if he disappoints."

Darcy looked down at his aunt. "Madam, you have long been vocal in censuring entails, of applauding your husband for settling his estate upon you for his daughter. As such, this insistence for a male guardian falls contrary to my ears – there must be reason for you to so alter your opinion. If you desire me to accept responsibility for my cousin, then tell me what it is you fear. Those are *my* terms, Madam, and they are not open to negotiate."

❖❖❖❖❖

Richard Fitzwilliam watched Darcy and Hewitt leave the room with some disquiet after agreeing to play host in his cousin's absence. But he found to his relief that he was yet able to keep his own counsel at the dining table after offering a round of Port. Uncle Gardiner, as Fitzwilliam had come to think of him, had received so glowing a description of Albion Park from Bingley at dinner that he now asked Sir James for an account of its history; and Henry Wentworth, having an interest in matters architectural and himself the owner of an ancient structure, entered their discourse with zeal. This left the Colonel free for introspection without causing affront, as Nathaniel Hewitt at present required no attention; he appeared to prefer his own reflections.

From the vague, lovesick smile the young man sported, however, Fitzwilliam could well imagine upon what subject young Mr Hewitt dwelt. Or rather, upon what person! Darcy would undoubtedly nudge him now to engage Nathaniel in some discourse to divert his mooning – the Colonel knew his cousin to have deep reservations concerning the rapport which had sprung up between Hewitt and Georgiana – but in truth, he had little heart to dampen that ardour. At least for that young man, the object of his occupation appeared to reciprocate his regard.

To push from his mind his own disturbing notions, he concentrated on recalling the circumstances of Gee's acquaintance with Nathaniel Hewitt. Darcy had related it to Fitzwilliam with mixed feelings following shortly after the event.

Darcy had taken his sister as an indulgence to Castleton where they had first visited the Norman castle high on the hill and followed it by taking tea with Wentworth at his inn.[1] While Georgiana had explored the ruins on her own, the wind had taken her bonnet, but a young man appeared suddenly and retrieved it for her. Darcy, coming upon them quietly, had noted the timorous attraction each found in the other, but as the siblings left shortly after, he had dwelt little on it – until, to his chagrin, the young man had arrived at the inn some time later. It transpired he was the young brother of a mutual friend of Darcy and Wentworth who was resting with that gentleman while he studied the peculiar geology of the Castleton area before travelling back to his college. Although Gee had been very bashful with the young man, her brother could hardly fail to notice how the pair built upon their instant fascination.

Two weeks later, Wentworth accompanied young Hewitt to Cambridgeshire and the two had called at Pemberley. Fitzwilliam chuckled to himself to recall that Darcy had contrived consecutive days of fishing and riding so as to keep meetings between Gee and Hewitt to a minimum, but still they found again an interest in each other. From that time, Nathaniel Hewitt had made point of calling on Darcy "on Wentworth's behalf" both at Pemberley and in town whenever opportunity allowed. He had made no overt claims upon Gee's company – he could not do so when she was not yet out – but few would mistake his interest on the infrequent occasions when luck offered an encounter with her. Certainly Gee could not mistake it, nor had she seemed loathe to befriend him.

And now his young cousin *was* out for all purposes, and at the least she would be so formally in a matter of days, and Nathaniel had the good fortune to pass the new year at Pemberley. Fitzwilliam could only wonder when – there was little doubt *if* – the young suitor and Darcy would come nose to nose. As one of Gee's guardians, he supposed he should join Darcy in deflecting trouble. The man had taken against the pairing intent on protecting his sister–yet the Colonel could not bring himself to it.

He saw little harm in the association and, in truth, he liked young Hewitt. The boy was somewhat odd in his pursuits – insects and fungi and the like – but an amiable enough fellow and of good family. And Georgiana liked him. He did not concern himself seriously that the pair entertained notions of a formal understanding – both were young, just embarking on their lives: Nathaniel preparing for his Tour where he would likely forget about this youthful infatuation and pass five or more years in blissful bachelorhood; Gee only now coming out, a season or two awaiting her to delight in the attentions of young gentlemen of good family before she gave her heart away. She would suffer no lack of suitors! Fitzwilliam's greater fear was that she might feel over whelmed by them all.

Perhaps as well just now he felt some kinship with Hewitt for they held one thing in common – each was a younger son with all the consequences of such. Not that he believed this accounted in any way for Nathaniel's interest in Gee; he had liked her well before he could know her fortune and, indeed, such things did not appear of any consequence in the boy's ambitions.

Fitzwilliam sighed. So simple a meeting, he envied them that. He did not know what might come of the friendship, but at least his young cousin was enjoying the unabashed admiration of a fine young man; and it seemed to help her shed at last some of the pronounced reticence she had retreated into after the devastation wrought by Wickham's misuse of her. Perhaps at last, the timidity and shame she had taken to herself after that debacle had now left his cousin, and in excellent time for her debut this week. For the encouragement of that newfound confidence alone, Richard would applaud young Hewitt.

Upon that thought, Mr Hewitt himself rose and, taking advantage of Darcy's absence, made excuse to join the ladies unremarked. This left the Colonel to confront his own demons yet again.

❖❖❖❖❖

The deadlock was broken when Lady Catherine said, "Sit down, Darcy," a remark he took to signal her agreement at last. When he had taken his seat, his aunt said nothing at first, apparently marshalling her thoughts as to how to begin.

"You have no leave to speak of this, Darcy; not to your wife, nor to Fitzwilliam. I cannot think what it will do to our family's name, our standing – *all* of our families – to have this become a matter of public gossip."

Darcy bristled at the inference, but checked a reply.

"No, do not berate me, Sir. You will soon see that I take such caution with good reason. You will see the torment which would be visited upon us; we should be shunned by society, our good name sullied for history. That *my daughter* should have fallen to the treacherou –"

"Madam." Darcy interrupted his aunt. "I take your concern, now pray impart this scandalous circumstance. If it be so ruinous as you proclaim, there will be no need for your cautions."

"Very well; I *shall* nonetheless rely on your discretion." She looked at her nephew but then, unable to meet his eye as the next words were spoken, she looked aside towards the windows. "It is that woman. Mrs Jenkinson. She is to account for it. My daughter falls too much under her influence. If Anne were to inherit outright, she would sign it over in an instant – all of it – bilked by a nefarious woman who preys upon the weak. And likely she will turn Anne out once she has succeeded if my daughter does not oblige her with an early demise."

"Aunt! Surely you grasp at nothing. Mrs Jenkinson has been companion, a devoted one from all observance, for some years. In my experience, charlatans do not take so long – no, nor work so diligently – for suspect rewards, no matter how substantial."

She looked back at him now. "She is not what she appears, Darcy. Do not allow her unctuous demeanour to blind you to the conniving viper within. I see her for what she is. She knew her prize from the moment I took her on and has never let pass an opportunity to ingratiate herself with my daughter to her own ends."

"Then why keep her employed? Why did not you send her away long ago when your suspicions were first aroused?"

"I thought to do so; twice I attempted it, the first only a few months after she came to us. I had my suspicions, but allowed myself, on confronting the woman, to be swayed by her earnest professions of innocence. It is my generous nature I fault; I was too soft."

"And the second?" asked Darcy, suppressing with difficulty a smile.

"Two years past, when the true horror of her insidious penetration into our lives could no longer be countenanced; I gave her an hour to gather her belongings and remove herself. But foolishly I did not prevent Anne from seeing her in the interim. It was a second mistake in the business – I shall not make a third!"

"Anne spoke up for her friend?"

Lady Catherine barked a pained laugh. "Would that were all; I might have reasoned with my daughter or time would have brought her around. No. She swooned and took ill until I feared for her life."

"So you relented again."

"I did, to my eternal regret, but with conditions forced upon the woman. I ceded to my daughter's outburst, Darcy, but if I had to do so, I wished to keep my enemy near me to foil her at every turn. She has attended *me* when I required it as well as Anne and is never left in doubt that I see her intrigue, her insidious perversions."

"And so you wish Fitzwilliam to marry Anne, thus at once removing the fortune from temptation of the companion and leaving *him* to achieve her expulsion."

"Yes. It should have been *your* responsibility had you honoured your promise. It may never have come this far had you married Anne years ago."

Darcy set aside the gibe, unwilling to raise the old argument. "Tell me, if they were to marry and the fortune taken out of the lady's reach, why should it concern you if Fitzwilliam, in compassion, might allow the ladies to maintain their present arrangement?"

"I trust that as her husband, Fitzwilliam will see the influence she exerts on Anne and cast her out appropriately. But if he does not, at least the marriage itself will prove the lie, no matter how others might speculate. It may be enough even for the woman herself to go off, finding her plans thwarted."

Darcy shook his head. "*This* is your scandal? That a woman who has shown devotion to your daughter's care for years may have designs on a share of her inheritance?" he asked, incredulous. "I cannot believe it!"

"Darcy, do not be such a fool! Must I particularise the disgrace for you? You are a man of the world, are you truly so naive?"

Before Darcy could reply, Lady Catherine set her face into an expression of intense distaste and said, "The woman has ruined my daughter, Darcy, with perversions. They have an... *unnatural...* relationship!"

Now Darcy did laugh, a quick ejaculation of incredulity, absurdity.

"Darcy! I assure you this is no jest; you *know* I have not the humour for it."

Darcy bit back his outburst, though still he could not credit his aunt's confidence.

"I wonder if you will laugh when your good name is dragged through mud, sullied as so much fodder for the gossips. Do you think I concern myself with this only on my own behalf? I can contain it while I live; I rely on you to do so after my death. For I will not, myself at the least, be forced to endure the sniggering, the shunning, the degradation of it then. But I would not see my family – nor my daughter – cut from society all the same. And if you care nothing of yourself, would you see your dear mother, for whom my daughter was called, so degraded? Have you forgotten the name of Fitzwilliam once belonged to her as well?"

"My *mother* is beyond all petty wants. Look here, I do not deny this might be cause for concern for you; I simply find it difficult to lend credence to such a notion. Surely you are mistaken!"

"No, I am not. I have..." she closed her eyes in revulsion, "I have incontrovertible proof. I have myself witnessed moments of intimacy between them when they believed themselves alone; intimacies that would put any question to rest immediately, that no lady should be obliged to speak of, no less to endure. I will *not* speak of them to you. I cannot. I suffered them in silence then, and I have said more already than I had wished."

Darcy was troubled now. He maintained some scepticism, yet saw that if what his aunt asserted was truth, it was indeed a situation to warrant concern. He gave little weight to her contention that Mrs Jenkinson sought the deBourgh fortune. If she had passed these years in effortless extravagance as a companion, Darcy might more easily credit that she could bide her time in the hope of such gain. But he very much doubted there was any ease in the woman's life, her charge to care for his sickly cousin not only a constant one, but done under the intense scrutiny and intervention of his aunt. And until recent revelations of Lady Catherine's heart ailment, there had been every expectation, given Anne's long-time health concerns, that his aunt should outlive her daughter. No, as such Darcy could not believe Mrs Jenkinson a swindler of that ilk – perhaps had she met Anne once on her own, but not with Lady Catherine presiding in presumed health at the time this supposed plot was formed.

This other charge, however, carried more troubling concern. If it were true, if Anne and her companion were... of such a nature... then it was desirous to put a stop to it at once. At the very least, containment of the fact was paramount. And there was always a chance that, if the woman did have fraudulent aims, she could use the threat of Anne's exposure to gain rewards.

Without endorsing his aunt's conclusions, Darcy agreed on the strength of her evidence that, if Fitzwilliam declined marriage with Anne deBourgh, he himself would undertake his cousin's custodial care; but only if Anne accepted his nomination and if he would have full discretion over subsequent disposition of her assets as trustee.

Lady Catherine squinted and drew her lips into a tight line, trying to decipher Darcy's intentions. "I have already designated them to your first daughter, Darcy. That is not sufficient for you?" She laughed thinly. "Or do you think to slight your own child to provide for Fitzwilliam?"

"You sully your nephew; you know as well as I that the gentleman would not accept such a thing even did I wish it. I merely signify that, as the inheritance is Anne's by natural right, I will retain the privilege to consider *her* wishes with regard to it. She may well have legitimate bequests to endow if asked her opinion." He shook his head and sighed. "As to slighting my own daughter, your notion is absurd. My children – whatever children God grants to Elizabeth and me – are my responsibility. I will see they are *every one* provided for sufficiently."

"And Georgiana's dowry –"

"Need not concern you. It has been determined and provided by her own father and abides until such time as it is wanted."

Lady Catherine remonstrated, attempted to settle it such that Frances Jenkinson might never see a farthing of the deBourgh fortune, but Darcy would accept no restrictions on his discretion. He reserved for himself the leave to consider the known wishes of Lady Catherine along with those of her daughter in settling their fortune. Alternatively, he again pressed his aunt to reconsider and name Fitzwilliam as trustee, either singularly or in concert with Darcy, citing the Colonel's good judgment, impeccable honour, and discretion, as well as the very practical consideration of his closer proximity to Kent to maintain oversight of the activities of Anne and her companion. Lady Catherine yielded only that she would take the matter under advisement, but in the end she did accept Darcy's terms for himself. Now it only awaited Fitzwilliam's decision.

❖❖❖❖❖

Fitzwilliam at that moment escorted the remaining gentlemen to the parlour to join the ladies for coffee. Only by strength of will had he managed during dinner to rein in his shock at the betrothal of Amelia Chaney to Henry Wentworth. But as they left the dining room now, the smile Wentworth offered the Colonel held no special feeling, even less any sense of prevailing over a rival, and that puzzled him. Had Amelia pledged herself to *him*, Fitzwilliam's joy would have been uncontainable. Yet Wentworth's mood seemed no more jovial than at any other time of their acquaintance.

This thought brought to him a curious observation. How was it that he himself was, with no undue hardship, keeping his grief at bay in the certainty of having lost Mrs Chaney? For he did recognise the loss and his mind, left to itself, dwelt upon it; but he had yet to experience the stab of pain he might expect. Could it be he did not reconcile the woman he knew promising herself to Wentworth, so quickly and in such a reversal of feeling as she had appeared to have undergone? There must be some mistake, a hope to which he could still cling. He had been convinced of her affection for him before Wentworth's arrival – an attachment that had grown slowly over months. If she could truly have set it aside overnight, then was she the woman he believed her to be?

Or perhaps his inability to feel was simply a numbing defence against that certainty. For he had heard her pledge with his own ears; there could be no doubt of it. Furthermore, she had conveyed pleasure in the promise.

Fitzwilliam had seen men lose limbs and yet express bewilderment at the lack, certain they could still feel an itch or ache where in reality the arm or leg existed no longer. Perhaps he suffered a similar resistance to believe the truth even in the face of his loss. When the evening passed and he sat alone in his room, would he then be assailed by the full force of the disappointment that seemed unreal to him now?

When the gentlemen entered the parlour, they were served coffee and, subsequently, Fitzwilliam made his way to the windows to look out at the night. There was just enough moon to give form to the landscape and the occasional shape of a small animal scurrying about or digging through the snow in hope of a morsel. After some moments of watching a hare, he realised he was not alone and turned as he was addressed.

"I hope it finds what it seeks," said Amelia Chaney. "I imagine it a very long and difficult winter to be deprived of sustenance." She paused as she shifted her gaze from Fitzwilliam to the creature outside and drew her brows together in concern. "I wonder if it has a family to care for."

Fitzwilliam replied that no doubt all the 'family' was out foraging and the two then fell into general converse. After some moments, he could not but note that Mrs Chaney seemed hesitant with him, yet at the same time eager to be amiable. He concluded that she meant to regain their cordiality such that, at some point in the weeks or months to come, she could announce her betrothal with the hope of his good wishes and no rancour between them.

He could not respond to her now with cold detachment – he cared too much for the lady to rebuff her; yet his recent knowledge could not allow him to renew their easy affability either. He puzzled again, even as they conversed, at her renewed good will.

He noted as well that, as he and Amelia were speaking, Wentworth was across the room, engaged in converse with Lizzy but often directing his gaze upon Fitzwilliam and Mrs Chaney with some interest. Small wonder, given that they could make no formal pronouncement of their attachment at this time, that the couple purposely maintained their distance. But again, Wentworth's demeanour as he watched his lady with Fitzwilliam suggested no contained violence of emotion, neither joy in his prize nor jealous regard that his former rival now held her attentions. Indeed, he wore a benign smile as he looked on them as if complaisant with the world. It was most curious and very disconcerting.

❖❖❖❖❖

Darcy returned to his company but left it immediately again upon being recalled to his engagement to assist Bingley with final negotiations for the purchase of Albion Park. The three men adjourned to Darcy's study to review documents Sir James's solicitor had prepared for the sale. But Darcy himself was now quite abstracted. Fortunately, the papers were in order, the gentlemen in easy agreement, and little was required of him for the business to conclude.

There had been no reticence on the part of Sir James, Darcy noted – Lizzy's concerns of the man reconsidering were unfounded. Whatever she had noted of disquiet in the gentleman must have had no relation to this event. Indeed, the only change of note to the articles of sale was one that Bingley raised and it delighted the seller.

Bingley and Jane had formed such affection for the elderly gent that they broached the notion to Sir James – and with no hesitation were accepted – that exclusive use of the gate cottage at Albion Park remain his for his lifetime, along with unfettered access to the gardens. The only argument ensued when Sir James insisted upon paying a reasonable rent for the rights; following which they shook hands on the purchase, agreeing to travel into Lambton the next day to arrange for Mr Atherton's clerk to make the required change to the deed of sale. They could then reaffix their signatures in the solicitor's presence the following day and adjourn to the bank to direct a deposit on the transaction. Their business concluded so handily, they returned to their ladies and a celebratory toast.

But although the entire party was cheered by the Bingley family's new acquisition, Darcy became increasingly troubled. His eyes were drawn against his desire to Anne and her companion, speculation floating to the forefront of his mind despite any attempt to keep it submerged. Could he discern evidence of his aunt's allegations in their manner? Was Mrs Jenkinson's touch as she helped Anne rise from a chair a bit too intimate? Did Anne's glance of thanks carry more than gratitude? He counselled himself to stop such conjectures but still they crept in and occupied his mind unrelentingly. He hardly noticed Mrs Chaney's concerted attempts to engage Retched, or Nathaniel Hewitt's quiet converse with Georgiana on the settee, or Kitty's wistful restlessness.

"Darcy, love, what disturbs you? Did not the negotiation go well?"

Darcy reassured Lizzy that they had gone very well indeed, but that his disquiet stemmed from another source, at once understood by his wife.

"Your aunt?"

He nodded glumly. When Lizzy asked again, he admitted to business of which he could not speak to her at present, and begged her understanding. His countenance was so grave that she forgave him instantly, though her curiosity was piqued beyond measure.

How he contained himself through the remainder of the evening he could not tell, preoccupied as he was over this recent intelligence. When they passed part of the evening in charades, he hovered in the back and participated minimally. But at last his guests began to show signs of retiring. When Anne and her companion bid them good night and departed, he nearly followed after them to request converse with Anne.

But in the end he did nothing, at a complete loss for how to ask his cousin if she and her companion were, indeed, illicit lovers. Much against his anxious curiosity, the intelligence he sought was such as to wait a night without changing anyone's present course; and he could not reconcile the possibility of overtaxing his cousin so late over his own want of enlightenment – it could not merit precedence. He would rely on his own counsel tonight and find a way to address this in the morning.

When everyone else had sought their beds, Darcy, Lizzy and Retched were the last remaining and they mounted the stairs together. Retched's mood was sombre, something of a surprise to Lizzy given the conciliatory attempts she had witnessed Amelia making towards the Colonel. She might have thought the gentleman would be pleased with those attentions, marked as they were by their singular preferment coupled with a happy ignorance of his rival. But though Lizzy tried to draw him out, Fitzwilliam remained silent as to the trouble which weighed upon him.

He attributed his mood to a concern to resolve with Lady Catherine their business, now that his mind was unalterable, at which point Darcy recollected to tell his cousin that their aunt was not only well enough to receive him, but expected him in the morning. Though this news was welcome to him, still Fitzwilliam's demeanour did not lighten at all. Had he shared with Darcy and Lizzy the conversation he had overheard between Wentworth and Amelia earlier in the evening – and the quite natural and inescapable conclusion he had drawn from it – they might have alleviated his distress; or at the least given him cause to question its import. But retaining his own counsel, he did not. When he parted from them to seek his room for the night, he was none the wiser nor settled in spirit.

---

1 "Pemberley Break: Gee's Day Out" – an original short story published as part of an anthology titled *Pride Revisited*, January 2013, CreateSpace Press.

CHAPTER FOUR

Wednesday, 2 January 1799

❖❖❖❖❖

FITZWILLIAM EMERGED from his chamber remarkably fresh and with purpose; looking forward if not to the coming discourse itself, then to its aftermath. With this matter settled finally, he could turn his efforts then to the more difficult and painful task of reconciling his heart to lost love, since any other possibility had been removed from him yesterday.

Amelia Chaney had been in his thoughts as he had drifted into unconsciousness last night, and her gentle smiling countenance returned unbidden almost as soon as he had awakened; but unaccountably – mercifully – she had not pervaded his dreams and he had slept well for several uninterrupted hours. The night's rest would serve him in his forthcoming meeting with Lady Catherine, which would no doubt require all his patience. Then he would concentrate on tempering – regulating – his feelings for Amelia.

And yet he remained bewildered on that subject. It came to him to wonder once again how he was able to consider the lady with such detachment; for he *knew* his disappointment to be great though still he could not bring himself to quite *feel* it. Was it this other business, so inextricably entwined, that kept the ache at bay? When the finality of his own choice not to marry Anne was achieved, would his heart then break from the sudden weight of Amelia's choice to do so?

She was never from his mind and, to his astonishment, nor had she vacated his heart upon this recent intelligence. One might expect that with the withdrawal of her preference she might take all of herself and leave a cold, dark void in his heart – and yet he could still feel her resident with each new beat. He could only think of her with love – bitterness held no place, not yet.

He had never before experienced deep love for a woman; could this be how it manifested itself? That so immediate upon his own disappointment he should still feel her a part of him? It made little sense when he considered it; the evidence of others he knew who suffered unrequited passions did not support such a conclusion. Darcy, for one, had weathered torments of every kind when Lizzy had first rejected him – he had been immediately inconsolable in his loss and his funk had been recognizable for weeks, months afterwards.

But this? This was as though his heart simply refused the proof of his own eyes and ears. It simply could not be true. *His* Amelia was not the person who accepted Wentworth. He could not feel a void in his heart because Amelia Chaney was still there. How was that possible? Reason told him it was not, and he awaited with dread the moment when that truth would come to him fully.

Recalling himself to his present task and resolving to think no more of that other until this business concluded, he glanced now at his watch – five minutes before the hour of nine. Perfect. He walked down the passage, aiming to stop at his aunt's sitting room. But as he approached he found someone had preceded him. His cousin Anne stood outside the door, swaying slightly to and fro with apparent indecision and wringing her hands together, so concentrated on her own thoughts that she was unaware of his approach.

He cleared his throat; she turned at the sound. "Richard!" Her anxiety heightened at seeing him.

"Are you unwell, Anne? Do you need assistance? Shall I call your Mrs Jenkinson?"

"No! Please, do not. I... May I have speech with you, Cousin?"

The Colonel hesitated, glancing again at the watch still in his hand. "I am expected –"

"Oh." She considered an instant, but then drew her eyes to his and, with determination, said: "I must speak with you, Sir, before you address my mother. It is urgent, I beg you."

Fitzwilliam could do no less than comply, given her agitation.

"You go, if I do not mistake it, to answer my mother finally on a matter germane to us both. Is not it so?"

"It is." He did not know what to say beyond the simple affirmation and fumbled about for words. But he realised this was no discourse to be held in an open corridor, particularly outside Lady Catherine's rooms. He pointed towards Anne's chamber and they proceeded there, he following her in and closing the door behind them.

This intimacy did not appear to disturb Anne; she scarcely noticed. She began to pace a bit, but then moved to a pair of chairs and seated herself, looking anxiously at Fitzwilliam until he took the other.

"I know, Richard, that you have promised not to speak of this to me," she began, "and I would not have you break your word. I will in its stead speak of it to you. I do not ask you for your answer to my mother's late proposal; but I do beg your favour."

Fitzwilliam was stymied, curious even in discomfort of the subject, as each minute ticked away.

"I want you," continued Anne, "to allow me to make you a proposition first. Then if you agree, I will speak with Mama."

"To... a proposition?"

"Yes." She was pallid, her skin nearly translucent in her state of nerves and her eyes red rimmed in apprehension. "Richard, I understand the reasons for my mother's proposal to you; and what is more, I well know *why* you must consider it." Fitzwilliam began to speak but Anne stayed his comment with a raised hand. "No. Please allow me to say this while I have the courage." At his capitulation, she went on. "I cannot truly believe you wish to marry me. And I confess I have never desired to be wife to any man! But if it is your inclination to accept my mother... well... that is, I know how well the deBourgh fortune may assist you –"

"Anne, no!" Fitzwilliam here intervened, unable to allow Anne to oblige them both by giving answer to a question he would never ask. "I beg you. I am mortified that you should be forced to such discourse, but as you have begun I must tell you honestly that I go to decline your mother." Now he looked away for an instant. "I am very fond of you, I have no wish to dishonour you, but the entire –"

"Oh, do not explain yourself!" Anne was smiling, near laughter. "Can this be true? You will decline?" A glance at Fitzwilliam's countenance was enough to confirm it. "Your relief at such a decision, I am certain, only can find its equal in my own!" Now she did laugh, a light feathery sound that nonetheless released heavy care. "I was so afraid –"

Fitzwilliam, astounded at this entire encounter, could only look upon his cousin as she squeezed shut her eyes. When she opened them again, she said, "Dearest Cousin, I have struggled these days, it seems to no purpose. Even as I hoped for the reply you have given me, I more feared and anticipated the alternative. I moved between extremes of action, even debasing myself to accept my fate quietly. In the end, I had settled on debasing us both by offering you a bribe of half my inheritance to reject me! That is what I hoped to speak with Mama about, what I intended with *this* meeting. But I did not think it through properly. I should have trusted that you are a gentleman, trusted in your honour – forgive me."

"My dear cousin, it is I who should seek forgiveness. I have been a selfish being, thinking only of my own part in this. Had I more honour, I should not have so long entertained my aunt to cause you this misery. I overlooked, gave no thought to what might be passing in your mind. I should never have agreed to secrecy. Had I behaved more like a gentleman, I would immediately have ascertained your opinion in the matter and acted accordingly. I regret that I did not."

"Come, then, let us forgive each other and be friends – we will say no more of who bears fault." She held out her hands to him, and he reached and took them in his own a moment. Her colour was beginning to return, and she smiled tentatively. She looked younger than her years suddenly to Fitzwilliam, with the care removed from her expression.

"Do you wish still to speak with your mother?" asked Fitzwilliam.

"I do, yes; I must – I must plead with her to give up aspirations of any match for me. But I do not now find it necessary to converse with her before your answer. Indeed, it is better if you conclude your business with her first – my words to her will be difficult regardless, though this decision makes them easier for not disappointing *you* materially."

They walked to the door together and Anne stood in the frame of it watching as Fitzwilliam approached Lady Catherine's and knocked. He glanced back at her quickly and saw her mouth the words 'thank you' as Dalton bade him enter.

❖ ❖ ❖ ❖ ❖

Amelia Chaney glanced around the breakfast room and wondered at Colonel Fitzwilliam's absence. She wondered if he would appear at all. Mr Darcy had mentioned in passing to his wife that his cousin was to speak with his aunt at nine. Amelia could only presume their meeting referred to his answer concerning Anne deBourgh, an 'answer' she herself was anxious to learn. Of course, she would never hear it through him; but she rather thought that Elizabeth Darcy would apprise her of it, aware as her friend was of Amelia's heart.

She glanced up from buttering her toast as someone entered, but it was not the Colonel, rather it was Miss deBourgh—another party wound up in this business whether she knew of it or not. Her countenance appeared untroubled, so perhaps she knew nothing of the morning's interview.

Amelia was startled out of her thoughts by a remark directed to her by Sir James. She responded to him earnestly and was drawn into conversation with that gentleman and Mrs Gardiner. But while she attended them, still she conjectured on the business ongoing or just concluded in another part of the house. She had tried to engage the Colonel last evening in discourse, to regain some of their earlier amity. He had been cordial certainly; he could never be less than so. But Amelia realised the measure of her former mistake in that attempt. While he spoke easily enough with her of nothings, gone was his enthusiasm, formerly offered so engagingly, to make her smile. He had looked about him at others in the room more than he had looked upon her. He had called upon no recollections of their former acquaintance that had peppered his speech in the past. And on the odd occasion when he seemed about to regain some of the spark of old, he would turn his glance to Mr Wentworth. And when he had turned it back to her again, his interest had diminished. In short, there had been nothing more than the civility which might be found among any two marginally acquainted guests at a house party.

But Amelia would not surrender to the challenge before her. She could not fault the Colonel for his careful regard after her own strange behaviour. Perhaps it was too late to recover affections; perhaps he was simply too much a gentleman to convey abruptly a decided lack of interest in a woman of capricious tendency. But unless she heard of an arrangement between Colonel Fitzwilliam and Miss deBourgh – until she knew all hope was exhausted – she would exert herself to win back his esteem. She could not give the battle up for lost. She could, she supposed, accept Elizabeth's offer of help, allow her friend to smooth a path to Colonel Fitzwilliam's regard again. But she would not do so. She would win his love on her own merits or not at all.

A little shiver went through Amelia at the last thought.

"My dear, are you chilled?" asked Mrs Gardiner. "Shall we have your shawl fetched?"

Amelia assured her it was nothing, and focused on remedying her inattention to the kind lady.

❖❖❖❖❖

"You are late."

"My apologies, Aunt. I was detained unexpectedly."

Lady Catherine looked up now from the small table at which she sat, in her hand a pen poised over a parchment. Her eyes narrowed in beady perusal of her nephew, her mouth set in a stubborn line. She did not speak as he stood under her inspection. Finally, she rose and walked over, still watching him, then passed him by and sat on a small settee. He established himself in a chair adjacent.

"I understand you have come to decision at last?"

"I have."

"Not half above time, I think. Well, what is it?"

Fitzwilliam swallowed now, the moment at hand. He felt no qualms about his choice, particularly after his late discourse with Anne. "I must with respect decline your offer, your Ladyship."

Lady Catherine shook her head from side to side. "Fool!" she spat

40

at him. She said nothing else.

"Perhaps. Your proposal is generous and who knows but a year ago or two or five I might have accepted. But I am a different man now –"

"*Man*? What kind of man shirks responsibility to himself, to his family?"

"I will not debate my decision with you, Aunt. You made me an offer, a generous one, but one which I cannot accept. There is the end to it. Your daughter, Madam, will always be a friend to me – as will you, I hope – to call upon my good will at need. But I will not – I cannot – accede to a union that neither of us wishes. Anne, no less than I, deserves better of us both, you *and* me."

"Do not presume to instruct me in what Anne deserves, Fitzwilliam; I am her mother! I know better than any –"

"I have no wish to quarrel, Madam. I gave you an answer last week which you bade me reconsider. I have done so but my feelings have not changed, nor can they. Anne, if she chooses to marry, deserves to do so for love, as do I."

"It is love which makes you weak, you must know."

"No." He smiled.

She drew herself up in her seat and tilted her head back slightly to gaze at him across her nose. "I suppose you will offer to your widow now with your newfound righteous advocacy of love?"

The smile receded. "If I should offer to any lady the business is my own; though indeed I have no present intention to do so. Your censure of Mrs Chaney is mislaid; she is not culpable for my choice."

"Hmmph." Lady Catherine sneered but could find no disguise in her nephew despite close scrutiny.

"Do you see that paper there?" she asked, looking towards the desk where she had sat when he entered. "Do you know what it is?"

"I do not, Madam."

"It is instructions to Mr Atherton for the disposition of Sir Lewis deBourgh's – my – property. He calls upon me this afternoon." She sneered at him again. "You see, I had little faith in you to make a rational choice. It outlines a directive that all my fortune, upon my own and Anne's death, will be Darcy's. I will make him custodian to *my* daughter and, in return, my fortune will go to *his* firstborn girl." She stopped long enough to look for a reaction and saw none. "I see you know of this intention already. Does not it disturb you? He who has so much already, to be handed this when you are in want?"

"Madam, your fortune is your own to disseminate."

"Yes! It is. And for your foolishness, you will not see a penny of it. It will all go to Darcy. It could have been yours. It could have made you. But you *will not see it*."

"Yes, Madam, we understand one another well." At that he stood, determining the interview to be over.

Lady Catherine looked up at him and said, "Do you know, I thought I should not be surprised at your attitude, I half expected this stubborn refusal. But to repudiate all I can offer you and still not claim your widow? You are *worse* than a fool. For you gain nothing at all for your stand."

His smile carried regret for her closed heart. "You are mistaken, Aunt. But what I gain I dare say you can not comprehend." He bowed to her and said, "I am relieved to note your health returned to you so soon. Good morning, your Ladyship!" and walked to the door.

"Not a penny," he heard as he closed the door behind him. "Do you hear me? Not a penny!"

Fitzwilliam made his way back to his room. He wished some moments to collect himself after his interview before making his way down to breakfast. As he overtook Anne's door, he noted it was open several inches and, as he passed, she opened it more fully. She had been watching, apparently, for his return. They did not speak, but he smiled at her and earned an answering one before she proceeded towards the stairs.

❖ ❖ ❖ ❖ ❖

Kitty Bennet sat in a most unladylike sprawl in a chair in Georgiana's dressing room, watching a few stray flakes of snow tumble about in the air out the window as the maid finished with her mistress and departed. Kitty had stopped at Georgiana's room to see about borrowing a tippet for her gown they had earlier discussed, and they had fallen into keen discourse about the ball that was now fast approaching. When Becca had interrupted to request instruction from Miss Darcy on some garments the young woman was to have reworked, Kitty had flounced into the seat to wait out the maid. Now Gee turned her attention back.

"Kitty," Georgiana laughed, "do you sit in such a manner? It is not proper! What would your sister say to that, or your aunt?"

"Probably what you say now," was the reply. "But I cannot help it – I am at odds with myself." Even as she spoke, however, she pulled herself up into an acceptable posture.

Georgiana, owing to an earlier comment Kitty had made, considered that she might bear some responsibility for her friend's mood and became conciliatory. "Kitty, I am sorry if I have neglected you these past days."

"Oh, la! Do not trouble over it," she replied with a laugh. "I should do the same if I were in love."

"Kitty!"

"What?" She looked at Georgiana, whose lips had parted in surprise, and who bore a blush upon her cheeks. "Will you tell me that you do not love Mr Hewitt?"

"I certainly will not tell you that I *do*."

"Ha ha," said Kitty. "That is not precisely a denial, now, is it!"

Georgiana looked away a moment rather than meet Kitty's challenge. When she turned back, she said. "I… I like Mr Hewitt. I… esteem him highly."

"You esteem him? You *esteem* him!" She began to laugh.

Gee went and sat on the deep windowsill and considered Kitty's remark more closely. Finally she said, "Yes, I do esteem him. He is very intelligent, always thinking about one thing or another. Oh," she added to stave off any possible teaze from her friend, "but never tedious in it. I like to listen to him talk of his pursuits."

"His pursuits," echoed Kitty, still smiling knowingly.

"He is a fine young man, Catherine," she protested then, "and I will not have you abuse him."

"I do not see it abuses him to note your fondness for the man. La – indeed, your protest rather makes my point."

When Georgiana's embarrassment had subsided, she said: "I do like him, Kitty. He is handsome, you must admit; but kind also, you can see it in his eyes at every moment. And he possesses every quality of gentlemanly conduct. He is just what a young man ought to be."

"Mmm," replied her friend. "I suppose so. Rather too serious for my taste, but if you like that sort… I could not love someone who was not more gay, for myself. Mr Hewitt is too much… well… too much like Mr Darcy!" Kitty, who had never yet overcome her awe of Lizzy's husband, still referred to him in this formal manner.

"He is nothing like my brother!" protested Georgiana.

"If you like. But I see it. They are both of serious nature, bookish and proper…"

Before she could say more, Georgiana, who felt vague misgivings in allowing her friend to continue in such a vein, countered with a question. "And what, then, Miss Bennet, do you wish for in a man, if not kindness and intelligence, and good regulation?"

Kitty laughed. "Dancing? Amusement? A disposition of humour?" She stopped an instant. "Those other things are well and good, I suppose. I grant you they have their place. But I cannot be sober and sedate all the time. I wish for a gentleman with a sense of… merriment in him!"

"Ah, someone like Mr Reavley, then?"

Kitty glanced now at Georgiana, losing some of her aplomb with the table having been neatly turned on her. "Well…"

"You must credit him with good humour, Kitty, you must or do him an injustice."

"Yes, I admit despite his profession he can be droll. But… well, I admit I am concerned still."

"Over what do you concern yourself?"

"I wonder: he is young now, only entering his calling. But what if his living is as a leech, bleeding him of his wit over time? What if the requirement to be bookish and serious and … and all those things of his office – what if they are to change him?"

Georgiana detected behind her friend's questions a sincere anxiety. "Kitty, all people change with time. We grow older, find our successes where we may; make mistakes and learn from them; suffer pain to endure and joy to cherish; and can only find us changed in some ways by it all. But I do not believe the essential character of a person alters so much, not without catastrophic inducement. A man with humour in his soul, or goodness – or sadly wickedness – will always have it thus. He may learn to temper its expression at need, or indeed reveal it after some long dormancy. But he does not lose his basic nature in the usual course."

Kitty's smile had faded as she considered her gentleman. Each girl was quiet a moment, as Georgiana's thought had moved her as well to do the same. But she did not think of one young man only. Her mind had formed unbidden a comparison of two men of her acquaintance – one the object of her current regard; and another whose false professions of admiration had nearly destroyed her prospects in life and could still. She closed her eyes and, for the thousandth time or more, thanked her brother – for sparing her the kind of life Kitty's poor young sister now endured – felt gratitude for such a protector, such a good man, a good brother. And she reflected that if, indeed, what Kitty saw were truly similarities between her own Fitz and Nathaniel Hewitt, it was a blessing to be appreciated.

Shaking her head to dispel the scoundrel who no longer belonged in her thoughts, she said to Kitty: "Shall we go to breakfast now?"

"Ah, yes!" came a grinning reply. "Let us… I am famished!"

❖❖❖❖❖

When everyone had assembled finally in the breakfast room, Darcy took assessment of how many of the party would travel to Lambton for various pursuits. Once having established that nearly all of them would do, he sent instructions for sufficient carriages and horses to be readied for an hour hence. He, Bingley and Sir James would visit Mr Atherton's clerk and avail themselves of the happy coincidence of his temporary residence in the town to finalise a deed of sale. The Gardiners would call upon their friend

Mrs Kettering. The ladies had shopping to attend to in preparation for a ball, upon which the two Mr Hewitts and Mr Wentworth gallantly volunteered to escort them and supervise their parcels for the exercise it would afford.

Anne elected to stay behind, after asking Georgiana to make some small purchases on her behalf; Lady Catherine remained sequestered in her rooms as did Susanna Hewitt.

Fitzwilliam, who had in a pensive state finally arrived for breakfast near its end, initially inclined to remain at Pemberley, to Amelia's disappointment. However, he had been handed a letter on his arrival which transpired to be from his new acquaintance, Major Soames, requesting discourse with him. The Major, it seemed, would ride to Lambton and await the Colonel in the Rose and Crown from twelve o'clock onward. And so the party was set. Darcy would secure a room at the inn for their use where, after their varied errands, they would all meet to drink tea.

A plan being now established, people began to drift off to ready themselves for the outing. But as Anne and Mrs Jenkinson made to leave the breakfast room, Darcy hurriedly asked his cousin if she might spare him a word. If she wondered at the unusual request, she gave little sign of it. She did not inquire as to his interest, but after only a slight hesitation when she glanced at her companion, she smiled and assured him of her attendance. He directed a servant to escort them towards his study where he would join Anne presently.

He returned to the breakfast room to alert Lizzy that he had some business with Anne and, should he not show himself when the rest of the party was ready to depart, they should go on ahead. He would ride and catch them up and, also, he hoped, perhaps find himself at liberty to then share with her the reasons for his distraction the night past.

From the moment Anne had arrived for breakfast and taken a seat at the table with Mrs Jenkinson, he had found himself unable to keep his eyes from wandering to the pair. Images he would rather never conceive had tried for purchase in his mind – such that he had realised he could not delay longer in ferreting out the truth of his cousin's relations – and this had prompted his immediate request for her time. He gulped down half a cup of coffee to fortify, and went to his business.

CHAPTER FIVE

DARCY STOOD outside his study door, refraining from opening it while he collected his thoughts. He had no clear idea of what he would say to Anne. In fact he questioned the sagacity of speaking to her at all. They had been acquainted all their lives – indeed had suffered together now and again the presumption of a match between them – yet theirs was not a snug friendship of shared confidences and comfort. Their nearest expression of warmth had been a letter Anne sent to Darcy on the occasion of his engagement to Elizabeth Bennet, assuring him despite her mother's outraged accusations that Anne was delighted at his match and retained her good opinion of him.

Given such a history, what lunacy had propelled him to set an interview with little thought to what he might say? He wished he had felt at liberty to speak of this entire turn of events with Lizzy and that his wife accompanied him now. She had become more warmly acquainted with Anne these recent weeks than Darcy had troubled to do over years. But his aunt's demand for concealment had still rung in his ears and despite a curiosity she did *not* conceal, Lizzy had not pressed him to explain his unease when they awoke in the morning.

Alternately, he wished he had not so precipitously approached his cousin at all. This, too, was a breach of sorts to his aunt's desire, he recognised; except he reasoned that as Anne presumably was aware what she engaged in, any mention to her would only take form of confirming what each knew. Also, Lady Catherine had agreed to his condition that Anne accept his guardianship. Tentative points of honour, he admitted, and they niggled at him even as he approached their meeting – he broke the spirit if not the fact of secrecy; yet he could not stand idle. But how to conduct this interview? He disliked at any time to engage in business without sufficient preparation; and the nature of this coming discourse only exacerbated his unease. He could not march in and demand to know if his cousin maintained an illicit affair with her companion! So what exactly did he think he could accomplish? Blast his aunt for making this his responsibility –

Taking a deep breath and placing himself in the hands of Providence, he settled his resolve and entered.

Anne awaited him in one of the pair of chairs near the desk, a shawl about her shoulders and rug tucked around her legs, the fire unlit. Darcy noted that Mrs Jenkinson occupied the second chair; but at his entry and seeing his countenance she immediately excused herself, vacating the place to him. Instinctively, Darcy's eyes went to the door as she exited to ensure it was fully closed, whereupon he berated himself for the action.

Darcy sat, and the cousins traded pleasantries of no consequence a moment. Then an awkwardness descended, the room eerily quiet in anticipation of difficult business. Anne drew her shawl closer about her and Darcy tapped his fingers idly on the chair arm as each tried not to look the other in the eye. Darcy got up and went to the hearth, stalling a bit by lighting the fire as he made apology for the chilled atmosphere. As it took hold, he could no longer avoid either his cousin or his purpose, and he returned to face his odious task.

Anne asked him then if her mother was the reason for this interview – had her health taken a turn for the worse. Darcy assured her such was not the case, but then admitted that her mother had provided the inducement for their intercourse.

"I hardly know how to begin," he confessed. "We, you and I... well, we have never..."

Anne laughed despite her nerves. "Cousin, I believe we both know of the offer my mother has made to Richard; if that is what you wish to speak to me of..."

"No, no, it is not. Or, only by way of other things." He shook his head, gathered his poise then, and said: "Anne, do you know why your mother is so concerned to see you married?"

"I presumed that, having somewhat recovered from *your* fancied defection," she coloured as she said this, "she looked about for an alternative. I am certain a spinster for a daughter is one more embarrassment to her."

"Not at all! Or, more precisely, that is not what urges her action now. She is concerned for you, for your welfare when she is... no longer able to assure herself of it."

"I can hardly believe she expects me to live so long——."

"But..." Darcy stopped. Lizzy had said that Mrs Jenkinson would tell Anne of her mother's overall condition, yet it appeared she had yet to do it. Should *he*? Or would it at this juncture only cloud other issues? He opted not to do so for the moment. "One can never know what the future holds, Anne. At any rate, she wishes to ensure that you are protected."

Anne smiled, a soft expression of informed resignation. "My mother gives little credence to my judgment. Oh!, I cannot fault her for it; I have brought it on myself. I have been content all my life to allow of it – finding it the easier road than to assert myself when my ailments so often claim my fortitude. I left myself open to treatment as a child and, indeed, I merit such judgment when it comes to business. But are there not other methods of protection than marriage? Could she not appoint someone to look after my affairs in the event of... well, if it should be necessary?"

"I cannot speak fully of your mother's motive, Anne. But I can tell you that she has in fact considered just such a trustee; that is, depending on your decision regarding Fitzwilliam."

Anne very nearly told Darcy that danger had passed; there was to be no marriage to Richard. But she held her news. It was for Fitzwilliam to confirm that he had settled things with Lady Catherine. Anne knew only his intentions, though they were enough to appease *her* anxiety. And she herself still needed to engage her mother to stave off any other match. Instead she laughed. "Do you mean *his* decision! For I am certain my own opinion carries little weight with my mother. Pray, do not deny it. I have not lived with her all these years without learning something of the nature of *Lady Catherine deBourgh.*" These last words she spoke in hushed and exalted tones more suited to the Vicar of Hunsford than to Darcy's shy cousin.

Darcy smiled before recalling his point. "Your mother is concerned that there are people who would strive to take advantage of you without protection, absent a guiding hand."

"Of that I have no doubt. If that 'guiding hand' be yours, Cousin, and you are concerned how I should like it, I can set your mind at ease – I offer no objection. Indeed, I should be grateful for such an advisor." She returned to her former thought. "I know that Mama detests Mrs Jenkinson and accuses her of all sorts of evil intent. It is only my strong attachment to Frances that has allowed her to remain with me, but Mama watches her with a will, looking for any fault to condemn her."

She had introduced the very person Darcy needed to speak of, yet still he was unsure how to proceed. His silence, however, and a renewed tapping on the chair arm, alerted Anne that she had struck on a point of interest. While Darcy hemmed and hawed and tapped his fingers yet again, Anne finally said, "Fitzwilliam, just say what you must. I doubt you can shock me, I am past surprise at my mother's notions, but your reticence is worrisome."

"Ahem," he said. "Yes, well, it seems that your mother believes... well, believes..."

"...that my companion connives for my fortune? That Mama will die and I shall foolishly give it all over to Frances only to then be put out myself? I understand more of my mother than she allows."

"Yes, that is part of it."

"Part? What more could there be?" Where Anne had addressed the issue to this moment with a sort of resigned familiarity, she now took on an air of real curiosity.

"She believes – she has asserted – that you and Mrs Jenkinson have a friendship that defies convention. Too close a friendship. That you are too much attached."

Anne did not speak, but yet had not heard anything so far to cause disquiet. Darcy closed his eyes and, mentally trying to stem the rising colour he felt all too warmly, he plunged in. "She believes that you and your companion have an... unnatural, intimate relationship." There, he had said the words to her.

He opened his eyes to find Anne smiling; her expression was calm as she replied to the charge. "Yes, I suppose she might think it. I love Frances, so very much." She looked down as her cousin took in the simple statement.

❖❖❖❖❖

Lizzy was surprised to find herself first down. Her younger sisters had been so anticipating this shopping jaunt that she might have expected they, at the least, would be fidgeting in the hall awaiting the others. She strolled casually into the breakfast room to find that she had been mistaken – Sir James sat there in his greatcoat, on the table a portfolio presumably of papers for the estate sale, to carry with him.

"Sir James," she said, to alert him to her presence, "we have had barely a moment to become better acquainted since your arrival. How do you find your stay at Pemberley?"

"Exceedingly charming, Mrs Darcy, my compliments. Do not fret, Madam, for my entertainment. I have been delighting in the amiability of all your party."

"You are generous, Sir. But then, I believe you also had former knowledge of some of our group, did not you?"

Lizzy was taken aback a bit with the gentleman's reaction. He started upon hearing it; stuttering in speech for an instant as he formed a reply.

"Former knowledge, Madam? I... er... from where can you take such a notion?" His eyes glittered with attentiveness.

"Why, I recall our first meeting in Nottinghamshire. You told my husband you knew Mr Darcy his father, and the Colonel's father; and knew of their sons as well."

If his initial reaction had puzzled Lizzy, she was no less so now to see him visibly relax.

"Yes, yes of course," he replied. "How silly of me to forget that. I did indeed have the pleasure of acquaintance with Mr Darcy's father and the present Earl, as well as *his* father."

"His father also? Then your association is of many years."

"Er... indeed," he replied until, thinking better of the impression he gave, he added: "but not an intimate one, no. Our acquaintance was slight; yes, very slight – I have not met with any of them in some years."

Something in his demeanour, generally appearing immune to pother, alerted Lizzy's curiosity, particularly when he then changed the topic with obvious intention.

"I very much enjoyed your musical evening two nights past. Mrs Eustace-Wittig's talent is exceptional, is not it?"

"Indeed. It was a delightful evening." She determined to bring their discourse back to its original topic, certain from something in his manner that a tale of interest resided in it. "But what a shame, Sir, that you did not arrive sooner. The Earl of ____ called upon us briefly – you might have renewed your acquaintance."

Now there could be no doubt of the gentleman's discomfort. His hastily proffered *'What a pity'* could not disguise that his opinion did not match his words.

Before Lizzy could contrive to dig more deeply into the meaning of this, however, Kitty and Gee came nearly skip-stepping into the room, talking excitedly of lace and ribbons and a peculiar hair ornament in the latest Spanish style remembered from the window of the circulating library. They were followed closely by the arrival of several gentlemen as well as Jane and Mrs Gardiner. Any opportunity to learn of Sir James's former acquaintance must be delayed, but this did not restrain Lizzy from considering it in her own mind. Indeed, she was to ponder it distractedly for much of the ride to Lambton whenever Sir James would smile awkwardly to catch her gaze upon him.

❖❖❖❖❖

"You... you love her?"

Some moments had passed during which Darcy tried to reconcile what he had heard. No part of him could have expected Anne to come out so simply and baldly to validate his aunt's accusation. He had maintained from the instant Lady Catherine had asserted the fact that there must be a mistake – unconsciously, he had sought this interview to refute the affair. And now here it was, not only proved, but admitted readily and... innocently done, if that were possible. He could not account for it.

"Is it so surprising," asked Anne, "that I should?" And indeed, she appeared perplexed that anyone would not presume the fact. When Darcy could make no immediate reply, she went on. "Frances Jenkinson has been my companion these eight years, since Mrs Chamberlayne left me. From the start we found common sentiment and she has been my friend; and, yes, it grew into love most naturally. Who is at my side to cool my fevers, to warm my hands when the numbness takes them? Who brings me the news of the world when Mama would shelter me from it? Frances is my companion from waking hours until nightfall. Why, I hardly think she has been away from me more than three days in all these years, present even when Mama is not! While Mama would have me conserve my strength in idleness, Frances encourages activity and I believe it to have been my saving grace. I doubt I would have lived so long without her ministrations, both to my person and to my heart."

She was warming to her subject now; Darcy was quite taken aback at her loquaciousness. "I love my mother, Fitzwilliam, do not mistake me; and I do not doubt she acts as she does in my interest as she determines it. But she is too protective – it smothers me; as often as not it is more to keep me from the world than the opposite.

"I must accept blame for much; I allowed it, retreated into it gladly at times. I learnt early on that only perfection is acceptable to Mama, and my afflictions sat heavy on her; she took my weakness as her own failure to produce superior progeny. She tried to accept my limitations and found guarded success by simply disregarding them publicly; manufacturing reports of excellence in all things while in actuality expecting nothing of me – *encouraging* nothing from me. But I soon learnt as well that if little was expected, then it followed that I bore no burden not to disappoint for lack of accomplishment. The arrangement suited us both."

Darcy considered his cousin in awe, never having given more than passing consideration to the consequences of the life she had led.

"My former companions were all my mother's creatures. But Fitzwilliam, Frances has been at once mother, sister, teacher and friend – my confidante in low moments, my advocate, perhaps the one person in the world who has ever looked upon me or *treated me as a person* – as a woman, an equal – rather than a surly invalid of mean understanding. I am only truly myself in her company. What sort of person would I be if I did *not* come to love her? Mama is jealous of her influence upon me because they differ in their opinions, and so she seeks to denounce Frances at every turn."

Darcy had to allow the truth of her description even as some part of him realised his own culpability. He had been content all these years to view Anne as something 'less than' as well: less than an ordinary woman, less than an interested, rational creature. Yet even as he could admit of this, he recoiled from the idea of her relationship with the companion.

"Anne, I am not without sympathy for such, and if Mrs Jenkinson has been all these to you, then you are fortunate in her friendship. But –" He stopped, fumbling about for a way to say what he must and losing the battle of keeping from his expression the evidence of his discomfiture. "But do not you comprehend the damage such a – relationship – can do, both to you and your companion? It is not natural, an abomination under Heaven – it cannot serve either of you well in God's judgment. And if it should be discovered, gossiped over, you would all suffer immeasurably – your mother, you, *and* your companion!"

Anne sat studying her cousin, an expression of total astonishment writ upon her face at his outburst. Then at once her confusion turned to horror; a deep flush began at her neck and quickly spread to suffuse her entire being. It would be difficult for an observer to judge which interlocutor wore the deeper hue.

"Cousin, no!" These words escaped her, but then she sat, moving her mouth as though in speech but finding no voice. Darcy was alarmed for her and considered calling for Mrs Jenkinson but then, in a rare gesture, he leaned forward and placed his own large hand atop her small one. The touch seemed to recall her to speech.

"No, Darcy, it is not true!" she cried. "Is that what you believe of us?" Her horror was plain to see.

"I will believe what you tell me, cousin," he said, confused now. "But this is what your mother fears."

Her hand flew to her mouth and she looked near tears. But as Darcy watched with concern, her hysteria released itself in laughter. She grasped her cousin's hand and squeezed it until waves of giggles subsided. When she could speak again, she said, "My poor dear cousin! What you must think! But I assure you there is no – We do not – No, you are mistaken – my mother is wrong!"

Uncertain yet what she was telling him, Darcy said, "But you have admitted you love Mrs Jenkinson."

"Yes, and so I do. She is the dearest person in the world to me; and I should be very content never to marry and to spend my remaining years with my dearest friend. But," the blush rose again, "no, you are misled that there is a more... unrefined... relationship than that of... of sisters!"

Darcy was at once relieved to hear it even as he began to feel shame for believing otherwise. But then he recollected his aunt's assertion that she had proof.

"Anne, why should your mother believe she has witnessed such acts of pervers... well, of... as would establish her opinion so firmly?"

His cousin looked down at her hands and his, but despite her mortification, she replied forthrightly after a moment's thought. "No person, no matter how sickly or frail, can live without human touch, Fitzwilliam – the wiping of a tear, the kiss of a sister, the warm embrace of a friend – the clasp of a hand," she added as she raised his by example. "But that is all Mama can have witnessed. It is her own insidious, suspicious spleen that makes more of it." She looked Darcy candidly in the eyes. "I pledge to you that is the truth of it."

Darcy smiled at Anne with genuine warmth, perhaps for the first time in his life. "Then, my dear, I am happy you take such comfort in your friend. And I shall set straight your mother's misunderstanding. Indeed, I am profoundly mortified at having been the instrument of raising the matter to you; I must beg your forgiveness."

They both stood as she granted what he asked. She made to leave. But before she did so, smiling, Anne said: "Cousin, will you oblige me in a request?"

"Certainly, if it is within my power."

An inkling of a thought, the merest shadow at this point, began to form in her mind. "Will you *not* disabuse my mother of her opinion? Will you allow me to tell her of her mistake? It is time I addressed my own affairs."

Darcy agreed, puzzled but willing – even relieved – to yield so much to his cousin in recompense for the intercourse he had forced upon her.

❖❖❖❖❖

It was a sight of some welcome interest to the good people of Lambton to see fully three carriages and two gentlemen on horseback roll into the town and stop at the Rose and Crown. No foreigners these, who would stop an hour at the inn and then move on. No, the lead carriage bore the mark of Pemberley – this was Mr Darcy's house party – and as the delegation passed, shop keepers along the street rubbed their hands in anticipation.

Everyone alighted except Mr and Mrs Gardiner, for that conveyance would continue on to drop them directly at Mrs Kettering's prim cottage. They were waved off by ladies and gentlemen alike before the group separated to their own pursuits on foot.

Darcy, Bingley, Fitzwilliam, and Sir James at once entered the inn and were greeted by its proprietor, following which he guided them up to a room he had set aside for their use.

"Is Mr Atherton within, Toller?" asked Darcy. "Or his man Sanders?"

"Yes, Sir, to both! I will notify them of your arrival and direct them presently." Before he departed, he excused himself but then added that he was much obliged to Mr Darcy this season. It seemed the Twelfth Night Ball at Pemberley had secured Mr Toller such demand for his rooms for a few nights that he had been obliged to redirect late requests to the Shepherd's Crook, as well as the Haddock Head, two lesser inns in the town. In fact, those establishments were now fully committed as well, in a season when anything but local custom would otherwise be scarce until Spring thaws brought travellers out once again.

When the innkeeper had finally departed on his errand, Fitzwilliam retreated to the bar to await Major Soames. Only a moment later, Mr Atherton and his clerk arrived, most happy to oblige Darcy in his request for legal assistance.

The ladies had gone off in two groups. Lizzy, Jane, and Amelia began their errands with Mrs Eyre in a small lane off the high street, where they had final fittings for the ball. They found great satisfaction with their gowns as only minor adjustments were wanted. Lizzy provided Mrs Eyre with the trim she had earlier purchased and they agreed on its sparing use to outline the gown to advantage and complement Mrs Darcy's hair. Mrs Chaney's dove silk would no doubt leave Lady Catherine appalled with its brightness and life, despite being in keeping with her status.

With a promise of delivery on Friday from the mantua maker, the three ladies retraced their steps to the high street to visit the haberdasher's.

As they approached the shop, a gentleman with a small parcel exited a milliner's directly in front of them, and turned to go on his way.

"Mr Reavley!" called out Lizzy. "How do you do, Sir?"

He turned and, seeing who addressed him, stepped back to them with enthusiasm and bowed to each in turn.

"Good day, Mrs Darcy – Ladies. What a fair day this is to meet with you!" Even as he addressed them, his eyes flitted in the vicinity for other possible members of their party.

"You are shopping, Sir?" asked Lizzy with amusement; and on his reply that he was engaged by his sister to pick up sundry parcels, she added with a wry smile, "I wonder if you have met with my own sisters in your errands, for they are about here somewhere."

Mr Reavley at once perked up to hear of it and, on its being suggested that he might in fact encounter those ladies – to offer due respects, of course – in the very haberdashery to which they now made their way, he graciously offered to escort them thither. On arrival, however, Miss Bennet and Miss Darcy were not to be found within. Mr Reavley, with obvious disappointment, then made to take his leave.

"Mr Reavley," said Lizzy as he bowed a farewell. "I wonder if, having satisfied your errands to your sister, you might return in something of half an hour. We have a parlour at the Rose and Crown where we will meet for tea and I should very much like it if you will join us there."

It was with a decided spring in his step that Mr Reavley afterwards made his way back to the vicarage.

The Misses Bennet and Darcy had indeed visited the haberdasher's, as well as the circulating library, where the Spanish hair ornament was purchased, the milliner's to complete Anne's commission as well as their own, and a jeweller where Georgiana had a particular gift to procure for Twelfth Night. Finding the perfect article, she left it with instructions for engraving and the two girls then went on for their own last fittings with Mrs Eyre, which destination they had in fact reached by the time Mr Reavley looked for them in their sisters' company.

The two Hewitts and Mr Wentworth who had graciously escorted them to the shops — waiting outside on the pavement while the ladies marvelled over the latest gewgaws and then bearing the easy burden of their purchases afterwards — had for this last stop separated from their charges to visit a tobacconist nearby. They agreed to abide there until Miss Bennet and Miss Darcy finished their fittings and wanted escort to the inn.

Back at the inn itself, while deeds and agreements of sale were finalised above, Colonel Fitzwilliam conversed with Mr Toller in the snug until his friend should arrive. This the gentleman did, in the company once more of Corporal Cooper, some half an hour after the Colonel's arrival. Fitzwilliam left the Corporal with the innkeeper and a tankard at the bar, and removed himself, Major Soames, and two brandies to a secluded corner table.

After an exchange of pleasantries, Major Soames came to his business. It was a favour he had come to beg. He had, after his meeting with the Colonel two days past, considered long his situation. When he had mentioned it in passing, it had been only a whim, the idea of selling his commission to follow his wife to Norfolk. But the notion had taken hold, and he was of a mind to act upon it. He was concerned, however, for the fate of Cooper. Since the Colonel had expressed regard for the soldier, the Major hoped that he might prevail upon his recent acquaintance with the ranking officer to see the Corporal well placed. "For he will wither if he stays here, Sir; that is a fact."

Fitzwilliam immediately agreed to use his influence to secure Cooper a better posting, but was bothered to hear of the Major's own decision. He spent considerable effort in conversation with his fellow officer, in the end gaining only Soames's promise that he would not make decision hastily without additional thought and would correspond again with Fitzwilliam before taking irrevocable action. The man had asked nothing for himself, only for his soldier. But Fitzwilliam had determined then and there — saying nothing to Soames for fear of raising a hope he could not fulfil – to also try to secure a change of posting for the Major. He simply could not abide the notion of a good man's walking away when so many were wanted.

By the time they had finished their discourse, Fitzwilliam noted Lizzy and her companions entering the inn. He rose to call to her, introducing the Major who, as a result, was invited as well to join their party for tea.

❖❖❖❖❖

"What is it, Dalton? I have no wish to be disturbed. Tell whoever it is to go away." Lady Catherine had not interrupted her writing when she heard the door opening.

"I am not Dalton, Mother."

Now Lady Catherine looked up from the table. "Anne!" She acquired a distinctly uncomfortable expression momentarily, then worked to convert it to a thin smile. "My dear, I fear you have come upon me transacting business. Do you return to your chamber, and I will come to you when I have finished my correspondence. We may drink tea together."

"No, Mama. I must speak with you, and it cannot await your letter."

CHAPTER SIX

LADY CATHERINE SAT in stony silence, her hard, dark eyes riveted upon her daughter. Her expression was completely blank. One might have expected to see any number of emotions spread across her visage: shock, relief, anger, seething resentment or even scheming determination; but the thoughts that occupied her mind at this moment could be known only to her – she kept them well guarded beyond a wall as impenetrable as iron.

Anne waited a moment more for some word, some sign from her mother of further discourse, but none came. She bowed her own head, but did not give in to a lifelong habit of wavering in wake of the force that was her mother. On this day, Anne would not be turned from her desire. She did feel some guilt; their history could not have prepared Lady Catherine for such an encounter as her daughter had brought. But despite some natural misgivings, she had maintained her position, not given ground. And perhaps the bulk of her guilt lay in the realisation that it had felt good.

When she looked up, nothing had changed. Still her mother regarded her with unfathomable intensity. Anne smiled, an acknowledgment more than capitulation, and rose.

"It is not my desire to make you cross, Mama; nor to cause you pain." No response came. The blank eyes had not flickered or shifted at all from the space Anne had vacated. "I will give you time to consider what I have asked." She walked slowly to the door, looking back for an instant as she exited, and breathed a sigh into the uncharged air of the hallway.

❖❖❖❖❖

Mr Sanders, his instructions given, left the room mumbling assurances that he could provide final documents the following afternoon. He was happy to have some alternate occupation as they all waited upon Lady Catherine's whim.

"Mr Atherton," said Darcy. "Thank you, Sir, for your services."

Atherton acknowledged that he should be ever available at Mr Darcy's call in Town.

"Will you take some refreshment with us? I believe Mr Toller has tea arranged – and possibly something more satisfying."

"I must decline, Sir," replied Atherton, glancing at his watch. "Indeed, your aunt anticipates my call in the next hour. I should arrange for my carriage."

As the gentleman exited, he was met full on in a collision with a breathless boy of perhaps ten years who had obviously flown up the stairs. It was the proprietor's son bearing a letter for the solicitor.

"Ah," said Atherton to Darcy. "As we speak of her, Lady Catherine deBourgh corresponds." He flipped a coin to the eager-eyed boy and, with the leave of the others, opened the missive immediately. Darcy could see it contained only a few lines; Atherton read them quickly before folding it again.

"It appears I am excused my business today after all," he said, flourishing the paper. "Her ladyship indicates she is not yet prepared to conclude our affairs." His countenance expressed bewilderment, mirroring Darcy's own. Knowing as he did that Retched had delivered his rejection that morning, Darcy wondered at his aunt's delay given her insistence the night before that they avoid any additional postponements. But he shook off his thought and extended his invitation once more. Atherton accepted now, before leaving to find Mr Folsom and inform the physician that Lady Catherine had recused his services also.

When they entered the adjoining chamber, Darcy's small group found they had been preceded by several of the others. Lizzy and Jane, sitting near the fireplace, were joined immediately by their husbands and Sir James. Darcy noted Fitzwilliam over near the windows with a gentleman unknown to him, Major Soames presumably. They were in speech with Mrs Chaney.

❖❖❖❖❖

"I am delighted, Madam," said Major Soames upon Fitzwilliam's introduction of Amelia. The officer studied her a moment and hesitantly offered, "I held a slight acquaintance some years ago with a Stephen Chaney, a Captain at the time, in Sussex…" His speech drifted off, ending in neither certain statement nor question, and Amelia smiled softly.

"My husband, Sir; or rather, soon to be so when you knew him."

"Then –" Major Soames stumbled in his speech, realising the awkwardness of the situation.

Amelia took pity on the man. "I lost my husband last year, Sir – to illness."

Amidst professions of regret, Mrs Chaney graciously assured him she had been fortunate in her friends who had materially lessened her burden of recovery. "Colonel Fitzwilliam, in particular," she said with a blush, "has been most helpful in seeing me established. I do not know what I should have done but for his assistance." The smile she offered Fitzwilliam was dazzling in its gratitude as she continued in his praise, such that Major Soames himself scrutinised his fellow officer a moment.

Fitzwilliam stirred uneasily under the regard, and hastened to change the subject. But as he conversed with them of trivial things, he heard again in his mind her words: *"lost my husband last year."* True, they had begun a new year only two days past and her statement was nothing if not accurate. But *'last year'* sounded so much more than 'seven months' – more final – as if her period of mourning were concluded or would be so quickly; and he realised that in very little time at all she would be free to announce her understanding with Henry Wentworth.

A small stab pricked his heart. And yet, he thought, she had followed those words with such fulsome tribute of him. What could it mean? *Ahhh, Retched,* he chided himself, *do not make too much of every word she utters; that road leads to your ruin.* Unconsciously, he shifted and moved himself a step farther from the lady's side.

He returned from this thought to find that the conversation had moved on. Amelia had engaged Major Soames in speaking of his wife and their impending child. The Major's countenance was suffused with joy as he spoke his anticipation and his hope to be reunited with his wife for the happy event. But Fitzwilliam noted that, though she showed every courtesy of attention to the words, Amelia herself bore some discomposure of spirit. He wondered if this talk of babies did not cause her some pain – if she carried concern of her own in that regard. It would be natural, he supposed, for a woman to wish for children; and faced with another marriage in the near future, the childlessness of her former union might give her pause.

Shaking himself again to stop thinking of Amelia Chaney in this manner, he was happy for the distraction at that moment of the arrival of others. Catherine Bennet came bounding into the room waving ribbons about, followed closely by a smiling Georgiana Darcy and their gentlemen escorts. A new energy infused the room and Major Soames announced that he should think of being on his way.

As he took his leave, Fitzwilliam decided impulsively to accompany the man and ride some short way back with him. It gave him an excuse to remove himself for a while from Amelia's disconcerting company. They gathered Corporal Cooper and, on exiting the inn, met with Thomas Reavley on his way to join the party.

❖❖❖❖❖

"Mr Reavley!" said Lizzy at the young man's entrance. "I am delighted that you join us."

Mr Reavley went immediately to her, greeting Lizzy and Darcy both with utmost courtesy and gratitude. He was then directed to a sideboard for refreshments where he encountered his friends.

"Good day, Miss Darcy, Miss Bennet," he said, pausing only for an instant to look at Kitty before moving on to greet Nathaniel Hewitt in his turn. He conversed with them all easily until he had procured a cup of coffee, and immediately following he excused himself to speak with Mrs Chaney. He stood with her by the windows for all the world as if he had no cares.

Georgiana looked at Kitty and gave her an encouraging smile and nod. Her friend stiffened – glancing at Nathaniel Hewitt in embarrassment, though that gentleman was looking elsewhere and had not caught the exchange – before returning her gaze to Georgiana with a nearly imperceptible shake of the head. To elude further such encouragements, she excused herself to go see Jane, but the ploy offered no relief. Her eldest sister at once smiled and glanced herself in the direction of Mr Reavley.

Kitty's complexion now rivalled the pink of her gown and she bounced just a bit on the balls of her feet while her eyes flickered towards the windows and back several times in a poorly concealed show of curiosity. Did he watch her at all? Was he even aware of her presence as he laughed with Mrs Chaney over some small amusement?

"Kitty, my dear, you have a surfeit of energy and I have been sitting here far too long. Come! Take a turn about the room with me?" Jane gave her little opportunity to choose; she stood and looped her arm through her sister's. With a shrug, Kitty began to walk with Jane.

But when they reached the windows, Jane greeted Thomas Reavley and stopped to converse with him, holding Kitty's arm firmly if somewhat squirming within her own. Mr Reavley commented on the full complement of Pemberley's residents in the town today, causing Jane to laugh as she replied that she expected after spending so much time together, the change of scenery if not company did them all good. "And we did all have shopping to accomplish," she added, looking to her sister, "for the ball."

Mrs Chaney then asked Kitty if she and Miss Darcy had been successful in finding what they wished which finally got the young woman talking. She reported happily that they were very successful, but then added that she and Georgiana had been unable to find the recent volume of *The Lady's Magazine* at the circulating library; they were disappointed since it contained articles specifically on the fashions to be worn at Court for the Queen's upcoming birthday celebration.

"Ah!" said Mr Reavley. "I do grieve to hear of this." When the ladies looked at him in some surprise at his regret over a trifle, he added: "You see, my sister has only finished that volume this morning, and I was to return it to the library for her, but in my haste I forgot it. I regret that I caused you unneeded disappointment, Miss Bennet."

"Oh," she said, smiling at him with her entire countenance. "It is nothing, Sir."

"To be sure, I cannot be sanguine while I feel responsible for causing your loss," he replied. "I shall go at once and retrieve it for you... and for Miss Darcy, of course."

Lizzy, who had approached the group while Mr Reavley was speaking, offered an idea of her own. "Mr Reavley, why do not my sisters and Mr Hewitt accompany you back to the vicarage? I am certain the air and activity will prove welcome to them" – she glanced at Kitty and saw a tiny bounce of anticipation – "and they will have the pleasure of calling upon Mrs Henshaw as well as retrieving the monthly."

Georgiana and Nathaniel Hewitt when consulted were immediately amenable to this plan, and so the four of them donned their outer garments yet again and left, three promising a return within the hour.

"Mrs Chaney," said Lizzy once the others had left, "Amelia – I have heard some news." She spoke quietly so as to be heard only by Amelia and Jane. "Colonel Fitzwilliam has this morning declined his aunt's wishes. My husband had it from him during the ride to Lambton."

Amelia took in a deep breath, but almost as soon as she did so, the burst of joy passed. Lizzy looked at her in question. "I am happy, of course, to hear of it, Elizabeth. Thank you for telling me. But I fear it may offer little difference for me in the end."

Lizzy squeezed Amelia's forearm in encouragement. "Do not give up. This is only just concluded. He will come around. At the least there is no obligation in the way of either of you, is there? There is time to revive his interest."

Amelia smiled, though perhaps none too confidently. "No, that is true. As long as both of us are unencumbered, there is time. There is hope." She glanced out the window now, and wondered if that were true.

❖❖❖❖❖

Finding themselves at leisure yet while they awaited the return of Colonel Fitzwilliam from one quarter, the Gardiners from another and the young people from a third, the gentlemen put down their tea and prevailed upon Mr Toller for a bottle of something stronger. Not long after, most of the gentlemen had gravitated to one side of the room where they held a lively debate over some news or other brought from town by those latest arrivals.

Jane and Amelia had settled in to quiet conversation in a long window seat, so Lizzy moved to a free chair by the fire to join Sir James Thornton.

"Are not you interested in politics, Sir?" she asked him.

"Always interested to an extent, Mrs Darcy," he replied. "But I am too old to enter the debates anymore." He tapped his chest and chuckled contentedly. "My constitution demands less contentious pursuits now; let the young men" – he nodded his head to the side towards the group – "take on the burdens of commerce and law. I shall enjoy the fine things in life more quietly." He held up his brandy as he said this, and they laughed together.

"The words of a wise man, Sir James."

They spoke companionably then for some time. Lizzy asked the gentleman about his family and he gave her a short history. His happy countenance clouded over slightly when he spoke of the loss first of his daughter, then his wife; but in the main he had enjoyed a life of infinite satisfaction.

"How is it, Sir, that you settled in Nottinghamshire? I believe your family home is in Gloucestershire, is it not?"

"Yes. But you see, I never considered Mickle Shearing my home." At Lizzy's start, he qualified his statement. "Or, not once I had finished my schooling. I had a brother, Mrs Darcy, an older brother; he should have inherited. So I never bound myself to our properties. I rather liked the freedom my second status afforded me, and I drifted through life as a young man until such time as a vocation might find me." He laughed and then looked at Lizzy, smiling at the memory.

"Oh, I was a rogue! But there was no malice in me – I meant well. I never hurt anyone, not with intention. I simply enjoyed life too thoroughly to settle anywhere for my own good. I seldom suffered for invitations – house parties of school friends, balls and dinners, and occasions requiring escorts. When additional gentlemen were required, as they always were at these gatherings, you know, I was called upon to fill the numbers. I had an easy manner, a way with flattery, and I danced divinely, I was told; mothers everywhere, I am certain, lamented what a catch I would be if only I had a sizable fortune!" He laughed again, but then his expression turned serious and he became so bound in his thoughts that Lizzy asked her next question three times before he heard her.

"And did a vocation find you?"

"No," he said, shaking off what had claimed him momentarily. "As it happened, my brother died before he could inherit, and suddenly I became *the heir*. I relinquished my indulgent life and determined to be responsible to honour the brother whose constant adherence to duty even from childhood had cleared the way for my own immoderation. I returned home. A year afterwards I married a sister to my brother's widow." He glanced at Lizzy and saw the question she would not ask. "No, I did not feel obliged to do so. I did what I could to offer comfort to Deborah in the beginning – they had only been married just over a year and she not one and twenty – and in time, her sister Grace and I, we came to regard one another with real affection."

He spoke freely enough for some minutes, then said: "Listen to me, rambling on when you asked only, I believe, how I settled in Nottinghamshire."

"Do not stop for my benefit, Sir; I assure you I find your history infinitely more worthy of note than the rate of interest to be gained on sugar cane or nutmeg speculation," Lizzy said, referring to her husband's group again.

"I think my tale is near its end," said Sir James. "Grace and I settled in at Mickle Shearing, I became responsible, and the months passed. But neither of us ever felt truly at home there, and when I visited Albion Park for the first time while on a survey of our properties the following year, I loved it the moment I set eyes on it. I just knew Grace would feel the same. When our tenant of some years left, we chose not to continue leasing the property and began to spend a great deal of our time there. After several years, when my eldest sister's boy came of age, we moved entirely, giving residence of Mickle Shearing to him until such time as all of it will become his. It was good for us, the move – too many memories in Gloucestershire – the change was good."

As an afterthought, he added, "My sister thought as much also. She always despised and resented that as the eldest she would never inherit, and was delighted to see her Roger established. I own Albion Park outright, so it is not under the same entail.

"You have such an air of complaisancy, Sir, when you speak of Albion Park. Can you truly pass it on now so easily?"

"Yes, it is time. You are young yet, Mrs Darcy, you and your family. Change comes naturally to you, flowing in and out like the tides while you simply adapt without notice. When you get to my age," he laughed, "you need a push now and again to recognise that you have been in one attitude too long. Your sister and brother are the push I needed. And I am convinced it was a blessing. I know they will honour the place, I can pass my time in town without care of whether it prospers still, and I retain use of the gate cottage so that I do not leave it fully. I am quite content, I assure you." He smiled at Lizzy full up to the eyes. "Perhaps I shall become a rogue in town once more to keep myself entertained."

"I should imagine you quite successful at it; you have enchanted all of us!" Lizzy laughed in return. "Sir James, your acquaintance with Mr

Darcy senior and Colonel Fitzwilliam's father," she asked then, "was that during your life of indulgence?"

"Not Mr Darcy, no," he replied. "I came to know him later, after I had settled in this country. A fine man."

"So I have heard. I am sorry not to have known him." She noted that Sir James did not address Retched's father at all, but she could not leave it there. Something told her to tread carefully, but she asked again: "But you knew the Earl in your youth?"

Sir James looked at Lizzy as if to gauge the nature of her interest, but after a moment he answered her. "Yes. He was not the Earl then of course, not yet. But we had mutual friends, from school and town, as one does. We often found ourselves in the same society and once, I was invited with some others to a house party on the occasion of his majority. But that was the extent of our liaison. We were not what one could consider intimate friends." His final words coupled with a pointed glance at Lizzy told her he felt the subject now closed. But her curiosity had the better of her.

"Then, if you were a guest at Buxborough, Sir, you must have known — or met at the least — my husband's mother and aunt as well?"

Sir James sighed. He was silent a moment before smiling slightly. "Not his mother, no. I believe Lady Anne Fitzwilliam was quite young, certainly not yet out. But Lady Catherine Fitzwilliam... yes, I met her there."

Lizzy was astonished. "But... She never said... Did not you recognise one another?"

"Mrs Darcy, it was a long time ago. Too long for me to remember a great deal and better that I not; and I surmise Lady Catherine prefers to retain her privacy. I entreat you to keep this between us. It is of little import and can serve no one to know that we were once acquainted. It was brief and..." he repeated himself, "it was brief."

Lizzy was certain there was more to his story than Sir James would say — she noticed he had not directly answered her question — but she had already stretched civility to the edge of impertinence. She could not press him further but instead — to make amends for her probing — offered to refresh his drink. He accepted and, while she waited for Darcy to fill the glass, she noted that Sir James passed his hands over his face slowly, up and down, as if erasing a memory.

❖❖❖❖❖

They began walking all abreast but, as they crossed the road to the narrow lane leading to the vicarage, the four separated into pairs along the path. Georgiana and Nathaniel Hewitt walked behind Thomas Reavley and

Kitty and, although they said nothing to their friends, Gee and her escort traded smiling glances now and then at the stilted intercourse of the couple in front.

Several times, Kitty began speech with Mr Reavley, only to have him offer quick reply and then turn his attention to his feet once more. Kitty would blush, screw her lips up in thought, and try again, interspersed with little reflexive coughs. After many such attempts, when they were just coming within sight of the vicarage gate up ahead, Reavley finally took the initiative after one series of coughs to ask Kitty if she suffered from the cold. It was as if a barrier had been broken. The two began a flood of laughing converse with one another that astonished the couple behind.

The chatter stopped as they reached the vicarage, and Mr Reavley entered first to announce their visitors. There was no need: Mrs Henshaw delighted to see the young ladies, expressing disappointment when they declined refreshment. The group spent twenty minutes trading gossip until Georgiana mentioned that they had promised to return within the hour, and the ladies stood to take their leave.

Mr Reavley remembered to ask his sister for *The Ladies Magazine* which she relinquished happily, calling to the girls' attention an article on French fashion alterations of particular interest. After promising the vicar's wife that they would call again soon, the young people began the walk back, Reavley accompanying them again as far as the circulating library in order to transfer the deposit of the journal to Miss Bennet's temporary subscription.

As they walked, Georgiana and Mr Hewitt – once again positioned behind the others – slowed their pace and fell behind. Kitty and Mr Reavley, now nattering away again like magpies, scarcely noticed until they reached the high street. The library was only a few shops down, and Kitty called back that they would go on ahead to transact their business, meeting the others outside the establishment in a few moments; then she skipped away without awaiting reply.

With their friends gone, the lane took on a stark but welcome silence. Enough snow still lay on the ground to mute footfalls, and there were at present no birds to call or other sounds of nature to disturb the utter comfort and peace in the air. The two walked companionably until Georgiana noted that Nathaniel had stopped. She turned to find him a few paces back, staring at her with undisguised anxiety.

"Mr Hewitt? Are you unwell?" she asked.

He did not respond at first, but then roused himself with an emphatic "No!" as he took the few steps to where Georgiana waited, now looking full of anxious concern herself.

"No," he said more quietly as he reached her. "No, indeed, I have never felt as well as I do now. If your sister Mrs Darcy had not provided this diversion, I would have been forced to find one of my own. If I may, Miss Darcy, I must speak my mind to you."

"Why, certainly, Mr Hewitt. I hope you will always feel free to do so!" Georgiana felt bewildered now.

Nathaniel Hewitt glanced down then, assessing the ground and looking as if about to descend into a kneeling position to better see whatever it was he concentrated on; but then he shook his head and stood straight again. "It is no good," he said, perplexing Georgiana even more.

"Mr Hewitt?"

"Oh, I knew I should make a muddle of this!" he replied, bringing a laugh to Georgiana until she realised his serious intent in the ensuing silence. She found his gaze steady upon her, their eyes meeting and locking in earnest – grey to hazel, hazel to grey.

"Miss Darcy," he began again, "I cannot defer any longer. This is not the most advantageous place for such an entreaty, but I shall burst if I prolong my silence further. You must allow me to tell you –"

He hesitated then, losing his train of thought or his nerve, or perhaps both. Georgiana continued to look up into his eyes, a sweet smile half-formed on her lips, a blush of winter air in her cheeks, the sun's low rays lending a glint of silver to her grey eyes.

"I shall begin again, shall I?"

Still bemused, Georgiana could only nod her agreement, not quite certain just *what* he was beginning.

"Surely you guess my intent – you cannot be unaware of my regard. Miss Darcy, since I met you so many months ago, you have scarcely left my mind. Your image drifts from my dreams to my waking thoughts, until here, in your company these past days, I can see nothing else. Truly, I *wish* to see nothing else." Now that he had begun, his words came in a rush. "I consider departing for my Tour and it holds no interest, no enticement if you will not be there. I cannot conceive of leaving at all if I do not first tell you..." he faltered a bit now, but drew a deep breath, and said: "...tell you that I love and admire you as no other. If you will not have me, there is no place for me in the world, in truth."

"Have... *have* you?"

"Yes. Miss Darcy – Georgiana, dearest, sweetest Georgiana – will you relieve me of uncertainty? Will you say that you can love me? Will you consent to marry me? If you will be my wife, I pledge to you here and now to spend my entire life deserving you! I –"

Georgiana could not help herself, she began to laugh softly. Immediately Nathaniel Hewitt's face dropped to an expression readying itself for the pain of rejection. She removed a hand from her muff, and placed it lightly upon his cheek; and a tear spilled over onto her own as she whispered, "Oh, Nathaniel."

His confusion became complete when her laughter stopped suddenly and her eyes, unclear now behind a haze as they welled up, nevertheless locked upon his. "I can love you, Nathaniel. I *do* love you. But yet I cannot agree to marry you, not like this!"

CHAPTER SEVEN

AS THE CARRIAGES pulled away from the Rose and Crown, Lizzy sat back for the ride, hooked her arm affectionately through Jane's at her side, and considered their younger sister sitting across from them. Kitty had returned to the inn from her errand wearing a smile that spoke of success in more than the retrieval of a lady's magazine. She wore it still, better than half an hour gone. Even Bingley sitting next to her noticed a change in Kitty's demeanour.

"I believe, Catherine, you must have found today's excursion to your liking?" he asked idly. "Were you able to obtain all you desired?" When her reply was a giggle followed by a wave of coughing, Bingley glanced in ignorant wonder at the ladies across from him, drawing laughs from them.

"Not yet, Brother," she giggled, when she could speak again.

This only confused Bingley further, until Jane leaned forward and placed her hand upon his. "Charles, dearest, do not seek to understand. Our Kitty finds herself in love and –"

"Love!" she said. "Oh, do not call it love, Jane, it is nothing of the sort!" Still, she beamed.

By now, Bingley had caught on. "Ah, Mr Reavley, then?"

"*Indeed*," replied Jane and Lizzy together with teasing emphasis while Kitty's complexion turned several shades deeper. The blush, however, had no effect on her smile or her fidgeting.

"Do I surmise then, my dear, that your vicar offered you the compliment of his attentions after all?" asked Lizzy.

"Yes," said Kitty, her eyes glinting as her head tilted back and her shoulder rose in a shrug; she was pleased with herself. "Do you know, he insisted on accompanying us to the circulating library again, and then lingered there with me until Georgiana and Mr Hewitt caught us up before he would return to the vicarage. And he insisted on paying the subscrip –"

As Kitty continued her excited narrative, Lizzy felt a quick prick of alarum and dwelt on her recent words: *until Georgiana and Mr Hewitt caught us up.* Where had they been to require finding the others once again? Of course, Lizzy trusted Georgiana implicitly and Nathaniel Hewitt was an honourable young man; nothing untoward would occur. Still, Darcy would not thank Lizzy if she had sent the four out together only to have Kitty in her newfound enthusiasm for Mr Reavley scheme to separate from them. Neither should have been without chaperone; she would take that up with Kitty later. Little wonder Georgiana had returned to the inn flushed and awkward in company.

When she returned to the converse at hand, Jane had asked their sister if Mr Reavley renewed his request for a dance on Saturday.

"No," said Kitty with a quick pout. But she could not maintain the attitude and began to laugh presently. "He requested *all* the dances!" She bounced repeatedly in her seat, startling Bingley yet again. "Of course, I told him that is impossible. I promised him only two and so he has claimed the first, and the last before supper. He is certain to escort me for supper then." She bounced again; this time an attentive Bingley was prepared for it. "If he dances well I might grant him one additional near the end," she said. "But *only* if he dances well! Though I cannot imagine he would not, can you? Oh, I do hope he can dance well."

Kitty continued on in this manner while Jane listened patiently and asked questions now and again. Bingley simply stared in wonder once more at his sister – her enthusiasms in full force never ceased to amaze him. Lizzy smiled and let her mind drift again.

She could hear the horses from the carriage behind hers, and it brought to her mind her earlier discourse with one of its passengers. How odd that Sir James had been reluctant to admit a prior acquaintance with Lady Catherine; odder still that neither had owned to it on first encounter. Then again, she recalled that he had only arrived in the turmoil of Mrs Hewitt's accident and Lady Catherine's attack; perhaps that accounted for it.

As her musing brought back the images of Monday afternoon and rested on the gathering in the drawing room, she suddenly gasped, the scene made clear. Sir James had arrived after Susanna Hewitt's injury but well before Lady Catherine's arrival. He had been in the room with them when the old dragon had entered – he had been talking with Lizzy herself and with Anne.

Lizzy covered her mouth with her hand to keep from further ejaculation as she realised that Darcy's aunt had stopped in mid-sentence and collapsed – at the very moment her eyes had settled upon Sir James!

No, she could not credit that Lady Catherine had fainted at sight of the gentleman; and yet, how could the two actions *not* be related? The more she pondered it, the more clarity the image afforded. Coupled with Sir James's reticence and insistence on circumspection, she could only conclude the connection of their youth must have gone some way beyond mere acquaintance. There must be a story there! And one, apparently, that neither wished to divulge. Sir James had asked Lizzy to ignore his revelation, but it could do no harm to ask Darcy if he knew anything of his aunt's history before her marriage to Sir Lewis deBourgh.

❖❖❖❖❖

Sir James found himself also reflecting on his converse lately concluded with Mrs Darcy. His hostess was quick, intelligent. He had not fooled her one whit regarding a previous connection with Cat – Lady Catherine deBourgh. If he were to maintain the lady's preference, he should practice thinking of her as such; and yet even after so many years, the diminutive formed on his tongue naturally as though it had hovered there all this time lest it might be wanted. But surely the more decorous name better suited the woman she had become – she was not his 'Cat' any longer.

Who would have guessed that at such an advanced stage of his life, he would encounter her again now, when in forty years their paths had never crossed? He closed his eyes, picturing the honey-haired virago she had been and instantly he was transported back through the years.

When Lady Catherine Fitzwilliam had sent round to him her curt farewell, admonishing him not to attempt to see her again and professing herself well rid of his attentions, simple James Thornton as he was then had been thrown. His blithe nature had gone into a tizzy of confusion – he could not believe the words that swam before glazing eyes. Surely it could not be. But he had met her brother in town that very afternoon; an awkward encounter leaving no doubt that James was no longer welcome to call.

He had remained in town some weeks, hovering around the edges of the Fitzwilliam family's society until this horrid miscarriage could be revealed and set right; but no such correction came. After little more than a month, banns were published for Lady Catherine Fitzwilliam and Sir Lewis deBourgh of Kent – and his own 'Cat' ceased to be.

James had tried then to return to his life of ease, but found he could not. He was excluded from a small number of engagements where the Fitzwilliams would be in attendance. And even when he was not excluded, he had no heart to fill his accustomed role of affable rake. Most painful were events they both attended – James would watch his Cat enter on the arm of her older betrothed and his heart would go cold.

When his friend Robert Deane sailed to the colonies, James made a hasty decision to join him for the journey. It was thirteen months before he booked passage to return, but the time abroad had served him well. On his arrival again in England, James continued to travel, spending time with friends in Scotland and the Lakes and... anywhere he would be unlikely to find the society of his former attachment. Then word found him of John's death; and his brother's passing forced him to return at once to Gloucestershire.

It was amazing, as he thought of it, that he had never encountered any of the deBourgh or Fitzwilliam families afterwards – part judicious planning, a greater part good fortune – and eventually he no longer thought of them, no longer concerned himself with their paths crossing. And now, all these years later, to encounter her again, each of them widowed, well past the age to renew old passions even had they been the same people. It seemed a cruel trick of fate. Should he have known better than to form an attachment to the Bingleys and, through them, the Darcys? No – James had been aware that Mr Darcy was Lady Catherine's nephew, but he had also heard of their estrangement. He could not have suspected... and it mattered little. It changed nothing.

He turned his mind a moment to Anne deBourgh: a slip of a girl and easily indisposed. She had inherited her mother's features; but her dark colouring and her delicate nature, these must have been her father's legacy to her. James reflected that but for an inexplicable reversal of fortune, she might have been *his* daughter.

He shook his head now, not wanting his thoughts to take him to melancholy musings on his own Emma, lost to him two years gone while giving birth to a stillborn son. He looked about the carriage for diversion. Wentworth and Edmund Hewitt were enjoying some mutual jest, so he moved on and settled his glance upon Nathaniel Hewitt opposite him. The younger Hewitt appeared to be struggling with a conundrum himself. Sir James wondered what was on the gentleman's mind.

Indeed, the object of Nathaniel's occupation rode in the third carriage of this small procession.

❖❖❖❖❖

Georgiana sat very still, pressed as far into the corner of her seat as possible in an attempt to elude notice. Thankfully, when she and Nathaniel had met Kitty at the library, her friend was in such a state over her own conquest of Mr Reavley that she had not noticed the change in Georgiana's mood. Then Kitty had proceeded to draw the attentions of the group on returning to the inn such that Georgiana's elevated colour and breathing could be overlooked. But Mrs Gardiner was observant by nature, and Gee was certain her countenance must shout her feelings if anyone should look too closely upon it. She chided herself to collect her resources and maintain decorum until this business could be concluded.

Fortunately, the Gardiners were engaged with Mrs Chaney at the moment, giving Georgiana the freedom of her thoughts. She gazed out the window to avoid being drawn into conversation; but as the scenery passed, she saw again only the quiet, snow-covered lane in Lambton where her life had changed forever.

He loved her! Above all others, Nathaniel Hewitt had chosen to love Georgiana Darcy – and if he were to be believed, he had done so since that glorious spring day in Castleton when the wind had taken her bonnet but given her a handsome rescuer.

Gee's stomach fluttered again to recall his proposal. She had been slow to understand his intention at first as he fumbled about. But then the words were spoken – *have me* – and in that instant Gee knew there was nothing she wished more in life than to be loved by this man; to love him in return. The feeling had been so heady as to elicit bubbly laughter from her by way of reply.

Then so quickly following, came the realisation that she could not accept this man unless there was complete candour between them. She had looked around her at the bright sky, the snow-covered hedge and lane, their breaths crystallising in the air between them – hardly the place for what must follow – and back to those earnest, supplicating, beloved hazel eyes; and she had screwed her nerve to do the right thing. Fear had replaced the elation in her gut as she offered to allow him to withdraw his pledge in all honour if he could not accept her, blighted as she was by a youthful indiscretion. She had watched his own countenance darken in doubt while she began to speak, to confess her shame. She had looked down at the ground when she finished, unwilling to see what must surely be his disgust.

And he had laughed – not with derision, but relief – and she had looked up involuntarily to see hope return to his expression. His eyes as the afternoon light struck them displayed the flecks of amber she had noticed at their first meeting, but now they carried warmth and true regard. He asked then if she was in earnest, that this was all that stood between their affections; and on her confirmation he had laughed again and called her his own 'silly goose'. The only anger he had conveyed was directed at Wickham for ill usage of a young and innocent girl trusting of a false friend.

Nathaniel immediately and with vehemence had assured Gee that nothing in her own conduct could be decried, nor could discredit her in his heart; he could not believe her guilty of anything more than ignorance of the ways of men. Unknowingly he echoed the comforting phrases her brother had used at the time of her shameful incident. And then he rendered his judgment: of course he wished still to make her his own, to safeguard her from such people in the world; and he asked her yet again to accept his hand, pledging his undying faith.

Absentmindedly now fingering the ties on a brown paper parcel of ribbons that lay in her lap, Georgiana closed her eyes and anticipated the ball on Saturday; pictured herself in the gown she had so lately been fitted for, her hair dressed and interwoven with these very ribbons. She saw herself descending the stairs to find a crowd of young men awaiting her at the bottom; and Nathaniel stepping out in front of them all to claim right of escort, eyes sparkling with appreciation of her form as he reached out to offer her his arm. In her fantasy, he led her to take their place for the first dance and every one turned naturally to this handsome couple. *Their eyes met in a lingering gaze as they awaited the music being struck, and found each other again and again as they moved through the steps, each touch of their hands releasing a surfeit of exhilaration...*

"I believe, Mrs Chaney," said Mr Gardiner with pleasure, "our young friend must dream of dancing, if her sighs and swaying are to be judged well!"

Georgiana opened her eyes then to see the carriage occupants gazing on her with undisguised amusement. She gulped down a blush as best she could and smiled sheepishly.

"Mr Gardiner," admonished his wife, "you have broken her reverie now!" She smiled at Georgiana. "Go on, dear, do not mind my husband – go back to your sweet dreams."

The blood fully rising to her cheeks now, Georgiana stammered something about having dozed and then turned to look pointedly out the window, determined to remain alert until they arrived home. As they made the turn into the gates of Pemberley, she noted on the snow the shadow of the carriage in front of hers, and wondered what *he* was thinking now.

❖❖❖❖❖

Nathaniel Hewitt watched the gatehouse recede from view as his brother's equipage covered its last half mile to the house. He was at once self confident and apprehensive, irresolute where to settle. To know that Georgiana Darcy loved him gave him the buoyancy of certainty; he felt capable at that moment of besting any challenge. Any, that is, except the one he would soon face; and therein lay his apprehension. He must gain the consent of Gee's guardians for them to marry before she would accept him.

There was no doubt of her eventual acceptance; she had assured him of that, of her love for him. *Her love* – would he ever tire of thinking of this jewel being his to claim? But she had made any formal answer to him conditional upon the permission of her guardians, and most notably of her brother. She could not – most adamantly *would* not – ever betray Darcy's trust a second time by entering any understanding absent his knowledge.

Nathaniel little doubted that Colonel Fitzwilliam could be convinced of this match easily, and Gee had agreed with this assessment. But her brother had the greater voice of approval; he presented by far the greater challenge. Georgiana had warned Nathaniel that his interview would require care. But as they spoke of it, she convinced him it was a surmountable obstacle – the necessary approval would be hard won but attained in the end. After all, she had reasoned, they were near in age, both of good family, and he with prospects in property and fortune which would be nicely augmented with her own substantial endowment. As importantly, Nathaniel's brother was a long-time family friend; that must bode well to speak for character.

And in the end, Georgiana relied upon her absolute certainty – borne out time and again in his actions – that Fitzwilliam Darcy only wished for Georgiana's well-being and happiness. When he saw the joy this match would bring to her, all the other considerations would join to support his blessing.

Nathaniel had believed Georgiana's assurances because he fervently wished for such an outcome. But now, sitting on his own and considering the all-important words by which he would make his appeal, his confidence began to recede. He would not underestimate the challenge – and he must find the words, the approach, that would prevail. It would be tonight, it must be, before he could think on it too much and his courage and optimism could wane.

❖❖❖❖❖

Darcy smiled down the length of the dining table at Lizzy and wished, not for the first time in the past week, that there were not a score of people separating them. It felt an age since they had shared an intimate meal – just the two of them – in the family room. He laughed quietly at this. He could recall periods in the last several years, while Georgiana was at school, when dining alone in the small parlour had seemed oppressive; he had longed even for mindless company to hold at bay his sense of loss and seclusion. Never an individual who minded solitary pursuits, yet those early years following his father's death were notable for an emptiness of spirit only realised later. Elizabeth had changed that. She had returned to him the sense of peace to be derived in being his own person. Now he craved those quiet meals, though always in company with his wife.

He sighed, as she noted his greeting and responded with a warm smile. Another week and they would have some relief – he could withstand another week. It was not as if he were entertaining strangers; these were all family and friends he loved or, at least, tolerated (this last as his peripheral vision took in Lady Catherine's sour expression) – but they had brought with them in this season a host of concerns. He could not too soon see *those* resolved. Perhaps now that Retched had refused his aunt – the source, he believed, of that sourness in her – and most of the turmoil in the house – they could return to a company in harmony for Twelfth Night. His patience would be tried sorely enough with just the bustle of the next few days and their ball on Saturday.

He caught Lizzy's eye yet again and swore she read his mind; there was in her glance a sardonic humour that chided him to behave even as she laughed at him.

Looking around the table to elude his wife's all-too-astute gaze, he settled on his friend Hewitt. Edmund's mood was lighter today, much more the companion of old. Darcy could only believe his release from his wife's side attributed the change in temper. Despite her injuries, Susanna Hewitt appeared content with her invalid status and the attentions it afforded; and certainly Hewitt was more jovial out of her company. Darcy reflected how easily he might have found himself in such a marriage and counted himself fortunate indeed.

And how satisfied as well he had been to learn Retched's decision. Notwithstanding the onus of any future responsibility for Anne's welfare, he would not see either of his cousins so saddled with Hewitt's obligations, especially now given his clearer understanding of Anne.

Looking at Anne again with that newfound appreciation, he could see one immediate benefit of Fitzwilliam's refusal. She sat with her companion, more animated in discourse than he had witnessed in years, appearing for all purposes quite happy with her lot. Or perhaps he had simply never observed her with such insight as he now possessed.

Not so her mother to whom Darcy now gave some consideration. Lady Catherine had joined the others for dinner tonight, insisting she was in fine health, but her temper was clearly out of sorts. She had sat imperially in the drawing room before dinner, speaking to no one but gazing upon them all with displeasure. Sir James had approached her genially for a few moments, but she had been quick to put him off. Now, Darcy spoke with her to pass the meal and she responded in brief retorts, but she was distracted – glaring not at Fitzwilliam, as he might have expected, but at her own daughter. Darcy determined not to attempt to comprehend; it would surely overtax his resolve of happy tolerance.

While he spoke of trivial things with his aunt, he glanced to Fitzwilliam and Amelia Chaney. He might have expected those two to have returned to amicability and was surprised to note that both looked at pains to maintain their discourse; he could not discern which looked the more miserable. He would leave them as well to sort their relationship.

Jane and Bingley at least were at peace with the world, happily engaged with Sir James at the other end of the table. And Kitty, too, could hardly sit still as she claimed Henry Wentworth's converse; Wentworth listened with his customary affability, clearly taking enjoyment in her enthusiasm. Next to her, Georgiana appeared distracted, quiet and withdrawn. Darcy wondered what was going through his sister's mind. She kept herself attentive to her meal, not speaking even to Nathaniel Hewitt on her other side. The young man was preoccupied as well, taking only furtive glances at Georgiana from time to time and then reverting to the place in front of him. Perhaps the two had experienced a disagreement. Darcy would not regret such a thing – he would find some distance between them more than tolerable.

His attention was claimed now by an address from Mrs Gardiner and he left off his survey of the table in good humour to speak with Lizzy's aunt and uncle.

❖❖❖❖❖

Amelia had contrived to sit on one side of Colonel Fitzwilliam for dinner, but now having done so, she was shy of him. Her efforts to engage his attentions earlier in the day had met with only partial success and that in no small measure attributable to his friend. But when Major Soames left, the Colonel had accompanied him – Amelia might almost believe he had been relieved to escape her company.

She could not fully credit his apparent reticence to maintain a discourse with her. She had expected it would require no small exertion to regain the gentleman's trust and interest; but her efforts, rather than inducing even small progress, seemed instead to drive him further into himself... this was not the Colonel she had come to know.

He had been engaged in light discourse with Miss Darcy, but now the young lady had given her attention elsewhere. This was Amelia's opportunity.

"Have you been acquainted with Major Soames for some time?" she asked him, hoping the reference to his friend would enliven the Colonel where other topics had fallen flat.

"A short time only," he admitted, "but I find myself more impressed with each meeting."

They began to speak of the Major's circumstances and, from that, the current state of the Prince's Army until, after a few moments, their conversation was quite natural, much like it used to be, sharing opinions freely. Feeling some advancement at last, Amelia became less tentative, more animated, and nearly happy. Elizabeth Darcy caught her glance now and smiled with encouragement. But then Amelia mentioned Mr Wentworth in an off-hand manner and it seemed a cloud descended upon Colonel Fitzwilliam's countenance. Within moments he had retreated yet again, perfectly civil but somehow vacant. She chastised herself for having mentioned Mr Wentworth even in passing, and sighed in frustration at their progress so instantly dissolved. Their glances and speech became stiff again and it was with some relief finally that Amelia saw Elizabeth stand to lead the ladies to the drawing room.

She took tea and spent some minutes being entertained by Miss Bennet's excited chatter. Miss Darcy joined them as well but stood by, content to give her friend the lion's share of conversation. If anything, Georgiana Darcy, while clearly sharing Catherine Bennet's happy anticipation of the ball, nurtured thoughts of closer consequence. She kept darting glances at the door, no doubt awaiting the entrance of her admirer, an air of nervous expectation shimmering about her person.

So much gay interest was wearing and Amelia realised she did not possess the wherewithal to further engage Colonel Fitzwilliam tonight. Considering that she seemed to have caused more damage than reparation, she decided to retire early and face her challenge again fresh in the morning. She saw an opportunity before the men rejoined the party of excusing herself, and took her leave.

CHAPTER EIGHT

A PECULIAR AIR seemed to pervade in the dining room after the ladies had withdrawn; or perhaps Fitzwilliam simply pulled the strangeness of feeling from his own unsettled spirit. Did he only imagine the edginess of young Hewitt? – the irregular pensive quiet of Sir James? – Darcy's deliberate affability cloaking a fracture in his equanimity? – the casual way that Wentworth seemed to scrutinise the Colonel? Was he more sensitive to the moods of others given his own of late, or were these all figments – his own creation from nothing?

If so, his imagination did not stretch to ascribe such heightened consequences to Charles Bingley. He wondered briefly with a chuckle if Bingley ever felt the weight of events. His even and amiable temper had never been found ruffled in Fitzwilliam's presence, and even now he chatted with enthusiasm to his uncle and Sir James as if the world presented itself for his enjoyment – a highly admirable quality in the man which more than served to offset any shortcomings in intellect or determination. He could understand the attraction for Darcy in their friendship, complementing contrasts from which both profited.

But of course Bingley must occasionally suffer poor spirits; no one was immune to them. Fitzwilliam himself generally was found to be more of Bingley's nature than that of his grave and taciturn cousin, although even Darcy, now debating a point of history with the Hewitt brothers, had grown lighter in his soul this year past.

It is only I, apparently, thought Fitzwilliam, *who grows more sullen of late. And it is time for me to reverse such attitude.* He knew he was reputed to possess, and indeed more often than not *did* possess, a nature similarly easy to Bingley's if perhaps not as constantly so; and he was determined to regain it. He *must* resolve finally his feelings for Amelia Chaney!

I will leave, he decided; then wondered from where such a thought had sprung even as he saw its merits. Removed from Mrs Chaney and her lover, he could make strides in reverting to his old character; he could grieve her properly and begin again. And he could offer the lady all that remained to him to give – the opportunity to engage Wentworth without the disquieting shadow of his own attendance. He would mention the timely business of Major Soames to incite an early return to London. Of course, he would explain all to Darcy, but his cousin would not begrudge him his early escape in the circumstance. He would understand too well, as would Elizabeth, even without a full accounting.

The more he considered it, the notion took on greater benefit in his mind. This party at Pemberley had not proved the restful, happy gathering he had anticipated, although it was through no fault of Darcy and Elizabeth. When he had first suggested to Lizzy that Amelia Chaney be included, he had not consciously understood it would serve a purpose beyond that the lady could find company in a difficult season of loss. He had not yet acknowledged – even to himself – his heightened involvement with the widow; nor could he have seen the complications of Lady Catherine's proposal in light of his revelation that he loved Amelia Chaney. But given those, and the further impediment of Wentworth's introduction, these days had taken on a grotesque perverseness. Why should he remain to see them through when all it could purchase was further disappointment? Why subject himself to the gaiety of a ball on Twelfth Night only to watch Amelia and Wentworth growing closer, in effect pouring salt into his wound?

If he spoke with Darcy tonight, he could leave in the morning and achieve some distance immediately. He would, of course, first ensure accompaniment for Amelia's later travel; perhaps she could journey to town with Georgiana and Mrs Annesley next month. He then would return to work with a vengeance and put women – one woman – and marriage and love out of his mind.

Could he do this? He could distract his mind with distance perhaps, but could he also banish her from his heart by leaving? Then again, had she not already withdrawn from it voluntarily when she accepted Henry Wentworth?

He considered this and was met again with the strange impression that still she occupied place there. He concluded that as long as he remained at Pemberley – resident with her and her curiously renewed affability – this sensation would continue. But it was counterfeit; it could only delay and thereby intensify his eventual pain. Better to separate now and face the ordeal squarely before worse damage could be inflicted.

Yes, he would leave the next morning. The decision made, he resolved as well to leave with his ties to Amelia broken cleanly and with honour; giving himself then a finality to occasion his full acceptance of the loss, to begin to *feel* it. He marvelled again that he did not experience the depth of anguish he believed he should. He needed to confront this betrothal frankly — if only, perversely, to prove to himself that he loved her through the acuteness of feeling which must surely follow at last. As long as his sense of loss was only in his rational mind, it was too easy to believe that a reversal was possible, to hold out a hope she would reconsider. He had found himself scrutinising every soft word, every smile she had proffered in the last day in the hollow wish that she cared as warmly as she had done — but it would not do. He needed to court the pain now, to accept in his heart that he loved and had lost.

The gentlemen were about to rejoin the ladies in the parlour, and as they rose, Fitzwilliam caught Wentworth's eye.

"Sir," he said, "I wonder, will you oblige me with a word?"

Wentworth acquiesced, simply curious as he slowed his pace while the others exited. Fitzwilliam heard also Nathaniel Hewitt asking Darcy for a word in private, and saw Darcy's countenance immediately sharpen in suspicious speculation; saw his cousin look back at him briefly with an indefinable question before then nodding to Nathaniel and turning towards his study with the young man. Fitzwilliam heard and saw this; but it did not signify with him. He was too intent now on his resolve to act in his own interests.

❖❖❖❖❖

This was the most difficult moment of his life! Worse even than facing his father's judgment that time, at fifteen, when he had left a grazing gate unsecured and three head of cattle subsequently had been lost in a ravine for his carelessness.

Nathaniel Hewitt stood facing a beast of mountainous proportion, concentrating on remaining straight and tall and concealing the slight quiver in his knees. Not the best impression to leave if one's legs should buckle and drop one to the floor just at the moment of making application.

Mr Darcy did not make it easier. His countenance had assumed a wary frown as soon as Nat had requested a word with him, and the expression had not altered one whit in the interim. The gentleman stood in the centre of *his* room, slightly taller than Nat; absolutely more solid and daunting with his formal stony bearing; his impeccably tailored cutaway of darkest blue lending his eyes a deep saturation to suggest the prospect of an imminent tempest; those same eyes now deliberately masked of all emotion but suspicion, and trained so very intently upon Nat; his only movement a slight pulsating twitch in his cheek.

Nat glanced around him very quickly, took in the study as he formulated the words he would use. Mr Darcy still did not move or speak, and Nat fought against a sudden need to sit down. A thought flitted through his head that he should have done better to solicit Colonel

Fitzwilliam's approval first — an easier challenge to build both his own confidence and an advocate with Mr Darcy. But he was here; Mr Darcy in fact awaited him... with waning patience.

"Mr Darcy – Sir," he began, turning his attention once more to the awesome face. He saw nothing malevolent in it, but neither did it offer any accommodation or eagerness to hear what surely must follow. All Nat's careful preparation was lost in that instant — articulation became secondary to getting the matter irrevocably spoken before he lost his nerve.

"Sir, I beg the honour... the privilege... to marry your sister."

❖❖❖❖❖

Fitzwilliam and Wentworth stood a moment, facing one another without speaking. The Colonel inwardly marvelled again at Wentworth's *nonchalant* manner.

"I depart for town in the morning, Mr Wentworth; I have business to attend for the Duke of York's Regiment that cannot be delayed." Fitzwilliam felt beads of moisture forming on his upper lip and his hands were clammy, but he would say what he must; it was the best restorative for him in the end. He drew breath again. "But I cannot leave, Sir, without offering congratulations to you."

"I thank you, Colonel." The rejoinder was offered instinctively, but then the gentleman appeared bemused. "Might I inquire for what I am to be thus cheered?"

Now it was the Colonel who was confused, and he stood mutely until he recalled that Wentworth could not be aware of Fitzwilliam's foreknowledge. In that gentleman's mind, no one yet knew of what had passed between him and Amelia; the pair had been silent on the subject of their understanding, aloof with each other even since reaching it.

Fitzwilliam coloured slightly, realising his error and that, to explain, he must admit to his eavesdropping. "Sir, I am obliged to beg your indulgence. On my way to dinner two nights past I found myself privy to overhearing some part of your converse with Mrs Chaney."

Wentworth waved an easy pardon as nothing and smiled, yet he appeared even less informed as to Fitzwilliam's meaning.

"I am aware, Mr Wentworth, that the situation requires discretion; that you would wish your undertaking to remain private until an appropriate time. And I assure you that my good will towards both you *and* the lady will silence me on the subject hereafter."

"Colonel Fitzwilliam, I do not fault your discretion, but I must tell you, Sir, I wonder still at your purpose."

Fitzwilliam frowned. This was not going as he might expect — Wentworth not at all quick to acknowledge his good fortune. The Colonel shrugged in frustration, and began more forthrightly. "I merely wish before my departure to offer you felicity upon your engagement, Sir. Mrs Chaney is a gentle lady who, as you know, has long held my good will; I am gratified on her account to find she will be well settled with as worthy a gentleman as yourself. I wish you both happy."

Henry Wentworth's eyes had grown round as Fitzwilliam spoke, his mouth dropping down in amused surprise. "Colonel," he began when he found his voice. "I believe, Sir, you labour under a misapprehension! As you heard our discourse, surely you must allow that the promise of a dance carries with it no greater obligation upon its completion!"

"A dance?" *Did the man toy with him purposely?*

"Yes, a dance. What did you —" The full grasp unfurled itself then and, at once, he hurried to say, "Oh, no, Colonel! Mrs Chaney and I have no such understanding as you believe."

"But —" Fitzwilliam was adrift.

"Whatever could you have heard to bring you such a conclusion?"

Not fully articulate, Fitzwilliam nonetheless gave account of the conversation which, even as he now related it, echoed as inconclusive to his ears; but ended by noting as well the embrace which had followed and lent credence to his construal.

"Ah!" replied Wentworth, laughing at once until he noted indignation mounting in Fitzwilliam. He explained that the embrace had been one of friendship only, inappropriate perhaps, but nothing more than spontaneous gratitude for some offered advice.

Fitzwilliam could barely take in the words he heard. His mind grabbed for lucid thought even as Wentworth chuckled kindly.

"Colonel, if I may offer *you* some counsel as well, not dissimilar to that I tendered the lady?" He did not wait approval. "In truth, Mrs Chaney is enchanting, and I might have allowed of earnest pursuit but for the intelligence very early learnt that her heart has been otherwise engaged for some time."

"Some time?" echoed Fitzwilliam, hearing the words without quite taking their full import.

"Yes, it seems a gentleman of close association — an officer in fact, who has offered great assistance to the lady these months — holds an absolute claim upon her affections."

"But, the past days —" Fitzwilliam still could not think clearly.

"Ah, yes. A mistake in judgment, I am certain she would confess; born of giving credence to pointed counsel to consider the gentleman's welfare, if I may speak on her behalf. But surely he will have noted her late attempts to make amends?"

Wentworth laughed again now to see clarity dawning in Fitzwilliam's expression; but this time Fitzwilliam joined him in it, a nervous, self-deprecating laugh. What a fool he had been to draw hasty conclusion! Even as the truth became evident, he realised some better part of him had all along apprehended there must be an extenuating consideration he had neglected. For in his own misguided rational conclusion, he could not feel the pain of loss, yet the proof of his error now sent his heart soaring with elation.

He alternately apologised and thanked Wentworth for correcting his mistake until finally they shook hands and made their way to the drawing room to join the company. Just before they entered, Wentworth said: "You may count, Colonel, upon *my* full discretion in this matter; but do I take it, Sir, that this late information alters your imminent business in town?"

Fitzwilliam smiled. "Indeed, my friend. I shall dispatch the errand by post. My business, I think, is here after all. I have some amends of my own to proffer."

❖❖❖❖❖

Fitzwilliam returned to the drawing room with a buoyant step, glancing about him as he moved to accept a cup of tea from Jane Bingley. He took in the room quickly, becoming aware immediately of several absences, including Amelia Chaney. Uncertain whether to be disappointed, he decided he would do well to take a bit of time and come to terms with his change in fortune before encountering her – no need to compound his behaviour of late with a foolish display. He walked over to Lizzy who dispensed tea on the other side of the table.

"She retired early," Lizzy said immediately with a dry smile.

Fitzwilliam saw no point in feigning ignorance with his quick cousin. "Is she well?"

"Well enough." Lizzy had taken in the change in Fitzwilliam's overall demeanour and added, smiling invitingly: "I venture she wants only the stimulation of attentive company for a cure."

"I have been something of a fool, have I not?" he said then in a low voice. "I have misjudged the lady."

"A common enough failing of late – you are not alone." She glanced towards Anne deBourgh across the room. "But Anne is in excellent spirits this evening…"

Fitzwilliam offered Lizzy a wry glance. "Darcy told you, then, of my converse with her."

"Yes." She laughed then as if she took delight in a private jest. "And of his," she added rather cryptically. But she sobered an instant later and placed her hand lightly on Fitzwilliam's arm. "I had little doubt you would choose wisely in the end, Retched; and I am glad to see this now resolved, or nearly so."

83

He smiled at the satisfaction he saw in her look as she continued. "I do wonder, though, at some new trouble that may be brewing in another quarter."

At his quizzical regard, she nodded towards the fire where Georgiana stood alone, holding her hands out towards the blaze with little awareness. Her glance, her complete concentration, instead was trained upon the door, her eyes round in anticipation, chewing on the corner of her lower lip in a show of suspended nerves.

Fitzwilliam in the aftermath of his revelation with Wentworth had forgotten that Nathaniel Hewitt had begged speech with Darcy; and it came back to him now with the realisation that those two gentlemen were amongst those not present.

"N-No," he said in uncertain denial. "Surely it has not gone so far!" he whispered. Even as he spoke, however, he considered the young couple these past few days; he could not recall seeing one without the other nearby such that to consider them a couple sprang easily to mind. He realised he had underestimated the serious nature of their courting – he might have seen it more clearly had he been more observant, less consumed with his own concerns.

"Oh, dear," he looked back again at Lizzy. At the exact moment that she said, "Poor Gee" he murmured "Poor Darcy." They smiled knowingly, nodded agreement, and Lizzy added, "Poor Mr Hewitt!"

He looked back at Georgiana again; there was no mistaking the nervous anticipation she wore.

"I fear you will have to direct some of your attention away from your own amorous pursuits to deal with this in the next days, Retched. Darcy and Gee are going to need you."

He grimaced, not at thought of his own part to play but for the additional strain this could only add to the general air of the season.

❖❖❖❖❖

Darcy sat in the study, his shoulders slumped in gloom, ruminating on what had just transpired and dreading the discourse he would have to initiate with his sister. He scarcely noticed when Lizzy knocked softly and entered; he did not acknowledge her. She took in her husband's stony distant gaze and furrowed brow, and the light greeting she had planned died on her lips. She recognised from the darkness of his eyes, which always took on that deep storm-cloud hue when he was troubled, that the interview Darcy had just concluded had not gone well.

Lizzy had been entertaining the ladies in the parlour after dinner when most of the gentlemen of their party joined them for tea and coffee. Fitzwilliam and Mr Wentworth had come shortly after the first group, apparently restored in good humour with one another; but neither Darcy nor young Nathaniel Hewitt had come in at all. This, coupled with her sister's apprehensive inattention to their guests and darting glances towards the door, did not escape Lizzy's notice. She realised that Mr Hewitt must have requested a word with her husband, and she well knew what a trial it might be for him, indeed, for them both.

Upon Mr Hewitt's return to the parlour sometime later in a purposeful (but ultimately unsuccessful) show of composure, Lizzy feared the worst. She spoke a quick word to Jane to see to any further refreshments; then quietly excused herself to seek out Darcy, finding his study door ajar, the flickering of firelight outlining in sharp angles his taut, unmoving form at the desk.

She crossed over to him now, wordlessly resting her hands on his tensed shoulder in a demonstration of compassion. Before she could venture a query as to his recent meeting, however, the study door flew open without ceremony and Georgiana marched in, her own eyes storm-darkened as well.

"*Why?*"

Her brother slowly turned his head to look upon Georgiana, but did not respond. The young woman repeated her vehement challenge. "Why? Why do not you even seek or consider *my* feelings in this matter? Can you care so little for my happiness?"

Darcy continued to stare at Georgiana, oblivious to everything else in the room. Lizzy slipped away from him and made her way to the study door that Georgiana, in her pique, had left open. She closed it against any inquisitive passers-by. She had considered for an instant only on which side of the door to place herself – wishing to respect this private matter between Darcy and his sister but, in the end, believing herself better served with firsthand knowledge of their encounter. She stayed quietly in the shadows so as not to draw attention to herself, however; this matter must needs be resolved between the two siblings.

Drawing up rigidly to his feet, taking a slow breath and a step towards his sister, Darcy spoke finally with studied control. "Georgiana, when you can address me with civility, I will discuss this with you. Perhaps in the morning when you have had a chance to consider –"

"No! We will discuss this now." Georgiana and Darcy each were startled by her stand and now stood transfixed until Georgiana, unable to meet any longer her brother's censorious gaze, glanced away. She looked over towards Lizzy with a silent appeal, but Lizzy shook her head, softening the refusal with an encouraging smile.

Returning her attention to Darcy, Georgiana began again quietly. "Brother, I know my mind in this. Mr Hewitt is – he has my regard and I his. You cannot deny us happiness."

"I can and must look out for your welfare, since you wilfully disregard it." Georgiana began to protest, but Darcy silenced her with his glare. Lizzy chewed inattentively on her thumbnail as she watched these two people she loved; the very air between them seemed to undulate. She knew that there was far more resident in the minds of both siblings at this moment than the strict question of Nathaniel Hewitt's merits. She studied her husband and noted the twitch in his cheek, his set mouth, pinched nose and glassy eyes—the signs of effort his control took. He would at all cost guard his tongue; he would never voice Georgiana's past ill judgment against her, though they all knew it took precedence in his mind and his sister's.

"Georgiana, you are too young to know your own heart, no less that of Mr Hewitt. You are not yet eighteen, only now coming out into society. He is little more in years, only come from university, certain of little about himself as well. There are any number of young men you will soon have occasion to meet, established men, more suited in temperament, more suited in standing than – "

"More suited? Suited to what? To whom? Mr Hewitt is a gentleman, of an old and respected family! In that we are equal. But he rises above – he is also of titled heritage."

"A second son."

"A nobleman's son, nonetheless. Why, he is the brother of your great friend! And you question his standing, his temperament?"

"I question the stability of his future!" he snapped – then, shaking his head at his lapse in control, he moderated his tone once more. "I know well what he can achieve by marrying Georgiana Darcy, but what has he to offer to you? He –"

"That is unfair. Nathaniel has no need of my fortune; he will have his own inheritance when he attains his majority. His mother's gift provides him with a small estate and another holding and the resources to keep them. Do you think so little of me as to believe no man could admire me but for my *endowment*?"

Darcy winced at the familiarity of reference Georgiana used in speaking of Mr Hewitt, but forbore to chide her for it. There were more serious points to make. "Certainly not! But he does not have those holdings yet! And what experience to gauge whether he will maintain them with any success? He is untried, Gee." As she looked to refute him, Darcy plunged on. "He is amiable enough, I grant you, when he leaves behind his butterflies and bugs. But that – "

"So that is your objection to him? That he applies himself to the serious study of nature, rather than reading the classics?"

"No! I have already stated my objections, do not twist my words. But consider, Georgiana, were I to consent to this match, would you be prepared to sit at home alone while Mr Hewitt takes lengthy and costly expeditions to remote jungles? Or is it your wish to expend your youth consorting with prehistoric organisms and petrified plant life and eschewing all of society while your husband discovers a new species of *insect*?"

"You are being ridiculous. Your conjecture carries little merit and does you no credit. Nathaniel is not nearly so aloof as all that." Georgiana glared at Darcy for a moment, and then a curious look stole across her countenance as she added with derision, "By your reasoning, brother, I might conclude that your opposition to Mr Hewitt is that he is too like yourself!" At Darcy's start, she continued. "Your method of escape may differ, but your attitude does not. When have the pleasures of society been more than a tedious responsibility to you? What ball ever gave you the satisfaction that a solitary ride with Parsifal offers?"

"That is entirely different. I have made my way in society; I am established and perfectly at ease in it." Lizzy covered her mouth with her hand and slid back a step deeper into shadow to hide the smile her husband's statement induced. Darcy, however, took no notice of anything but his sister's uncharacteristic fit of pique. "And it is not my character in question here!" He drew himself up to a daunting posture to signal that debate was at an end. "Nathaniel Hewitt is a perfectly adequate young man, but I will not accede to this match. You are both too young to know your minds or your hearts, and there is no assurance that he will make something of his life. I cannot countenance a match with so little surety of success, and your very behaviour tonight has served to remove any doubt from my mind that *your* judgment is not balanced and cannot be relied upon. That is all I will say on the matter."

Georgiana stood still, gauging her brother's resolute deportment. Grief overspread her countenance and she whispered, "When will you see that one mistake in judgment, even so large a one, can teach a person better discretion? I am not that child anymore, Fitz." Darcy stood rigid in all his imposing size, his eyes hardened and his jaw set. Lizzy noted the pulsing in his cheeks, the grinding of his teeth the only sign of life noticeable for some moments.

Georgiana, one could see, tried to present a similar stubborn stance, and Lizzy thought with a prick of cheerless humour how so like one another they were at that instant, this dark and brooding husband of hers and his fair, willowy sister. But Georgiana's attempt to remain unyielding was broken by an involuntary quivering of her lips. Without another word, she turned and with a show of dignity made her way to the door. She opened it to leave, but at the threshold she turned to look again at her brother. His continued impenetrable scowl broke Georgiana's silence.

"You will never judge any man good enough, brother. No one can meet your exacting standards; yet you would sacrifice my happiness to keep me a girl under your protection. I will end my days a bitter old maiden, with a paid companion and a parrot for diversion. And all to assuage *your* displeasure at the thought that I could find happiness in being dependent upon someone other than you!" Georgiana stopped suddenly, as startled at the venom in her message as its recipient had been. Her face reddened, she raised tear-stung eyes briefly upon the effect her words had produced in Darcy, and she ran from the room.

CHAPTER NINE

GEORGIANA GAINED her rooms with little awareness and flung herself onto her bed. She lay there some minutes trembling. Becca came in from the dressing room, but before she could begin to ask her mistress's wishes, she was dismissed with a curtness that Georgiana would later regret – particularly as her maid, before slipping out of the room completely, retrieved a large paisley shawl from the dressing closet and draped it across Gee's shivering form with a gentle hand.

Now, Georgiana curled her legs up and drew the shawl around her more closely, gripping one edge tightly in her fist. She was as unaware of her body's movements as she was of her feelings, a number of which raced through her with none gaining purchase. She must simply be dead in spirit – yet how could such lack of sensation hurt so? She raised fingers to her cheek and was astonished to find her face dry. She could not even cry – for despair, for anger, for anything.

She did not know how long she lay there before the need to do something overtook her. She should talk to someone, someone who could help her. But who? Instinctively, she knew Kitty would offer little assistance. Nor could she talk to Lizzy, though the desire to do so was strong. But Elizabeth must be bound to support her husband in his decision, whatever her own opinion; and Gee could not tolerate any defence of her brother now. Her feelings about him were too tangled. And to tell anyone else of this was unbearable – humiliating.

She desperately needed to see Nathaniel, but that was impossible. Her brother would never allow of it and some part of her realised it would only cause both of them additional pain. What could they possibly say to one another?

Retched? Would he – could he – advocate for her? She had presumed when Nathaniel had first proposed that Retched might support her desire; but even as she wondered the answer formed. It was too late;

her brother had pronounced his judgment and her own subsequent outburst would not have opened his mind to reconsider, regardless whose argument was put forth. Perhaps if she had talked with Retched first for his approval... but then, she had also presumed Fitz would acquiesce after putting Nathaniel through his paces – she could well be wrong about the position her cousin would take, too. It mattered little; Retched was downstairs and to see him she would have to see the others. She could not face anyone now, certainly not Nathaniel and – even less so, Providence spare her – her brother. There was no one. She was utterly alone.

If she could not speak to anyone, she could at least try to make sense of her own feelings. She would write in her journal – perhaps setting down her pain in ink would help her to make sense of her jumbled feelings, her rage at her brother's unreasonable intransigence. How could he do this to her?

She sat up slowly, her muscles achy and strangely nonresponsive, and got off the bed, wrapping the shawl around her shoulders against a chill she felt through to her bones. She crossed to her ladies' desk and perched on the edge of a chair there but, rather than drawing out her journal, her hand reached for a letter she had received two days past from her companion, a cheerful note expressing disappointment that she would miss Georgiana's coming out, but wishing her friend joy at her Twelfth Night ball. Gee fingered the missive for an instant, recalling the delight it had given her to read – she had answered it only yesterday with an excited anticipation that now seemed a cruel hoax.

Without conscious thought, she let the letter drop, pulling out a sheet of paper, pen and ink. *Dearest Mrs Annesley*, she began and then, as the ink flowed across the parchment, the tears followed suit, spilling down her cheeks.

❖❖❖❖❖

In the close air of the study Georgiana's charge echoed. Lizzy did not move at once, but held her breath and watched her husband for a sign of his temper. When at last he sighed to expel his own breath, arrested as his sister's last words had assaulted him, Lizzy moved to him. His eyes reflected only pain and confusion; gone was the certainty that had given him fortitude only a moment before. She took his hands in hers, detecting a slight tremor in them as she did so.

"How can she say such things, Elizabeth? How can Gee believe I could ever act against her welfare?"

"Fitz. Georgiana is hurt; she needed to lash out and wound in return. She loves you above all others–"

"Except, apparently, this boy!"

"No, not even this boy. Perhaps one day, and certainly in a manner very different from what is natural with you, *that* will never be supplanted. But not now, not yet." Lizzy chuckled with forced lightness and squeezed Darcy's fingers, drawing no more than the beginning of a recalcitrant grimace from the farthest edges of his lips. "Darcy, *you* have been her world all her life. Now she finds herself in love with a young man – a man she admires and respects – and you deem him unworthy. Her pain is increased for suffering two losses at once: the first the life she considers with Nathaniel; the second your faith in her. She is never unmindful of your love, but she wishes for more – she wants to *deserve your respect*. You have been everything to her, and she is smarting at your absence of trust in her judgment… and she is right."

Darcy, who had begun to let go of the tension a bit as Lizzy spoke, balked and seized up at her final words. He glowered at her from under thick brows drawn together sharply. "What can you mean, she is right? Do you so doubt my intentions as well?" he sputtered.

"I do not, you know I do not. Your motives are pure and honourable and come from the deepest love for your sister." She hesitated, then: "It is your reasoning that is blinded."

"My… my reasoning! My reasoning is faultless! Both of them are too young… too unworldly… too untried… too…!"

"Perhaps. But there is real affection there, you have seen it, I know you have. Is that not a basis upon which to build these other things? The boy is from a good family; he will be well situated. It is true, he has not yet proved himself; but is not this a failure of youth, rather than character or profligate living? Do you know of any defects in Mr Hewitt's behaviour? Darcy, he is not Wic—"

"Elizabeth, please!" Darcy closed his eyes as if to shut out any more debate on the subject, in scant control of his composure. Silence hung in the study, a palpable charge in the room. Finally, inhaling deeply and releasing it in a sigh, he said. "I do not reject Hewitt from any personal animosity; nor do I equate him with that… that other. And yes, of course I see affection between them. I blame myself for that –"

Lizzy took breath to argue, but Darcy placed his fingers on her lips to still her comment. "Yes, I do blame myself! I have allowed the acquaintance, provided the means to be in such close company, when I should have known, did know, that it would lead to intimacy.

"But she is young, and has been sheltered so much of her life. She has yet to come out, has not met any one other than Nathaniel Hewitt. What kind of guardian would I be – what kind of brother – to acquiesce to this when she has not had opportunity to consider others? When I have yet to assess what others might offer to her? It falls to me to ensure that Georgiana marries well, to someone who will respect and protect her, provide for her, as well as love her."

Lizzy's smile was sympathetic, but contradictory. "Did all your opportunity to consider others turn you from loving *me* when once we had met? Was I the best on offer in worldly attributes –" she laughed; "— a wilful, contrary country girl, not much accomplished; only tolerable in appearance and of little standing and less fortune? And would you argue now that marrying for affection served either of us ill?" This time, it was Lizzy who stilled her husband's would-be reply; she cupped his face in her hands, placing her thumbs lightly over his mouth. "No, you need not say. I know the answer to this as well as you."

Darcy's words were stilled, but Lizzy could see his mind working, going through all the arguments raised by the women he loved. She slid her thumbs to the sides of his mouth, replacing their touch on his lips with a kiss, before walking to the window to give her husband his thoughts.

After some moments, Darcy crossed to the window as well and stood behind his wife, placing his hands on her shoulders. The silence lengthened. "Will you go to her? To see that she is... that...?" he asked finally.

"No." At her demur, Darcy turned Lizzy towards him to challenge his wife. She forestalled him.

"Fitz, you must go to her yourself. You need your sister to know that you are a *loving* tyrant." She coaxed a rueful smile from his irritation. "And Georgiana needs for you to understand that she adores you even as she reaches out for independence. Do not allow this rift to widen from neglect. You are too much one to the other, whatever your final judgment in this matter."

Darcy dropped his head to his chest, reaching up a hand to pull at the tension in the back of his neck. He looked to Lizzy suddenly older than his thirty years. She wished at that moment that she could weather this storm for him, and felt helpless to alleviate the pain he wore in dulled eyes that, moments before, had flashed with indignation. She drew him into an embrace, holding him tenderly in the quiet room, until his body began to lose some stiffness and he responded by enfolding her in his arms. He rested his brow atop her head and they stood thus for some time.

But Lizzy knew, ultimately, that it was not she who could proffer the succour he needed now. Stepping back slightly, she gazed at this man who could be so obdurate, so infuriatingly intractable – yet so passionate in his loyalty and affection and his attention to family duty. She gently reached out to a random lock of hair falling across Darcy's brow, persuading it up to its proper place before she whispered: "Go to her, my love. *Talk* with her."

Lizzy felt his arms slide limply from her and knew that her husband had heeded her meaning as well as her words. She lifted his hand, placed a light kiss upon the banded ring that had been her wedding token to him, and left him to compose himself while she returned to their guests to make his apologies and Georgiana's for their early retirement.

❖❖❖❖❖

Lady Catherine's mood was only partly tempered by a few winning hands at quadrille. She had been of foul disposition since she had condescended to dine with the company, and two courses of a flawless repast had not sweetened her one bit, nor had lively conversation following. Sir James wondered at this. Surely his continued presence amongst the party could not account wholly for the lady's sour spirit. She herself had encouraged him to remain and, indeed, she had been at liberty to ignore him for the most part before abruptly soliciting him for a diversion of cards in the evening.

Mr and Mrs Gardiner had happily made a four for the rounds, partnering one another with the natural ease of a familiar relationship. This had left Sir James to partner with Lady Catherine, and he wondered if the pairing brought to her the same memories they evoked in him: a younger man and woman by far, bearing over the breadth of time only a token likeness to the present ones; but who had regularly repulsed all challengers, delighting in the contest for its own sake and feeding as if instinctively off each other's play; minds and strategies in concert. It had been over just such a game shortly after their introduction that James Thornton and Lady Catherine Fitzwilliam had recognised kindred spirits, had begun to move from concerted minds to concerted hearts. James shook his head to dispel such recollections.

Though she played quadrille still with a shrewd will to win, the woman seated opposite him now bore little else in common with the lively, smiling beauty of his memory, his Cat. This Lady Catherine wore a continual scowl and limited her discourse to finding fault: society had grown tedious; servants required continual surveillance to ensure their honest labour; trades-people no longer knew their place or betters, an opinion James found peculiarly objectionable given their table partners, though the Gardiners had the grace to allow the matter to pass unchallenged. Even her intimate acquaintance was not spared, her speech peppered with vague references to unreasonable and ungrateful relations. In short, it seemed to Sir James that the world no longer conformed to Lady Catherine's expectations and she bore it as a personal slight that it did not see fit to do so.

That some unpleasantness existed between the lady and her nephew Fitzwilliam was clear, although Sir James had no evidence as to its origin. But her frequent glances at the colonel since his entrance were filled with disdain. The gentleman for his part ignored them; indeed he appeared in fine spirits.

Still more surprising to James were the expressions Lady Catherine bestowed upon her own daughter. Anne deBourgh was such a slight, ill creature; how could anyone look upon her with less than compassion? Having witnessed two days past the young woman's distress after Lady Catherine's collapse, he could not imagine that Anne was not devoted to her mother; and he rather presumed the latter required little effort to bend the unassuming Anne to her will. Yet now the young woman sat in conversation with several other ladies, and Lady Catherine frequently subjected her to ill scrutiny. Anne occasionally returned the interest, watching her mother with a quizzical nervous air, saying nothing.

In order to mitigate the pall of Lady Catherine's sour temper as their rounds progressed, Sir James engaged Mr and Mrs Gardiner in conversation and now, somehow, the topic had come round to the extended time Sir James had passed in the American colonies in his youth. He regaled his friends with stories of a land and people at once familiar and alien – settlements and towns fashioned after their own but with a looser mode of custom; of French trappers and red savages; opportunities for anyone not faint of heart; the taming of a wild country – and as he told his stories well, his audience grew. The Bingleys and Miss Bennet came over to listen, even Miss deBourgh and her companion, everyone with eager questions. For nearly an hour, James entertained them all, the card game given up somewhere along the way, to Lady Catherine's displeasure. She remained, however, to listen, though she neither asked questions nor made comment. Perhaps her own thoughts had taken her back to recall the events that had encouraged Sir James's journey.

James abstractedly noted when Nathaniel Hewitt entered the room; the young man cast a tragic glance at Miss Darcy before moving to a secluded corner and but moments later, he and his brother withdrew for the night. As this had been preceded by the abrupt departure of Miss Darcy and as Mr Darcy continued absent, James feared the worst for the young lovers. *Oh dear,* he thought, as he returned to his narrative of the colonies as they were then; *how fortunate I am to be beyond an age for this business of love.*

❖❖❖❖❖

The first thing Lizzy noted on returning to the drawing room was that Nathaniel Hewitt had gone, as had his brother. She hoped they were together. The younger man had looked decidedly discomposed when he had entered after his encounter with Darcy, and she worried at how he fared. If Edmund Hewitt could not alter the disappointment his brother suffered, he at least knew Darcy better than most – he could appreciate what Nathaniel had undergone and offer some perspective with his comfort.

Despite his persistent objection to Nathaniel Hewitt's suitability for Gee, Lizzy could not believe Darcy had been rancorous with the young man. Firm certainly, probably cold in a reined in, reasoned approach; but with no outright display of animosity. His equanimity would not have been excited by young Hewitt in the manner it had with his sister and any strength of feeling would have been most carefully contained. Still, Darcy's very businesslike approach and tightly held emotions would have posed a formidable obstacle for a young man already made anxious by the undertaking he had set himself. She had no doubt Mr Hewitt might be feeling something akin to having survived – barely – an act of surprising a sleeping lion in its lair.

Fitzwilliam observed Lizzy's return and suspended a game of chess with Wentworth to approach her. Lizzy chuckled at the camaraderie the two men now shared – something had transpired between them to erase their tacit rivalry. She made a note to ask him about this later. But for now, his anxious expression as he reached her inquired of graver concerns.

She acquainted him with what had occurred with Georgiana, watching him shake his head in consternation as she proceeded. Asked whether he ought to intercede with either of his cousins now, Lizzy advised against it. "Darcy is only now on his way to visit Gee again."

Fitzwilliam accepted her opinion even as she added, "You may well be wanted in the morning, however."

Grimly, he agreed; then described events in the drawing room during Lizzy's absence. Young Nathaniel had taken up residence in the darkest corner of the room, staring out the windows into the black of a moonless night. Beyond a tortured lingering gaze at Georgiana as he passed by – a slight falter in his step as if he debated speech with her – he had engaged no one. This much Lizzy had seen for herself; it had prompted her own egress to seek her husband.

Fortunately, though, much of their party was engaged in conversation about the room and few others noted young Hewitt's tenuous hold. Fitzwilliam himself may not have done so had he not been alerted to circumstance. He had been standing in discourse with Edmund Hewitt and Wentworth – all three had recognised Nathaniel's mood, and were taken with disquiet on the verge of a leap into alarm on the boy's behalf.

After a few moments, Georgiana, who had stood frozen all the time since Hewitt's return, uttered a strangled cry and fled the room. Her departure seemed to break Nathaniel's resolve completely. He had slumped in his bearing with eyes squeezed tightly shut, and leaned towards the window, laying his forehead on the cold pane.

Instantly, Edmund Hewitt had gone to his brother, speaking low to him while obstructing the young man from curious view of the others in the room; and very quickly after, Hewitt had made excuses for both of them for the evening and led Nathaniel out.

"Oh, dear," whispered Lizzy. "It was so bad?"

"It might have been worse. Much of our party was distracted by stories of Sir James's travels in America. Besides Hewitt, only Wentworth and I, and your Jane I believe, took any peculiar note."

"I am thankful for that. The poor man's humiliation must be severe enough without suffering it widely. I wonder he came back here at all after his interview."

"Ah, he must put a good face on it, I think, show himself a man. Except that he had not fully reckoned his disappointment until he saw Georgiana."

Lizzy looked about the room, her gaze stopping at Anne particularly before returning to her cousin. "I begin to regret our ball on Saturday, Retched, with all these unresolved intrigues. In fact, I begin to understand Darcy's abhorrence of large house parties!" Despite the words, she laughed and was joined in it by the colonel.

To alleviate some of the tension Lizzy must feel, Fitzwilliam related to her his earlier conversation with Wentworth, finishing with a promise. "You will suffer no further angst for my account, dear cousin. I have done with it. I am determined to spare you additional worries and, in that pursuit, will do all in my power to afford a happy end for at least two of your guests."

❖❖❖❖❖

Darcy moved towards Georgiana's rooms with leaden feet grown heavier as they approached nearer. Elizabeth had been right: he could not retire tonight without attempting reconciliation with his sister. He fervently wished for this. His heaviness lay instead in the fear that he had no idea how to achieve such appeasement. He could not give Gee what she wished of him; he could not approve this match.

He found himself now, for the third time on the day, facing a confrontation totally unprepared. Squaring his shoulders in false courage, he knocked on the door and waited.

There was no response. He knocked again, louder this time, to the same result, then moved on to her sitting room door next down. No one answered here either. Vaguely he registered the oddity that at the least Gee's maid did not appear, and he returned yet again to the bed chamber door, this time calling out to his sister even as he knocked. She may not wish to see him but surely would provide some reply, if only to spurn him. When met with continued silence, he began to worry. He could, of course, force his admission; but he would not do so. His sister's apartments were her own – he would not violate that sanctuary with uninvited entry. But the longer he stood outside, the more his concern for her grew.

He had just determined to send for Elizabeth to enter on his behalf, fearful for Georgiana's welfare, when the panel door at the end of the hall opened and Georgiana came through from the other side. She gasped as she saw her brother, and stopped. He was so relieved to see her that he barely wondered at her coming from the servants' corridor. Both seemed rooted in place, unable to move, unable to speak, studying each other with pained care.

Darcy deliberately relaxed his posture in wordless supplication and, after a moment, Georgiana began to walk slowly towards him. When she was only a few steps away, she stopped, looking down; but not before Darcy noted her tear-streaked face, dark circles forming already under swollen eyes. He swallowed hard, pain warring with resolve and his better senses.

"I delivered a letter to Mrs Reynolds for posting," she stammered finally, her voice husky, still looking down, "and did not wish to encounter anyone" – explaining the unusual direction she had taken.

"Yes," Darcy replied with a small nod and then both were silent once more. Georgiana's arms hung limply at her side, while Darcy's clasped hands fidgeted unconsciously. After an interminable age of a few minutes, Georgiana looked up from the floor and the siblings' eyes met and held. An instant later she was in the protection of his arms, sobbing convulsively into his chest while he lowered his cheek to her head, held her tightly, and fought back his own heavy emotion. Fleetingly, he recalled an image of a moment nearly identical to this only two years before, another consolation following Georgiana's near-elopement. But this time could not be more different – this time, the adversary was not so easily discernible or agreed upon; this time he attempted to give succour to a pain he had himself inflicted.

Gradually, Darcy's senses returned to him and he realised where they stood. At any moment, their house party might begin to retire and the corridor to fill with onlookers, either guests or servants. He could spare his sister that much. Georgiana was still much out of her senses, the sobs once unleashed showing no sign of ebbing. He shifted his arms, lifting her into them easily, and carried her to her room, no longer requiring permission to enter.

Reaching the chaise in her sitting room, he gently placed her on it and when, head still burrowed into his chest, her hands grasped him more tightly as he made to rise, he sat with her. She curled herself into him as she had done so often in childhood when she had been vulnerable, frightened – Darcy rocking her gently – and the two waited in silence for her weeping to expend itself.

CHAPTER TEN

Thursday, 3 January 1799

❖❖❖❖❖

LIZZY OPENED HER EYES in the darkened chamber. She lay facing the windows, but still she knew with certainty that Darcy did not occupy his place on her other side, nor had he done all night. She had awakened briefly on several occasions hearing his step, but each time had found it only a phantom anticipation. She was not surprised at his absence.

She rose now, drawing a robe around her for warmth, and pulled back the draperies. The sun had not yet crested above the hill; the faint light of predawn offered only an outline in the garden of grey snow tinged with a pink cast. It should be clear today; the sky appeared cloudless – but the cold penetrating through the panes of glass was searing in its intensity.

She could sleep no longer despite the premature hour, yet was unready to call for Alice and dress in the cold and dark. Chancing that no one would be about so early, she made her way downstairs, proceeding directly to the library. As she placed her hand on the door knob she noticed the leather tie around it, alerting servants not to enter and disturb its occupant. And as she knew she would find, Darcy was there, sitting near the hearth though he did not regard it any more than the forgotten book his hands picked at unconsciously.

He glanced up from his wool-gathering when she had crossed half the distance between them, and he held out a hand to her. She noted how cool it felt despite his nearness to the fire he had maintained. She squeezed his hand to warm it and he pulled her closer, around to the front of the chair and onto his knee. Even as she leaned in to his embrace, she noticed his dishevelled appearance. His coat lay on the floor, his waistcoat was wrinkled and unkempt; his cravat which had been discarded on the piecrust table adjacent appeared stained with tears. His hair was rumpled from running his hands through it (repeatedly no doubt), falling every which way across his skull and brow – quite an appealing look, she appreciated silently, if only his expression were not so tormented.

"Have you not slept?" she asked.

He shook his head; then, "What time is it?"

"Not yet half five."

"So late?" He smiled vacantly at her.

"Late!" Lizzy looked at Darcy's face but realised he was distracted, his words had a perfunctory ring to them.

"Yes," she smiled. "While you have languished here in the comfort of the library, I have already bathed and dressed, scolded two upstairs maids and the scullery girl, made three shirts for Mrs Henshaw's charity box, assisted Mr Norris on the farm in birthing five piglets, and repaired the garden wall from our storm last month."

"Mmm," came the reply.

Lizzy snickered silently, the convulsive movement drawing Darcy's eyes to her where, taking in her night apparel, the words finally found purchase. "You –" he began incredulously, and then comprehended her mockery and shook his head. This time he was present in his smile.

"Shall we begin again?" asked Lizzy, smirking.

In answer, Darcy tightened his arm around her, drawing her close for a kiss.

"Ack!" she grimaced a long moment later, and turned up her nose. "You taste of old stockings! What have you been drinking?"

"My dear, I will have you know it was a very rare cognac!" he protested.

"Not rare enough, I daresay. I hope you have not any more of it," she replied; but she had succeeded in drawing him out.

"Only the one; it was Fitzwilliam's gift to me for Twelfth Night. He thought circumstance timely to present it last night, and we made short work of it then... or this morning I rather suppose." He shrugged slightly, his mouth pursed in a smirk. "It *was* rather ghastly after all."

"Ah, so he did find you."

"Yes. We resolved nothing, but passed a few hours." He studied Lizzy now, screwing his face up into a frown. "Silk? Cotton? Or Wool?"

"What?"

"The hosiery! And how long have you made habit of chewing old stockings?" he teazed.

"Oh, I stuff them in my mouth quite regularly – to keep from laughing aloud when you talk in your sleep."

"You never do! And nor do I!"

They both laughed now, if his was not free of care. To prove she bore no aversion to her husband, Lizzy kissed him again; and then snuggled into his chest. He held her protectively, but a slight reflexive gasp escaped him.

"What is it?"

"It is nothing," he whispered. "Only I ended the night in just such repose, but with a less sanguine young lady in my arms." Idly, he picked up the cravat, still damp.

"Ah!" Lizzy sat up enough to see her husband's face. "And were you able to assuage your feelings and hers?"

"A bit." He described his encounter with Georgiana – they had spoken little and settled less; but had at least forgiven their immediate offenses to each other if they could not come to agreement on the larger ones. He sighed discouragingly.

"That is no mean achievement, my love. Do not chastise yourself – the rest will come."

"Perhaps." He sighed again. "It will not be the same for us, though, Lizzy, I think. Not ever again. This will live on between us. I cannot consent to what Gee desires, and she cannot forgive me the refusal."

Lizzy considered briefly trying to clarify Georgiana's desires; perhaps Darcy might find it palatable to consider the issue with a somewhat more dispassionate, disinterested party. But she noted the pain in his eyes, and chose to defer introducing any argument for now. He had passed a sleepless night for thinking of his sister's distress, and was not ready for such discourse; she had no wish to pain him further and chose instead a conciliatory path. "Understanding may elude her, but she *will* forgive it. You must talk with her of this when you can both reason better; and then give her time, Fitz. She is hurting."

"Mmm."

Not quite the comforted response Lizzy could wish for, but at least Darcy stopped berating himself openly. "What will you do now?"

After a long moment of silence, Darcy sighed and stood, lifting and setting Lizzy on her feet as he did so. "I am going to take my wife back to our chamber –"

Lizzy proffered her best alluring smile, but Darcy tempered her thought immediately by completing his own. "Neither of us is fit for the staff to encounter," he said; "and when I am newly dressed, I believe I will take Parsifal out." She fell into step with him and they exited and mounted the stairs together in a half embrace.

When they gained their chamber, Darcy saw his wife back into their bed to warm her and went to his dressing room. He returned only a moment later, however, having chewed a few sugared cardamom seeds in the interim; and he obliged his wife with a renewed display of affection, replacing her earlier taste of him with a sweeter memory before calling for Grayson. Before departing, he leaned down to graze her ear with his lips and whispered, "Remind me when next we are in town to send to Crook & Besford's and order you some new stockings."

❖❖❖❖❖

Some three hours later, Lizzy had dressed, selected her attire for the remainder of the day, reviewed the day's menu, and now received a summary from her housekeeper on preparations for the ball on Saturday. It certainly appeared that all was well in hand.

"It will be a grand evening, Mrs Darcy," said Mrs Reynolds. "If I may say, oh, the good it does my heart to fill this house with gaieties once again."

Lizzy smiled. "Even with all the extra labour?"

"Pish-posh," she replied immediately. "It is never a bother. Why, all the staff and servants have jumped up to do their part. They are as excited as any guest, hoping to catch some glimpses of the festivities and fashions arriving. I caught Sally and Martha singing while they polished the silver this morning!" she chuckled.

Lizzy shared in her amusement, but her smile turned to a slight grimace a moment later. "I begin to think few above the servants anticipate the event happily." At Mrs Reynolds's quizzical regard, Lizzy deemed it proper to share with her housekeeper the sad events transpiring the night before. After all, not only had Mrs Reynolds known – and cared deeply for – Georgiana since her birth, and Darcy nearly since his own; but there was bound at some point to be discussion of the rejected suit amongst staff, and Lizzy would have Mrs Reynolds forewarned so as to minimise gossip and conjecture.

"Ah, I did fear something of the sort," she acknowledged. "I had wanted to ask. Miss Georgiana surprised me late last evening, appearing in my office with a letter for posting today –" she noted Lizzy's curious expression, and added, "—to Mrs Annesley." She shook her head at the memory of Georgiana's appearance. "She was very distraught, poor child. But she would not tell me what had transpired. I did wonder if her gentleman had thrown her over, but now I see it is much worse than that." She shook her head again and said almost to herself, "Oh, dear. Poor Miss Georgiana—and poor Mr Darcy."

"Yes, indeed. And I am afraid this will cast rather a pall on proceedings. How Georgiana will manage I confess I have not the will to ponder."

❖❖❖❖❖

Georgiana herself would wonder the same.

Thoughts seemed to move to the forefront of her mind at random, vying for consideration. She had little will to direct them and less to deny them, though she had tried on waking to hold them back before realising it a futile exercise.

The first to assail her was the certainty that she could not face the breakfast room this morning. She lacked the strength to maintain a mask of composure; the least greeting would likely set off tears. It occurred to her as well, if not so consciously, that even if the others had not been told explicitly of last evening's events, as surely was the case, most would know something of them. They would have deduced it from any number of telltale signs: her own mood and Nathaniel's, her brother's extended absence from the company. She groaned to think of having to endure all those silent opinions. She could no more weather the judgments in their glances than their pity, although on reflection, the latter would be infinitely worse.

She called for Becca and asked her to take Mrs Darcy word that she would remain in her rooms the morning. Her maid's quick acquiescence, coupled with an expression comprised equally of astonishment and concern, sent Gee to her looking glass as soon as the girl had departed. She stared in dull horror at the wretch who looked back at her.

Little wonder at Becca's reaction. Gee was a fright. She knew, when she had sluggishly opened them earlier, that her eyes bore the effects of crying, but had not quite credited the extent of damage; they were swollen half closed and red. Her complexion, generally clear and apricot-hued, was blotched with mottled colour and two blemishes were coming out near her mouth. She had fallen into a troubled sleep still in her gown – trying now to remember finding her bed at all and failing – and it was wrinkled and bunched askew. Pity Becca, trying to make something of it again!

This thought led to a recollection of the manner in which she had sent her maid away the night before and she felt ashamed of it. As the young woman had just returned from her errand, Georgiana immediately apologised. She and Becca were of an age together and had often traded confidences; they had become as much friends as the inequality of their positions allowed. Rarely was Gee short with her and now she sorely regretted her earlier curt manner.

Thankfully, their good relations brought swift excusal from Becca. A few moments more found Georgiana telling her troubles to the girl. To her surprise, she also found herself drying Becca's tears rather than the reverse; she supposed she had cried herself out after all.

The maid chastised herself after a moment of crying and drew on all her skills of management. "I have arranged breakfast, Miss, to be sent up on the hour. Not a moment to lose to put you to rights again, so we had best be about it." With that she left, returning a few moments later with a robe for Georgiana. "There is a hot bath waiting for you, Miss, and a cold compress for your eyes."

Georgiana allowed herself to be led away, grateful both for the initial display of compassion evoked in her maid and that it had been cut short in favour of pragmatism now. As her mistress soaked in the bath, Becca prepared her attire and prattled of silly things, occasionally drawing a smile from Georgiana. But though some part of her responded, still Gee felt the weighty intrusion of other concerns.

The remorse she felt for her treatment of Becca was as nothing compared to that she felt for Fitz. She had been angry, upset – yet how could she have flung so carelessly at her brother the accusations she had done? Even through her own intense emotion, she had seen at once the pain they caused him; the effect had astonished them both. And then she had turned and fled, unwilling and unable to apologise.

But why should I apologise? she thought now. Why should she not feel anger and resentment at his callous disregard of her desires? He had pronounced judgment upon Mr Hewitt without so much as a thought. If he cared nothing for Nathaniel's distress, did her own feelings matter so little to him? He was totally unreasonable and... tyrranical!

Then again, he had come to her after their quarrel and had not hesitated to comfort her with soothing words. And Georgiana had needed no encouragement to seek that comfort, folding herself in his arms as she had always done when she was frightened or sad. An image flashed through her mind of a little girl, barely beyond toddler and still in the nursery, being informed of her mother's passing – understanding little at the time but the great reassurance his solid grasp had promised that he would not leave her as well. And some years later, after he and Cousin Richard returned from their father's burial, she had curled up in the large wing chair with him in his study and felt that same sense of continuity in his firm embrace. Time and again as lesser calamities or fears would assail her; Fitz always enveloped her in safety and love until she overcame them.

Most recent had been his intervention when she nearly ran away with Wickham. Fitz had been so angry – she had never seen him so awesome in rage, it had frightened her – and yet not one word of it had been directed at her. Even as she had realised her ignorant mistake and suffered both the humiliation of what she had nearly done and the devastation of an aborted first love, her brother had never once blamed her, but had shown her only compassion. He had taken the blame upon himself, in fact: for his own neglect of her, his failure to protect her, leaving her too easily swayed by the schemes of Wickham and Mrs Younge. And he had gone about comforting her again tirelessly, night after night when the tears came. In all this time, not once had he spoken to her of it, recalled it to her memory nor laid any blame at her feet.

Until the night past. Oh, he had not spoken the words; but it was there between them. Her poor judgment. Her youth and immaturity. Her inability to recognise the worth of a man. The accusations, the doubt in her astuteness, had not been absent for lack of being spoken aloud.

But he was *wrong* this time. How could she make him see it? She was not a child any more. While Fitz had found his own way to love in the last two years, Georgiana had grown up – why, she had even offered *him* helpful comfort; he had acknowledged it to be so. She had recognised the mistaken feelings she had believed constituted love and more – had learnt much of the true nature of love – through Fitz himself, through Fitz and Elizabeth. She had come to understand genuine feeling born of well-founded respect; passion emanating from true regard.

She found these things so easily in Nathaniel Hewitt, felt all this for him, and she *knew* he returned it. She *knew* him to be a good man, to be right for her. To even recognise the stabbing pain in her heart at the idea of being made to reject Nathaniel was crippling, she could not allow herself to think on it. With all her remaining will, she blocked acceptance of the eventuality. It was too much to bear.

She sighed, removing the compress from her eyes to rub at them. How could she make Fitz recognise that she was capable of prudent discrimination, she was no longer that silly girl? One answer came to her: she must stop behaving as one. She must stand on her own feet, control her emotions, and speak from reason rather than emotion. She must stop running into the protection of his arms every time she felt hurt, no matter how strong the pull to rely on him. If she wanted him to think of her as a woman, she must begin to act as one.

Her heart, fresh in its pain over being denied Nathaniel, could not bear losing her brother as well. And yet this was his fault! It need not have happened at all if only he would listen to her heart, see what she saw in Nat Hewitt. Once again, her anger at Darcy was raised.

I will not dance with him at the ball! As soon as the thought arrived, she gasped, drawing a glance of concern from Becca. *The ball!* What new misery to add to her overburdened heart. How could she attend a ball? A ball where she was meant to make her entrance to society – to be at once hostess and honoured guest – to make the acquaintance of eligible men who would ogle her and make love to her brother for her hand and her endowment? A ball that Nathaniel must surely attend without the right –

the permission surely – to approach her. It was untenable, she could not bear it. Her daydream of the previous day in the coach was proved a foul lie.

Nathaniel Hewitt would be the only gentleman at the ball she could not see – and the only one her heart would wish to do! Oh, however would she make her way through this?

❖❖❖❖❖

When she arrived in the breakfast room, Amelia felt surprise and wondered if she had misjudged the hour. Only Elizabeth, the Gardiners and Sir James had preceded her, though it was already a bit after ten o'clock. She hesitated a moment in the doorway, bemused, but then Elizabeth glanced up and immediately welcomed her in with good wishes on the morning.

As Amelia moved towards the sideboard, Fitzwilliam came in behind her, stopping to greet those at table. Elizabeth waylaid him a moment, taking him to task in some manner over cognac to which he laughed heartily in reply. Amelia, her back to the others as she procured a cup of tea, closed her eyes and smiled absently. She loved the sound of the Colonel's laughter – it rolled naturally and easily from his chest, infectious in its pleasure even when she did not comprehend the jest.

"What daydream has induced such a pleasing smile as this?"

She turned, startled, to find him standing at her side now.

"Good morning, Mrs Chaney," he added belatedly. His glance had something of a tentative question in it, his brows drawn in and raised but his broad smile and his manner open and friendly.

"Good morning, Colonel Fitzwilliam," she replied and felt colour rising in her cheeks. To stem her embarrassment – and defer his question – she held out the cup to him. "Tea, Sir?"

He took the cup, thanking her, and she looked away, grateful for an instant to busy herself with securing another. The Colonel apparently was content to stand yet and watch her in the task. When she had done, he reached for her cup as well, offering to deliver it to the table while she filled a plate for herself.

She selected a slice of cold ham and a roll, then as an afterthought, a few dates and a mandarin orange. When she turned to join the others, she stopped in hesitation an instant. Colonel Fitzwilliam stood at the far end of the table away from all the others, holding a chair out in anticipation. The two cups of tea rested, one at the table's end and the other at the next place on the long side. She looked first at the Colonel, then shifted to Elizabeth. Lizzy's smirking glance was encouraging and she nodded almost imperceptibly. Amelia turned back to Fitzwilliam, and went to join him. He held her chair and, when she had been established, he excused himself to collect his own breakfast.

She busied herself with her tea while wondering at Fitzwilliam. Delighted, yet somewhat anxious at this development, she found her hand trembling as she held her cup, and she replaced it carefully on the table, grateful for the moment alone to collect herself. She took a deep breath, uncertain how to feel.

All too soon, he had returned with his own repast. Amelia glanced once more down the length of the table, but the others gave her no notice; they were engaged in their own interactions. To make light conversation, she said, "We are a small party this morning."

"Yes," he replied. He smiled, but there was some restraint in it. "Likely we will remain so."

She puzzled at the cryptic remark, and he began to speak again in a very low voice. Although he leaned in close to her as he spoke, still she strained to hear him. "I may as well tell you," he said, "for I think we shall all require some compassion in the next days."

He told her in as succinct a manner as possible of the past night's events, taking care to keep the information spare so as not to expose his cousins more than necessary. "Darcy has gone riding, so Lizzy tells me," he finished. "I imagine he will be gone the morning as is his way. And as for Georgiana, she does not feel up to society at the moment – nor young Mr Hewitt, I gather."

"Oh, dear!" whispered Amelia to him, as she felt overwhelming compassion for the young lovers, forgetting immediately her own concerns. "Is there anything I can do for Miss Darcy, to be of use in some manner?"

"I think not, not at present. I have just come from Georgiana's rooms, but her maid sent me away, suggested that perhaps I might try again in a few hours. I cannot believe she – Georgiana, that is – will have passed a restful night."

Shaking her head in agreement, Amelia's compassion was redirected. "And what of you, Sir? How do *you* fare?"

Fitzwilliam was taken aback at this. He felt no surprise at Mrs Chaney's consideration for Georgiana, but that she concerned herself with his own feelings next astonished him – and warmed him – greatly. He found himself then revealing his muddled emotions to her: his heart commiserating with Georgiana even while he understood Darcy's reservations; guilt over not having realised the stage to which his cousin and Mr Hewitt had come; an empathy for Mr Hewitt, recognizing some of himself in the young man; how he wavered in his reasoning yet needed to fall on one side or the other of the issue.

His responsibility as one of Georgiana's guardians required that he form an opinion. And when it came to it, he would support Darcy's decision in the end, for without the approval of both... But how far he might attempt to influence the man he was uncertain. For although he knew his cousin to have valid objections, he also would not have adopted such an air of finality. He liked Nathaniel Hewitt; he had witnessed Georgiana's joy in his company. He was not convinced that it could not come well in the end if the match were carefully nurtured over time.

"Have you spoken to your cousin of this?" she asked; "Mr Darcy, I mean?"

"We passed several hours last night with a bottle of cognac –" he began; and though still she did not understand the significance, Amelia recognised at least the source of his early converse with Elizabeth. "I listened to his reasoning, could find no fault in it, nor personal malice. He was not of a disposition for debate then. But Darcy..."

Amelia waited. Fitzwilliam seemed to struggle a moment with how to finish what he had begun. He studied Amelia's countenance a moment, then said, "Darcy is by nature a serious man; he takes his responsibility for all this" – he swept his hand in an arc that encompassed the room but so much more – "as a sacred trust. And even more his sister's safeguard. Utterly commendable it is; though at times he takes too much on himself in his determination to protect her. But then, it is an aweful charge."

He sighed then. "When I left him in the small hours of the morning, we determined to speak of it again tonight, he and I. I will attempt to bestride the ground on both sides until I see a clear path. But first I must see Georgiana, to hear her on the matter. I have no wish to redouble her pain, but I cannot see my own part in this without understanding hers. Perhaps I can best serve both my cousins simply by bringing them close enough to speak to each other."

Amelia struggled to restrain herself – she wished nothing more now than to reach out and place her hand atop Fitzwilliam's as it lay inert on the table, to offer comfort that would ease the lines in his brow. But she had not the right. To give herself occupation, she picked up her mandarin orange. Taking her knife to pierce the skin, she found it thicker than expected and exerted herself.

Suddenly, Fitzwilliam roused himself and forced a smile. He glanced down, took the orange from her fingers and punctured the skin handily. He peeled it in an instant, and began to separate it into segments for her as he said: "It seems this season has been fraught with complications, does not it?" He hesitated an instant and then said, "There is another word I would speak with you, if I may have the liberty –"

Amelia was leery but curious. She nodded; "Of course."

Fitzwilliam looked down the table then and Amelia's eyes followed as she ate an orange segment. She had not realised that while they had been talking, others had finally joined the breakfast party. Lady Catherine, her daughter and companion, Kitty – they were still only half the entire company, but Amelia had been so absorbed in the Colonel's account she had not heard even these enter. But still, she and the Colonel had relative privacy removed from the others as they were and, as she returned her attention to him, he cleared his throat.

"Mrs Chaney," he said, and she noted the warmth her name held in his speech; "I fear that the good will we have shared, you and I, has... well, has suffered of late." He looked down, wishing to say more, but when he looked up again, his expression was tentative, careful. Amelia's heart seemed to race in anticipation as finally he added, "I regret this. I blame myself. I should like very much to recover our friendship, if you are amenable."

Amelia stopped breathing. Had she heard correctly? Was Colonel Fitzwilliam offering her the very thing she had wished for these last days – the opportunity to make amends for her neglectful behaviour? She forced herself to inhale slowly and, noting finally the hesitancy in his expression as he awaited reply, she smiled. "I should like that very much, Sir."

❖❖❖❖❖

Lady Catherine had spent a restless night, unable to sleep for her troubles. She was unaccustomed to being forced into action objectionable to her; she had vowed years ago on the day following her wedding to command her own destiny and had done just that. She had learnt to understand the manner in which the world worked and she used her knowledge well, refusing to allow herself vulnerabilities. In doing so, she had prospered, had proven herself, secured her family's standing in the most acceptable society.

Yet now she found herself thwarted at every turn. The world was changing, and not for the better. The next generation – to include her nephews, even her own daughter – set little value in convention, and it would be her bane. Their attitudes would spell the destruction of the propertied class, the ruin of English society, everything she had passed a life building.

She glanced down the table and scowled. Fitzwilliam had professed Mrs Chaney to have no part in his rejection of Anne, but there he was, mooning over the woman like a besotted schoolboy. Had he no sense of propriety? Had *she*, to encourage him so when she was not even free of her widow's garb? Yet Lady Catherine was prevailed upon to condone such behaviour, to reward it by giving Fitzwilliam the means to secure a life with the woman.

Darcy was little better. Had he met his duty from the start to marry Anne, none of these subsequent measures would be wanted. But he had allowed his baser desires to make a match, turning his back on a duty to merge their families' fortunes. She might grudgingly have forgiven him this – for the sake of family – but now he balked yet again, on principal, from supporting his aunt in a manner that could increase her land, his influence, his importance in society. It was negligence at best.

They none of them understood duty, sacrifice for the greater good. None of them.

Her eyes flicked to Sir James. She wondered now what had ever drawn her to him. Had he altered so much with the years, or had she? He was entirely too tolerant, with no sense of preservation – blithely turning his estate over to his nephew to confine himself to a small property, and now giving even that up for a set of rooms in town when he should be enjoying his last years in comfort. Her father and brother had been right all those years ago, though it galled her to concede so even to herself – but the man had no ambition, nor sense of pride.

Perhaps she would have done better to encourage him to leave when he offered; she had wanted to prove that the past had little claim upon her. But she had dreamt of James Thornton the last two nights, adding much to her disquiet. Her dreams were not fantasy, but recollections of a former life that held little relevance to her now. They were not welcome.

And now her own daughter had turned on her – a final insult – it was too much to bear.

Anne's betrayal was the worst. Lady Catherine had spent the past thirty years sacrificing for her daughter – bringing in specialists to attempt to cure her; agonizing over the possibility of losing her each time she suffered a bout; curtailing or even completely disregarding seasons in town, exiling herself to Kent for the improved air; always attentive to Anne's every need at the cost of her own.

Her husband had been content with seclusion at Rosings; he had always found tedium in the social rounds. But Catherine had not bartered for retirement in the country when she had accepted Sir Lewis deBourgh. She had borne it – all of it – for one reason: her daughter.

She had sought to make her life bearable with industry – by concentrating on refurbishing Rosings to establish one of the finest houses in the country, and becoming involved in bettering the lives of the community nearby. The cost to her of this diminished life was one she had paid in silence. But she had exacted her own price as well – over time she had forced Sir Lewis to give her control of the estate which, though her method of persuasion had been underhanded, even he had admitted she was better suited to manage. And from the first, she had made every decision, taken every action, with an eye to securing a future for Anne. Now this was how she was to be repaid? It was unconscionable.

"Mama?"

Lady Catherine's thoughts interrupted, she swung her head to the side to her daughter.

"I wondered if you have considered our discourse," offered Anne in quiet tones so as not to be heard widely.

"Hmmph," said Lady Catherine. But Anne did not cower under her glare; she only fidgeted in her chair and glanced down briefly before asking again in a small voice.

"Have you considered my request?"

"Do not press me, Anne," she snapped and, indeed, this time her daughter blanched and looked away.

Lady Catherine rose immediately and, after long consideration of Anne's averted face, she began to make her way to the breakfast room door. As she walked from the room, she was joined by Sir James.

"Lady Catherine," he greeted her; she stopped to face him. "You are very short with your daughter, Madam. Are you not well? Surely she cannot have given cause to warrant such enmity."

"You appear to be very well acquainted with my daughter for having only just been introduced."

"I recognise distress, Madam, without intimate acquaintance – hers *and your own*. If I may offer you any assistance –"

The expression of earnest concern Sir James wore caused Lady Catherine to hesitate an instant, but no longer. Then she drew herself up quite formally to cut him off. "My relations with my daughter, Sir – my business of any sort – are no concern of yours!"

He did not respond directly. He studied her a moment, curious. "Have you turned so hard with the years? What can have happened to the girl I knew?"

"That, Sir, also does not concern you."

"No. It does not," Sir James replied with sadness, bowed slightly and took his leave.

CHAPTER ELEVEN

RICHARD FITZWILLIAM exited the room bearing a permeating smile. He felt his equanimity much restored and, for the first time in several days, believed that happiness was within his reach. His converse with Amelia Chaney at breakfast had gone very well indeed; the concern she expressed only confirmed, in so much more meaningful a manner, Wentworth's declaration that Amelia held affection for him.

But he would take care with this second chance, would move slowly to ensure that no wrong-footed word or act could once again threaten her feelings, or his. He pictured her smile just now as he had taken his leave of her. It was enough to know that the two of them had time to acknowledge and explore their desires.

He had taken his leave to delay no longer in his business on behalf of Major Soames. With that purpose he made his way to the library where, after procuring writing instruments from a footman, he settled at the drum table and prepared the requisite correspondence for express to Horseguards. On finishing, satisfied with his proposed plan, he addressed his missive to Lord Danvers; John Merriwether was a particular friend and they shared views on the current condition of the Army. Fitzwilliam knew he could rely on Danvers to speak well for him on behalf of Major Soames.

This discharge of obligation now set into motion, Fitzwilliam faced another much more personal in nature. He should attempt again to speak with Georgiana since she had not sent for him after his earlier call. He roused himself to leave on this charge and, as he did so, he met Lizzy coming into the room.

"Retched," she said, "have you a moment to spare me?"

He replied that he should like nothing better, but she took note that he consulted his watch.

"Do I keep you from some purpose?"

"Not at all. I merely thought to try if Georgiana will see me; but I have been turned away once – there is nothing to suggest better fortune now."

They spoke for a moment then of the young woman. Lizzy, too, had ventured to console her sister just before breakfast and been put off by the maid with an apology. She offered a hope that Fitzwilliam would meet better success, "for she should not too long isolate her person – she will make herself ill with her thoughts in such seclusion."

Fitzwilliam gestured towards a pair of chairs nearby and, as they settled into them, Lizzy said: "...but Gee is not my reason for our discourse now. I wish to speak with you of Lady Catherine."

Fitzwilliam wondered if Elizabeth desired a first-hand account of his late meetings with his aunt and so was surprised when in its stead, she asked, "Are you acquainted, Retched, with your aunt's early history?"

"Her early history!" he exclaimed, bemused. "Why ever do you ask?"

She chuckled, and then related the conversation she had heard after breakfast between Lady Catherine and Sir James. Their discourse had confirmed Lizzy's previous suspicion, that they were previously acquainted. The gentleman had found her greatly altered, apparently.

Fitzwilliam laughed. "I have learnt very lately, dear Eliza, that it can be no good thing to draw conclusions from overheard conversation!" He proceeded to tell her of the mistake he had made with Wentworth, able to speak lightly of it now in view of subsequent events. His telling was good humoured enough that it took them briefly to speak of his renewed friendship with Amelia. Lizzy delighted to see him smile again as he spoke of his lady; though she exploited every opportunity his speech afforded to teaze him over it. She expressed no doubt they were finally on a path to accord and added her satisfaction that Lady Catherine's interference had been repudiated.

Her remarks brought back to Fitzwilliam a comment Wentworth had made as well, that of Mrs Chaney unwisely following false counsel, and at once he realised the source of the advice that had caused his lady to withdraw from his attentions. He felt anger towards his aunt certainly, but more so at himself. Had he considered as he should that Lady Catherine would use any means to achieve her desires – not only with him, but anyone who stood conceivably in her path – Amelia might have been spared such a role in the affair. He might have averted even a temporary estrangement. He felt angry, too, that if he had maintained his first inclination to refuse Lady Catherine's proposal rather than giving it a week's credence, there would have been no occasion for misunderstanding at all.

He must apologise to Amelia for his aunt's behaviour and his own, and make it up to her somehow for failing to credit that some external interference accounted for their rift. He said something of the sort to Lizzy, but she wisely reminded him that as he and Mrs Chaney found themselves in concert once again, perhaps he should confine himself to that happy state.

"But Retched, with regard to your aunt, this morning's was not the first occasion to cause me wonder." She moved back in time, telling him of her conversation with Sir James, which satisfied nothing but intrigued her the more; then recalling both the timing of Lady Catherine's collapse so closely following the gentleman's arrival on Monday and that Sir James when first he met them, had admitted to a prior acquaintance with Fitzwilliam's father.

Despite his earlier caution, Lizzy had captured his interest now. He sifted through his memories, finally admitting, "I do not recall ever hearing Sir James remarked before by my father or, indeed, anyone in the family. But that is not so extraordinary. More than that I cannot say."

"But do they ever speak of her — of an attachment prior to her marriage to Sir Lewis deBourgh? *Could* Lady Catherine and Sir James have formed such a one?"

"I suppose it to be possible. Now as I think on it, I recall once shortly after my uncle died, I heard it commented to my aunt – Lady Anne, that is – that Lady Catherine, for all her devotion to his memory, had seemed in life to share little in common with Sir Lewis."

"Do you recall Lady Anne's reply?"

"I do, surprisingly. She said that the gentleman had been Hobson's choice but that, once having accepted him, my aunt had entered into her marriage with a vengeance. Strange words, do not you think?"

"Indeed."

"I wonder," mused Fitzwilliam now, caught up in Lizzy's curiosity as well. "Do you know that my aunt and my father have little to say to one another?"

"Yes; do you know why that is?"

"Not with any certainty. It has been so all my life, I cannot recall a time when they did not suffer each other's company. She has returned to Buxborough no more than half a dozen times, I think, in all these years since establishing in Kent, and never stayed longer than required. And moreover, my mother has said that after she married, Aunt Catherine never spoke to her own father again but once, when her brother Charles died young. I always supposed the cause lay in Sir Lewis's direction; I thought nothing of it at the time. But do you suppose there is something in that to speak to this present conundrum?"

"I wonder..."

They speculated a few moments more, but Fitzwilliam could recall no further evidence of explanation.

When finally Fitzwilliam left to seek out Georgiana, they had come to no conclusion, but Lizzy had determined yet again to ask Darcy for his recollections.

❖❖❖❖❖

Georgiana slipped through the entry, pulling the door closed behind her quickly, and breathed out in relief. The stables were not warm, but at least she was out of the frigid wind that had escorted her from the house; she had quickened her steps the entire way to escape its biting company. The light inside was dim, but she would know her way in the dark, and she proceeded now down the centre passage until she came to the third bay from the end.

She had moped much of the morning in her rooms, until she could not rest there another moment. But neither could she face any one; and so she had thought to escape for a short while with her beloved Comus. Becca had worked miracles with Georgiana – between a steaming bath, the cold compress for her eyes, and her sympathetic ministrations – such that Gee no longer cringed at her reflection in the mirror. If she chanced to meet someone along the way, she would not immediately reflect the horrors of the night she had passed; though still she fervently hoped to encounter no one. And indeed, she had been fortunate. She had met only Bryce outside in the paddock and she had been able to hide her countenance in her layers of covering then; what remained on display would be put down to the effects of the wind.

Even before she came within view of it, Gee heard a soft nickering at her approach. Comus knew of her presence and knew, moreover, that it was *he* she came to see. The colt was full of itself, but she loved it dearly. She knew he would make her feel better – feel something, if only for a few moments, other than despair – even if such visit resolved none of her troubles. And her heart did lift just a bit as soon as she saw the dark head appear over the gate at the front of the enclosure. He lowered his muzzle to graze her outstretched hand, and she felt tears rising. But these were soft tears of gratitude for the regard in which this noble beast held her.

She passed some time with Comus, talking softly to him and stroking his forelock after she had given him his requisite treats. She whispered to him of her confusion, her pain, knowing that this confidant would neither judge nor lecture her. And to her surprise, she felt somewhat better for doing so. She was quite unaware of the passage of time, until a waft of cooler air reached her and she looked up to see the stable door closing and then a lamp making its way in her direction.

When it neared, she could see the outline of a person she knew must be behind the lamp, and several steps closer on, the person resolved itself into Richard Fitzwilliam.

114

He did not speak immediately. He gave her the courtesy of not gazing upon her too closely but rather glanced about him until he reached Comus's stall himself. He turned to hang the lamp on a post hook, and only then did he allow his glance to meet hers, punctuated by a brow raised in question as to his welcome.

Georgiana turned back to Comus, but greeted her cousin civilly enough. "He has grown since you were last here, has he not?" she asked.

Fitzwilliam smiled and agreed. "Indeed, you will be riding him soon enough."

At that, she turned to her cousin and walked into his open arms. They stood in embrace without words until Georgiana, feeling suddenly awkward, stepped back again.

"My dear, I have no wish to compound your disappointment...," he began, and before he could speak further, she glared at him, her lip quivering.

"So you share my brother's judgment! Are you sent to make me see reason?"

He took no offense. "I am not sent at all. I come out of concern for you," he said and she looked down, knowing she had leapt to conclusion as he added, "to comfort if I can; to speak of this if you wish it."

She screwed up her face as she considered his offer. Talking to Comus had lifted her spirits a bit; might not it help to talk with Retched? Or would his opinions only cause her additional pain? She deliberated only a moment before glancing about her. She walked a short way to a hay bale, where she turned and sat upon it with purpose.

Fitzwilliam took the gesture for a decision. He went to join her, first stopping to pick up a horse blanket. He extended a hand and pulled her up when she took it, laid the blanket across the hay, and they both sat.

Neither spoke immediately. Then, tentatively, Georgiana asked, "How does he fare today?"

Fitzwilliam was uncertain at first to whom she referred, but he considered the tenderness in her inflection and replied accordingly. "Not well, I suspect, although in truth I cannot tell you. His brother and Mr Wentworth left with him early this morning –"

"He has *gone*?" Her voice now carried alarum.

"Only for a few hours, Gee. I am certain they have his welfare in their plan. They will have found an inn nearby and do what they can to help him. But they will return for dinner, all of them."

Gee was placated, if not happy. She had concentrated so much of herself in not thinking about Nathaniel that she had not considered how he must be feeling until the query had slipped out with her cousin. It opened up all their disappointment again. She was certain she could no longer shut out thoughts of him. But neither could she wish for him to leave Pemberley despite the pain his proximity must afford her.

When Fitzwilliam did not offer criticism of Nathaniel Hewitt's suit, she blurted out at once: "Oh, Retched, how can he *do* this?" Her voice contained both pain and anger.

Fitzwilliam had no confusion this time as to whom she referred. "My dear, he thinks of your welfare – always; do not doubt that it resides uppermost in his judgment."

"Then you do share his opinion?" The eyes she raised to him were forlorn, her voice absent of life. "There is no hope."

It fell to Fitzwilliam now to respond and he suffered the weight of it instantly. He could drive all hope from his cousin, leaving her bereft; or assuage her feelings knowing it might only delay the inevitable heartbreak. He little knew if Darcy would entertain any debate; and, in the end, as it would require the approbation of both Georgiana's guardians for her to marry, it mattered little if he would sanction it when Darcy did not. But to declare what he would have done put him at odds with one of his cousins, in between them with no manner to bring them together. And this disagreement, he saw, bore the capacity to tear apart a bond that had sustained brother and sister through much. He considered with care his reply.

❖❖❖❖❖

"Kitty, dear," said Mrs Gardiner, "do stop your fidgets."

Kitty sighed and sat down again, picking up her work but paying it little mind. She had come to the drawing room when she could find no other occupation to make the time pass, but this offered no improvement other than someone to share her boredom; or rather it seemed, someone to irritate with it.

She had awakened this morning in high spirits. Only two days until the ball – she became giddy contemplating it. But the excitement of anticipation had quickly been tempered following breakfast by the reality: it was *still* two days until the ball, and Kitty was at odds as to how to make the time pass.

Half their party had not come to breakfast; those that did were largely out of sorts or subdued and retreated to their own pursuits immediate upon its conclusion. She herself had gone to visit Georgiana but had been turned away. The maid had said her mistress was indisposed and not expected to quit her rooms today.

Kitty knew from Georgiana's demeanour the night before that something upsetting had occurred. For that matter, her friend had been acting strange since their journey into Lambton the day before, though Kitty could think of no occurrence in particular that would account for such a change. She had appeared distracted, however; had shown no curiosity at all concerning Kitty's reconciliation with Mr Reavley for all her earlier teazing.

She wondered if Georgiana and Nathaniel Hewitt had fallen out – they had not spoken much at dinner the night past, and the gentleman also made himself scarce today. Or, worse, could it be that Mr Darcy had separated the couple? Although these thoughts occurred to Kitty, she did not dwell on them beyond a few moments. She had not the discipline for reasoned conjecture. She would perhaps attempt again to visit Georgiana later and ask what had transpired. Besides, she suspected that whatever had caused her friend's withdrawal would not serve to maintain her own mood.

When she had left Georgiana's door, she had gone next to the north parlour and spent a bit of time plinking at the pianoforte. But without Georgiana, it could not hold her interest and, as they had no further entertainments planned, there seemed little point in practice.

She had thought then that she might visit the stables, had she a greater interest in horses; or perhaps simply a brief turn out of doors. But she had gone to the window to ascertain which cloak might be warranted, only to quickly decide against any outing at all. The wind rattled the casement, blew swirls of loose snow about with ferocity – not a day to venture out, however briefly.

Finally in a state of desperate boredom she had come to the drawing room to pass time amongst the ladies within. This had maintained her for a short spell, for Jane had received a letter from Mama and some moments were passed hearing of home. Kitty wondered very briefly as her sister began to read the letter whether she would have done better to remain at Longbourn for Christmastide but pushed the idea aside. Truly she must be bored to even conjure the thought.

It seemed Mama had made up her disagreement with Mrs Long, to Papa's express disappointment. Mary had finally obtained the long-awaited new courtesy book of Robert Grey and had taken nightly to reading from it interspersed with offering her own critical remarks. Maria Lucas had called the other day to say that their old bay had finally died. They would wait until spring to replace the horse. The letter continued on in similar manner.

Yes, Pemberley even on a cold, tedious day was yet preferable to being at home. And in any event, if she had remained at Longbourn, she would not now be awaiting a ball. This reminder had engendered restlessness again. Kitty paced to the windows to look out, then to the fire to warm her hands, then back to her chair; repeating the movement several times until finally it provoked Aunt Gardiner's present chastisement.

She glanced now at Amelia Chaney, sitting at a small writing desk as she penned a letter to her brother. Perhaps Kitty might engage Mrs Chaney in some discourse when she had finished her correspondence.

This was her mood when the drawing room door opened, but when it only admitted the housekeeper, Mrs Reynolds, Kitty looked down again at the embroidery in her hands with resignation. An instant later, her tedium fled.

"Oh!" said Mrs Reynolds on discovering Lizzy was not within. Jane indicated her sister might be found in the library with Colonel Fitzwilliam, to which the housekeeper replied, "Thank you, Mrs Bingley. We have a visitor, Madam – will you receive him? Mr Reavley has called."

Kitty's head snapped up, her sewing forgotten and all her ennui flown from her. Mrs Gardiner chuckled even as Jane answered.

"By all means, show the gentleman in," she smiled; and, as he entered, "Mr Reavley, how nice to see you! We find ourselves quite in want of pleasant diversion."

❖❖❖❖❖

"Georgiana," began Fitzwilliam, taking her hand into his as he spoke, and she closed her eyes against what was to come. "I confess I am of two minds in this." He noted a tiny spark in them as she opened her eyes to him.

"Then you are in favour of this marriage?" she said, her tone too expectant for his comfort.

He squeezed her hand, saying, "Do not make so much of it. I simply allow for some doubt in opposing it fully."

"But you must tell him so!" she cried, before modulating her voice and adding, "Will you tell him so?"

"Georgiana." Her face fell.

"You will not. You will not oppose him."

He laughed at the presumption, not without humour. "I assure you I do oppose him now and again when I am certain of my ground. But in this I am not."

She hesitated; her expression reflected uncertainty as to whether she could tolerate his answer to the query her mind formed. But finally she asked, "What is your opinion, Retched? Will you tell me – if I had come to you first to ask your consent – what decision would you have given?"

He smiled down at her. "My dear, I will not answer you so particularly now; but I will tell you what you might wish to know." He sighed. "For a start, I like your Mr Hewitt." Before his cousin's desperate desire could read too much into the statement, he added: "Moreover, from my observance I believe Darcy likes him, as well."

"But..." Georgiana did not go further, uncertain what to make of this.

"But liking the man does not on its own signify." He squeezed her hand again. "I have observed you these last weeks and I believe you tender

118

strong affection for the young man; this speaks to me in his favour. And I must add that I am convinced of Mr Hewitt's admiration for you." He smiled. "This too gives good evidence of judgment for his part."

"I do love him, Retched. We are..." She considered what she had meant to say and Fitzwilliam was certain that when she spoke again, she had altered her words, moderated them. "We are well suited in every way for particular happiness."

Fitzwilliam nearly laughed at this – the stilted words, the business manner – but he knew she was trying to appear objective, unemotional, and so he refrained with a will. "So it would appear; and on the face of it, I might approve the match for these things."

"But..." Her voice carried resignation.

"But your brother raises some valid concerns." He sighed now, feeling himself the sting of his next words. "One cannot live solely upon love, my dear. One must have the means..."

"We do have the means! Nathaniel is to have a property, and with my dowry –"

"Yes, yes I know." It was more than he and Amelia could have, and yet he hoped to make a life with that lady when her mourning was complete. Therein lay some part of his reticence to deny Georgiana. "But your brother is right to question Mr Hewitt's stewardship, being as young and lacking in experience as he is.

"And there is yet the question of *your* youth as well, Georgiana." She began to shake her head in denial, and Richard added: "I do not question your judgment, my dear. I see some of the attributes in Mr Hewitt that commend him to you. But you have not yet entered the world. How can you be certain, with your limited acquaintance, that there is not another gentleman who might offer you love as well, and more? Who might, in fact, be better suited? I do not question Mr Hewitt's character; no, nor yours – and nor does your brother; we reserve ourselves only regarding the certainty with which you place your heart and your trust so completely in him without benefit of wider intelligence."

Georgiana was quiet, reflecting on his words. There was a stubborn set to her chin that gave him to understand she refuted his reasoning; but yet she did consider it. After a moment, she looked up at him and studied him carefully.

"You would have said yes." It was a statement, not a question. Despite his having admitted of concerns, she had recognised that in Fitzwilliam's speech but, although he would not confirm it to her, he could not deny it to himself. His own experience of late gave him to weight love heavily in this matter, and he knew it would have tipped the balance in his mind. But this did not necessarily constitute good judgment—he recognised that as well. He made no reply.

"You must tell him so!" she repeated. "Will not you speak to him for me? Will not you make him alter his decision?"

Fitzwilliam sighed. "I will speak to Darcy of my own opinion; I have done once, and we meet again tonight. But do not expect my words somehow magically to alter his resolve, Georgiana. I have said that I endorse some of his concerns, and I must speak candidly of these as well. If there is any possibility that he—that *we*—should amend our judgment, then *you* must accomplish the alteration; you must convince us both that our concerns are without foundation."

"It is impossible," she whispered. "He will not listen to me as you do."

"Do not you think you are being unfair? Have you tried to speak to him rationally of this? Have you listened to him any more than he to you?"

Georgiana looked down at her hand in Fitzwilliam's and did not answer immediately. Then she said with some petulance, "Why is he so stubborn, Retched, and intractable? It overawes me. He makes it so difficult to talk to him at all. Yet you do not intimidate me – you listen to me, you credit me with reason. Why can not Fitz be more like you?"

"Ha!" Fitzwilliam laughed, but it was short lived, only until he took her complaint seriously, and answered it such. "Do not compare us, Cousin, not to the disadvantage of either. You would have your brother just as he is, and you know this." Her stubborn pout suggested she was unready to concede such a thing.

"Gee, can not you show Fitz some compassion?"

This surprised her. "Compassion? Why?" she asked, though her tone carried less edge than before, more curiosity.

"My dear, I have had the easy task all these years. Yes, I also was appointed your guardian, and I hope I have acquitted myself well in that regard. But for all purposes, mine was the easier road. I could saunter into your life bearing gifts and a ready laugh or, when needed, an ear to listen and a chest to cry upon, or counsel. I could afford to make a friend of you. And afterwards, I sauntered away again. But Darcy –" Fitzwilliam stopped a moment to choose his words.

"Fitz has had to be all things for you – your brother, yes; but also your father, your mother, your mentor, your protector; even as he found his own way. That left little room for friendship as well. The charge was amplified for him. He has had both to discipline and to comfort; guide and nurture; at times dry the very tears he provokes. This is no easy undertaking, you know it well. You could go to him with any fear – but who could he turn to when he doubted the way? If he wished only to indulge you as a brother, yet he must instruct you as a parent. If he loved you too well, yet he must on occasion subjugate that to reason for your good. He has assumed your custody, your protection, as a trust far too long for him easily to relinquish it now when your need of him diminishes."

Georgiana contemplated the idea, and Fitzwilliam could see her expression soften.

"Can not you try to allow of this? Can not you allow him to falter in his step now and again? He has want of your regard, Georgiana, as much as ever you have needed him. Perhaps you can begin there to find your way to a new understanding."

"I will try," she promised.

❖❖❖❖❖

Thomas Reavley had brought a trap out in the freezing clime ostensibly to bring to Mrs Darcy some parcels his sister had promised at their last meeting; but he was quickly – and easily – pressed to remain for refreshment. Lizzy had returned to the drawing room only moments after his arrival. She thanked him for his gallantry to brave the cold on such an errand – profusely and not without some laughter given the trifling nature of the parcel contents – and following, she had sent for chocolate and settled in to small conversation while they awaited the warming beverage.

Kitty's ennui had dissipated at Mr Reavley's entrance. She sat demurely on the settee beside Jane now, a half smile on her countenance, for all the world engrossed as she listened to the young vicar describe the condition of the roads. Mrs Gardiner caught Jane's eye and the two shared a wordless amusement.

Having dispatched both his errand to Lizzy and a report of the weather, Mr Reavley then remembered yet another purpose for his call. He pulled from inside his coat a thin, flat parcel and held it out to Kitty. She removed the outer wrap to find the latest month's copy of *Gallery of Fashion* and nearly squealed in delight.

"Fortuitously, I was browsing the... er... news periodicals... at the library this morning when this was put out for display. Of course, I procured it immediately, certain that you – and Miss Darcy, of course – would wish to avail yourselves of the latest news."

Kitty's colour heightened and she giggled briefly before consciously composing herself. "Thank you, Sir. That is most kind of you to think of us, Miss Darcy and myself."

"Do you know, the colour plates are really quite extraordinary."

"Do you often peruse ladies' fashion magazines, Mr Reavley?" chuckled Lizzy, her tone light enough to take the sting from the observation.

"Oh, I... I happened... to turn a few pages... as I awaited my turn at the counter," stuttered Mr Reavley, before smiling in defeat. Then he said, "But truly, I had not previously realised the quality of art represented in these publications."

He was spared further embarrassment – although in truth he little minded the teazing – by the arrival of refreshments. Mrs Chaney had now finished her letter and joined the others; they all passed a delightful quarter hour in general converse, Mr Reavley and Kitty trading glances and smiles from time to time.

When she had finished her chocolate, Lizzy walked to the window to gaze out at the garden and a moment later she called to Kitty and Mr Reavley to join her there. She pointed out to them a rabbit burrowing near the hedge as though it should be of curious interest to them before idly wandering back to her chair. And under the moderately watchful eyes of her sisters and aunt, Kitty and Mr Reavley found opportunity for discourse.

❖❖❖❖❖

Darcy sighed as he approached the stables, uncertain whether in anxiety over what awaited him or from relief to be nearly home. Most likely, it was both. He had set out early that morning with Parsifal and together they had circuited the outer perimeter of Pemberley, or nearly the whole of it. The hours had afforded him a great deal of thought, much of it disturbing in nature; but they had culminated in a decision, or rather confirmation of what he had known even before setting out.

In his mind, he could not expunge the image, the sound and feel of Gee's anguish last night. He had held her for an age while she clung to him and wept; wishing he could say the words that would revoke her grief but knowing he could not. He could only whisper soothing words of little meaning and less conviction. He had held her until the weeping ceased and, finally, she slipped into sleep from exhaustion. He had carried her then into her chamber, had settled her on the bed and pulled the counterpane to cover her. He had stood looking down at her quieted form for several moments, until she moaned in sleep and drew her knees up. He had left her then, taking his regrets and confusion to the library to ponder. But morning had brought him back to the same concerns.

Parsifal was so accustomed to the route they had followed that he had needed little guidance; Darcy had given it scant thought until, when he had attained the lane that led towards Lambton, he had redirected the mount to take it, in order to meet at the appointed hour Bingley and Sir James at the Rose and Crown. They no longer required his attendance; Bingley was perfectly capable of completing the purchase of Albion Park without his help. But his brother had requested him specially, and he had obliged. Mr Sanders had finalised the deed transfer documents and, in his presence as well as Mr Atherton and Mr Folsom for witness, all parties had signed. They had then arranged a bank draft deposit, and retreated to the snug at the Rose and Crown for celebratory drinks.

But Darcy was restless, anxious to have done with the conversations he knew he must initiate to conclude this business of Nathaniel Hewitt. Only then could he begin to resolve the rift with Georgiana. Since he had travelled to Lambton independently, he took his leave of the gentlemen early, riding with purpose back to Pemberley.

The air had changed since his morning jaunt; the temperature had plummeted and wind nipped at exposed flesh. He did not retain the casual pace of his morning ride, but travelled with all haste, smiling unthinking at his first view of the house with welcome smoke curling up from its chimneys. Now he dismounted Parsifal and led him in to the relative shelter of the stable block, giving his equine friend an affectionate pat before turning him over to Bryce who had materialised immediately to take charge of the horse.

Before he turned to leave, Darcy glanced down the length of the enclosure and stopped. There was a lantern near the end and, in its faint illumination, he could see two figures seated on a bale of winter hay: Georgiana and Fitzwilliam. He stood a moment, deliberating, before expelling a breath and walking slowly towards the pair.

CHAPTER TWELVE

AS HE APPROACHED more closely, Darcy acknowledged his cousin and sister, but stopped advancing when he gained Comus's enclosure. He reached a hand out and the colt acknowledged the greeting with a butt of its head, then began to investigate his person. Darcy smiled and, surprisingly, heard both Fitzwilliam *and* Georgiana chuckle. "He was well named, was he not?" he asked idly.

Fitzwilliam replied. "Indeed; you took well the measure of the rascal."

"Oh, not I," said Darcy, smiling and nodding at his sister. "Gee chose the name almost from first acquaintance." He laughed and pushed the horse away from him playfully as he addressed it: "God of Revels, indeed. Chaos and Excess. Well, I have no treat for you today, it serves nothing to look."

"Here." Georgiana reached into her muff and pulled out a twist of brown waxed paper which contained still two slices of apple. She held it out to her brother with a tentative smile.

While Darcy offered the animal its treat, Fitzwilliam glanced at Georgiana and, sensing no untoward reluctance in her composure, he withdrew his hand from hers and stood. He considered that this place where his cousins had passed so many happy hours together could perhaps prove just the place now to reconcile them. "I think it time I returned to the house," he said with intentional lightness. "The ladies must be in need of diversion – and I would not have them forget me from too long an absence."

When he had gone some small way, Darcy called to Fitzwilliam and moved to catch him up. "Cousin, when *I* return, I would speak with you of this matter," he said in a low tone.

"Yes, of course. You will find me in the billiard room." He made to leave but stopped when Darcy added, "Is Hewitt within, Edmund, that is? We need have word with him as well."

"He was not." When Darcy looked surprised, Fitzwilliam said, "Hewitt and Wentworth departed before breakfast this morning, taking young Hewitt off with them. I do not believe they have returned as yet. The horses were not brought in while I have been here."

"Mmmm," considered Darcy. He nodded, asked Fitzwilliam to detain Hewitt if he returned, and his cousin left. Darcy took a measured breath before turning around to join Georgiana on her makeshift settee.

❖❖❖❖❖

On their way once more finally — after a delay caused by a wheel which had mired in a rut — Nathaniel leaned back in the carriage and closed his eyes, squeezing them tightly to try to block the memory of Georgiana standing by the fire. It persisted as if sketched permanently before him.

It was no use. All the persuasive reasoning, all the drink in England for that matter, would not drive away the image of the expression she had worn when he had returned to the drawing room the night past. He could wish now that he had followed his instincts and gone directly to his room after... after. His absence would have given her the report of his downfall just as surely as their wordless encounter had done; but he would have been spared having to see his own anguish reflected in her grey eyes, her face crumpling with disappointment — disappointment in him.

He had failed — utterly, miserably, damnably. Failed to convince Mr Darcy of his worth to marry his sister; failed to gain them the future together they both desired; failed her. How could he ever look upon her again? Or she him? Would his final memory of her gentle eyes be always wrenched by their expression of disappointed alarum he could not forget? Would he ever be able to think on her again and see instead the shy smile she had bestowed when she declared her love for him?

Surely her faith in him was lost now, as if it mattered when *she* was lost. Mr Darcy, on reflection, would probably send him away today, despite Wentworth and Edward's contrary opinions; and Nathaniel could almost hope for the expulsion. Indeed, he himself had wished to leave immediately last night, but Ned had talked him out of precipitous action. This morning, early, his brother had returned to find him still in his evening clothes, fumbling about numbly in useless activity, and he had taken Nathaniel in hand. He had directed his man to clean the suffering man up; then he and Wentworth had carried him off before too many people were about.

They had travelled south in weighty silence for over an hour to an inn where Wentworth was known. He procured them a room for their use and a hearty meal. It might have been gruel for all Nat ate of it. Once they were established, Ned coaxed from him details of the unsuccessful application that Nat could only gulp out to him the previous night. His senses dulled, they did not prevent Nat from noticing the cringing glances his brother and friend shared from time to time; though they did not interrupt his narrative as he took them through his declaration to Georgiana in Lambton to his abject repudiation by her brother. When he finished, he rested his elbows on the table and dropped his head down into his hands.

No one broke the silence for a moment before Ned exhaled slowly. "Nat, I could wish you had told me what you had planned. I might have warned you if I could do nothing else."

"Warned me!" Nat bristled despite the mildness of his brother's rebuke. "Warn me not to love her? Impossible! Not to offer for her when I cannot comprehend being with any other?" He glanced somewhat guiltily at his brother when he said this, aware of Ned's own marital circumstance. "Not to endanger your amity by presuming to insinuate myself on your friend's property?" he added bitterly. "You have no need to tell me I do not deserve her, Ned; I am all too aware of my shortcomings."

"Nat," replied his brother, glancing at Wentworth for corroboration. "Of course I do not think you unworthy. But Darcy is –" He stopped, uncertain what to say, and then finished with, "I would have tried to advise you. *We* could have advised you," he added, including Wentworth this time.

This garnered Nat's attention despite himself. "How so?"

Wentworth barked a laugh. "Nathaniel, Darcy is not a man to approach on such business without preparation – he dislikes surprise in the conduct of his affairs and, where his sister is concerned, he is... extremely careful."

"How could he be surprised? I have been in company some time; I made no secret of my admiration for Miss Darcy. Surely *you* noted it!"

"Yes," his brother answered. "And I dare say my friend did, too. But yet I did not guess it had gone so far. Perhaps I should have done; but I did not realise your imminent intent. How much less would Darcy see what he could not wish for."

Nathaniel's head snapped up at this, ready to take issue, and his brother held out his palms to stave off offense. "Nat," he said, "Miss Darcy is not out in society yet, for your attentions to be so markedly directed. Did you consider to ask Darcy for permission to court his sister?"

"No," came a grudging reply.

"Then perhaps you can accept that he might be taken aback by such a precipitous appeal as a marriage offer, regardless of your qualities. It disadvantaged you from the start."

Nathaniel was not disposed to concede anything; he merely reverted to a glum sigh and offered, "It would have mattered little. He would only have denied consent to court her then."

"Perhaps. He might have cautioned to give Georgiana the opportunity to enter society; he might have contrived to know more of you himself before consent or denial. He might do any number of things that would not so perfectly dash your aspirations. And *you* might have courted Darcy a bit as well while you made love to his sister – given him a chance to like you for himself. "

"Oh, what use!" cried Nat. "It is all so nonsensical. I mean, he is not even her father! He is *only* her brother."

"Ha! If that is what you believe, then truly you do not know Darcy well enough to beard him in his own den."

"Be that as it may," said Wentworth now to mollify a bit, "the deed is done. What precisely did Darcy tell you? Did he offer reason?"

"Something of her youth and mine."

Ned and Wentworth waited, but Nat had no more to add.

"That is not so bad," Ned finally offered. His brother looked at him in astonishment, and he clarified. "What I mean to say – if that is the worst of his objections, it is a condition overcome by time." He hesitated, as if to say more might offer hope without foundation.

"No. You did not see his countenance, feel the air in the room. His judgment was irrevocable."

"Did he forbid you to speak with Miss Darcy? Send you away immediately?" asked Wentworth, well aware of the answer.

"No." After a second he added, "not yet."

"Do not you think he would have done so immediately if he found you so flagrantly offensive?"

But Nat just shook his head, before cradling it in his hands yet again.

They spoke to him in this manner for some time, trying to draw away from him his raw emotions and offer perspective on the circumstance. When that had little effect, they ordered ale to ply him with drink and dull his senses. At first he only became more morose.

He sat awhile saying nothing, staring into his drink with tortured eyes. When he spoke finally, he wrenched out: "I must leave; we must leave, brother!"

"You know I cannot, Nat. Susanna cannot yet travel, and moreover –"

Nathaniel cut him off. "I will go alone. I will borrow your horse, Wentworth, if you will give it to me."

Wentworth and Edmund exchanged glances. It was Ned who replied. "Nat, I cannot allow you to leave on your own; not in this state of mind. You need to consider carefully –"

"But I cannot stay – it is untenable – a torment to remain and watch Miss Darcy from a distance, unable to be with her, to speak to her."

Between them, Edmund and Wentworth convinced Nathaniel to wait a day. Ned promised to speak with Darcy that evening and find out if he could his friend's full mind in the matter. If his brother still felt compelled to leave after another day of consideration, then Wentworth would go with him. Grudgingly, Nat agreed, but then he added: "But Ned, when you speak with Mr Darcy, do not plead for me, I beg you! I would not have you debase the Hewitts in such manner – nor prove the man's argument for taking up what I could not accomplish myself. Allow me to preserve what remains of my pride."

His brother agreed, and the three then set out to drive the matter from Nat's head with drink and talk of other things. And for a time, his distress was muted if not forgotten. In this temper, he might almost believe his brother's intimations that perhaps all was not lost.

But now, as they journeyed back to Pemberley, all his emotion flooded back to him and with it came his certainty of doom. His misfortune had no ease, no relief... no hope.

❖❖❖❖❖

As he made his way to the house Fitzwilliam thought about nothing but gaining it quickly. With the sun dropped down behind the hill, the bitter cold had worsened. But when the footman closed the door behind him and took his greatcoat, he began to consider his cousin's request for speech. Darcy's expression had contained regret, but Fitzwilliam had noted resolve as well. He wondered what their speech would accomplish – if Darcy was prepared to apprise Edmund Hewitt of his thoughts now, then Fitzwilliam had little confidence his own opinion could alter his cousin's decision. But he would attempt it; he owed Georgiana that much. Perhaps Hewitt might attempt it as well, to speak for his brother.

He entered the drawing room to find the ladies present but, as expected, Wentworth and the Hewitts still had not returned. He went to warm his hands by the fire and was joined shortly by Mrs Chaney.

"Were you able to see Miss Darcy?" she asked timidly, uncertain of her welcome in the business.

"I was," he said. He smiled at her and, glancing back first at the others, said in a low voice. "Georgiana and I spoke, although I could offer little by way of tangible comfort. But I believe it did some good for us both."

"Then I am glad," she smiled.

Fitzwilliam looked back again at the assembled company. Lady Catherine had joined them during the afternoon and sat now expounding on some subject, drawing a range of tolerant remarks from her audience. She continued pointedly to ignore her nephew but her presence brought back to him his earlier conversation with Elizabeth. He turned so that his back was to his aunt and the others, not to be overheard.

"Mrs Chaney," he began, then faltered and hesitated before continuing. "It has become known to me of late that you were accosted by my aunt in unfortunate consequence of... a certain matter." He noted Amelia's embarrassment; it matched his own. "I must apologise – I wish to make amends for her behaviour, *and* for mine not to have prevented such an egregious affront."

"Colonel, I beg you," she said with some discomfort, flicking her eyes towards Lady Catherine. "The less remarked, the better, truly. You have nothing for which to express regret. My own comportment has not been without blunder."

They regarded each other awkwardly, and then Fitzwilliam offered her a warm smile. "Madam," he said, "my behaviour towards you these recent days has much to account for." When she coloured and looked away, mortified, he added, "But I will content myself to renew our amiability. However..."

At his qualifier, Amelia looked up at him with some unease.

"However," he repeated, "at present my cousins require my attention. They are, as you may surmise, in strong disagreement and I am concerned for them – for Miss Darcy in the next days."

Amelia immediately conceded that it was to his credit to be so concerned, anticipating him to add that she would interpret no relevance from any absence or distraction on his part. He smiled, grateful that she understood.

"May I make a request of you?" he asked.

She nodded, smiling; and he proceeded to apply for the honour of the first dance at the ball on Saturday.

Amelia's face clouded over and she cringed. Fitzwilliam could only wonder at her reticence, until finally she admitted, "I regret, Sir, that I cannot. I have already made promise of the first dance – to Mr Wentworth." She spoke the name softly, uncertain of its reception; and was taken aback when Fitzwilliam began to laugh as at a wonderful jest.

"Of course!" he cried. "I should have known." He glanced about him quickly in embarrassment at his outburst, nodding to a few in the room who had looked up at his ejaculation, and then returned his attention to Mrs Chaney.

Amelia screwed her face up in bemusement as he explained. "Madam, I have yet one additional confession I must make to you," he said, still laughing. He admitted then quite sheepishly to having overheard her conversation with Wentworth a few nights past, his misunderstanding, and the late converse with Wentworth that had corrected his mistake. Mrs Chaney at first dropped her mouth in astonishment and seemed appalled, but gradually her expression softened to one of comprehension and, ultimately, of embarrassed humour.

"So you see," he finished, "I did know of your previous commitment for the dance. However, if I may be so bold – are there others perhaps for which you have yet to promise yourself?"

Smiling broadly, she replied. "Sir, I have promised none beyond the first." She dropped her eyes, adding softly, "They are yours to choose."

❖❖❖❖❖

Darcy looked to his sister for permission and she nodded tentatively. He sat next to her in the place Fitzwilliam had vacated. They were silent a moment.

"Do you detest me?" Darcy kept his gaze on Comus.

"Yes," she answered, but immediately she smiled sadly and said, "No," looking at him and drawing his eyes to her. "I never could," she whispered.

He matched her affecting smile for an instant. "And do you truly believe I think so little of you?"

This question she was not as quick to answer. Her countenance showed her mind at work. "Perhaps, in some ways."

He felt the sting of this, but it was no more than he had expected; and he had asked knowing the answer could injure him. He left it for the moment.

"Georgiana, it occurs to me that your appearance last night in my study" – they both winced at the memory – "was immediate enough that you had no speech with Mr Hewitt."

She looked down at her hands. "It required only his countenance and his avoidance to guess your answer to him." Darcy nodded, as she added, "I was not wrong."

"No, indeed you were not. Would you hear my reasons?"

She appeared torn as tears began to form and blur her vision. "Will knowing them mend my heart?" As soon as the words were spoken, she regretted them. She took the handkerchief her brother held out to her and said, "Forgive me, brother. That is unfair. I will listen, of course."

Darcy spoke his reasons – the same concerns Fitzwilliam had offered; the same he himself had raised the prior night. But despite her certainty that he was wrong, Georgiana could sense a difference in the tenor of their speech today. This time he took care to speak softly; to explain himself fully, as he might have done with Fitzwilliam, or with Lizzy – there was little of disapprobation or decree in his tone. He might have been thinking aloud. And on the few occasions where she mounted disagreement, he listened to her. It changed nothing, but still he listened; she could see him taking in her words. It was a start.

"Will you send him away?" she asked quietly then.

"No... though I cannot speak to his desire to remain, I will not encourage his departure; unless you wish it."

She shook her head vigorously that she did not. "I am confused, Fitz. I cannot easily think on Mr Hewitt, and know nothing of how I shall find the wherewithal to address him again in company – but yet I cannot bear the notion of his leaving so soon." Tears began to slip down her cheeks – not the wild, racking sobs of the night past, but slow and gentle, spilling over in a slow trickle as her eyes welled with them – and she asked: "Will you excuse me, brother, from dinner tonight? I shall try to compose myself to resume my duties to our guests tomorrow."

"Certainly, my dear, you are excused. Do not trouble yourself with our guests for now – but look after yourself." He paused. "Georgiana... I *do* credit your discrimination; I comprehend why you would be... fond... of this young man. I hold no enmity for Nathaniel Hewitt, you must know. Indeed, I like him well enough." Now his bearing changed; he stiffened slightly as if to steel himself from an odious memory. "I know that this is not as it was... before."

She looked at him, searching his countenance. "Do you, Fitz?"

"I do!" He frowned in thought. "You have changed in these last months; do not believe I am blind to it. You have matured into an admirable young woman, both in your heart and your reason. Indeed, you outgrow need of me." He hesitated as his own eyes began to glaze over. "It is difficult for me to accept this; I will try, truly, but you must be patient with me. When I look at you, I still see my Gee, and I incline only to protect you. You must correct me when I would forget."

She smiled at him now and whispered, "Thank you, Fitz. It is difficult for me, also." She glanced down, placed her delicate hand upon his and squeezed it in mutual comfort. When she looked back up at him, she said, "But... is it possible... that is, can I still be your Gee now and again? For I confess being a mature woman is not always tolerable to bear."

With a smile to break a heart, he moved his arms around her, and they sat thus a moment. Then she pushed him away gently, wiped away her tears with his handkerchief, and asked: "Tell me, then – what else *did* you say to Mr Hewitt?"

"I did not forbid him your continued acquaintance if you wish it, nor banish him. I was civil in every way. I merely rejected his suit —"

"Merely?"

Darcy sighed, and apologised. "Forgive me, I did not mean — of course it is no small matter to you, nor to me. But I have said I like the young man. Who knows but had he come to me a few years from now with the same request — each of you having more experience of the world, a wider acquaintance — I might have viewed it differently. But as it is —"

"A few years!" she said, and laughed grimly. "Tell me, brother, did you wait years to offer for Lizzy once you knew you loved her?"

"Georgiana, my love of Elizabeth is a different thing entirely."

"How is it so? I love Nathaniel just as you do Lizzy."

"I do not doubt you believe it so now. But Gee, I had passed several years in society. I was well acquainted with every manner of young woman to find Elizabeth superior to them."

"But *she* was only twenty; not so much older than I."

"Enough so. She had been out for some time — had suitors before me. Indeed, I suffered by comparison with the gentlemen of her acquaintance at the start," he laughed grimly. "I know you care for Mr Hewitt and I see your pleasure in his company. I am not unmoved, I confess, by your appeal and by your strength of affection for the boy. But, my dear, how can you know with certainty that you love him above all others, if you have yet to acquaint with others? How can either know that he will provide for you well when he has yet to provide for himself? I cannot approve a match based on youthful affections so early ignited, when a commitment to marry is for a lifetime. In this I must remain unmoved."

Darcy stopped there, considering whether to say more. When Georgiana did not argue further, but sat in resigned silence, he chose not to continue — he would take care to say nothing that might spark hope if there were none to offer. He little doubted that they must speak of this again, and soon, when she had considered arguments to his objections. But for now, it was enough that they could speak at all.

"Come," he said as he stood and offered his hand to her. "Shall we return to the house and a warming fire?"

She took his hand; they stopped together for a final moment with Comus, and then pulled close their outer clothing to brave the walk back.

❖❖❖❖❖

Frances Jenkinson could only stare at Anne deBourgh, uncertain of an appropriate response. She had noted, of course — it had been plain enough to see — a coolness between Anne and her mother since yesterday; but she could never have guessed this to have been the source of it.

Anne herself sat looking quite complacent, awaiting her friend's approbation. And indeed, Frances could only applaud that Anne had made a step to take charge in any mode of her own affairs. But in this manner? It was... astonishing!

Fast upon her surprise came momentary outrage at the allegations upon her own character that featured in Anne's story, but this ran its course in only seconds to be supplanted by humour. She had apparently never given Anne her due; perhaps her companion had inherited some of Lady Catherine's mettle after all. And she could well imagine the scenes: both the awkwardness of Anne's discourse with Mr Darcy and the bizarre confrontation with her mother that followed closely upon it.

Frances asked, "What was your mother's answer to this?"

"She has not given one. She... considers my request."

Frances shook her head in wonder. It occurred to her then to wonder also what effect this would have on Lady Catherine's condition, and she ventured to ask Anne how her mother had appeared following their discourse. She had suffered no palpitations, shortness of breath, or other effects from Anne's revelations?

"No," replied Anne, her countenance acquiring a wary frown. "Why do you ask?"

Frances sighed. It was past time; and she carefully revealed to Anne the debilitating heart ailment her mother suffered. As she spoke, Anne recoiled in surprise, gasping and drawing her hand to her mouth. Her brow creased in worry; she listened in this attitude until Frances had done.

"Why did not you tell me?" she asked in horror.

"She would not allow it. She still does not."

Anne shook her head angrily. "You as well, Frances? I trusted you to be the one person who would not withhold the truth from me, would not shield me while believing it for my own good! Is there no one I can put my faith in?"

Frances apologised and explained as best she could the considerations she had faced. Eventually, Anne forgave her; and immediately after began to fret. Could she have caused her mother harm? She had felt proud of maintaining her conviction in the face of her mother's displeasure, but she would never forgive herself if her actions caused Lady Catherine to suffer a collapse, or worse. Should she withdraw her petition?

In the end, with the counsel and comfort of her friend, she decided not. Despite outrage at being forced to act against inclination, Lady Catherine had not experienced a relapse and she certainly had not appeared weak this morning when she snapped at Anne. Indeed, she had always seemed to thrive on conflict; certainly she stirred enough of it herself.

Perhaps some part of her even recognised and applauded that her daughter had learnt something of her mother's example of tenacity. Anne would remain steadfast to her wants.

"And now," said Frances, echoing Anne's thoughts, "we await her decision?"

"Yes. Now we await her decision." She smiled at her companion.

❖❖❖❖❖

The Hewitt carriage approached the stable yard as Georgiana and Darcy set out to walk home. Darcy noted it was unoccupied; the driver had discharged its passengers at the house. He hoped they would have dispersed before his sister's entry and, but for the cold, he would have slowed their pace to ensure it. Georgiana's cloak and gown were not adequate against the wind; Darcy unfastened his greatcoat and drew her in to his side, pulling the coat around her. They huddled together beneath it and quickened their step.

When they entered the house, the Hewitts and Mr Wentworth had only just shed their outer garments and remained yet in the entry hall. They turned towards the newcomers at the opening of the door and, as Georgiana emerged from under Darcy's coat, she and Nathaniel Hewitt saw one another and stood stock-still. Young Hewitt could only gape, wearing an expression of startled alarm while Georgiana dropped her eyes immediately, her cheeks inflamed with colour.

Mr Wentworth recovered first. "Darcy; Miss Darcy," he greeted them, nodding at each in turn. "The cold permeates one's bones today, does not it?"

"Indeed," replied Darcy, before greeting Edmund and Nathaniel Hewitt quickly. Nathaniel did not reply; he appeared to be in something of a stupor.

Fortunately, Lizzy approached just then from the stairs and took stock of the awkward encounter. Rushing over, she exclaimed, "Georgiana! You are chilled through! Come, let us get you warmed at the fire." She slipped her arm around the young woman's waist and led her unprotesting away, offering a reminder to the others that the dinner hour approached. Darcy noted in his grateful relief that his wife did not take Georgiana to the drawing room, but immediately to the next set of stairs, mounting them for their private quarters. His sister now under capable care, he turned his attention to the gentlemen.

Nathaniel Hewitt still did not speak, but retained his gaze upon the floor tiles Georgiana had so recently occupied, his expression blank. He struggled, one could see, to maintain it thus, his complexion having taken on a greenish tinge.

Edmund Hewitt began to explain to Darcy, more to relieve the awkward clime than from necessity, where they had passed the day. While he was so engaged, Henry Wentworth watched the stairs. As soon as Lizzy and Georgiana had reached the top and turned for the next level, he took his young friend in hand.

"Let us be on our way as well, Nathaniel. It grows late and we should not tarry — we do not wish to delay the dinner hour."

Nathaniel had looked towards Wentworth upon hearing his name, and sluggishly responded, rousing himself to depart with nothing more than a curt nod in Darcy's general direction.

"Forgive him his manners, Darcy," said the elder Hewitt as the others moved out of hearing. "He does not think to offend..."

Darcy waved it away. "I quite understand."

Edmund Hewitt then laughed sheepishly and offered, "We thought to give Nat false comfort in drink, but I fear it took him more fiercely than it should. My brother has not enjoyed the years you and I have had to gain tolerance."

Darcy acknowledged this with a nod as Hewitt added, "He will sober sufficiently for dinner, Wentworth will see to it."

The reminder of this obligation prompted Darcy to mention that they, too, should retire to dress, but he first secured Hewitt's agreement to meet with him and Fitzwilliam directly following the dinner hour.

CHAPTER THIRTEEN

AS WAS BECOMING all too common of late with so many preoccupations, conversation at dinner tended towards being isolated between pairs and low in tone as reflected the general mood. In order to keep herself amused, Lizzy moved her interest around the table to speculate upon the moods and musings of the party.

Situated immediately to her left, Nathaniel Hewitt's thoughts posed no challenge at all. He held two: Georgiana, at whom he could not refrain from darting pained glances down the table, and his own misery. Lizzy had been surprised when Nathaniel appeared for dinner; she had not anticipated he would master the composure to do so. Clearly, from his expression as he considered Georgiana, *he* had not expected *her* attendance. Before they had come down from dressing, Darcy had confirmed to his wife Nathaniel's condition on his return earlier. As such, she rather thought his presence now to be more of drink-induced bravado and less of good sense. Yet here he was – suffering in such an appealing manner.

To his credit, the young man tried to converse with her, aware he had been afforded a place of honour (an honour arranged partly out of compassion and partly to separate him as much as possible from Georgiana). But he had not the wherewithal in reason to maintain discourse for long and no heart for it.

Jane, to his left, also attempted to engage Nathaniel Hewitt; Lizzy could perceive her thoughts also with ease. She knew her sister too well to doubt that Jane assumed some of Hewitt's pain in a sympathetic attempt to lessen his. When she conversed with him, her voice held a peculiar lilting softness as though to speak more stridently would wake the sleeping beast of remorse in him. Jane once had had good reason to comprehend the sensation of lost love he bore so prominently. No doubt she now regarded Nathaniel with an earnest hope that his suffering would, in the end, bring him the same happiness and contentment she now enjoyed.

When she was not trying to draw out Mr Hewitt, Jane conversed with Uncle Gardiner at her other side, as well as with Bingley and their aunt across the table. Despite their elation at finding themselves owners of an estate – now wanting only the deeds to be proved – still the Bingleys faced their own dilemma.

Sir James had indicated that, as he was to retain the gatehouse at Albion Park for his use, he could effect a move and turn the estate over to the couple by early March, and they were anxious to become settled in to their new home quickly. To preclude strenuous travel for Jane so near her confinement, the Bingleys would remove from Netherfield as soon as feasible in February and reside at Pemberley until their home was ready – an occurrence Jane anticipated with delight but for the odious requirement to apprise Mama of the entire business.

Indeed, Mrs Bennet was like to be inconsolable for the loss all at once of her eldest daughter, a favoured amiable – and tolerant – son, her grandchild to come, and her status in Meryton as an intimate of Netherfield Park with, as she perceived it, an open invitation to call. And it *would* prove an ordeal, for Jane especially, to inform her parents and suffer its effects.

But as Lizzy considered it, her own sympathies shifted. For Jane and Bingley, the suffering would last perhaps a month until their removal, although that in itself would require fortitude (and an ability to turn a deaf ear that Jane lacked) – but Papa and Kitty and, even more so Mary, would bear Mama's histrionic behaviour far longer. Lizzy made a resolution to be more attentive to Mary for a while, would write to her more often. She would invite her sister to make a visit but was certain their mother would never allow of it in her 'time of need'; Mama had grown quite dependent upon Mary for her comfort since Jane had married. Papa, too, would miss his elder daughter greatly for himself, although he would say little of it. Lizzy predicted he would be a more frequent visitor to Pemberley in the next year, however.

Uncle Gardiner came next in her perusal, and Lizzy conjectured that his prime concern tonight was to enjoy cook's elegant course. A man of moderation in all things, he nevertheless felt compelled to sample as much as he could and always left the table complaining that he would not require sustenance for a week before presenting himself promptly for breakfast the following morning. Dear Uncle Gardiner! Welcome at any time, his solid presence in this party especially had proved a calming and rational relief amidst the chaos. And how delighted Lizzy had been to find a friendship of note developing between Edward Gardiner and Sir James Thornton.

Tonight, her uncle applied his good sense to a solution for Jane's problem; he well knew the fits his sister would parade. But the only counsel he could conjure was for Bingley or Jane to write to Mr Bennet immediately with the grand news – thus being out of range of Mrs Bennet's reaction until she had time to calm a bit. Lizzy smiled and wagered with herself that Edward Gardiner also wished to spare *himself* his sister's distress, since he and Aunt Gardiner would travel back to Longbourn with the Bingleys by way of returning to town.

Jane, feeling some guilt already at having announced through correspondence her being in the family way, was loath to use this method again. As such, it was certain the Gardiners would not stop long in Hertfordshire on the return; some emergent trouble with the business or the children would no doubt require their departure almost immediately upon arrival, only to then resolve itself cleverly before her uncle ever alighted in Gracechurch Street.

Mrs Jenkinson posed something more a challenge for Lizzy to interpret. She was quite animated tonight, an elevated temperament to suggest a light spirit; likely she had finally unburdened herself to Anne regarding Lady Catherine's heart condition. But it must be more than that: Frances Jenkinson's eyes shone with good will and – could it be pride? – when she glanced across the table at her companion. Lizzy began to wonder if Lady Catherine's conjectures concerning the relationship between her daughter and Mrs Jenkinson might not carry merit after all, whether Anne in her naiveté realised it.

Mr Atherton surprised Lizzy. When Darcy was in Lambton earlier in the day, the solicitor indicated that he had been summoned finally to attend Lady Catherine that evening, as a consequence of which Darcy invited both Mr Atherton and Mr Folsom to dine. When the two men arrived, Mr Atherton had struck up a discourse with Kitty of all people, and had appeared content to attend her frivolous ramblings – so much so that he had offered his arm as escort for dinner and now sat between Kitty and Mrs Jenkinson, conversing with both in equal measure.

Kitty kept up her part of the discourse by chattering on about the latest fashions from France, a topic concerning which Mr Atherton was astonishingly well informed. It seemed Mrs Atherton was French by birth and maintained frequent correspondence with her relations there.

Kitty had rebounded well from her earlier boredom. Mr Reavley's call had been just what her spirits wanted, and after his departure she had pored over the *Gallery of Fashion* as much for the plates as for the notion that the gentleman had held the magazine close to his heart as he carried it to Pemberley... to her. No doubt the distracted smile that played about her lips now had its source in a different gentleman altogether than the aging solicitor to her right, regardless how well informed in the matter of true India muslins.

Mr Folsom did not trifle with Miss Bennet; he reserved his comments for Lady Catherine to his left. When they did not speak, he looked about him abstractedly as if to determine how he found himself here at all. He could be in town to celebrate Twelfth Night with his own family for all the purpose he served in Derbyshire. He *must* wonder why ever Lady Catherine called him to accompany Mr Atherton and, indeed, Lizzy wondered the same.

True, he *had* been called upon for his services since his arrival. But Lady Catherine's collapse a few days past could not have been anticipated by the lady, as it had transpired to be a simple swoon (the cause of which Lizzy now believed with certainty) and, since then, she had very adamantly refused the physician's attentions. He had called as courtesy to check on Anne and Susanna Hewitt a few times, but the local Mr Grimes would have done as well for them, despite Mrs Hewitt's lamentations to the contrary.

Lady Catherine for her part conversed with Mr Folsom in the manner of a grand lady to a retainer of long standing – at once familiar and formal, and with every expectation of agreement from him. Perhaps in the end that had been the reason she commanded his travel to Derbyshire – the mere fact that she could when others seemed to defy her at every turn. As soon as she thought it, Lizzy chastised herself; such a notion was unfair. It was entirely possible that Lady Catherine had summoned Mr Folsom out of concern for her own health in light of the controversy she had initiated with Richard Fitzwilliam.

But even as she limited her speech to her physician, Lady Catherine's attentions encompassed far more. Lizzy could see that the lady's eyes darted about the table. *I wonder if she is engaged in the same enterprise as I*, thought Lizzy, but then dismissed the idea. Lady Catherine's thoughts were wholly the result of her own mood, her expression changing as she considered one or another of the party.

The grand lady studied Georgiana briefly with a curious eye, no doubt wondering at her niece's sombre mien and lack of appetite, before moving on to Fitzwilliam and Mrs Chaney. To these, her expression was one of disgust. Most curious, however, was the manner in which she regarded her daughter. One might have expected her to exhibit relief that Anne had refuted any notion of an unnatural liaison with Mrs Jenkinson; and yet instead her glance spoke of anger and resentment. And even those emotions gave way to anxious concern whenever Anne and Sir James fell into discourse, as if she would prefer the two had never met. What possible harm could she find in an amiable acquaintance between them?

After several attempts to take the measure of Lady Catherine, Lizzy gave it up as a futile effort that could yield only a throbbing head for her trouble.

She did muse for a moment, however, upon the intelligence she had earlier gleaned from Darcy. She had asked him what he knew of his aunt in her youth. He had few details and could recall no names ever mentioned either to confirm or refute Lizzy's certainty of a prior understanding between his aunt and Sir James. But he did relate two memories which could have bearing.

The first was confirmation of Fitzwilliam's earlier recollection. Darcy's mother, Lady Anne, had indeed uttered the cryptic remarks Fitzwilliam had mentioned, in the same comment admitting that her sister had suffered a disappointment in love before her marriage to Sir Lewis.

The second event which Darcy recalled had occurred shortly before Lady Anne died. She had been grievously ill and Lady Catherine had arrived some days prior to look after her, but spent much of her time sending the well-run household into an uproar. Mr Edward Darcy had been near to banishing her but for Lady Anne's wishes. Darcy, then sixteen and called home from school, had gone to visit his mother with poorly concealed ill humour one afternoon, where she had coaxed him into revealing an altercation with his aunt. All his pent up frustrations then came pouring out and, after relieving himself of his complaints, he asked his mother why Lady Catherine always must make herself so disagreeable.

'My dearest Fizzle,' she had replied, using her young daughter's name for him that brought a smile still to her illness-ravaged countenance; 'you must forgive your aunt and show her always respect and affection. She has not been blessed with the good fortune I have had. When we were little more than your age now, Catherine's heart was well and truly broken. It did not mend in the exact manner it had been, she was forever altered. Her spirit returned as temper and will, but for all that she is yet a good woman – she is my sister, my Kitty, inside. She has lost much over the years – her father, her brothers – do not you renounce her as well. When I am gone, you must promise me you will maintain a connexion with your aunt; promise me you will try to love her if you cannot like her. Promise me, for the sake of the sister she was to me and the constant heart she once possessed.' And he had promised to try.

Lizzy had learnt much from this recounting to explain Darcy's complex relationship with his aunt. His mother's sickbed plea was not something he would toss away lightly. It explained his forbearance, his passivity for so long when Lady Catherine pushed marriage to Anne, even why he continued his customary Easter visits to her year after year. But whether it also could explain anything of a former acquaintance with Sir James was pure conjecture.

Passing over Darcy now – Lizzy knew his mood too well to require supposition – she studied Georgiana. Gee was another whom she had been surprised to include in dinner; she had presumed the young woman would feel disinclined and, indeed, Darcy had indicated his sister had earlier requested exemption.

When Lizzy had escorted Gee upstairs, she had stayed with her a short while and had managed some speech finally. Gee had shown reticence to confide in Lizzy at first, which puzzled her even as she determined to use gentle persuasion to loosen her sister's tongue. To constrain her emotions too long would not serve Georgiana, or at least that was the reason Lizzy gave them both for her meddling.

When Gee did speak, it was to relate the conversations she had shared with Fitzwilliam and then her brother in the stables – and Lizzy felt a relief to match the young woman's that the siblings had reconciled some of their discord. Once Gee had begun to speak of this, it had unleashed a torrent of words and feeling that, once ended, embarrassed the girl; and she had apologised for placing her sister in any position of disloyalty to her husband.

But Lizzy had laughed when Georgiana suggested that she must agree with Darcy regarding a match with Nathaniel. '*Must I?*' she had replied; then went on to explain that a wife was never obliged to agree with her husband in every thing. '*Perhaps I must abide by his judgments, but I assure you I do not always share them.*' She had smiled wickedly and added, '*and even as to abiding them, there are times when that can be got round as well...*'

She had left it at that, with a gentle teaze that perhaps they should keep that intelligence between them; this had raised a brief, ingenuous smile from Georgiana. Still, the young woman had some things to learn before acquiring the condition of marriage, and Lizzy could not but partially agree with Darcy that Gee was not ready. She managed, however, to offer needed comfort without, in the end, having to divulge her own opinion on the matter; eluding any question of challenging her husband's rationale.

Whatever had possessed her sister to attend dinner at the last moment, Georgiana did not enjoy it. She ate little and, though she tried only to look down at her plate or to her brother or cousin when speaking to them, her eyes drifted too often up the table, to settle on Nathaniel Hewitt. It clearly caused her pain to do so but, rather like the tongue that cannot keep from roaming to an inflamed tooth, she felt his presence as a continual ache and could not stop herself. On the odd occasion when her glance met with Nathaniel's, Georgiana would revert her gaze to her own place quickly, struggling to keep anguish from her countenance.

Now and again and with mixed success, Fitzwilliam would intercept one of those mutual glances and engage in trivial speech with Georgiana to defray a rush of torment. To his credit, Darcy also maintained speech with Gee throughout dinner to occupy her, but it was clear that despite their having reconciled somewhat earlier, her brother still was too central a source of her pain to allow him to distract her now when Nathaniel Hewitt was in view as a constant reminder. All in all, Lizzy credited her sister well for the level of equanimity she *did* maintain, but she predicted Georgiana would retire for the night none too long after the last course had been cleared from the table.

Fitzwilliam, although an attentive servant of his cousin's need, could not restrain his delight at being in Amelia Chaney's good graces once more. When he turned to face the lady, his entire countenance would suffuse with hopeful optimism – in sharp contrast to his young cousin on his other side – and now and then, when Lizzy caught his eye, she had only to raise her brows teazingly at him to raise *his* colour several shades. She could not hear the discourse Fitzwilliam and Mrs Chaney shared, but she could see it was warm. Lizzy wagered once again that an understanding – this time a formal understanding – would not wait the year of mourning; she doubted it would wait the couple's departure for town in a week's time.

Amelia Chaney's mood was easily read as well; it mirrored Fitzwilliam's. While she was very pleased indeed that these two had found the way back to each other, Lizzy had to admit to herself that they were not nearly so interesting when merely making love to one another. She did not begrudge them their happiness; only a source of intrigue and amusement.

But Sir James Thornton, on Amelia's left, offered great intrigue. Clearly, he had known Lady Catherine in the past and well beyond mere acquaintance. Lizzy might want proof of it, but she knew it as she knew her own name. It only remained to determine how to prise the tale from the man, as it would never come from the lady in question. Lizzy set herself a challenge to draw him out.

Sir James was especially attentive to Anne this evening; he had made point of offering to escort her in to dinner and sit by her side. His glances moving between mother and daughter held concern, but he wore only a smile as he drew out his dinner partner in converse. Lizzy studied the two – an unmarried woman, beyond an age where marriage might be expected; and an aging, widowed gentleman – and a wild notion flitted into her head. Could this gentleman seek to find in the daughter what he might once have wished from the mother? As quickly as the idea entered consciousness, she dismissed it as ridiculous. No, Sir James's kind heart simply reached out to Anne in friendship, perhaps born of her relation to an old acquaintance, but no more than that.

Yet Anne responded well to the elder man. She was positively loquacious tonight; clearly in high mood. No doubt relief concerning Fitzwilliam accounted for much. But Lizzy could not but wonder if there were more to her light heart, given her earlier observations of Mrs Jenkinson.

Henry Wentworth offered no intrigue for Lizzy, but he did draw speculation into his character. Thoroughly likeable, easy in conversation – in fact, he could be quite outspoken, a trait Lizzy found refreshing – nonetheless there was something about the man that stirred compassion in her. She supposed it might find a basis in his having given up on Amelia Chaney just lately, although she had never supposed him as serious in intent as Fitzwilliam in that regard.

But a man of Wentworth's temperament was suited to a wife and Lizzy wondered how greatly he felt the lack of one. He was not an entirely handsome man, but other attributes more than compensated for this – why was he still single past the age of thirty? For some reason, it came to Lizzy that Wentworth could have been an excellent match for Charlotte Lucas as she was once – they could have been well paired with his intelligent, easy manner and her kind heart and pragmatism. Not for the first time, Lizzy regretted Charlotte's having settled for William Collins, however much her friend seemed content with her circumstance. This gentleman might have offered her love as well as the comforts of her own home. But no sense wishing for impossible things; Lizzy could only hope Wentworth would find his own 'Charlotte' one day.

At present, Wentworth consoled himself in converse with Bingley. Lizzy smiled as she regarded her brother. He had been elated all the afternoon at finding himself now a man of property awaiting only the filing of documents, and he and Wentworth engaged in a discussion of the practicalities of moving household goods, servants, and livestock; not that there was much of the latter to concern them. But Wentworth enjoyed the acquaintance of many tradesmen who specialised in such work and Bingley was happy to avail himself of his friend's recommendations. Lizzy smiled as she contemplated Bingley, marvelling as always at his modesty and good humour; a better husband for dear Jane could never have been devised.

And a better wife for Edward Gardiner could never have been found than Margaret Carswell, as she had been formerly. Lizzy could not measure the gratitude she felt for this woman who had from Lizzy's youth set an example of all that was gracious, good, and wise in a lady. And if her aunt had not enjoyed some roots in Derbyshire, Lizzy might never have found herself at this table, mistress of Pemberley and wife to Mr Darcy. She owed much to Margaret Gardiner, indeed, for bringing them together when their own natures had worked against them.

At the moment, her aunt was asking Edmund Hewitt after the welfare of his wife. He offered that Mrs Hewitt convalesced well, thanks to the attentions of Mr Grimes, Mr Folsom and Mrs Darcy's staff. Lizzy noted that even as he spoke with Aunt Gardiner, however, Mr Hewitt gave some part of his attention across the table to his brother. Lizzy surmised that he was more concerned for Nathaniel's welfare at the moment than for his wife's, his brother's on the whole being the more volatile distress. Occasionally, he smiled at Nathaniel as if to offer him fortitude; and now and again, he would glance down the table to Darcy. When he did this, his expression took on wary thoughtfulness. Most likely, he wondered at the meeting he was to have with Darcy very soon.

Lizzy wondered a bit at that as well. Darcy had mentioned the assignation to her before dinner, but would not say what his intentions were – only that he felt it necessary to offer to his friend some discourse regarding his brother's suit in the hope of settling the matter with the least amount of misunderstanding or resentment in any of them. He would only say that he had it in his mind how to address the circumstance; and promised a very curious Lizzy a full recounting before they retired.

As she considered this now, she glanced down the table to find her husband's eyes fixed upon her. She wondered at the intensity in his gaze until, as he nodded at the table, she realised that, while she had been occupied in the survey of their guests, they had all quite done eating. Darcy's silent reminder (and smirk) was for the lady of the house to adjourn proceedings. Immediately, she smiled all around, suggested that it was time for tea, and rose. Her guests followed her example.

Given that several of the party had business to conduct during the evening, the gentlemen would forego their customary hour of port, and everyone, with three exceptions, adjourned to the drawing room. Nathaniel Hewitt, upon a quick word with his brother, left it to Edmund Hewitt to offer excuses and retired immediately. Only a moment following his departure, Kitty approached Elizabeth, asking her leave to escort Georgiana to her chamber and remain with her there for as long as Miss Darcy might wish it. Gratified by her sister's sensitivity, Lizzy of course granted the request.

❖❖❖❖❖

Darcy having granted his aunt the use of his study for her business with the solicitor, he suggested the library for his own. While Edmund Hewitt made a brief diversion for an obligatory call upon his wife, Darcy and Fitzwilliam settled themselves with glasses of port – deemed the only libation of merit for their business – and Darcy then proceeded to preface for his cousin what he had in mind to say to his friend. The Colonel concurred; he offered some small considerations which Darcy adopted at once, but in the main he could not fault anything of consequence.

As Fitzwilliam refilled their glasses and added a third to the tray, Edmund Hewitt arrived. He took the drink with gratitude, something of a nervous smile playing about his mouth. The smile became correspondingly more nervous when Darcy raised his glass.

"To friends and good company," he said – an innocuous enough remark as it went, until he followed it immediately. "In service of our own friendship, Hewitt, I intend to be frank regarding this thorny matter of your brother."

CHAPTER FOURTEEN

Friday, 4 January 1799

❖❖❖❖❖

NATHANIEL HEWITT came downstairs and detoured to the breakfast room before leaving the house. Breakfast itself would not be served for two hours yet, but Mr Darcy always had early beverages made available, and a tazza of fresh fruits on the sideboard. Nathaniel's plan was to gulp down some coffee, then cut an apple into pieces to take to the stables and share with Comus. The colt seemed the only connection he might maintain with Miss Darcy since her brother had denied his suit two nights past. Georgiana would not defy Mr Darcy's judgment; she had barely spoken to Nathaniel in the last day, indeed had avoided his company as he had hers. His hope was dashed and, in his dejection, if he must remain at Pemberley he would seek any manner to retain some part of her to himself by courting the animal she doted upon. He intended still to convince his brother to allow him to leave as being best for all concerned. Ned had not visited him the night past which led Nathaniel to believe no good had come of his discourse with Mr Darcy.

He drew up short on walking into the breakfast room, then, to discover that rather than the vacant premise he had expected to find, three pairs of eyes turned to mark his entry.

"Oh!" he said. "Forgive my intrusion, Sir. I did not expect the room would be occupied at this hour." He bowed stiffly, uncertain of his welcome with Mr Darcy for having been bold enough to declare love for the man's sister.

"Not at all," replied Mr Darcy with a solemn air. "Come in, Mr Hewitt."

Nathaniel glanced from his host to Colonel Fitzwilliam briefly and, finally, to his own brother. All *three* gentlemen wore serious expressions;

they had obviously been in conference. But Edward nodded to endorse the invitation, and Nathaniel joined them at the table, although he remained standing.

"We are just preparing for a ride, brother."

"Why do not you come along with us?" offered Fitzwilliam.

"Oh, I... er..." stammered Nathaniel, flicking glances at Mr Darcy.

"Yes, do accompany us," seconded that gentleman. He wore no smile, but his tone was cordial.

"I am without my horse, Sir." As soon as Nathaniel made the excuse, he regretted it. What an ignorant dolt he must sound. From the time he had spent there, he had as much reason as they to know that Pemberley had an amply stocked stable with any manner of mount to be had at will. But as he silently chided himself for the stupid remark, Mr Darcy only smiled shrewdly.

"I believe we can rectify such want and supply you with adequate substitute," he said, kindly ignoring Nathaniel's reddening countenance. "Or you may ride Wentworth's if you like, as you are acquainted with it."

"Mr Wentworth does not accompany you?"

"No," said Edward. "Mr Bingley and Sir James have petitioned his opinions this morning on some business."

"Well, then, that settles it," said Colonel Fitzwilliam with a hearty smile as he stood, "what say you?"

"Yes, yes of course," answered Nathaniel, being unable to refuse, and attempting to convey happy acquiescence despite an odd premonition, as if he were a fly just landed in a spider's lair without yet realising he was caught fast.

The four of them walked to the stables and three chatted amiably while Wentworth's blood bay was saddled to join the other waiting mounts; Nathaniel busied himself with assisting the groom. Then the quartet of gentlemen rode off towards the wood and up onto the ridgeline.

❖❖❖❖❖

As she approached the door to the north parlour, Kitty could hear the music – some sort of sonata or etude of soft, plaintive notes. She hesitated before entering; perhaps her friend would not welcome her presence now. And she had to ponder, even did Georgiana consent to her company, whether *she* felt up to the challenge. She had little experience in comforting such distress. Oh, she had weathered her mother's upsets all her life, it was true – but even then, she stood on the periphery most often, watching as Jane or Lizzy or Mary attended to Mama, and generally complaining about the disruption to her own plans that her mother's indispositions caused.

And then, they were different somehow from this quiet grief that she had witnessed last night in Georgiana, and again now. This more resembled Jane the first time Mr Bingley had left Netherfield without her knowing – indeed she had believed it impossible – that he would ever return. This was *real* heartache.

The night prior she could not help but notice Georgiana's mood at dinner and she had offered to go with her to her sitting room following. She had stayed with her friend for a few hours. Georgiana had not felt inclined to speak much of her own ills, but rather asked Kitty to distract her with conversation, and they spent some time talking of Mr Reavley's visit. That is, Kitty spoke of it, while her friend made a half concerted attempt to listen well. She had managed to raise a smile from Georgiana a few times, especially in relating how Lizzy teazed Mr Reavley over his intimate knowledge of fashion plates. But when she had finally taken her leave, Kitty had sighed in relief to find herself free of the melancholy air of the room.

Now, she scolded herself for her reticence, turned the knob, and slipped into the parlour. It frightened her to face this intensity of sorrow, but Mr Darcy's sister had become her friend. Even though the younger of the two, Georgiana had often offered advice or compassion for disappointments that, by comparison now, seemed silly. Kitty could not abandon her friend when genuine, overwhelming worries assailed her; even if she had no notion of how to help.

Georgiana sat at her pianoforte with her back to Kitty. It might have been any session of practice if her posture did not betray her – a slight slump of the shoulders and her head slightly tilted as she watched her fingers move along the keys. While Kitty stood to watch, she saw her friend wince a time or two, as though she had struck some sour note that Kitty could not hear. The music sounded perfect to *her.* She watched a moment as two hands moved quite independently of each other, one producing a haunting melody and the other an accompaniment in some minor key that gave the entire piece the feel of a lament. Not accomplished in music herself, nonetheless Kitty could appreciate the skill with which Georgiana caressed the keys to produce such notes.

She approached quietly and when she had covered most of the distance between them, Georgiana noted Kitty's shadow as it moved across the instrument, and she turned. Kitty stopped lest she was intruding, but Georgiana smiled a sad welcome, even as her fingers still maintained the music.

"I never will comprehend how it is you do this," said Kitty with a smile, joining her then at the pianoforte. "It is beautiful – so sad."

Georgiana laughed with little mirth at this. "There is the trouble, Kitty," and she stopped, placing her hands in her lap as she turned to her friend. "This is supposed to sound a playful movement, if I could only render it properly!"

Embarrassed at her blunder, Kitty began to colour and coughed once; the effect of which was to raise a genuine smile of humour in Georgiana. Kitty reached out tentatively and placed her hand atop Georgiana's. "I wished to find how you are this morning, if… well, if you wish to come to breakfast with me."

"Is it the hour already?" asked Georgiana, twisting around to glance at a long-case clock. Her countenance assumed a contemplative frown. "I do not know. I… well, I do not think I can meet… him yet."

"I do not think you will, Georgiana. Lizzy told me Mr Hew… he… went riding this morning; with his brother and Colonel Fitzwilliam and Mr Darcy."

"*Riding!* With my *brother?*"

❖❖❖❖❖

The men had crossed the ridgeline and continued to an outlying expanse on the eastern edge of the estate. Its owner, a Mr Grantham, had offered sale of over one hundred acres to Darcy to raise capital to offset the man's debts resulting from death duties; Darcy surveyed the property with an eye to consider its purchase. He had already received report of its arable properties from his steward, but he wished to supplement this information with his own assessment. His initial impression was favourable; however, he had some few concerns he wished to consider as well.

After traversing the length of one boundary, the riders picked a way through a copse of trees to the other side of the acreage. At one point the path narrowed to allow of only one horse abreast and, after Darcy had gone through, Fitzwilliam and Hewitt had hung back and motioned Nathaniel to precede them. When the young man emerged again into open field, it was to find that he was alone with Mr Darcy. His brother and the Colonel had not immediately followed.

A knot formed in Nathaniel's stomach as he realised the separation had been by design. His suspicion was confirmed when Mr Darcy, noting his glance back at the copse, smiled wryly and said, "You need not concern yourself for your brother. My cousin has known these lands since our youth – they will make their way back easily enough."

"Yes, Sir." Nathaniel swallowed the knot which now worked its way from his stomach to his throat. He had been well and truly lured into a lion's den, and his own brother had been party to it. How could he have done so? – colluded in such a thing? Edward might make his way back unscathed, but would *he?*

"And you need not look like a hare run to ground." Darcy laughed. "I will not bite your head off."

"No, Sir" was all the reply Nathaniel could muster.

"I merely wish for your advice."

"My *advice*, Sir?" Nathaniel was truly put off balance now.

"Yes. On one, perhaps two matters, as it happens." Mr Darcy smiled at his companion, but it did little to put Nathaniel at his ease. He could not know that indeed Darcy was attempting to form a rapport between them; but that the gentleman's own unease with the discourse he was about to initiate made his friendly overture awkward.

"It is my understanding that you are a naturalist, Mr Hewitt – a natural scientist – and have acquired admirable knowledge in the field."

"I am no expert, Sir, not yet; but what knowledge I possess is at your service."

"Good." Darcy then asked the young man for his opinion on the land they now surveyed. When once Nathaniel overcame his astonishment – and relief – at the subject under discussion, he dismounted and walked over towards the dry-stone wall, where protection from drifts had left some space of ground without snow cover. Crouching down for ease of inspection, he began to point out some facts he observed in the soil, its dormant vegetation and indications of ground life. He was able to relax as they held a lively debate of the property's likely uses, and his nervous inclination receded. His opinion that the land could be used either for grazing or certain crops without undue preparation, citing the apparent soil quality and natural plant coverage, was considered seriously by Mr Darcy as Nathaniel returned to his horse and remounted.

Finally, after several moments of such exchange, Mr Darcy said, "Your eye is good, Mr Hewitt; you do indeed possess formidable knowledge of details."

Nathaniel smiled, pleased and proud of the acknowledgment, until his companion went on.

"However, one must consider details in a broader context when making decisions on the care of precious... resources," said Mr Darcy, and looked to Nathaniel. "The overall consequence of a collection of facts when brought into confluence with one another is paramount." He then went on to point out to Nathaniel, though not unkindly, the dearth of acceptable wind breaks, that additional drainage would need to be introduced for farming, and other drawbacks to the property, concluding that it might take as many as three to four years to produce a good yield, or two years at least for superior grazing. His ease in discussing such things was impressive to the younger man, though in truth, Nathaniel understood that Mr Darcy's purpose in the exercise had been to ascertain Nat's acumen, having no cause to persuade of his own.

"In the end," said Mr Darcy finally, "it is a good property. I will offer for it, though less than is asked to accommodate improvements and the reconstruction of two tenant cottages. But the investment is a sound one, if properly prepared in the near term for future gains." He paused an instant, considering his last remarks; then looked directly at Nathaniel. "Your instincts were good." The simple statement, delivered with a genuine smile of approbation, gave Nathaniel a disproportionate measure of pride.

The feeling subsided yet again as he realised that Mr Darcy was studying him as though making a decision.

❖❖❖❖❖

Lizzy noted the relief in Georgiana's countenance when she peered into the breakfast parlour before entering it after Kitty. The expression lasted only a moment before reverting to a thin mask of normalcy overlaying heavier emotion. But Lizzy herself felt relieved that at least Darcy's sister did not remain in seclusion this morning. She offered her own sister a smile of thanks for her part in rousing Gee, drawing a beam of delighted satisfaction from Kitty. A wicked idea flitted into Lizzy's mind: Kitty was taking on quite regular acts of selflessness of late. If it continued, the surprise her family usually felt upon encountering one was in danger of disappearing altogether.

Cook's kitchen had produced some lovely hot rolls this morning and each girl helped herself to one with honey, and to a cup of chocolate that offered to the room a wisp of rich aroma rising from the delicate china. While Kitty's roll disappeared with all speed and soon was augmented with another, Georgiana's was picked at. But still, Gee entered into converse with Jane and Aunt Gardiner and, if she was not fully herself, she was able to come out a bit.

This relative calm was threatened with the later arrival of Fitzwilliam and Edmund Hewitt. Georgiana froze in the act of raising a bit of honeyed roll to her lips and watched the air behind the two men, as such unmindful of the particular glances she received from each of them. She relaxed only when Mr Hewitt deliberately closed the door behind him; but even then, she was watchful for it to reopen.

Lizzy intervened. "Mr Hewitt – Colonel – good morning! Did you lose my husband in a snow drift?"

Fitzwilliam laughed and returned the intelligence that Darcy and Mr Nathaniel Hewitt had not returned with them; they were inspecting the Grantham acreage yet.

"Ah!" said Lizzy, adding, "Good; I am relieved then that I should not have to expend myself in the tedious hope for an early thaw."

The thaw in Georgiana's demeanour, however, lasted only as long as it took her to realise that, if it was unusual for Nathaniel to ride with Darcy in company with the others, it was even more so that the two men

150

should have remained alone together. The application of her attention was riveted upon her cousin when he sat next to her at the table with his repast. When the room's occupants had reverted to their various newspapers, letters and conversations following the Colonel's arrival, Georgiana ventured to address Fitzwilliam softly. "Retched?"

"How are you this morning, my dear?" he asked, offering her a benign smile.

For answer, he received the full concentration of two rounded grey eyes filled with appeal.

He smiled reassuringly at her, and spoke in a low voice. "There is nothing to concern you, my dear. They only remained behind to talk."

She did not appear mollified by this intelligence, but he would not say more; the only conclusion she could draw was that her brother, as he had done with her yesterday, had decided to explain to Nathaniel why he had been denied. No alternative explanation came to her with any claim to reason.

In fact, Fitzwilliam took care to say no more to Georgiana. He knew, as did Hewitt, to whom he glanced now in guilty conspiracy, the nature of Darcy's discourse with Nathaniel; but little purpose would be served to apprise his cousin of this. He could not know how the young man would react – he could become angry and leave Pemberley this very day as like as anything – and Fitzwilliam did not wish to heap further concern on Gee unless it could not be avoided.

❖❖❖❖❖

"Hewitt," began Darcy, "... may I take the liberty to call you so?"

"Yes, of course, Sir."

Darcy nodded and smiled, not unaware of the disparity in their addresses. "Two nights ago, Hewitt, you came to request the honour of my sister's hand, a request I denied you."

"I did, Sir." Nathaniel looked to Darcy as if wavering between defending his actions and a wild dream that the decision had been overturned.

Darcy quickly continued in order to dispel false hopes, having no wish unduly to torment the young man. "I have not rescinded that denial. I would, however, have speech with you further, to clarify my position. That is," he added, "I wish to account for the grounds upon which I base the refusal."

Nathaniel realised that Darcy did not often make habit of explaining himself, and found the present turn of their discourse greatly discomfiting. But he gave his attention mindfully to his host.

"My responsibility regarding marriage for Miss Darcy..." he shrugged at the formality, given the intimacy this young man had already

151

achieved with his sister, "is based upon three primary concerns, but *all* these deriving from a desire for my sister to be both well settled and find contentment in a union. My three concerns are these: Is it a good match in all possible ways? Is my sister certain of her feelings and inclinations in the matter? And is the gentleman worthy of her?"

At this last, Darcy noted that Nathaniel squirmed a bit. And it came to Darcy that, as much as the subject matter might cause this unease, perhaps his young companion also did not find such serious discourse easily attended while sitting a horse. He himself was perfectly at home astride Parsifal, but perhaps it gave him unfair advantage. He dismounted therefore and invited Nathaniel to do the same. They continued their converse as they walked with their mounts, the activity giving each of them a welcome excuse to speak without overmuch direct eye contact.

"I will address these in order. Firstly, the match. Your family is titled, an honour your brother inherits along with properties. You are a younger son. However, that in itself is of little consequence. Our families both are long established. As such, a match may have merit – *provided*," he said, "my other considerations are met."

Nathaniel hesitated an instant, uncertain whether his participation in this meeting was welcomed, but youth and the desperate hope that all was not lost spurred him on. "Sir, I am a second son, it is true. Yet I will inherit a modest estate from my mother's family; I will not be without property of my own to provide, nor sufficient income to keep a family."

"Yes. Yes, I am well acquainted with your competence. Suffice to say such a match would not be considered a poor one. Secondly, as to my sister's disposition in the matter." Darcy hesitated himself before continuing, loath to speak to this man or anyone of Georgiana's intimate feelings, uncertain whether either had the right of such an assumption. "As you chose to address my sister before soliciting my acquiescence, we both know that Miss Darcy is disposed to favour your suit."

He noted that Nathaniel coloured a bit at this, and he could not bring himself to excuse the oversight; he allowed himself the satisfaction of the young man's squirm of discomfort. "I am not unaware that she tenders some... admiration... for you. My concern is not so much whether those... sentiments... are sincerely felt; but rather that she has sufficient knowledge at this time to truly understand the basis for her regard on short and accidental acquaintance."

He stopped walking with his horse now and looked directly at Nathaniel, who had also stopped. "My sister is not yet eighteen. She has yet to be introduced to London society. Her first entry into *any* society, such as it is, will be tomorrow night. Until recently, she has led a protected – privileged – life. I can not countenance an obligation for her before she has had an opportunity to understand in full the prospects open to her, to make the acquaintance of people of the ton – yes, and possible suitors – and to be certain for herself that *when* she chooses to marry, it is truly a choice, entered into freely and happily, but on sound basis as well, rather than the first agreeable man she has chanced to meet."

Darcy felt decidedly uncomfortable now in revealing personal intimacies, but forced himself to go on. "I have been so smiled upon by fortune as to experience the joy, Mr Hewitt, of a match of true affection with Mrs Darcy. I will settle for no less than the same mutual regard for my sister when coupled with other appropriate conditions."

Nathaniel appeared to consider seriously his companion's words as Darcy watched – perhaps he even considered his brother's marriage by contrast – and finally he replied with all solemnity, "I would wish the same for your sister, Sir."

Darcy's lips turned up minutely at the selfless reply. "And can you see that she has not yet made acquaintances broad enough for me, as her guardian, to be certain she can know her mind... her heart?"

Grudgingly, the young man acknowledged the point from the guardian's perspective. Darcy said, "I concede that my sister likes you, Nathaniel. And I trust that her feelings are sincere. You should well feel gratified that she bestows them upon you, and I do not fail to credit *you* that she does. She is not capricious in nature; she does not do so lightly." He smiled at Nathaniel at this last, before becoming serious once more to press his point. "But I would have her certain, before she names it love, that she has become acquainted with life in a wider society, that she possesses sufficient intelligence to make informed judgment."

Nathaniel nodded in understanding, if not in agreement, his expression holding still a determination to believe their affections were strong and genuine, and belonged unassailably to them alone.

"Hmm," said Darcy, starting to walk again now to make his next point easier to impart. "And so to my last consideration – is the gentleman *worthy* of her?"

"Sir, I beg you, do not use such a term to judge, as I am certain to fail of the test."

Darcy laughed aloud, raising an indignant glare from the suitor. "Forgive me. I intend no offense. I have no doubt you are earnest and, indeed," he said, trying to assuage the indignity the young man suffered at being made sport of, "I laugh at myself as much or more. I hazard that *I* shall be hard pressed to find *any* man full worthy of my sister."

This tempered Nathaniel's resentment, and both men shared a quiet, nervous laugh in conciliation. "However, make no mistake," said Darcy then, "I do have a concern of you that I feel it fair you should comprehend."

They stopped walking again naturally and faced each other.

"My sister, as you are no doubt aware, brings with her a formidable dowry which only adds to her more personal attributes."

Nathaniel could not withhold reply. "Sir, I swear oath to you on my honour, it plays no part in my care of your sister. I had no knowledge of her endowment when I first came to love her, and –"

Darcy cut him off, wincing unconsciously at the youth's expression of affection. "*Yes*, to your credit, I believe it does not influence your *regard* for Georgiana. But my point nonetheless is related to her fortune, and to yours as well."

Nathaniel hesitated, stopped and started a few times before finally offering: "She has told me, Mr Darcy, of her former mistake, in Kent..."

"She *told* you this?" Darcy was incredulous. "*What* did she tell you precisely?"

Nathaniel was clearly nervous now, visibly wishing he had not yielded such information. Quietly he answered, gathering courage as he spoke. "That she became enamoured of a gentleman, a family friend, and believed her admiration returned until your intervention saved her from what would have been a miserable fortune-seeking alliance, a dreadful folly, she is certain of that. That she was grateful you interceded in his deception before she made a horrid mistake in succumbing to false and pretty words. That in consequence she would never consent to a match without your express approval. Nothing more, Sir."

"The scapegrace in question was neither gentleman nor friend, though he wore the ruse of it easily enough." Darcy could say no more for a moment, thinking back to how close he came to losing his sister to that bounder. *Nothing more?* The fact that Georgiana had confided as much as this to Nathaniel Hewitt impressed upon Darcy more than any other thing both the gravity and earnestness of his sister's trust in this young man; her courage in making so frank a disclosure to maintain honourable regard between them. And it did not escape Darcy that it spoke well of Nathaniel – his suit being unaffected by such a close call with disgrace, and his unsolicited admission of the intelligence now.

As if he understood this, Nathaniel added, "I have not spoken of this, Sir, to any other; and it shall never be raised by me again after this meeting. It changes nothing in my admiration for Miss Darcy, indeed she is blameless. I only wished you fully to comprehend my acquaintance with this history."

"Indeed." Darcy grimaced before emerging from his dour reverie and reclaiming control of their speech. "I am grateful for your disclosure. But you do mistake my intentions in raising the issue of her endowment."

"Sir?"

"I must be persuaded before giving my consent for Georgiana to marry, that her welfare is in the hands of a gentleman who can manage his – and her – competence well; a good steward who will provide a comfortable and secure life for her and any marriage issue. I *will not* give my sister over to the care of a spendthrift, a gambler, a rogue."

"*Sir*, I –"

Darcy realised Nathaniel had assumed an insult to his own person. This was not easy for him, and he had taken yet another misstep. "Forgive me, it is not my intention thus to accuse you; it is clumsy of me to express it in such a manner."

Nathaniel stood stiffly, unsure for but an instant, then nodded a pardon and tried to smile.

"However, you do bear the guilt, Mr Hewitt, of youth and inexperience. You have only just completed your education, why – you are only now taking your grand tour, are not you?"

"I am, Sir."

"Yes. And so you see – at least for my part as Georgiana's guardian – you are as yet untried. You are amiable; it may surprise you to know that I like you well enough." He nearly laughed at the smile Nathaniel tried so hard to stifle. "You are intelligent, well schooled, and I daresay, you have an earnest *desire* to prove successful. I find no deficiency in these attributes.

"But in your lack of experience I can point to no assurances that you will manage your estates well, tend your family and those under your care with respect, and preserve your family, your properties, your duties to society. My sister's welfare is a sacred trust. I will pass it only to the care of a man who can prove to my satisfaction his potential in these attributes."

They were silent then, both turned inward in meditation. From their expressions alone, anyone might have thought them a mirrored reflection despite their differences in age and physical stature. Finally Nathaniel made to reply. Myriad questions and defences came to him, but he chose simply to ask: "Why have you told me this, Sir?"

"Because your care of Georgiana is heartfelt and as such I was wrong to deny your application without doing so." At the expression of hope that lit Nathaniel's eyes, Darcy threw up his hand in caution to stay him. "I have *not* reversed my decision. I do, however, have a proposition to put forward."

"A proposition, Sir? What is it?"

"I wish – I insist – that Georgiana enter society freely, with no obligation to any man—and take time either to be certain of her continued affection for you or to form alternate attachment. Furthermore, I wish to see you demonstrate your capacity to fulfil your duty—as a gentleman and as prospective husband for my sister."

Nathaniel could not help but smile as he said, "Thus the test this morning?"

Darcy smiled with warmth in return of the boy's understanding. "Partly. But that trifle only secured you this discourse. You will leave in the new year for your grand tour as planned and Georgiana will enter society as planned with no obligation between you. Upon your return, conditional upon my sister's wishes being unchanged, you may choose to establish yourself here, at Pemberley, aligning yourself to work with my steward – under my oversight – in the management of this estate for a period of one year. You will be worked diligently, but you will not be a labourer; you will be a guest in my home with all the requirements of gentlemanly conduct demanded of such. You will be allowed within reason to pay court to Georgiana, but with no privileges above other suitable candidates beyond the natural advantage of residing here. You will, as a gentleman, take no unfair advantage of the circumstance, of me, or – most assuredly – of my sister."

That the entire notion had taken Nathaniel by surprise was writ across his countenance such that he could make no comment when Darcy paused for a deep breath before continuing. "At the conclusion of this year at Pemberley, presuming your own wishes to be unchanged and if I judge you to be of good character, good management, and sincere regard – and granted of course that Georgiana still desires to consider your marriage offer – then you may advance your petition again and I will reconsider. If however, my sister during that period should take a preference for another gentleman, you will accept her choice without protest; and may, in such circumstance, break our contract without debt on my part nor discredit on yours."

Darcy had finished. He had not known how, when they had set out that morning, he would be able to make himself say all he had done; but somehow when the time came it was more palatable than he might have thought. He did like Nathaniel Hewitt; what he had offered was a hard bargain, he knew, and it now remained to see a measure of the suitor's resolve. He found himself with no little surprise hoping that the young man in front of him would have the character to accept what Darcy had delineated. He had, at the least, shown the disposition to listen to it all before rushing in with judgment.

When Nathaniel did reply, it was brief and circumspect. "A singular proposal."

Darcy acknowledged this with a bow from the neck.

"You ask a great deal of me, Mr Darcy."

Darcy swallowed the lump forming in his throat and tried to ignore the stinging behind his eyes. He answered slowly, carefully articulating each word. "As do you, Mr Hewitt."

Nathaniel smiled. "Fairly answered, Sir." He was quiet again, looking down in thought. Indeed, Georgiana's regard was not a prize to be lightly taken. "Am I correct to presume you have discussed this with my brother?"

"You are; and with my cousin who is also Georgiana's guardian. Edmund and the Colonel will support *your* decision. Your brother believes your father will do so as well."

The younger man nodded. Neither man spoke now as Darcy watched Nathaniel Hewitt consider the various aspects of their discourse. Finally: "I accept your proposal, Sir; but with three requests."

Darcy narrowed his eyes, wondering what the boy had in mind.

"Firstly, may I have leave, Sir, during my tour abroad, to correspond with... you or the Colonel... as to Miss Darcy's welfare?" Darcy chuckled, but assented.

"What else?"

"With respect, Sir – one full year of tutelage is a great period, perhaps excessive. I might suggest that three months could as well confirm the assurances you require of my aptitude for stewardship. Would you consider an assessment at that time, and I shall abide then with your decision either as to a contract fulfilled or the requirement for additional tuition?"

Darcy scrutinised Nathaniel very carefully with a daunting expression; the younger man could not determine if it reflected arrogant resentment at the liberty he took to negotiate, or amusement at the presumption. "Three months might suffice to indicate your aptitude perhaps, but with no surety of application." He studied Nathaniel another moment. "Very well, an initial assessment after *six* months."

Nathaniel could not refrain from a small sigh of relief and accepted the compromise.

"What else?"

Nathaniel hesitated, then finally and sheepishly asked, "May I, Sir, request the honour of Miss Darcy's hand for the fir... *second*... dance tomorrow night?" He blushed as the question escaped him.

"That is a request to make of my sister, Sir – but if she grants you it, I can find no objection."

"Yes, Sir, thank you." Nathaniel relaxed a bit and smiled in anticipation.

"I have one last request, Sir."

"Another? You indicated three stipulations to my proposal."

"Yes. But as we spoke, one further occurred. It is this, Sir: may we now return to the stables? It is deuced cold out here!"

Darcy laughed aloud, and realised as he did so that he was feeling the chill as well, from his cheeks down through his boots. They mounted their horses but, before starting out, Darcy looked upon the young man with serious consideration a moment and then slowly extended his hand. Nathaniel met him halfway and shook it as Georgiana's brother smiled.

CHAPTER FIFTEEN

DARCY APPROACHED the breakfast parlour, glancing at his watch; a bit late but most would still be at their leisure there. He would check here first for Georgiana and, if she had not come down this morning, then he would go to her rooms. He noticed the door was closed – unusual, but he thought little of it. As he placed his hand on the knob, he halted a moment to organise his thoughts and his countenance.

When he entered, the eyes of all assembled glanced up. Many then returned with no ceremony to their news or conversations, but several kept their attention trained upon him in various aspects of interest: Hewitt, Fitzwilliam, Lizzy – and Georgiana, whom he was gratified to see in attendance sitting between Catherine Bennet and Fitzwilliam. He greeted the company at large and moved to the sideboard for a cup of coffee. At least, that had been his intention – a hastily consumed warming drink before requesting speech with Georgiana. He felt it incumbent to tell her of this late development and would stop for no more than this.

But the aroma of fresh hot rolls assailed him – a scent that, mixed with the honey adjacent to them, carried him happily back to childhood – and he succumbed, carrying a plate and his coffee can to the table. A few moments' deferral would be acceptable. The stimulation of his morning's ride and subsequent negotiation had given him an appetite.

He went to sit next to Lizzy who startled him by asking immediately if Mr Nathaniel Hewitt did not accompany him. The question itself posed no surprise, it was rather the volume at which she directed it. Glancing to her and then following her gaze to his sister, he realised that Georgiana still watched the now-open door with some apprehension.

"Ah," he said, replying similarly to Lizzy so as to be heard down the table. "He did so as far as the stables, but he remained there in converse with the grooms. I imagine he will be along in half an hour or so."

Georgiana visibly relaxed again, eliciting some contrition in Darcy for allowing his hunger to postpone a meeting meant to allay her anxieties. He despised seeing her so skittish in her own home, and this resolved him. With a sigh, he pushed aside the roll, took only a sip of coffee, and stood again abruptly, requesting speech with his sister.

The suddenness of his request caused Georgiana to glance first at Fitzwilliam, then to Lizzy, in an appeal for any explanation. Darcy realised he had only exacerbated her unease. Now he smiled to soften his countenance and added that his study was comfortably warmed with a fine blaze.

Fitzwilliam rose to assist his cousin from her seat, squeezing her elbow in reassurance as he did so. She was surprised then when she moved to join her brother that Fitzwilliam did not accompany them, but she followed Darcy's gesture for her to precede him from the room.

If much of the party ignored this exchange, there were three who certainly did not. Georgiana had left the room and, just before he would have done also, Darcy turned at the doorway, looked from Hewitt to Fitzwilliam, and offered a deliberate nod and a smile, with another pointed acknowledgment following to Lizzy. He did not remain to witness the relief and pleasure his communication had elicited.

"Georgiana," Darcy started when they were seated by the fire in the study. His tone sounded formal even as he smiled, causing his sister additional disquiet at what was to come. "Gee," he altered his approach; "I have had long discourse this morning with Nathaniel Hewitt. Indeed, I requested he ride out with us today for that express purpose."

Georgiana's eyes enlarged in question – was he to tell her that Nathaniel would leave after all?

"I made him a proposition I would inform you of; for it will require agreement on your part as well."

❖❖❖❖❖

"We are friends, are not we?" Nathaniel said, giving Comus a light chuck of affection. "Will you show kindness to your friend in the new year? Keep a watch over her for me; do not allow another to come between us?"

Even as he spoke the words, however, he was confident that he and Miss Darcy could weather this challenge. It was not an unqualified consent from Mr Darcy, but yet it was hope. No, it was more than hope, far more! It was a promise – a contract – as long as certain conditions were met; and he had no doubt at all that he would meet those placed upon *him*. It only remained for Georgiana to continue steadfast in her affections. And despite the lure of a social season in town, or two as it more like would transpire, he had faith in her – in their love for one another.

As he considered it, although he had envisioned in the passion of first love a more immediate and absolute outcome, reason asserted that this end had much to commend it. In truth, he believed quite firmly that both he and Miss Darcy were of an age to know their minds and their hearts – he must disagree still with Mr Darcy on that point – but perhaps they *were* too young yet to take up married life together, though not the promise of it.

He had not expected to fall in love so young, had not well considered the reality of settling in to a life together, before even his grand tour was accomplished. He had not given this a thought when his heady ardour had given sway to his proposal to Georgiana; reason had played little part in the proceedings. He only knew that he must be assured of a return on his own affections, of securing a promise.

A part of him understood that he was unseasoned and the experience of this tour would better prepare him to get on in the world. And though it stung his vanity to have it so blatantly acknowledged by Mr Darcy, his practical skills in managing property *were* untried – the opportunity to apprentice at an estate of Pemberley's order was one any number of his friends would envy if they could admit of it. It would serve him well; and all the while he would reside with her – take his meals with her, enjoy her society of an evening – with the certainty that in a matter of months after they would be married. Being so near her in anticipation may prove a torture, but what sweet torment!

Miss Darcy, too, deserved the chance to move in society before becoming a matron, to have the joys which most young women of her status were afforded. Were they to marry without her doing so, would she come to regret what she had relinquished to marry him so young? Marriage would change much in their lives; should they not begin each with full conviction that neither had sacrificed anything to do so?

But here, he had somewhat more difficulty putting reason ahead of passion: his mind drew sketches of his lady engaged in all the events of the upcoming season, conversing and laughing and dancing her way through balls and concerts, promenades and plays. Yet the arm upon which she hung for escort would not be his. The ear that thrilled to her laugh would not be his. The eye that appreciatively watched her descend the stairs at the theatre would not be his, nor the smile that greeted her with every turn of the dance.

Bad enough if he were to reside in town this year, being forced to *share* her attentions with other gentlemen. But to be so far removed from it all, to know that she experienced wondrous things in which he could not be a part, this stirred misgivings in him. He was jealous of those nameless, faceless gentlemen; that was much of it certainly. He trusted that Miss Darcy's love for him could not be supplanted – she would remain steadfast, he must believe it.

Although Mr Darcy had stipulated that no formal understanding would oblige them during this period, he was certain that in Georgiana's heart, as much as his own, the contract already bound them. But it was the idea that she would experience these things without him that gave him pause – that they would not share the season as their own, each minute she passed in the company of another, a begrudged minute not given to him.

He chastised himself now for such thoughts as he conceded another slice of apple to Comus. He would have experiences as well while on his tour; when they were reunited they would fill hours with stories of them, but they would all pale beside those that the two of them together would then enjoy for a lifetime. He was being nonsensical. Their love was strong and too much their own for time or circumstance to be their enemy.

As Mr Darcy himself had pointed out, the overall consequence of discrete facts when they came together was important; and this agreement served everyone well. Nat would spend a year abroad (he now quite happily decreased a prior plan of two years) without any need for uncertainty of what awaited him upon his return: his Georgiana and a short apprenticeship on a rich estate before assuming his own smaller one upon his majority. And when he established residence, finally, at Markham Hall, he would soon after provide it a mistress as well. His mother would like that *very* well, and that she would approve of Miss Darcy he was certain.

Miss Darcy, in the interim – his sweet, shy Georgiana – could engage all the joys of the season knowing that Nathaniel awaited her. She would not feel so much the pressures of combing through potential suitors to come away with a suitable match – she had made one already and it promised constancy in love *and* safekeeping. And Mr Darcy could sanction the match with confidence when he had proven his ability to provide that security.

He wondered now how long he had passed with Comus, but the colt only eyed him greedily in response when he asked. Had it been long enough for Mr Darcy to find his sister and tell her the news? Did she yet know that they had been granted a perfect reprieve? Nathaniel could barely wait to see her, to share this reversal of their fortunes. Briefly, his face clouded as he wondered: will Miss Darcy accept the terms of this arrangement? What if she does not? But he quickly dismissed the notion. Of course she would embrace it! If the alternative were for them to be apart, how could she consider any other course!

With a last affectionate swipe at the colt, Nathaniel fastened his coat again and made his way out of the stables. He could wait no longer. As he made his way towards the house, he considered Mr Darcy. He felt quite sympathetic towards the man now. His future brother had been fair in the end. After all, he had only been protecting his sister and Nathaniel could not decry him for doing so.

❖❖❖❖❖

Georgiana gazed on her brother in total incomprehension. She could not have heard him correctly. Surely he did not just inform her that he had reversed himself! It was impossible. Her nerves these last few days must play tricks with her. And yet...

Darcy scrutinised her for a reaction but saw nothing more than a dazed young woman, speechless, her brow furrowed in bemused consideration. "Georgiana?" he prompted her. "Is this plan acceptable to you?"

Within seconds, she had travelled through a myriad of expressions: from incomprehension to disbelief; disbelief to suspicion of misunderstanding; suspicion to hope; hope to the confirmation she read in her brother's eyes; and then to cautious joy.

"Yes! Yes, it is acceptable!" she cried as she rose and stepped quickly to Darcy, startling him by throwing her arms about his neck. "It is wonderful! You are the best of brothers! The best guardian! Yes!"

All this was spoken while she clung to her brother tightly, nearly choking the breath from him. "Gee," he said finally, peeling her arms from him and pushing her back a bit to see her countenance more fully. His eyes met hers and, though they were gratified with her reaction, they also held serious counsel. "This is not unqualified consent; you do understand this?" He repeated certain conditions to ensure she comprehended the parts both she and Nathaniel Hewitt must play to earn his formal approval. She made herself a comfortable seat on the arm of his chair, leaning affectionately in to him with her hand upon his chest for support as he spoke. When he had done, she replied.

"Fitz, you do not err in this trust. I will abide by your wishes – we will abide by them – for however long it takes to give you the surety you require. He will prove his worth to you, I know it well. And I only want the chance to love Nathaniel... er, Mr Hewitt."

This last gave him some bit of concern and he impressed upon her that she was to be receptive to the acquaintance of others, to include other gentlemen. "I do not make this stipulation as some punishment of time, my dear, but for you to consider frankly if Mr Hewitt more deserves your favour than any other. I would have you certain; I would have you know it for your own benefit much more than mine."

She promised him to try, emphasising that at their ball the next night she would ensure she gave to Mr Hewitt no greater liberties than propriety allowed. She placed her hands into his earnestly to stop his unwitting wringing of them, then they spoke a few moments more until each understood the other fully and accepted their parts. All the while, she could not withhold the joy from her countenance and his own lightened to see it.

"Gee," said Darcy finally, serious once more. "Regarding the ball –
we are engaged, you and I, to open the dancing tomorrow night." He
hesitated, even as she nodded agreement, then said: "But I shall relinquish
you to Mr Hewitt for your partner if you prefer it."

She was struck by the significance of this tender and moved by it;
but her reply was immediate and gratifying to her brother. "No! No, I
must dance with you for the first – we must!" She felt somewhat
embarrassed then by the outburst and tried to moderate the import of her
words. "I suppose you expect me to think it very generous of you to offer,
Brother, but I see through your intent! You seek to save yourself the
requirement of dancing at all!" She laughed, tentatively at first, then with
more vigour when he joined in. "You never find the activity much to your
liking, but you will not escape your duty so easily."

"My dear, in this instance duty is in fact my honour and my
pleasure."

"Fitzwilliam," she said now, and he noted her grave mood in the
way she pronounced his name.

"Yes?"

"I... I have been mortified by my thoughtless words to you these
last days, ashamed; I do so regret them. Even before this happy turn of
events, it saddened me to think we could have reached such an altercation.
I must tell you... I wish you to know how much..." Her eyes began to fill
with her emotion and he blinked his own to diminish the prickling behind
them.

"Do not think on it further, Gee. They are only words and easily
forgotten."

She knew this to be untrue, but allowed him to comfort her and
himself with the avowal nonetheless. "I could not love anyone as I do
you," she choked out finally.

"I know, my dear," he acknowledged, attempting as they embraced
an easy manner belied by the catch in his voice. "I well know your regard."

"Now, off with you," he said finally in some embarrassment. "I
have an interrupted breakfast to attend to, if there are any of those rolls
remaining!" As he stood, he chuckled and added: "And you have a gown
arriving today for a ball, do not you?"

Georgiana smiled in utter delight and offered her brother a kiss
upon his cheek before tripping lightly from the room.

❖❖❖❖❖

"Wherever do you go to gather your wool, Lizzy?"

"My wool?" she asked, and realised she had been listening to
Bingley without the least comprehension.

Lizzy had remained at the table for a while following Darcy's exit with his sister. She had tried to insert herself into conversation again, but her mind would wander of its own choosing to the study. Her curiosity was manifest. The breakfast hour nearly over, everyone had finished and would be moving on shortly; as such, she felt she too could slip away without offense. She offered Bingley a quick apology and followed after her mind.

She made her way to Darcy's study and leaned against a wall outside to await Georgiana's egress. While she waited, she ran through her imagination what might be transpiring. She knew from late night conversation with Darcy what he had considered proposing to Nathaniel Hewitt, but so many variable details could have altered his intention at the last, or Mr Hewitt's reception. Apparently, from his pregnant acknowledgment, some agreement had been reached between the men. But what precisely they had agreed upon, and how Georgiana would view it, was a source of considered interest to Lizzy. She hated to see Gee so unhappy but, even more, hated what this had wrought between the girl and her brother.

Fortunately, she did not have long to bide her time in useless speculation. The study door opened and suddenly Georgiana was there. "Lizzy!" said Gee, barely stopping her progress; "Is Cousin Retched in the breakfast parlour still?"

"I believe so. But –"

"I must see him," she said, and disappeared as abruptly as she had turned up. Lizzy could only laugh at her shadow, Georgiana's presence had been so fleeting. But she had noted a change in her sister's demeanour, all trace of anguish dispelled. Lizzy walked into the study and was rewarded at seeing her husband in quiet humour.

"May I presume we are a happy household once more?" she asked.

"Do you know," Darcy replied with some wonder, "I believe we are!"

Lizzy crossed to him and searched his face for any lingering complications, but was satisfied in seconds that his equanimity matched his words, and she smiled. "Was it very difficult for you? To speak with young Hewitt, that is?"

"I thought it should be, but in the end, no. He was quite amenable." He laughed now, and began to tell Lizzy of the intimidating start to their converse; a mood he now felt some guilt for engendering as he had also to admit he had derived some satisfaction from turning the tables of surprise on Mr Hewitt. But by the time he reached the end of his narrative, it seemed both men had formed a modicum of real accord, and Darcy could not contain his gratification at how Georgiana had taken the news.

"So," he concluded, "Mr Nathaniel Hewitt is happy; Fitzwilliam and Edmund Hewitt are happy; Georgiana is happy once more and does not disown her tyrannical brother –" He laughed, but Lizzy detected more of relief than anything in his tone.

She put her arms lightly around his waist, his own coming up instinctively to draw her in, and she looked into his eyes. "And how are *you*, Mr Darcy? Are you happy as well in the end?"

He considered very little time before replying that he was, indeed, happy. In fact, following these encounters, he found himself actually desiring that Mr Hewitt would fulfil his part. "They *are* young, Lizzy; I do not regret these precautions. But I do believe in a few years time, Nathaniel Hewitt has it in him to be a good husband to Gee, and a welcome brother to us. I am content."

"Why, husband, how very reasonable you are! I am inordinately proud of you, Mr Darcy." She took in his wide smile now, the glint in his eyes returned since trouble had flown them, the lines of care smoothed out from his brow. He appeared to have shorn the years his recent worries had added to his mien of late. She tightened her embrace, rose up on her toes and kissed her husband, prolonging it when he would have drawn back a moment later.

"Mrs Darcy!" he exclaimed, surprise matched by pleasure.

She whispered to him, "Do you know, you are very handsome when you are being eminently reasonable. I find the attraction nearly impossible to resist." She initiated another kiss, this time neither requiring coaxing. A moment later, Darcy chuckled.

"All this past year of marriage, it seems I have been expending my efforts very poorly indeed. I have wasted much time in useless gestures of romance when all I needed to elicit your passions was to engage in commonsensical judgment!"

Lizzy smiled beguilingly and asked if he had made any other practical decisions of late.

❖❖❖❖❖

Henry Wentworth shook his head and smiled as he watched Colonel Fitzwilliam and Mrs Chaney speaking together. He was happy that they had resolved their misunderstanding, thinking them well matched in temperament. He fully expected that little time would pass before he would hear of an impending marriage. Their pairing seemed most natural and they would do well with one another.

As he considered the couple, he wondered – given his initial interest in the widow himself – whether *he* might ever find a 'natural' partner. He had had his share of flirtations over the years and, despite his choice to follow his father in trade, his family connexions and fortune guaranteed no dearth of plain or impoverished gentlemen's daughters willing to find him acceptable. He chuckled in suspicion that most of them believed that once they were wed, he could be cajoled into giving up the inns for a complaisant life in town. He had yet to meet any lady, however, who elicited the depth of interest reflected now in Fitzwilliam's countenance, or the contented pleasure in Mr Bingley's. Even his friend Darcy, had become, amazingly, more confident and easy since his marriage to Elizabeth Bennet.

Watching the Colonel and his lady in intimate speech, he could wish for such a woman. He was only one and thirty, hardly beyond an age to be found attractive. All his friends were now settled. Indeed, it seemed many of them made it their business to direct him to a similar state. His own sister continually paraded young women before him. And the notion did appeal in abstraction. But he rather fancied that he would only engage the matrimonial state with a woman he loved for herself, and hoped for the same in return. And therein lay his problem. Love had not found him.

He could feel deprived at such condition, but then his thoughts turned to his friends the Hewitts: Edmund Hewitt, married to a woman of mean understanding while hopelessly in love with the wife of another; and Nat Hewitt now. *He* had found love quite by accident, but look at what it had brought him. The poor boy – and for that matter, Miss Darcy as well – was miserable. That family had not fared so well under the influence of Eros. Perhaps Henry Wentworth should not incline for something as likely to bring pain as pleasure. His life was full enough in his friends, in his sister and her brood; he would not wish for trouble.

❖❖❖❖❖

Fitzwilliam was about to rise and pull out Mrs Chaney's chair for her when he felt arms moving around his neck from behind. An instant later Georgiana's cheek was pressed against his own as she murmured, "Thank you, Retched!"

Lady Catherine greeted her niece's enthusiasm with a disdainful remark about the over-familiarity and lack of propriety exhibited so cavalierly by young people. Kitty marvelled at her friend's remarkable change of temper. Edmund Hewitt eyed the young lady and smiled broadly from across the table and Fitzwilliam rose, taking Georgiana's hands in his as they slid from his shoulders. She was near to bursting with the desire for speech and, as the curious eyes of those who remained in the parlour now watched them, he led her to a corner of the room for privacy.

"Thank you," she whispered again. "I cannot know how you convinced him; I shall not wonder, but you have restored me to contentment."

"Ah," Fitzwilliam replied. "My dear, how very much I should like to warrant your gratitude, but I cannot claim such an honour. It belongs squarely with your brother."

"You did not speak to him last night?"

"I did, my dear, but I assure you Darcy made proposal for this scheme before ever I spoke a word, or Mr Edmund Hewitt for that matter. Your brother only asked our thoughts and consent, and those we could give freely."

Georgiana accepted this news with great reflection as Fitzwilliam added: "If any can lay claim to having influenced your brother, my dear, it is you yourself! I am certain your feelings stirred his resolve. As much as he desires your interests furthered, your happiness is principal in that, as it is for me, as well."

She squeezed his hands. "I *am* happy, Retched, inordinately so." They spoke a moment in low tones to confirm the agreement Darcy and Nathaniel Hewitt had reached. Fitzwilliam raised his brows to hear that Darcy would assess Mr Hewitt's capabilities after six months of apprenticeship, but in all other respects the details of accord were as he expected. He delighted in the turn of his cousin's temperament – she positively glowed with uncontainable joy.

❖❖❖❖❖

When Lizzy and Darcy emerged from his study to make their way back towards the breakfast parlour they met with a stream of activity. Mr Atherton, Mr Sanders and Mr Folsom had just been announced to Lady Catherine who now led them to purloin use of the study again for her own business. It seemed Lady Catherine's instructions of the day prior had been finalised and they met to verify, sign, and secure documents.

Darcy wondered only briefly what, in the end, his aunt had decided before consciously releasing such thoughts. Whatever she had done, he would hear of it – and deal with it if necessary – soon enough. He did extend an invitation to the gentlemen to attend the ball on the following evening, but they declined. They were quite anxious to return to town as soon as may be possible and would leave in the morning if not, indeed, this very afternoon.

Fast upon the arrival of the London gentlemen, came the delivery of ladies' gowns and accessories and Mrs Reynolds led a bustling command of servants to sort and carry the linen-bound parcels to the appropriate chambers. The mantua maker would no doubt be along shortly to begin last fittings and instructions to the maids for pressing and maintenance.

Finally, the Darcys were waylaid again upon meeting the Gardiners, the Bingleys and Sir James in animated discourse outside the breakfast room. It seemed Uncle Gardiner had expressed in passing his eagerness and his wife's to view Albion Park after Mr Bingley took possession, perhaps next summer. Whereupon Sir James suggested that they need not wait so long. He planned his own return on the coming Monday and in no time issued an invitation to his new friends to call as his guests. Within moments a plan had been devised.

The Gardiners would indeed follow Sir James to Nottinghamshire – and Jane and Bingley with them! They would all return to Pemberley on the following Friday then, to retrieve Kitty before setting out Monday a week for Longbourn. In this manner, as well as enjoying an acquaintance with Albion Park, the Gardiners could assist the others in a cataloguing of its contents. Sir James would gain agreement as to what items he might wish to remove to the gatehouse or even to London and what might remain, such that Jane and Bingley might better plan their own requirements.

As much as Lizzy rued the loss of even a few days' visit with her relations, the plan had merit for Jane and, of course, Lizzy and Darcy gave their leave with grace when Aunt Gardiner asked if they should mind the temporary defection. Mrs Gardiner offered to remain behind if her niece wished, but Lizzy would not hear of it.

By the time they had quit this last diversion and arrived again in the breakfast parlour, only Kitty and Georgiana remained within, sitting with their heads close together at one end of the table in excited chatter concerning the ball which had once again become an event of gleeful anticipation. Darcy's dish and coffee from earlier had, of course, been removed from the table; but he noted with hungry satisfaction that food still resided on the sideboard. He made his way there, a slight rumbling emanating from his stomach to answer the call of the few remaining rolls. No sooner had he carried a new dish and coffee can to the table where Lizzy awaited him than another arrival was marked.

Nathaniel Hewitt wandered into the room still in his greatcoat, perhaps uncertain of whom he might find there. But it was obvious as soon as his eyes lit upon Georgiana that he had found all he sought. She had looked up at his entrance and the two now were transfixed in their attentions, awkwardly silent for want of a means to express what they felt. A moment more and, spurred perhaps by Kitty's giggles, Nathaniel had managed to cover his moon-eyed discomfiture enough to greet Lizzy and Darcy, before returning his gaze to the young lady.

Darcy considered the young man briefly and then turned to his sister, noting her expression. He looked at his wife, then down at his dish. Sighing, he stood up and offered his hand to Lizzy, saying, "My dear, if you can spare me a moment, I should like a word... perhaps in your sitting room?"

She rose at once, a laugh hovering about her mouth, but maintained her decorum as they exited. Before she could say anything to him, however, Darcy turned back and leaned in to the parlour once more. "Catherine, we have need of your assistance as well," he said to the further astonishment of his wife.

When Kitty came out into the corridor and looked to Darcy in a confusion of purpose, Lizzy took pity on him. "Kitty, it is I who need you. Will you oblige me, please, and take a very important message to Mrs Reynolds?" When Kitty nodded idly, Lizzy leaned towards her sister and whispered something to her. "Immediately, please!" she then said aloud. Bemused by the instruction, Kitty nonetheless shrugged and walked off to find the housekeeper to impart the request.

"What errand did you set her?" asked Darcy.

"You will see very soon," replied Lizzy with a sly smile. "Come, let us go to my sitting room."

"Lizzy, my love, you do know I had no purpose in mind?"

"I know it very well, Mr Darcy; however, I *do* have purpose in mind, and I wish you to oblige me in this."

"Very well."

They mounted the stairs to the private wing and as they approached Lizzy's sitting room, she said to him, "Do you recall my remarking only moments past that I find you very handsome when you are being reasonable?"

He glanced at her warily and confirmed the recollection, as she grinned. "Well, I have decided you are equally so when you succumb to romance."

They had come to her sitting room now and as they entered he replied. "I have no notion what you mean, Elizabeth."

"Of course you have! Do not come the innocent with me, Mr Darcy. You are not made for disguise. I know perfectly well you contrived to allow Gee and Nathaniel a moment to themselves." She noted his reddening countenance, though he admitted nothing. "Do not fret – I will not tell anyone of your flagrant breach of propriety. But I do adore you for it."

In reply now, Darcy took Lizzy in his arms and gazed into eyes that gave back the truth of her words. He kissed her once, and would have done again but his intentions were disrupted by a knock upon the door. Lizzy smiled as seconds later on being bid to enter, Mrs Reynolds appeared rolling a tea cart – on which lay service for coffee, a bowl of honey and a cover that revealed, upon being removed, a serving platter heaped with steamy hot rolls.

CHAPTER SIXTEEN

THE AFTERNOON passed in a flurry of activity for the ladies while the gentlemen enjoyed the leisurely pursuits of the billiard room, the cold spell having discouraged going farther afield. With six final fittings to accomplish, the mantua maker found employment for nearly three and a half hours. In addition to Miss Darcy, the three Bennet sisters and Mrs Chaney, Miss deBourgh had elected of late to have one of her gowns remade for the ball. Most of the work had been accomplished already by Mrs Eyre through written instruction; but Kitty and Georgiana had purchased for Anne in town a few days past a card of elegant lace with which to edge her hem and sleeves. This formed the greater part of finishing required now.

When finally Mrs Eyre made her way to the laundry to counsel the maids on garment care, the ladies gathered in Lizzy's sitting room for some refreshment. Now that the household was a happy one once more, the ball was again a topic of great anticipation, seeming all the more imminent and real for having their gowns at hand. Mrs Gardiner was as delighted as the rest – she had not attended a private ball in years – though she would make do with an old gown re-trimmed. She and Lizzy shared a quiet word of satisfaction to see that Miss Darcy had regained herself. And it was apparent from their private giggles as they occupied the settee that Kitty was happy to have her friend back as well.

While they were at their refreshment, they received a surprise visitor in the form of Mrs Hewitt. It had occurred to Mr Grimes to arrange delivery of a wheeled chair for the woman, encouraging her to remove from her bed for short periods during the day as she was able.

Immediately upon her arrival, the talk shifted to her condition. She sat at something of a tilt upon several cushions, having winced, moaned, or complained outright at every turn of the wheel as her maid pushed her carefully into the room; yet she would not be denied her moments of attention. Apparently, the individual calls the other ladies had taken turns to make to her sick bed during the week were grown insufficient to her sense of self importance. When she had learnt of this gathering, the ladies for once meeting on the same floor as her room, she had insisted upon being made of the party in her new conveyance.

After some moments, Jane attempted yet again to introduce converse of a different nature and, in so doing, mentioned the fittings they had just completed. This set off Mrs Hewitt on an anguished outburst that soon settled into a whimper. It seemed she had specially commissioned a gown in the latest of French fashion from her own dressmaker in town – "Mrs ___, you *know* of course, I paid her *36 shillings* for it, *imagine*! But I *always* say one *reaps* what one *sows*, and she *is* the very *best*!" – and was distraught to believe that she would not have opportunity to show it to advantage at the Darcys' ball. Indeed, it would have been the talk of the evening, she was certain; people would have remembered her attendance for months on the strength of it, forgetting all the other ladies present while preserving her image.

"Why, Mrs Hewitt," replied Lizzy to this claim with a sweet smile, "You do yourself disserve. I am certain your participation at a ball would be unforgettable regardless of your attire."

Susanna Hewitt thanked Lizzy for the compliment while Jane and Amelia Chaney traded quick glances and Kitty surreptitiously turned her face into the upholstered side of the settee. "Perhaps you might still make an impression in your gown, madam," said Lizzy, "at a future date. I am certain you will be back to your old form in time for the upcoming season."

"Ah!" cried Mrs Hewitt. "I could do *no* such *thing*, Mrs Darcy! Why, it should be *hopelessly* out of *fashion* by such *time*! The very *idea* of such a *thing*! No, I *fear* I shall have to have it *remade* to some other *purpose*. But *such a loss*!"

She was so distraught at the notion that Kitty now suggested Mrs Hewitt direct her maid to bring it to Lizzy's sitting room, where at least the half dozen ladies present might admire it as it deserved before it was forever altered. Even as Mrs Hewitt declined with celebrity, lamenting that it could not be sufficiently admired without it being on her person, several eyes moved to Kitty while she coughed in embarrassment. Lizzy's glance at her sister was laced as it were with a hint of startled admiration.

❖❖❖❖❖

Lady Catherine remained seated at Darcy's desk a moment when her callers had left, fingering a copy of the papers she had just signed. Mr Atherton had questioned some of the provisions for disposition with regards to her daughter; he had insisted upon a codicil for Anne's express endorsement, given the unusual nature of the bequests in regard to Sir

Lewis deBourgh's prior intentions. Lady Catherine had agreed; she assured her solicitor it would take little persuasion to gain Anne's approval. But she had rejected the notion of calling Anne in to their meeting; she would speak with her daughter first alone. Mr Atherton raised objection yet again, but eventually acquiesced. He had dealt with Lady Catherine too long to expect anything more or less. The gentlemen now returned to Lambton to prepare their departure for town, and would stop at Pemberley again on their way to witness Anne's signing and secure copies to have proved with the Prerogative Court of Canterbury.

Gathering the various documents together now, Lady Catherine made her way to her own sitting room whereupon she directed Dalton to summon Miss deBourgh for an interview. While she awaited her daughter, she thought about what she had just done.

She had acquiesced to Anne's request, with one exception. It galled her to have done as much as she did but, in the end, it would serve. She could live with this outcome, she thought, then chuckled coldly to realise that indeed she would not. But most of her own requirements were met. Rosings would stay intact, *and* in the lineage of the Fitzwilliams if not in her own family directly. Of that, she had been most adamant. Where smaller properties and investments went was of less interest to her, but Rosings had been *her* triumph, *her* glory, made much more prosperous than could have been done under her husband's hand alone. And it would remain as the monument to her sacrifices through the years.

She wondered now why she had given in to her daughter in large part. Had she recognised that Anne would never have a child of her own regardless of whether she married; indeed might very well die in the attempt? If that were true, what point in her marrying and ceding the property to a stranger? Or had Lady Catherine simply grown soft with the prospect of death hovering? Had seeing Sir James again – triggering unsettling memories in her dreams – played its part?

Those unwelcome thoughts were interrupted by the arrival of Anne herself. She took a chair adjacent to her mother's, a tentative smile offered, but neither spoke until Dalton had left the room with an admonition from her mistress that they were not to be disturbed under any circumstance.

"It is done," said Lady Catherine. "My Will, with an addendum for your endorsement."

"I see," said Anne, looking down into her hands folded into her lap. She seemed hesitant to ask anything.

"I have done what you have asked – for the most part."

At this, Anne's eyes came up, searching her mother's with curiosity, but Lady Catherine merely held out some papers and said, "Would you read it for yourself or shall I tell you?"

Anne hesitated; then took the proffered document, but did not look at it. "You may tell me."

Lady Catherine described the arrangements then in order, earning only a nod now and again from her daughter. Occasionally Anne glanced down at the document in her hands, but did not follow each point minutely. She trusted that her mother held nothing back. When Lady Catherine came finally to the disposition that deviated from Anne's request, the young woman met her mother's eyes in a long perusal; but after a moment she nodded to this as well in a pronounced manner. She had achieved so much of what she had asked that accepting this one stubborn insistence seemed little enough to cede. It was acceptable.

When all had been said on the matter, Anne commended it and agreed to endorse the codicil when the solicitor returned. She smiled then, returning the papers. "Thank you, Mother. You have given me great ease."

"Hmmph," was the reply she received, but it was not without affection.

"Mama," Anne began, hesitant again.

"What is it? Do you have yet more to demand of me?"

"Only information."

"What do you wish to know?"

"Two things: firstly, why did you not tell me of your heart ailment?"

Lady Catherine made to answer coldly, but noted her daughter's concern. "I saw no cause to worry you needlessly. As you can see, I am quite strong; there is nothing to warrant dwelling upon it."

"But your collapse –"

"That was nothing, I am fully recovered. You may ask Mr Folsom yourself this afternoon; he tells me my heart beats like a lion's. I have no intention of putting these provisions," she said as she lifted her documents up, "into effect too soon."

Anne was unconvinced and finally, to relieve her daughter's concern and depart the subject, Lady Catherine admitted that her recent attack was unrelated to her heart condition; she had suffered something of a shock upon seeing Sir James at Pemberley all at once and had simply fainted. Her deepening colour and obvious discomfort at confessing to such a weakness finally served to persuade Anne.

Anne lowered her eyes once more. "You have struck upon the other information I wish to know. I have noted you these last days with Sir James and came to suspect in your glances and your peculiar avoidance that you knew him before. Will you tell me of it?"

Lady Catherine's face set in stubborn resistance, but it was not sustained. The appeal in Anne's expression, coupled with the finality of settling her will and the persistent memories she had suffered of late, conspired to loosen her tongue.

"Yes, I knew him. It was a very long time ago, a time it does neither any good to recall. We were very young."

"You loved him."

"Yes."

Both were silent now, Anne considering this and her mother mulling over whether to say any more.

"Did you love my father as well?" was all Anne finally asked, although she had sensed the answer all her life.

"Hmmph." This revelation of her feelings to her daughter did not come easily to Lady Catherine. In stilted speech, she replied. "I... learnt to like Sir Lewis deBourgh, I understood him in time and he understood me. In that regard we respected one another. That was sufficient."

"How sad to think of it."

"Not at all." Lady Catherine now regained her customary tone. "Love, as you might have noted, only confounds people. It cannot provide for your welfare, cannot change your life to advantage. It effaces reason. It can only cause one pain. It has no place in marriage."

Anne's face screwed up in dissent, but she chose not to wage a futile argument. Instead she asked, "Why did you marry him?"

"I first met Sir Lewis deBourgh in town, one of my earlier inclusions in a dinner party of my father's. I acted as my father's hostess that night as my mother was indisposed. Sir Lewis became infatuated with me instantly; but he was so much older than I, I scarcely gave him a thought. I was in the midst of my first season, with the whole of London paying court. I lacked no attention from gentlemen. But Sir Lewis had determined on that first evening that he would have me; and each subsequent chance encounter – or chance as I thought them – made him more desperate in resolve. I was cordial to him out of respect for my father, but I felt little more for him then."

Her words came smoothly, as though she spoke of events just passed rather than years distant – brought to her lips easily by the memories that had assailed her for days. "At a house party at Buxborough, then, I met James Thornton as he was; a second son, few prospects, but full of charm and confidence. We came to admire one another, it is true; we enjoyed some months of courting."

"But my father was a friend to the Earl."

"Yes; or at least a political ally. He had connexions in society, connexions my father found desirous to satisfy. In short, he wished to retain Sir Lewis deBourgh's good will; and Sir Lewis deBourgh wished ... for me."

"They forced you to marry him?"

"No!" Lady Catherine's denial was violent; "persuaded, perhaps, of the merits of such a union. But I entered upon it freely enough. Your father had won his desire and was happy then to rest on his laurels. I was not. I had won connexions, and I used them to my advantage. I learnt to appreciate what I had obtained; and I obtained a life I desired. It was a good union – we each derived our pleasures from it before he died."

Anne might have asked more but her mother's tone held a finality that suggested she would say little else. "Then... Sir James... might have been my father."

"Yes, I suppose he might, had circumstance been different. But it was not. Do not romanticise the man now, Anne. I assure you I do not! I think little enough on him," she finished, though her reaction upon seeing him again after all these years held contrast to the idea. She drew a breath and said, "Your own father was Sir Lewis deBourgh, and he it is who deserves your sympathy. He was a good provider to us, a good father to you."

"Yes, of course," defended Anne. "I would not think otherwise of him." But her thoughts strayed back to her mother and Sir James; to what might have been. Her mother would not appreciate Anne's emotion, but still she felt empathy for Lady Catherine... and following, tremendous guilt over the way she had behaved in the last two days towards her.

"Mama," she said, spurred to a confession of her own before thinking it through, "I lied to you."

Lady Catherine's eyes sharpened now, returning her swiftly from the past, her attention riveted upon her daughter.

Anne squirmed a bit under the scrutiny, but continued. "It is not true... about Frances and me, I mean. You have no cause for concern. We are not... We do not... I only confirmed your suspicions of us to gain advantage. I threatened to make public an illicit relationship to persuade you to grant my requests." She looked down at the floor, her face flushed. "I regret the deceit."

Silence overtook the room. Close on the heels of her confession, Anne realised the danger of it. Her mother could rip up the documents in her hand and all would be lost. She had succumbed to an uncharacteristic vulnerability in her mother's narrative, and now in a moment of emotion may have threatened all she had achieved. What ever would she do if she had forfeited everything by losing her reason?

A small idea had begun to form in her desperation that perhaps she had lost nothing after all. Whatever the truth of Anne's relationship with Frances Jenkinson, her mother had with little provocation believed it untoward. How much more readily would others be willing to believe it as an indecency as well? Whether true or not, to put the story about would cause the same damage. She considered now whether to voice this notion, when she heard an uncharacteristic sound.

Lady Catherine was laughing; not the patronising amused snicker she bestowed now and again on her acquaintance, nor the light trill she was known to affect in the company of her friends to signify mild amusement. This was deep and strong, coming from well within. Anne looked up at her mother in astonishment.

When the convulsion had ebbed, Lady Catherine fixed her daughter with a look not of outrage or betrayal, but far more benevolent, perhaps even admiring. She smiled sardonically and said, "Well, there is no mistaking – you are *my* daughter."

❖❖❖❖❖

"Your library is most impressive, Mrs Darcy."

"It is the work of several generations of my husband's family, Sir. I do not believe any subject under the sun cannot be found here in some measure. When my father visits us, I am always assured of finding him here from the close of breakfast – indeed, it can be a challenge to remove him again for dinner and other necessities."

"He sounds eminently reasonable," laughed Sir James. "I hope to have the pleasure of Mr Bennet's acquaintance one day." He glanced about him. "I dare say I hardly know where to look first to choose some diversion."

"I should have the same difficulty were I not a creature of habit. I confess I maintain a small selection of my favourites in my own parlour to resort to when the challenge here is too daunting."

He chuckled. "And what might I find among your favourites?"

"Ah, now you invite me, Sir James, to admit my follies and vices! For if pressed, I must admit to a partiality for popular novels."

Now he laughed outright. "I hesitate, in consideration of offence, to avow that I am not surprised in the least, madam. But I will not admonish you for it and hope no umbrage is taken, for it is my own partiality as well for which I make no apology."

"Indeed? Have you yet read the second novel of Miss Harriet Lee? *Clara Lennox; or the Distressed Widow*, published so recently?"

"I have not yet had the pleasure. I did very much enjoy *The Errors of Innocence*."

"Well, Sir, if such is the entertainment you now seek, I can remedy your want."

"Delightful! I accept."

"Then wait with me a moment and we shall go together for it. I must only retrieve first a book for Mrs Hewitt."

"How does the lady in her misery?"

Lizzy smiled sweetly as she perused the shelf. "In her misery, Sir, she is perfection itself."

Sir James was quick enough not to mistake her and laughed. "I rather expected as much from her husband's pronounced relief whenever he joins the party."

Lizzy found the title her guest had requested quickly enough and as she and Sir James walked up the stairs, she found herself relating to him the news of Susanna Hewitt's wheeled chair and visit to the ladies earlier. His amusement was evident despite her attempts to relate the story without particular judgment. When they reached the landing, Sir James waited patiently while Lizzy delivered the book to the invalid; then followed her to her sitting room to claim his own.

"Please, sit with me a moment, Sir James." Lizzy pointed to a chair as she handed him the novel.

Sir James obliged and they spent a few moments discussing Mr Sicklemore's recent novel, *Edgar; or the Phantom of the Castle*. They both agreed to its merits, particularly as the first publication of so young an author. They agreed as well that it borrowed much in style from Mrs Radcliffe and in plot from Shakespeare. Sir James found particularly amusing the title. "Something of a misnomer I think, as we find any phantom strangely absent throughout and the castle referred to only in speech. Perhaps a better title would have been 'Remorse in the Priory', but that hardly draws one in with such romantic promise."

Lizzy now mentioned the book she had just given to Sir James. *Clara Lennox* and its plot of young lovers divided by disapproving parents owed some inspiration to Shakespeare as well. When Sir James expressed his anticipation to begin it and looked to rise, Lizzy said, "I cannot but wonder, Sir, if our party at Pemberley might not offer a story to rival this one."

Sir James continued to smile, but it was set in place as he said in too light a voice, "How is that, Mrs Darcy?"

"The notion of lovers separated by time and distance finding each other once again."

The comment found its mark; Sir James paled visibly. "Mrs Darcy..."

Lizzy apologised, but then pressed him politely. She had put enough evidence together to realise that Sir James and Lady Catherine had been well acquainted at one time; and his own reticence on the subject implied the nature of that acquaintance. She assured Sir James that if he chose to tell her his own tale, she would relate it to no one beyond her own husband; but though she could apologise for unabashed curiosity in the matter, she could not seem to quell it.

Sir James considered a moment before, with a sigh, saying, "Our 'story' as you call it lacks the stuff of novels. It is common enough." He proceeded then to tell Lizzy of his history with Lady Catherine Fitzwilliam, as she was then.

They had in fact met at Buxborough, although they had been aware of each other from the summer before. But neither had suspected from that distant glance that they would form an attachment; indeed each had been prepared to do no more than tolerate one another based upon presumption and first impressions. Lady Catherine must have been eighteen or nineteen, Sir James hardly much older. By the time he had quitted Buxborough, the two were inseparable.

They continued their courtship in town, under the wondering gaze of a society which had believed he would never settle upon one woman. And in a short time, he proposed and she accepted. They had told no one. Lady Catherine's father had been recalled to their estate during that time and must be petitioned first; and so they had waited a month for his return enjoying the blissful awareness of what should come to pass. As soon as the Earl had arrived, James had sent round a request for a private interview with His Lordship. He received no reply.

Nor for several days afterwards had he seen Lady Catherine. She did not appear at any of the events; and her brother, the present Earl, fobbed James off when he would approach him, only saying she was engaged elsewhere. Then one day, James had met her out walking in the park with her companion and they had contrived a diversion for some speech in privacy. It seemed her father had arrived with the news that they had selected a husband for Lady Catherine, one propitious to the family. She was miserable, swore she would not have the man, could never love him. But they would press the matter, her father and her brother both. Her brother it had been who warned their father of Sir James's too close interest, and her general freedom had been curtailed.

Here Sir James tried to end his narrative, but Lizzy cajoled him into continuing, promising again her utmost discretion. Sir James admitted that he had acted then from desperation, honourable in intention if not practice. He had asked Lady Catherine to run away with him, to be wed in secret, certain that upon their return, the marriage would be accepted and prepared to risk the consequence if it were not. And she had accepted readily.

They set a date three days hence – she was to meet her dressmaker and would not be expected back for several hours – and he passed the interim in making their escape ready. She did not appear as anticipated, though he waited hours after she should have done. When he returned to his rooms, he had a note from her. She was being watched too carefully, but promised to write again as soon as she found another opportunity to escape. She begged him to remain close by, to be ready to fly at a moment's notice, and he had done just that. He had waited until he thought he would go mad from the tedium, though in truth it was only three days more. Then another letter arrived.

This one was short and to the point. It expressed her desire that he not see her again. She had been mistaken; she did not love him enough to consider marriage to the life he could offer. She wished for more in society, and she warned him against public petition of any claim upon her. It was her prerogative to reconsider his proposal and she had done so and found him wanting.

He had been incredulous at first, refusing to accept it. He compared the writing in the note with her prior one; it was the same and he could detect no strain or other alteration in it. Then later that day, he had chanced to meet her brother in the street – odd though it was that he would find the gentlemen in his area of town – and it had been made clear that he was unwelcome to tender any additional attentions upon his sister by her own choice.

And that was that. Lizzy asked him if they had encountered one another again, and he replied they had done on a few instances in the several weeks following her note, only amongst greater company. But then a month after their suspended elopement had come the announcement of her marriage to Sir Lewis deBourgh by special license. James Thornton had chosen to exile himself in America; and he had not seen Lady Catherine again until their meeting at Pemberley this past week.

"How awful for you," said Lizzy.

"Not for me, no, dear lady. I have long ago come to terms with the episode. All in all, I think it best. I have been happy for many years. I found my Grace, and we lived the life we were meant. And I am certain Lady Catherine as well has long reconciled her own path."

Lizzy mentioned that Lady Catherine may have done so, but she appeared for most purposes to have disowned her father and brother from that time, cutting off nearly all contact after her marriage. This saddened him to think of it as he recalled that her family had always been paramount to her discernment of herself, her lineage a particular source of pride. He asked about her health now, and Lizzy confided that condition as well; given what Sir James had disclosed, it seemed a small breach.

"I suspected as much from events," he replied. "I am sorry to hear of it."

"Sir James," Lizzy began, then paused before plunging in; she was too curious to hold back. "When you see her now, both of you widowed and needing answer to no one, are you at all inclined to renew a... friendship, with Lady Catherine?"

His smile was bittersweet, but with regret over the past rather than the present. "No." There was no hesitation in the reply. "I have changed.

We have changed – too much to try to reclaim what once we felt. We are not the same people. It is better to leave the ancient past untouched, I think."

❖❖❖❖❖

"Darcy," Lizzy asked after relating to her husband what she had learnt that afternoon, "do you think if she had married Sir James, your aunt would be different now?" She had pondered the idea once and again since Sir James had told her their history. She thought she might have felt differently about Lady Catherine with this knowledge – more forgiving perhaps or compassionate – but was surprised to find she did not. The woman's hypocrisy in her judgment of others blunted any compassion that might have been due her for events occurring years ago. Whatever circumstance may have been forced upon her then, still she had some discretion in how to meet it and, indeed, it had been many years since she had gained a large measure of independence when her husband had died. Her actions and attitudes were her own, and accountable as such.

"Yes, of course," Darcy replied. "How could she not fail of it?" As Lizzy tried yet again to commute this into some empathy for the woman, he noted the consternation in her face. "But I should not spend my time regretting the woman who might have been."

Lizzy glanced at him in some surprise.

"My love, circumstance may have added greatly to the woman my aunt has become. But it cannot answer wholly for it. She has had within her – she must have done – a cantankerous proclivity all along; it did not spring to life fully formed only from her disappointment in love. We cannot know but that, had she married Sir James, she might still be much as she is, except differing disappointments would have been called to account for it. And in that case, we might feel obliged either to pity or despise what it would have made of the gentleman's disposition as well."

He smiled now, and Lizzy laughed; instantly giving up all conscious thought of Lady Catherine deBourgh and only somewhere deep within registering briefly that she could still take some pleasure in disliking the woman.

Darcy came now to sit with his wife, taking a hand from her lap and lacing his fingers through hers in complete contentment. Both were dressed for dinner but not required downstairs for nearly half an hour and they enjoyed their customary pre-dinner quiet time. After a moment, Darcy closed his eyes and leaned his head against the high backed settee. He did not doze; merely enjoyed the serenity of the room's air. He remained so until he heard Lizzy chuckle, and he opened one eye to find her looking at him in good humour.

"What do you find so amusing now?" he asked.

"Not amusing so much, only... nonsensical, I suppose. I was considering that, given all the uproar of these last weeks, we are fortunate to bring Christmastide to a close with such contentment."

"Bite your tongue, Lizzy!" admonished Darcy. "Do not court additional trouble by proclaiming us free of it too soon."

"Darcy!" she laughed. "Can you be superstitious? You, a man of the world?"

"I merely see no cause to tempt disaster."

They both chuckled at this. But Lizzy said, "I suppose we are fortunate our house party is not larger. There is no one remaining to suffer calamity. Bingley can now claim an estate; he and dearest Jane will be established less than five and twenty miles from here. They both will prosper, I know, from being farther removed from Mama."

Darcy only nodded, leery still to give in to optimism. Lizzy said, "And Aunt and Uncle Gardiner have made a new friend into the bargain in Sir James. Kitty has found contentment with, of all things, a vicar and he, to my delight and Kitty's, with her."

At this Darcy rolled his eyes heavenward. "I suppose before too many months have passed, I shall have yet another Bennet sister residing within five and twenty miles." But his tone held no disgruntlement despite his words, and Lizzy smiled at the assessment. "Would you mind terribly? If Kitty were to marry Mr Reavley?"

"It is not I who should mind, but the vicar," Darcy exclaimed. "But no, I should not mind if he does not. It might even offer some amusement to be a spectator to such an odd coupling."

"Fitz!" The admonishment was only half-hearted before Lizzy continued with a summary of her guests. "Mrs Hewitt continues to convalesce and we should be able to send her on her way in mere months." She laughed at the horrified expression she had induced in her husband, and hastened to qualify that she jested; Mrs Hewitt herself had that afternoon expressed her hope of being returned to her home and children within weeks. "And in the interim, you have your friend Edmund Hewitt to hand with few calls upon his time.

"Georgiana is in love and, all owing to the very commendable sacrifice of her brother's peace of mind, she and her own Mr Hewitt themselves enjoy sweet dreams of the future."

"Not so much a sacrifice after all," admitted Darcy, and he squeezed Lizzy's hand. "I only needed reminding that I cannot hold Gee's affections by holding her a child in my heart forever." He gazed sincerely then into Lizzy's chestnut eyes, his own earnest in concern. He moved his hand to place it over his wife's abdomen. "Will I be so obstinate, do you think, with our children?"

"Of course," she laughed. "After all" – she adopted his tone from their earlier discourse of his aunt – "you have had within you a proclivity for obstinacy all along." As he replied with a rueful sigh, she added, "but our children – and I by the way – will love you for it; or perhaps despite it."

They kissed then, forcing another intermission in Lizzy's recounting. When they broke apart, they enjoyed the silence for an instant before Darcy prodded her, chortling as he asked: "Who remains in your accounting now?"

"Hmm? Oh, yes, my account. Let me think." She smiled. "Retched and Mrs Chaney are once again in harmonious accord. I should be astonished if we do not hear of some formal understanding there very soon. You must admit they are well matched in temperament."

"My cousin certainly believes so; I cannot decry it."

Lizzy ignored this. Darcy harboured yet some small resentment towards Amelia Chaney for causing pain to Fitzwilliam, even as he understood the source and circumstances that led to her actions. But he would come around fully in time when he saw Amelia's contrition and the joy she would bring to his cousin.

"Anne is content not to be coerced to marry Retched and, as it appears, not to marry anyone. Lady Catherine must be content to know she was mistaken in her daughter's own proclivities." Lizzy laughed again to think of it, though still she harboured some suspicions about Anne and Mrs Jenkinson. She would not voice those concerns to her husband, however. Let him remain as naively content as Anne herself to believe the woman's protestations.

"We have still to learn, however," cautioned Darcy, "my aunt's decision regarding her Will, and her daughter's future. She may yet cause Anne – and us, I might add – some great inconvenience."

"Yes, but however she incommodes us, or you rather, you will administer it admirably. And I refuse to believe she would coerce Anne again into a match. Her first two attempts caused her suffering enough, I think, to attempt a third.

"And so, we are left with Lady Catherine and Sir James. That puzzle is solved, and we are assured that there will be no attempt to resurrect old feelings."

"You have forgotten Henry Wentworth, my dear."

"Not at all. But Mr Wentworth is the one person who has remained amiable throughout Christmastide despite his role in Fitzwilliam's misunderstanding. And unless he has developed a mad, consuming passion for Mrs Reynolds in these last days, I feel confident in asserting that we are safe from any trouble in that quarter."

Darcy laughed at the idea and, grudgingly, conceded to his wife that they might breathe easy. "But I shall reserve judgment until our ball is safely dispatched if you do not object."

"If you must. I, on the other hand, am impatient to restore every body, not greatly in fault themselves, to tolerable comfort." Lizzy glanced at the clock on the mantle. "Shall we to dinner, Mr Darcy, with our happy company?"

They rose, but before moving on, Darcy embraced his wife. "And what of you, Mrs Darcy? Are you happy as well as we move into this new year?"

"Mr Darcy, I could not possibly wish to be more so than I am at this moment." She smiled. "And you?"

Eschewing mere words, he instead expressed his agreement on the occasion as convincingly and as warmly as a man violently in love with his own wife may be supposed to do.

❖❖❖❖❖

When they arrived in the drawing room, Lizzy and Darcy found that only Georgiana had preceded them there despite the distraction in Lizzy's sitting room that had delayed their coming down. As they entered, Gee turned to them from the fire with a beatific smile. They barely had closed the door, however, when it seemed there was some commotion in the corridor without – Mrs Reynolds in agitated discourse with another person, a woman by the timbre of the voice which grew in volume as it approached the room.

The voices stopped abruptly and immediately following, the door opened to admit Mrs Annesley, of all people. Her eyes alighted on Georgiana and, without even acknowledging Mr and Mrs Darcy – such was her single purpose to comfort Georgiana that she did not notice them – she rushed to her companion and drew her into an embrace. "Oh, my dear friend!" she exclaimed. "Forgive me for being away when you have had need of me. But I came as quickly as I could do."

Georgiana was at a loss for words not wholly connected with her being barely able to breathe within the confines of Mrs Annesley's ample bosom. When at last her squirming for air resulted in her release, still she could say nothing. She had completely forgotten in her recent joy the letter she had rushed off to Mrs Annesley only two nights past, and was mortified now to have caused the lady to cut short her own family visit and return prematurely to Pemberley. Georgiana's chagrin, when Mrs Annesley now looked upon her countenance, only served to confirm the woman's belief in her suffering.

Darcy was nearly as bemused as Georgiana, being unaware of his sister's recent and hastily penned missive to her companion. But Lizzy realised at once what had occurred and stepped in to sort out everyone's understanding. She explained quickly to Darcy that Georgiana had written in her anguish to her friend on Wednesday – a description he as quickly matched to a memory of seeing Georgiana emerge from the servant's hallway late that night after delivering her letter to the housekeeper – and then went on to reassure Mrs Annesley that the situation had since been resolved to everyone's happy acceptance.

Mrs Annesley looked to Georgiana for confirmation to find the young lady shaking her head vigorously, a smile of embarrassment offering apology for the alarum she had caused until she found her tongue again to express her regret. When once this had been conveyed and the companion had refuted any notion of resentment at her early return (for she confided that while she loved her family, she did not find it restful to pass too much time amongst them; the household always seemed fraught with misunderstandings, calamities and clashing sensitivities) she remembered herself to greet Mr and Mrs Darcy properly. Following this, she apologised to them for her own early and – as it now proved – unnecessary return to disrupt their party.

"Not at all, Mrs Annesley," replied Darcy. "It speaks immensely to your credit that you wished to be with Miss Darcy in an hour of need." He assured the lady of her status at Pemberley and that she was a welcome addition to its residents; at which time Lizzy then pressed her to join them for dinner. When it was agreed, Mrs Annesley gave a last hug to Georgiana, this one in relief at the restoration of her friend, and began to leave to hurriedly change into dinner attire. Fortunately, she had a gown at hand and would not have to rely upon those packed in her travelling trunk.

Just as Mrs Annesley reached out towards the door, chuckling all the while in amusement at the turn of events, it opened under a hand from the other side, and she stepped back again to allow for the admittance of this new personage. Their eyes met and the happy smile upon her countenance froze in place.

Mr Henry Wentworth filled the door frame, stopped in the act of entering, his hand still resting on the latch handle and his own countenance fixed in place in an aborted general greeting. They stood thus for a moment, staring into each other's eyes with unequivocal attraction, until finally he stammered, "Oh... uh... good evening... uh, that is..."

Lizzy and Darcy looked immediately to one another in disbelief. "Not another?"

CHAPTER SEVENTEEN

Saturday, 5 January 1799

❖❖❖❖❖

AS SUDDENLY as the cold snap had arrived two days past, it moved out again, bringing mild air behind it. It bode well for guests who would journey from any distance to Pemberley for festivities. Less auspicious was the cloud cover that accompanied the warmer temperatures. Even a waning half moon if the night were clear might have offered some welcome light to travellers; but it seemed they would have to rely heavily on their coach lamps.

Darcy had directed that lanterns be maintained on the drive from the gatehouse, but little could be done beyond the estate, where illumination would be most wanted. In an effort to ensure at least some measure of protection, he had engaged several men to ride in pairs along the main road from Lambton throughout the evening – locals who held intimate knowledge of the terrain and tenuous points along the road, they were glad of the employ in mid winter while their fields were fallow.

The mild clime, coupled with mounting anticipation of the night's festivities, gave to everyone a restless vigour evident even at the breakfast table: heels tapping rapidly on the floor to match the rhythm of anxious fingers on the table; much to and fro for contemplating the prospect from the windows; an impatience with the news being reported in the papers. There was a bustle of activity throughout the house from the wee hours as staff and servants made ready. But the residents found themselves with several hours to pass before they could begin their own preparations and much which they might find to occupy their time would only put them in the way of maids and footmen and sundry others. The suggestion of a walk therefore was eagerly embraced, and those few who declined – Lady Catherine, Anne and her companion, the Gardiners – repaired to their own rooms.

While the residents took the air, the house was in the throes of being transformed. The ballroom had been opened the previous day and now every surface which had not been yet cleaned thrice received further attention. Chairs were set up around the perimeter; music stands erected in the upper-story niche for the musicians; fresh boughs installed for decoration and trimmed with cones, berries and ribbons; fireplaces at either end set, with large greenery sprays established on the mantles above; and chandeliers readied with six-hour candles. The full-length windows leading to the outer balcony were scrubbed and its terrace cleared of every trace of snow, ice, leaves or debris, in the event brave souls wished to venture out for air.

The North parlour was arranged for conversation groups or music for those who did not partake of dancing, Georgiana's piano festooned in fresh greenery, the Christmas fire alight still though much reduced. As had been done for the musical evening early in the week, the dining room and its adjacent parlour had been opened to each other and set for supper use. Two additional parlours had been opened into one for use as a card room, set with tables and chairs, stocked with cards and fish and the occasional board for chess, backgammon or draughts. Three smaller rooms on the ground floor would provide dressing rooms for ladies and gentlemen to repair their appearance on arrival and storage for outer garments and shoe changes. They were fitted with long looking glasses and appropriate amenities. The smoking room was aired and stocked.

The kitchen had been active for some days in the preparation of light refreshments, supper dishes, beverages. As people were in some cases travelling a distance, the supper on offer would be substantial. Darcy had spent an hour or more at first light in the cellars with Naismith and Mrs Reynolds, directing the use and timing of wines, champagne, brandies, sherry and port. Negus and Wassail and ale-based nog were prepared. The aromas from all this activity reached even the main house now and again with the continual opening of doors between service and living areas.

Usually unseen in the execution of their duties, an astonishing number of servants were to be found everywhere from first light: polishing, buffing, dusting, setting fires in all the grates and stocking coal or wood; rearranging furniture, straightening draperies, rolling carpets for storage. Pemberley's permanent staff had been augmented with day labourers for the occasion. Again, a ball for the gentry meant welcome winter income for a few days for the local populace. They would return the next morning to assist in restoring the house to its customary arrangements.

❖❖❖❖❖

At half past one, a cold luncheon was laid out for any of the residents who wished it. They would not dine in the evening, and it would be several hours until supper. Most drifted in to partake of some meats or cheeses to sustain them, before drifting off again. Maids and valets and under-servants traversed the corridors to provide hot water for baths.

Mr Butler was to come at four to begin formal preparations by dressing the ladies' hair and so, before he arrived, Lizzy and Darcy took the opportunity to gather some of their near relations for a private celebration. Offering gifts on Twelfth Night was a favourite part of Lizzy's holiday observance and she had discovered (to no surprise it must be added) that her husband's anticipation had been no less than her own.

Edward and Margaret Gardiner, Jane and Bingley, and Kitty joined Lizzy in her private parlour, Darcy entering soon after with ratafia for the ladies and brandy. While they sipped and expressed their wishes for the year, they exchanged gifts.

Lizzy and Jane had, it seemed – in keeping with frugal habits of long establishment – chosen to continue a tradition of making gifts for one another. Jane's to Elizabeth was an embroidered needle case and, inside with an assortment of the useful tools, she had tucked a small parchment with some private sentiment. In return, Lizzy had taken a simple trinket box and embellished its top and sides with scrollwork and dried flowers before sealing it with lacquer. On the bottom, she had penned an inscription to her sister. From Kitty, they each – Jane, Lizzy and Aunt Gardiner – received an embroidered handkerchief.

Bingley's eyes widened in delight at the desk globe Darcy offered him – vowing even as his fingers began idly to spin the orb, that it would be the first installation in his study at Albion House.

"How perfectly delightful, Bingley," Lizzy could not refrain from laughing, "Darcy has offered you the known world in its entire just at the time when you are settling down finally to one tiny spot within it."

Bingley then presented Darcy a burlap-wrapped bottle and, unwittingly, a guffaw when it transpired to be the same "rare" Cognac that Colonel Fitzwilliam had given to Darcy two nights before. Lizzy's outburst of laughter then required some explanation; and came as well with an admonition that, should the gentlemen share the libation presently, they should expect no wifely affections for some time after. The men were undaunted, although they did wisely decide not to sample the vintage then and there.

The Gardiners then gave to Lizzy and her husband a Chinese vase of polished stone; simple in design but in an extraordinary lapis colouring immediately lauded by all. A similar object the shade of emeralds then found its way to the Bingleys. Lizzy proclaimed at once that it should rest on the demilune table in the hall near the drawing room – to replace a certain urn that had suffered accident only a week before. But she wisely chose to keep it there in her own parlour until after all their guests had departed.

Jane's gift to her aunt was a cameo brooch – a Romanesque woman emerging from helmet shell, with silver filigree setting, the whole eliciting tears of appreciation from its recipient. The tears only increased when Margaret Gardiner next received Lizzy's gift: a Kashmir shawl in fine light wool, woven through the middle in a loose and lacy pattern, then growing closer in weave towards the ends where a thick border of paisley design provided interest. It was agreed all around that the cameo could not have been better matched to the shawl had the sisters colluded in their purchases.

Bingley and Darcy *had*, it was found, been in collusion with regard to Edward Gardiner. Their uncle found himself the proud owner now of a full kit of fishing gear, to be maintained exclusively for his use when he visited Derbyshire and, now as well, Nottinghamshire. Immediately he began to conjecture how soon he might return to test his skill with it. His wife shook her head in resigned amusement.

Kitty previously had received her rose-coloured gown from the Darcys; and her dress for the ball that night had been courtesy of Jane and Bingley. But Lizzy and Jane together had one other item to proffer: a pair of pink quartz crystalline earrings that would complement well her new attire. She squealed in delight, then repeated the approbation when her aunt and uncle gave her a pendant which matched the earrings.

It was not long after that a maid brought the news of Mr Butler's having arrived some while ago. He had completed fashioning Miss deBourgh's hair, had nearly finished Lady Catherine's, and would be ready for Jane, followed by Kitty, very shortly. Kitty could no longer contain her excitement that the time had arrived to prepare for the evening, prompting Jane as they exited the parlour to suggest Mr Butler start next with her. More squeals brought a chuckle to Lizzy as they receded down the passage.

❖❖❖❖❖

Lady Catherine considered her reflection in the mirror. She wore her morning gown yet, would not don her ball gown for some time. But with her hair dressed, jet beads following the contours of her upswept greyed tresses, and a hint of colour at her cheeks and lips, still she presented a formidable aspect. She had never possessed the kind of soft beauty that her sister had offered, but in her day there were few gentlemen who, having gazed upon her, did not return for a second glance or more. 'Handsome' more fitted her description – but compellingly so. And she had not lost that with the accumulation of lines and creases and the experience of a life.

She was tired, it was true; but no one could suspect it. She did not let her guard fall from the moment she rose in the morning until she retired alone at night, of that she was confident. As such, it pained her now to admit to any show of weakness; it had disconcerted her to prepare her will. But she had always done what was necessary, now as at any other time. She supposed she could take some comfort in knowing nothing would be left unfinished if she were to expire – *yet I have no intention of doing so for a long while*, she thought as she took a deep breath.

"Dalton!"

"Yes, Your Ladyship?"

She had appeared immediately, apparently hovering just on the other side of the connecting door until wanted. Lady Catherine smirked to herself. Dalton at least understood her place and her duty; she had come to know her mistress well over the years, anticipating her moods and her requirements. She directed her maid now to request the presence immediately in her sitting room of several individuals and, when Dalton hesitated a few seconds, she added: "Tell them I have important business, but I shall not take up more than a moment of their time."

When Lady Catherine moved into her sitting room a quarter of an hour later, they were assembled: Anne, Fitzwilliam, Darcy, Elizabeth. The last was not necessary, but in the end Lady Catherine had included her; what she had to say would affect the woman's children – and in any event as her nephew would immediately share his business with his wife, she may as well hear of it firsthand. The ladies appeared in various stages of readiness for the evening, as she herself did. The gentlemen, having an easier preparation not yet begun, appeared as always.

"I will not keep you," she said as she perched on the front of her settee and waved a hand at the others to sit. Elizabeth and Anne complied; the two men remained standing, moving in behind the ladies.

"As you all are aware," she said, flicking a glance at Lizzy during an instant's pause, "I have directed my will be prepared. Mr Atherton is to have it proved on his return and, presuming I survive the next week, it will be established." She looked from one to another of them. "I would have you know its content."

❖❖❖❖❖

Lizzy and Darcy had been about to embark on a call to Georgiana before the summons came from Lady Catherine. They made their way hither now upon leaving their aunt. Time was passing and the need to begin their own preparations for the ball was at hand. A considered reaction to their aunt's news would have to wait its turn.

Gee's maid answered the door, offering that her mistress was in the sitting room with Mrs Annesley. The two were closeted together, reviewing no doubt events of the past days of their separation. They rose when the Darcys arrived.

"I must be on my way," said Mrs Annesley, "or I shall find myself last down."

"I believe Alice has finished working her magic on your gown," said Lizzy with a smile after greeting the companion.

"Ah, good. Then I shall be wanted for the fit," she replied, as she took her leave with a smile at Gee.

Not having anticipated beforehand to attend the Pemberley ball, neither had Olivia Annesley arranged proper attire for the occasion. But after meeting Mr Henry Wentworth, there was no question of her missing the event. The gentleman had monopolised the lady's attentions all the last evening and this morning again from breakfast, Lizzy noted, and all to Mrs Annesley's apparent delight. Jane, who was closest in height and form to the woman, had offered one of her own gowns for the cause; and Lizzy's maid, Alice, who was quite deft with a needle, had been happy to assist in some minor alterations to suit. A bit of trim now and it should serve.

"I think, Gee, that your recent fears for Mrs Annesley's welfare have been unwanted," chuckled Lizzy when she had gone. "I doubt we will have her here at Pemberley for much longer, by her own choosing!"

They spoke for a moment of the extraordinary attraction instantly formed between Mrs Annesley and Mr Wentworth while Darcy only shook his head in strained belief. When he reminded his ladies of the march of time, they settled to their purpose. Lizzy offered Georgiana her gift first – a reticule in cream duchesse satin. She had trimmed it in Belgian lace and formed a criss-cross pattern on the sides in seed pearls. Gee rose immediately to hug her sister – "It is beautiful, Lizzy" – before offering her own gift.

Lizzy found an antique hair comb with long prongs of horn and a heading of gilded metal overlaid with delicate filigree. The only embellishment was a square-cut tawny topaz set into the centre and flanked on either side by small oval garnets; a simple design for a lady of unpretentious taste. Darcy remarked of how well it would look in his wife's chestnut hair and she could only agree delightedly.

Darcy then made to proffer his own gift to his sister, but Lizzy forestalled him. Claiming necessity of finishing her toilette, she took her leave. In truth, the recent reconciliation between brother and sister was such that she wished to leave this time to them – a gift that cost her nothing beyond unsatisfied curiosity. She placed her hand on Darcy's shoulder, arranged to meet him in her parlour when they were both ready to go downstairs, and left. As it happened, on her way she met Mr Butler being escorted down the corridor, come from Mrs Chaney. Lizzy offered herself as his next; afterwards he would see to Miss Darcy as his last on the day.

TESS QUINN

When Lizzy had gone, Darcy invited Gee to sit with him on the chaise. No doubt the thought occurred to both of them how different the experience felt from a few nights past. Now there was only renewed affection between the two and perhaps some new understanding. Any bitterness had been resolved and relegated deliberately to the past.

Darcy wordlessly held out to his sister a small parcel even as she offered one of similar size to him. He nodded for her to open a square silk-covered box of pale green, little more than a hands length in size. Stitched into the top was "Thos. Gray" in the same thread. Gee recognised it as from the jeweller in Sackville Street, and her hand began to tremble as she made to release the catch at the front of the box. She lifted the lid and glanced briefly again at her brother as she began to move aside a soft cloth covering its contents; she gasped upon seeing what lay within.

Nestled within an oval depression in the deep green velvet lining was a string of pearls. They were graduated in size, one large pearl holding place in the centre, with graded ones moving up the string, knotted in place on their silken thread. The smaller orbs were flawlessly rounded and faultlessly matched in size with their counterparts for symmetry. But the most remarkable characteristic was the colour of the nacre. The pearls were of the palest grey such that their translucent patina shone silvery as the light struck them.

"I thought of you immediately on seeing these, Gee. They are the very hue of your eyes in the sunlight."

At the moment, Georgiana's eyes were filled with tears. She could not speak.

"Do you like them?" he asked, anxious to have chosen well.

"They are perfect, Fitz!" She appeared hesitant to touch them, and her brother reached over and drew them out of the case by their clasp. He held them up for a moment to her view before opening the catch and bringing them to his sister's neck, fastening them again behind her while she held her hair to a side. Her hand moved up to graze them with fingertips as she smiled at Darcy. "Thank you, brother."

She blushed as he said, "You look very elegant, my dear," his gaze admiring and his voice expressive. To cover her awkwardness, she pressed him to open his gift.

The leather box, only slightly smaller than hers, revealed two items within; each well wrapped in linen. As he unbound the first, he was perplexed to find his father's pocket watch, and he looked to his sister for explanation.

"I confess I had assistance – but do not blame Grayson, Fitz; he only helped me with an eye to your satisfaction."

"You cajoled Grayson into taking this for you?"

"Yes. Two months ago in fact – I kept expecting you to note its disappearance but hoped, as it did not work properly, you would not seek it out. You can see it works now. I took it to Mr Tregent in the Strand and he was able to repair it properly."

Darcy might wonder how Georgiana had learnt of such a distinguished watchmaker, but suspected that to be the involvement of his valet once again. "I cannot consider of a more meaningful gift, Gee. Thank you."

"But there is more," she replied, nodding at the remaining linen-protected parcel in the box. Smiling, he picked up an item much the same size and shape of the first. He drew his brows together in wonder. "Go on," she said.

Unwrapping the linen quickly now, he found not another watch, but a case. Its top held a lightly etched trellis design, superimposed upon which was engraved a 'D' in the centre. "I hope you will begin using Papa's watch, Fitz. With a protective case, it will not prove too fragile, I think."

"Not at all. Of course I shall –"

He was clearly moved at her thoughtfulness as she urged him to open the case to place the watch inside. He did so to find an inscription on the inside cover: *"A brother, as it were, a second self. Ever your affectionate, Gee."*

As he blinked back a stinging behind his eyes, Georgiana said, "I do hope Aristotle does not object to my purloining his words for my own purpose."

Darcy leaned to his sister to kiss her brow. "If he takes objection, my dear, I shall come to your defence; on that you may depend." His quietude spoke the depth of his pleasure in the gift.

❖❖❖❖❖

Richard Fitzwilliam – newly shaved, bathed and rejuvenated – regarded himself briefly in the shaving glass. His countenance was at rest, reflecting neither joy nor sorrow, simply reflection. *You*, he said to himself in his mind, *are a fortunate man, Retched; wealthy in your friends, in love and –* And with the thought came a dazzling grin.

He had endured every emotion under the sun these past few weeks, it seemed, but now it all came down to this. He had been restored to Amelia Chaney's heart and he had every intention of remaining there. Tonight, he would begin a subtle but concerted courtship with the refreshed hope – a realistic one – that in a few months time she might agree to become his wife. That thought alone brought him joy. All else merely increased his blessing.

As Tipton handed him a steady stream of clothing articles and fussed about him, Fitzwilliam thought of the house party, and how at last the dramas which had plagued them all had seemed to find resolution. The spirit of the season finally had smiled upon them all. Besides his own elated mood, Georgiana would make her first public appearance tonight in excellent spirits – in love and with a prospect of happiness before her to temper her reticence at entering the social whirl. His cousin Anne had not looked better in years, nor as content in her maidenhood.

And when he thought – as he would do quite naturally when reflecting on his own good fortune with Amelia – of his friend Wentworth, he could only laugh at the jest Providence had played. Henry Wentworth had needed only one glance at another widow in the form of Mrs Annesley to join the ranks of lovers in the house.

As for his aunt, the Colonel was near to believing that, despite her curt recitation of intended settlements, Lady Catherine had formed a temper not only of resignation but of acceptance – even contentment for as much as he ever considered her capable of that condition. She had certainly astonished Fitzwilliam with her pronouncements. While Tipton tied his cravat, he considered the meeting recently concluded.

"I shall not keep you, nor shall I open for discussion what I am about to relate. Neither need I caution, I trust, that the intelligence is private in nature. It is done and, to my mind, irrevocable. The time for debate of the matter is passed and I shall not entertain any." Lady Catherine glanced from the seated ladies to her nephews behind them.

"Firstly, you should know that my daughter Anne is in full agreement of these provisions, having formally endorsed a codicil to the effect." She glanced pointedly at Darcy as she added, *"Mr Atherton is convinced she does so of her own choosing, without coercion; and she may tell you the same here now."* Lady Catherine did not, however, defer to her daughter, but plunged on.

"In the event of my death, given my daughter's..." she hesitated an instant, glancing at Anne before choosing her words, *"reticence... to engage in business, she has requested that you, Darcy – and you, Fitzwilliam – will act jointly as trustees on her behalf. As you have done so amicably for my niece all these years, I trust you will do the same for Anne."*

Fitzwilliam was surprised at this; he had expected as much to be laid upon Darcy, but not his own inclusion. He would, of course, agree and serve Anne as he was able.

"My primary concern, I need not remind you, is my daughter's welfare. Secondary to this, the preservation of Rosings. With exception of some outright bequests to faithful retainers and such, upon my death the entire estate is at the disposal of my daughter under the guidance of my nephews – for her lifetime."

Everyone's eyes were drawn to Anne at this last. She appeared content enough, smiling and nodding slightly, with no resentment at her mother's inclination to speak for her.

"Anne has pressed upon me her insistence to remain unmarried. When I have passed, she wishes to vacate Rosings Park, removing nearby to Tetley Grange to reside

with her companion." Lady Catherine's controlled demeanour slipped for an instant into one of disbelieving perplexity at such a notion before returning to an expressionless mask. "Should Anne predecease her companion, the Grange will remain in possession of Mrs Jenkinson during the remainder of her own lifetime, along with an annual allowance for its maintenance." Here she had stopped as she raised her brow at her daughter, but Anne remained silent, accepting this one alteration to her request that Frances be given the Grange outright. "Upon her demise" (Fitzwilliam could not but note that the idea gave his aunt no distress as she shifted her glance to Lizzy) "Tetley Grange is to become the property of your eldest daughter, Darcy. Should you have no daughters, then of your second son. In the event of neither eventuality, it shall revert to Rosings' holdings."

Elizabeth glanced at her husband as Darcy replied, "As you wish, madam."

"I have not finished." Once again, Lady Catherine shifted her gaze to Elizabeth. "I have directed that four investments of £5,000 each be established. These will, in whatever amount they may grow with interest, be granted to each issue of Darcy — save the direct heir — upon attainment of the age of majority."

This provision too evinced no surprise from Fitzwilliam, though clearly it registered on Lizzy's countenance. "Any issue beyond these will receive no provision from me," she concluded, nodding now at Darcy. As these investments totalled the intended dowry set aside for Anne, the colonel presumed this was their aunt's method of disposal, with Anne's approbation. He was mistaken.

"Now, as to the disposition of the bulk of the estate, it shall be as follows. My daughter was assured an endowment upon her marriage of £20,000 outright. This sum, upon his own marriage, is to be settled upon my nephew, Richard Fitzwilliam."

Fitzwilliam started in amazement and he began to stammer an objection, but he was cut short by Lady Catherine. "I will brook no debate, as I have said. My mind is set in this." She involuntarily glanced at her daughter, and Fitzwilliam looked down to see Anne regarding him with a beatific smile. This had obviously been her doing, although how she had accomplished it he could not imagine. He closed his mouth, made an effort to push down his embarrassment at being the only man of his acquaintance to be endowed in the manner of a lady, and tried to accept the gift gracefully as he stumbled out a brief word of thanks. Some part of his consciousness noted that Darcy's hand, resting upon Lizzy's shoulder, gave it a squeeze.

"Hmmph." Lady Catherine appeared to derive some satisfaction at her nephew's awkwardness. But then she cleared her throat. "Finally, Rosings and all its assets and income — less individual stipulations as noted — will, upon both my own demise and my daughter's, become the property of Richard Fitzwilliam's eldest son."

Amidst the collective 'ah's of those assembled, she pressed on. "I have given my concerted efforts to enhancing Rosings to what it now amounts; I would have it maintained by a Fitzwilliam. It will remain in your trust for your son," she directed at the colonel, "until he is of age, of course. If you have no son, your eldest daughter shall inherit. And if you should have no issue, it will be joined to the Pemberley estate through Darcy's eldest." With a brief glance around her assembled party, she concluded. "That is all."

Still in something of a stupor, Fitzwilliam attempted nonetheless to offer his aunt some gratitude, but she rejected it once more and hurriedly indicated that she had a ball to prepare herself for, dismissing further ejaculation. She rose and swept from the room in silence.

The remaining four departed together then, and stood a moment in the passage coming to grips with their fortunes. Anne regarded Fitzwilliam with a sly smile until he impulsively embraced her, and she laughed. "Are you truly in concert with these dispositions, Cousin?" he asked her.

"Oh, yes! I am most pleased with them," she assured both men. Darcy clapped Fitzwilliam on the back, Lizzy offered him an embrace and following, they all went their own ways to their own musings.

An hour later, the Colonel still was amazed at the news. He could never have hoped for such a boon, particularly given the acrimony of his late communications with his aunt. But whatever her motives – however Anne's sudden assertiveness had influenced Lady Catherine – he would look to the future with greater confidence now. Clearly, his aunt had tried to eschew any expressions of gratitude, but he would find ways to proffer it somehow; little ways beginning with a sincere attempt to like her better.

❖❖❖❖❖

Darcy began to turn as he heard Lizzy enter the room behind him but his movement was arrested on beholding her. She was singularly lovely. He had admired her hair earlier – a simple chignon at the back, now with her new comb nestled within it; while soft, loose tendrils curled about her face – but with her attire for the ball complete, the whole of her appearance made his heart skip its beat.

Her gown was a creamy white silk of character, set wide upon her shoulders and the neckline dipping to form a deep vee at her bosom. His eyes lingered there a moment at the merest teaze of delicate coppery-gold lace plaited as an inset. The high waist was ringed with bugle beads of a deep burnished gold, and the same circled the hem in two offsetting scalloped tiers; once more a few caught the light, tucked in to the convergence of scallops in short capped sleeves. Darcy could not, of course, have described the gown in such detail; he knew only its effects.

When she reached him, finally he stirred himself to turn to her completely, saying, "Was ever there a lovelier vision in all of England? I am an inordinately fortunate man, Mrs Darcy."

Through her grin of gratification, she replied, "I could offer the same observance, Mr Darcy. You are quite handsome tonight in your new waistcoat." She fingered his coat lapels as she gazed up. "Its blue embroidery draws my admiration immediately to your eyes."

He straightened in pleasure even as he dismissed her compliment. "I assure you, madam, *my eyes* will see little tonight but you!" He kissed her in greeting, then again. He raised a hand tentatively as if to caress her head but, mindful of Mr Butler's efforts then, he allowed a finger only to trace a curl at her cheek and lowered it again.

"Do you regret that we did not keep to fancy dress tradition for our Twelfth Night ball?" she teazed him.

"Good heavens, no!" he replied immediately. "You are perfection just as you are. And in any event, can you possibly imagine I should welcome the requirement to attire myself as Julius Caesar?" He laughed. "I prefer to cloak my tyranny in the form of a gentleman with a beautiful lady at my side. It is the only way I shall weather such an event as tonight."

Lizzy admonished him to make an effort to enjoy himself this evening, but then said: "As I was readying myself, I kept thinking of your aunt's singular announcement. What do you make of it? Apparently, your championing of Fitzwilliam was to some effect!"

"I could not be more satisfied. But I doubt *my* arguments held sway. I rather think Anne turned her mother's resolve, though I will be deuced to understand quite how. Nonetheless, whatever her reasons, it is well done."

"I agree. I could almost feel some remorse for the epithets I have hurled at your aunt these last weeks."

"Almost?"

"Mr Darcy, you can hardly expect more than one miracle to show itself in a day! And I should not wish to draw your attention too much from her astonishing good deed."

"Then, madam, if that was your design, you should *never* have donned this gown!"

Smiling, she crossed now to the settee where two parcels rested on a small side table. "Come," she said, "permit me to give you my Twelfth Night tokens while we have time still."

He joined her, grabbing up two small parcels of his own from the mantel.

"Me first!" she said, thrusting the smaller of her gifts towards him. Setting his down, he took it and removed the protective linen covering to reveal a book bound in faded red leather. It was in superb condition and he turned it over to the front to see the title: *An Account of the Life of Mr Richard Savage*, in a first edition printing before Samuel Johnson's name had been associated with the publication. The author here was 'anonymous.'

"Wherever did you find this?" he asked in amazement. "I have been searching for just the thing!"

"Yes, I know. I wrote to all your book sellers some months ago and alerted them that if they found a copy, they should come to me," she laughed.

Before he could take it into his head to sit and begin reading the book, she offered him the second parcel. It was largely flat, about a foot on each side, and he removed the wrap to find two thin boards. Laughing at Lizzy's expression of impatience, he slipped off the top of them to reveal beneath a series of simple drawings. There were four in all, hastily rendered but, given the landscape they represented, more potent for their simplicity. "This... this is the edge just northeast of Pemberley," he said as he studied them closely.

"It is. That young artist you liked so well at the Royal Academy, Mr Turner? It seems he passed through the area to visit a friend in Yorkshire, and made these sketches. I was fortunate enough at the bookseller to recognise the location. I thought perhaps you might like to commission a painting on the strength of them. He does paint light so well."

"Perhaps. But these are wonderful just on their own. I shall see them framed together for my study."

"I am pleased you like them."

Darcy felt it necessary as well to express his pleasure without words, such that it was some moments before he got round to offering Lizzy the first of her gifts.

His air of expectancy now spurred her to reveal it quickly. Nestled within a small wooden crate was a teardrop-shaped vial of amber liquid. The label read simply 'EBD/438.' With a curious glance at her husband, she withdrew the bottle, handing him the crate, and removed the stopper. The air immediately around them was sweetened with fragrance.

"Darcy! It smells like... like..." She concentrated a moment with closed eyes: "like Hertfordshire!"

His laughter was the more enjoyable for being profound. "Yes!" he said, when it had subsided. "I suppose it does. More to the point, it smells of you. At least, of you when I first met you... in Hertfordshire, of course. That delicious melding of pears and wild dill and I do not know what else. Intoxication."

She passed the bottle under her nose and inhaled. "It is wonderful."

"It is rather. And it is your very own. Do you see the label there? EBD? Elizabeth Bennet Darcy. Floris will sell it to no one else without your express consent. And the 438 after? The number of mixtures it took before they could achieve the right scent. You would not imagine some of the ghastly aromas I endured sampling for weeks on end until it came together. At last, as my olfactory sense was worn thin, they sent one of their perfumers to spend a week in Hertfordshire – to Meryton in fact – to understand my description. Of course, they did not have you to complete the scenario, but I think in the end it is much as I recall."

He took the bottle from her now and, first dipping the stopper in to coat it, he applied dabs to his wife's pulse at the neck and wrists, taking the time to follow each dab with a soft kiss. "Mmm," he mused in perfect bliss. "Yes, this is quite as I recall."

Lizzy kissed *him* then, well and truly. But after a moment she said, "Now, Mr Darcy, since undoubtedly you commissioned this intoxicating fragrance for your *own* pleasure, where is a gift for *me*?" Her eyes glinted with her teazing. Reluctantly he released her but his enthusiasm was regained as he retrieved the last parcel and held it out to her.

She grazed her fingers over the top lightly, across the name 'Rundell & Bridge," before moving them down to the clasp at the front. Raising the top, she was presented with a necklace in burnished gold resting on an ivory satin cushion. It was fashioned very simply with delicate looping links. In the centre were three perfect teardrop garnets, set a few inches apart, and in between them, rounded diamonds. Accompanying the necklace in the centre of the satiny nest were earrings, each with a diamond round followed by a drop of tear-shaped garnet. The set was exquisite.

"May I, Mrs Darcy?"

Lizzy was uncharacteristically speechless, but she nodded her agreement. Darcy moved around her to hook the clasp at the back, indulging in a few more well-placed kisses in the process, before turning her to him again. She reached up to run her fingers over the gems even as he did and he took her hand in his. "They are perfect for you."

She moved to the mirror above the mantle and gazed at her gift even as Darcy brought her the earrings. As she removed the ones she had been wearing and replaced them with these new drops, Darcy told her that the gems had been his mother's. They had been part of a decorative collar – quite ornate and admirable if you liked the sort of thing – but too old, too fussy for Elizabeth Darcy. And so, he had commissioned them to be reset to reflect his wife's tastes.

"They reflect it *quite* well." Lizzy tilted her head as she studied the necklace, watching the garnets move with her and glint with firelight. "I could not have chosen better."

"Mmm." Darcy sighed heavily, placing his arms around his wife only lightly to avoid disarranging her gown. "Perhaps we should make our way downstairs now, wife... before I am moved to cancel this ball altogether..."

In the event, they did go down, but not before Lizzy thanked Darcy suitably for her adornments. He held her shawl for her as they walked and she pulled on her gloves. "So," she asked, her face alight with joy: "what manner of surprises await us tonight, I wonder!"

CHAPTER EIGHTEEN

5 January 1799 – Twelfth Night

❖❖❖❖❖

AT LAST THE BALL was imminent! Staff once again blended into the walls, labouring out of notice but for smart-liveried footmen at the ready. The house shone bright and welcoming. And most of Pemberley's residents were gathered again in the drawing room, passing the minutes in small conversation until the first carriages bearing guests for the evening would arrive.

It was surprising, given her earlier anxiety for the hour to show itself, that Kitty was not amongst the early arrivals. She and Georgiana were the only ladies yet to show themselves. Glancing around the gathered company, Lizzy thought what a handsome assembly they made – the gentlemen in their dark coats, the only appreciable differences amongst them being in the cut of their collars and the pattern of their waistcoats – and the ladies, with few exceptions, largely in white.

Lady Catherine, of course, was not attired in white; but even Lizzy had to admit that Darcy's aunt wore her widowhood well if without necessity. Still tall and fair-skinned, her appearance was nothing short of dramatic in stark black brocade, with jet beads catching the light here and there. She wore her hair in the fashion of her own day – quite high and full – yet it suited the gown and the woman. If a smile were to draw up her mouth and eyes, she might have power yet to garner an older gentleman's appreciative interest. Her daughter stood with her in sharp contrast wearing a simple blush velvet gown trimmed in Spanish lace – as understated as her mother most assuredly was not.

Alice had indeed worked magic on Olivia Annesley's donated attire. Lizzy would hardly have recognized it had she not known of the arrangement. Jane's open gown had been recut through the neckline to

200

accommodate Mrs Annesley's height and edged in primrose coloured satin to complement a petticoat border of embroidered primrose flowers around the hem which had been used to lengthen the gown. Certainly Mr Wentworth was approving, as he hovered close about the lady.

Jane could draw admiring eyes whether in a shift of burlap or a confection as her current one. Tonight, the barest suggestion of green tint in her gown lent softness to her complexion – she was peculiarly suited to green – and underneath, white silk Lustring to tease the eye as it moved and gleamed in candle light. Bingley's pride in his wife was writ across his face; he gleamed as she did.

As attentive as Wentworth was to the lady of his peculiar interest, Colonel Fitzwilliam rivalled him. His eyes had widened in appreciation when Amelia Chaney entered the room; indeed she looked lovely. Her gown of grey was cut square across the bosom and lent softening with a border of soutache swirls in a deeper sooty shade, this repeated down the edge of the overskirt and matched in hue a ribbon at the waist. A narrow form of the ribbon's twin weaved through her hair, its deeply-hued colour contrasting honey lights in her tresses, and a small dark feather arching low over her knot of curls. And of course, the natural blush upon her cheeks at Fitzwilliam's concerted gaze only enhanced her appeal.

She wears the colours of a bird, observed Lizzy, *and Fitzwilliam assuredly is the hawk this dove has well and truly lured tonight – mourning could seldom prove so attractive an enticement!*

Lizzy sipped at her sherry, wishing to pace herself. It would be a long evening and not yet begun in earnest. She squirmed a bit as she felt movement within her, drawing Darcy's questioning gaze.

"It is nothing," she reassured him with a smile. "Your child merely wonders when supper will be made available."

Darcy's smile was diverted when the door opened – he was, as Lizzy knew, anxious for his first glimpse of his sister in her finery. It was not Georgiana who entered, however, but Kitty.

Lizzy glanced at her sister, then immediately at Jane and Aunt Gardiner in turn to see her own surge of admiration mirrored in their countenances. Kitty appeared every inch a lady! Mr Butler had tamed her thick hair into tight curls atop her head with one long lock dangling down the right side to teaze her shoulder. A cerise-tinted feather rose up from the same shade of bandeau, fluttering as she walked. Her gown in a creamy shade was of a cut to slim and lengthen her form, giving an appearance that concealed the effects of her healthy appetite. She had always favoured rose for her garments and tonight, a net overlay descending from the waist was strewn about with delicate embroidered crimson flowers as though she had picked a handful from a field and then tossed them into the air to land upon her gown haphazardly.

"My dear Catherine, you are very elegant this evening," smiled Bingley as she approached, causing something of a disruption in the overall effect as she giggled and hopped in delight.

"Kitty, did you chance to see Georgiana at all?" asked Lizzy. "It is nearly the hour for our guests to arrive."

"Oh, yes, she is just outside. She tries to get the better of her nerves and was in the passage taking deep breaths when I came along." Kitty's intelligence was useful if somewhat indelicate; but fortunately, only her sisters and their respective husbands were within the hearing of it.

Lizzy looked at Darcy who had already taken Kitty's words. "I will go to escort her," he said. But before he could take two steps, the young lady entered under her own devices; and if those who had come before were resplendent in their full dress, the effect of Miss Darcy's entrance brought gasps from ladies and gentlemen alike.

She entered quietly, tentatively, her head held high more of training and will than of nature as her eyes tried not to settle on any person in particular. Her fingers ran unconsciously across the fringe of her light shawl and her lips were somewhat pursed in hesitancy.

Lizzy followed Darcy's quick glance towards Nathaniel Hewitt to notice that the young man's mouth was open, his eyes fixed in rapture on Georgiana. Darcy himself collected his wits and walked to his sister, linking her arm through his and placing his free hand upon his chest as he whispered something to her. Their smiles mirrored each other, as broad as their countenances would allow and earnest enough to warm the room without want of the fire and myriad candles. Murmurs of approbation were heard around the parlour; and still Nathaniel Hewitt stood transfixed. Finally, Darcy moved to break the enchantment, leading Georgiana to the group he had just departed.

"Gee," smiled Lizzy. "How truly lovely you are!" Georgiana blushed with delight while Kitty giggled on her behalf. Lizzy chuckled to consider that poor Darcy had just begun to reconcile accepting his sister as a woman, only now to encounter her as a most beguiling river sprite!

Georgiana's lithe form was complemented with perfect grace by a gown in the Grecian style of silk tissue shot through with silver threads. Three layers of the delicately sheer argent fabric draped from her high waist to end in differing lengths – an open tier to the knee, then closed at mid-calf and the last ankle-skimming layer curving into a modest train in back – giving it a graceful fall and shimmering movement as she walked. It was trimmed all around in silver as well and tied in front with a silver cord and tassels. Satin slippers peeked out from her hemline and silver armlets adorned her just above the reach of her gloves. Her head was ornamented simply with bandeaus of frosted silver and the only jewellery she wore was the string of lustrous grey pearls her brother so fortuitously had bestowed upon her that afternoon – shown to advantage by her slender, long neck and a bodice cut in a broad curve that was echoed in the sweep of her train. Her grey eyes, surrounded as they were with silver raiment, took on that same bright hue themselves, glinting in the various lights in the room and adding to the sensation that this was an otherworldly nymph just risen from her watery abode and shedding droplets gaily in the sun. She was bewitching.

Fitzwilliam joined their little group now, taking his cousin's arm. "My dear, how very proud am I to claim kinship with you tonight! Why, I doubt I shall be so fortunate as to claim a dance this evening for all the gentlemen who will clamour for your favour."

Georgiana flushed and with utter sincerity objected. "Surely you exaggerate, Retched. But at any rate, I shall be very cross if you do not, for I have set my heart upon dancing with you both." She looked from Fitzwilliam to Darcy, still attached to her other arm, as she said this; bringing from each of them smiling assurances that nothing would induce them to disappoint her desires.

A moment later, with some reluctance, Darcy relinquished his hold on his sister and Fitzwilliam led her off to greet the others in the room, stopping last at the Hewitt brothers. The younger gentleman finally had regained his senses, though still he riveted his gaze upon his lady and, as they began to talk with one another, no observer could doubt that in his mind, he revelled in his good fortune. Even Lady Catherine had nodded in approbation when Georgiana had curtsied a greeting to her.

The resident party now complete, it was only moments before Naismith entered to indicate that the first carriages were arriving. Darcy finished his brandy, Lizzy left behind her half-full sherry glass, and then – collecting Georgiana as they passed – the denizens of Pemberley went out to receive their guests.

CHAPTER NINETEEN

DARCY LED GEORGIANA to their place at the top of the dance while remaining couples filled in the line. He smiled to alleviate her nerves, and if he were honest, his own.   As much as he disliked the spectacle of what they were to embark upon, he felt some relief that it was time to begin; he looked forward to being able to move – even in the slow pattern of a minuet – after standing for an hour receiving his guests and engaging in inane chatter. He surmised Georgiana felt the same.

Lizzy had weathered it, enjoyed it even, far better than he and his sister had done, but even she had sighed happily to see the steady stream of humanity dwindle to a trickle and then cease.   The three of them, as Naismith and Roberts had closed the main doors with an air of finality, had arched their backs to stretch, taken a few deep breaths, and offered each other revitalizing encouragement before joining the revels then in full swing.

Nathaniel Hewitt had hovered patiently in the general vicinity of reception during the entire hour, attempting to appear in happy converse with people from time to time as he surreptitiously maintained a protective eye on his lady. It would seem, with the vagaries of a young, passionate sort of love, that simply to observe the object of his devotion attending to duty admitted of superior pleasure to the gentleman than any other activity to hand. Finally, Darcy had delivered his sister to Nathaniel's eager converse, then allowed himself a foray on the refreshment area for a quickly downed brandy before accepting a glass of sparkling wine from a passing footman and joining the fray.

He had walked round for a few moments to ensure all passed smoothly. Then he had signalled to the musicians who brought to a close the movement they had been playing while the crowds had milled about. With Lizzy at his side once again and Georgiana nearby, he had quieted the room quickly with his resounding voice. He had welcomed them all yet again on behalf of himself and his family, wished all an excellent Twelfth Night of revels, and then declared that the dancing would now begin, causing the room to fill with excited twitters as ladies made to pin up their skirts. By her express request, he refrained from any particular mention of his sister; the significance of the evening for her was known well enough without proclamation of it.

As Darcy had taken Georgiana's hand to lead her to the dance, Fitzwilliam had claimed Lizzy for a partner; they stood nearby in the line, with Mrs Chaney and Wentworth following. Nathaniel Hewitt was now paired with Olivia Annesley – they having made fast friends on their short acquaintance. While the rest of the dancers paired off, Darcy contented himself with gazing across the line at the most important ladies at the ball, and in his life: his wife and sister – gold and silver tonight – equally remarkable to his eyes. He felt no impropriety in giving the much-heralded Darcy pride an airing for the evening.

❖❖❖❖❖

Looking across at Thomas Reavley, Kitty felt both excitement and nerves. Excited that finally the ball had arrived and dancing was about to begin, she felt nearly as if this evening marked her own coming out, although she had been attending assemblies and parties for a few years at home. But tonight felt different, a buzz of excitement humming around her. It was the most exalted ball she had ever been fortunate to attend, and only her second private one; she wanted to miss no detail of it, no dance or conversation, so that she could regale Lydia with every particular when next she wrote to her sister.

When guests had started to arrive, it was all she could do to keep from rushing out to await the arrival of Mr Reavley with his sister and Mr Henshaw, so anxious had she been to present herself to his eye in her finery. Her sister Jane had taken her in hand, counselling that a bit of discretion might yield gratifying pleasure when the gentleman came seeking her out; and so it had proved. Kitty had mingled with the Bingleys until the young vicar entered the ballroom and, seeing her, had made directly for her. He had scarcely eyes or greeting for Jane or Bingley, so concentrated was his attention – and his approving smile – upon Kitty. It gave her a heady rush of feeling.

Yet if she were excited that the moment for dancing was upon them, she also felt nervous as she faced Thomas Reavley, being uncertain if he would pass this test. She so wanted to allow of her attraction to the man, but there were impediments. She had pushed aside the most grievous of these, the facts of his being a vicar and of modest income. *In truth, it could not be less than Wickham's, could it?* Mr Reavley's easy temper and quickness to engage in laughter had allowed of his reprieve, even as at times Kitty little understood the sources of his enjoyment. And he certainly looked handsome in his formal attire, his open countenance anticipating the first notes of music with undisguised relish.

But this last impediment – or rather requisite – would not be overlooked. Could the man dance? He may talk of it with great enthusiasm, but she knew from painful experience at the Meryton assemblies that such eagerness in a partner did not always translate to skill. Yet she did so wish to care for Mr Reavley. She could never love a man who was not accomplished in dancing equal to his enjoyment of it; and now she was about to discover. Of course, these early dances were rather sedate in nature and she wished she had engaged him for one of the country dances after the supper hour when the livelier steps would more surely test his merit; perhaps few would notice if she allowed him to engage her then once more. But if he tripped over his feet now – or worse, over hers – there would be no question of granting another; she might even have to reconsider their engagement for a second one before the supper break! It all hinged on this first – and now the moment had arrived at last!

❖❖❖❖❖

Edward Gardiner eyed his wife and considered what a satisfactory life he led. His business prospered, he enjoyed good health and the wonderful company of friends and relations, and he was most blessed in this woman who stood across from him. Margaret Carswell had been a goodly number of years younger than he, but yet had chosen him over a trio of younger admirers some fourteen years past. She had given him four children, the delight of their lives, suffering with the last a chronic joint malady that now forced limitations upon her exercise. Yet still she retained a sense of humour and her comely figure; and it was the latter which drew forth a smile now as they awaited their first and likely their only dance of the evening. In her simple gown of creamy lutestring, she rivalled many of the ladies present tonight – all of them, to his heart.

She stood now returning his smile with great affection, always a lady eminently sensible yet caring and attentive and capable of cogent discourse on all manner of topics; and Edward was ever grateful that she had singled him out these many years gone to receive her affections. Indeed, in her ball gown tonight and with joy informing her expression for the evening's festivities, she looked to him unaltered from the young woman of twenty he had wed. He made a note in his mind to take her out more of an evening, perhaps a subscription at Drury Lane or the concerts at Vauxhall or Ranelagh.

❖❖❖❖❖

When the line appeared set, Darcy glanced up to the conductor and nodded. Then at the direction of Maestro Martinali, the introductory strains of the minuet began, and the Darcy ball was formally under way. Darcy had still to reconcile that the graceful lady with whom he stepped the bouree and coupee was his gangly, shy little sister. This woman opposite maintained an elegant smile and performed the slow ceremonious movements with consummate grace. Only her eyes, as they met his now and again, displayed less than full assurance, gave a glimpse of his Gee. This new Georgiana was a revelation to be admired.

He was not the only gentleman to take notice, nor was Mr Nathaniel Hewitt, whose eyes strayed up the line to Georgiana whenever the progress of the dance allowed. Many gentlemen standing about the room noted Miss Darcy with admiration. Indeed, Darcy had received remarks from several as the guests had been arriving. He had found himself gritting his teeth in a fixed smile as he listened while her attributes were recited as though she were a thoroughbred at Tattersall's. On more than one occasion, he had been moved to intimate politely that there was every possibility of an established claim upon the lady's affections. He began to find more to appreciate in young Nat Hewitt's ingenuous nature. After all, he had at one time given some consideration of Bingley as a fair match for Georgiana, and Mr Hewitt had something of Bingley's easy temper but it was combined with a studious and steadfast nature uncommon to his youth.

❖❖❖❖❖

As Kitty relinquished Mr Reavley's leading hand to cross in front of him and turn down the outside, she raised her own to her mouth to stifle a giggle and had to concentrate on keeping her promenade stately. She was giddy with joy! Mr Reavley had so far acquitted himself with his dancing prowess that Kitty was sorely tempted to take him up on his former request of all the dances of the evening. What little the vicar lacked in competency of movement he covered well with enthusiasm and he managed to retain his feet. Perfection of form he had not – but neither was he an embarrassment as a partner and Kitty found it well enough. She met him again now and offered her hand once more for the return up the middle, wishing that the music might never end.

"And so, Miss Bennet," addressed Mr Reavley as he took her hand, "I trust my humble abilities cause you no embarrassment?"

"Why, Mr Reavley," she blushed and, noting the glitter of amusement in his eyes, replied, "do you seek reassurance, Sir, or idle flattery?"

"Ha! I suppose I merit such rebuke, but perhaps a little of both." When she did not respond, he added, "Is this the only answer I may expect?"

Kitty started to reply, then stopped, determined to offer a controlled and ladylike reply. She made yet another cast off and then during their final turn together, pronounced: "Your skill is adequate with these slow processions, Mr Reavley. But I shall reserve my judgment until I see for myself if you can dance a reel or a jig."

"Alas, then, that we are not engaged for such a one," he said. "Unless…"

Kitty smiled flirtatiously. "Vexatious, indeed, Mr Reavley; but not, I think, an insurmountable hindrance."

The dance ended and they acknowledged one another, before the strains of the second were struck. As they waited their turn, the gentleman took up the issue once more.

"May I, then, have the happy anticipation of claiming you?" He hesitated only an instant with a smile. "For a country dance, that is?"

"Mr Reavley! Already we are engaged for another before supper – whatever would people say?"

"They would remark only, I am certain, that I am a most fortunate gentleman this evening."

Now a giggle did escape Kitty as they continued without further converse. When the dance ended, they were approached by a gentleman from the local area who requested the next. She accepted and left her vicar with his question yet unanswered but for the smile in her crinkled eyes as she turned away from him.

❖❖❖❖❖

By the time the first of the opening pair ended, Georgiana had relaxed into full enjoyment of the moment. Between light-hearted commentary from her brother and Lizzy as they progressed, and Darcy's assured movements through the steps – he was, after all, a well-schooled dancer despite his preference to abstain as often as he may – Georgiana had managed to forget that the eyes of nearly a hundred people watched her. She relinquished caution, and the silvery sparkle of her filled her features as she took Darcy's hand to step into the second dance of their set.

"Thank you, both," Georgiana giggled spontaneously, looking from Darcy to Lizzy when they had bowed to each other finally as it ended. "That was more to be enjoyed than I had imagined!" Lizzy in turn laughed at the surprise Darcy evinced in having to agree completely.

In the interim while partners were changed, several gentlemen young and not so young looked on, their countenances ill concealing that they sought an opening to request a dance of Miss Darcy. But her brother, glancing over heads, found that of Nathaniel Hewitt nearby and it took only a slight inclination before Nathaniel was at their sides taking Georgiana from her brother. Had the musicians not struck the warning notes of the next set at that moment, one might have heard in the vicinity a collective sigh of lost opportunity.

❖ ❖ ❖ ❖ ❖

"Mrs Darcy?" asked her husband, offering his hand. "Will you honour me, my dear?"

"What! Such a contravention of decorum from you, Sir? You know you cannot dance with your own wife and seek to teaze me."

"Hang decorum," he replied. "I am perfectly in earnest. What silly prohibition finally to find a lady with whom it is not a torture to stand up only to be disqualified for the mere coincidence of having married her." When she only laughed in reply, he added, "Notwithstanding, I have heard no whisperings of disapprobation against Bingley or Mr Gardiner, and they each have danced with their wives. This *is*, after all, a private ball."

"But how much more egregious, Sir, for us to follow their example when we are hosting the evening's entertainments!" she teazed.

Darcy glanced about him. "I can espy no young ladies standing on the side for want of partners now; surely we might be forgiven." His expression took on a glint of mischief. "How if we affect to imagine ourselves strangers?"

Lizzy smiled broadly, the only encouragement required, and Darcy repeated his initial invitation.

"Why, Mr Darcy, I would be delighted if you find you can endure another so soon after the first."

"I shall suffer through, Madam; after all, I must maintain a watchful eye on our young swain here," he added, smiling at Nathaniel Hewitt and Georgiana standing nearby.

"How utterly romantic, Sir!" replied Lizzy with a chuckle. "How could any lady possibly refuse such an elegant and heartfelt proposition?"

The dance began and, as they crossed one another, Darcy said to his partner, "There is *only one* lady present," – and as they crossed again – "to whom I should wish to proffer romantic propositions –"

"Indeed?" countered Lizzy a moment later as they passed yet again. "Do you point her out to me, Sir..." "...I should like to witness the woman who can capture your heart..." "...She must be a great beauty to merit your particular notice!"

"I once was foolish enough to pronounce her merely tolerable, but..."

"...but you revised your opinion?"

"I did; it was not long before..." "...I found myself meditating on the very great pleasure..." "...which a pair of fine eyes in the face of a pretty woman can bestow."

They were separated then, weaving around their neighbours, but as they finally passed again, Darcy said, "In point of fact I believe you to be..." "...well acquainted with the lady..." "...perhaps you might be persuaded to assist me..." "in securing her affections." He paused in his steps to raise her hand to his lips and place a light kiss upon her fingers.

And when they came around yet again, she teazed, "Take care, Sir; such breaches of propriety and under so many eyes..." "...may compel you to marry me."

"Were I not already most unreservedly wed, madam, I should oblige you with alacrity."

❖❖❖❖❖

"Colonel Fitzwilliam," said Mrs Chaney as they moved off for some refreshment after their dance; "it has been some while since I have enjoyed such an evening. Once again I find myself in your debt for arranging my invitation to Pemberley."

"No, no, Mrs Chaney, I will not allow of it. There are to be no debts between us – only contented pleasures arising from the gestures of friends."

She curtsied slightly by way of reply, and he added: "I take satisfaction, Madam, only from having been the *means* of introduction; for I believe you and Elizabeth have found much to form a friendship between you, have not you?"

"Yes, I believe so – I hope for it, certainly. I like Mrs Darcy very much, and her sister, Mrs Bingley. Indeed, I find all your relations delightful."

Fitzwilliam's brows elevated in surprise. "*All?*"

Colour rose into Amelia's cheeks. "I... that is,..." she stumbled; and Fitzwilliam chuckled.

"Madam, I seem to have placed upon you an untenable burden of reply. I withdraw the question."

Her blush deepening, Amelia said only, "I do hope to be afforded opportunity to continue the acquaintances made here, Sir."

"Oh, I think you have little cause to doubt of it." Now the colonel's colour rose to match Amelia's. "I am certain Elizabeth means to further the intimacy," he said with awkwardness.

It was with some relief, perhaps on the part of both, that Colonel Fitzwilliam now was addressed by a gentleman known to him who lived near Buxborough. He asked after the colonel's family and then, upon being introduced to Mrs Chaney, engaged her for the next dance – undoubtedly, his aim from the start in approaching them. Fitzwilliam watched her departure with a reminder to himself not to proceed too hastily.

❖❖❖❖❖

The Darcys had been petitioned by a local squire to submit to his daughter's talents and had passed the last minutes duly admiring Miss Kingsbury's self-accompanied vocals. The young woman did possess a certain charm in her singing with, sadly, little else to recommend her person, resembling perhaps too much her father in face and form. Fortunately for her, however, she was Sir Robert Kingsbury's only heir and with eight thousand pounds outright upon her marriage she enjoyed a share of local suitors. Having now discharged their compliments, Lizzy and Darcy were returning to the ballroom when they happened upon Georgiana with Edmund Hewitt.

"What! You do not dance?" Darcy asked his sister. "Surely you do not lack for partners! I would not believe it."

"Indeed she does not," replied his friend. "I partnered her myself for the last, and must take the fault for depriving her further."

"Nonsense," said Georgiana. "Mr Hewitt has been kind enough by my request to walk out here with me to find some calm."

"Do you not enjoy your first ball?" asked her brother.

"Oh, yes! It is wonderful, Fitz! And much as I might have dreamt it to be. I find it all a bit overwhelming, if truth be told, and require only a moment to take a breath."

Finding within himself little argument against such feelings, Darcy left his sister to her respite and took his friend off for a stout drink while Lizzy remained with Gee. When she pronounced herself ready to return, they walked together companionably, making use of the ongoing dance to observe others as they went.

Seeing Mrs Annesley, Gee asked Lizzy, "You do not mind that I wrote to my companion and caused her early return?"

"Not a bit. It was perfectly reasonable that you did so." She glanced over at the lady smiling at Henry Wentworth. "I dare say from appearances, neither does *she* mind. I am certain that the question of Mrs Annesley's future has been taken from our hands."

"Yes, I believe I have lost my companion, or will do soon." Georgiana's expression momentarily clouded.

"You may well have to make do in the future with only me, I fear. Will I suffice, do you think?"

"Of course!" Georgiana replied immediately. "In truth, I suppose I do not need Mrs Annesley any more. You are my sister! It is only that I have grown fond of her in these two years and rely upon her good sense."

"That is to be expected, Gee, and quite natural. But you need not lose your friendship with Mrs Annesley. As Mr Wentworth and your Nathaniel are great friends, it falls within reason still you will meet each other from time to time." She paused a moment as a thought occurred to her. "I do hope she does not marry too soon. We rather relied upon her seeing you through the spring and summer in town."

"I can postpone another year."

"No. She will not forsake you, nor will we. With your brother, and Mrs Annesley, you will be well able to enjoy your season. And do not forget Fitzwilliam and perhaps Mrs Chaney as well. Surely Mr Wentworth will not act so quickly. Perhaps he too will choose to enjoy a season." She laughed to think of it. "You may be required to act the chaperone yourself!"

"Do you think so?"

Lizzy laughed again, but then considered it. "Perhaps it could work to your advantage, my dear. I am certain that Nathaniel will correspond with his friend during his journeys. What better way to secure word of him now and again than to have Mr Wentworth at hand."

This notion held considerable appeal to the younger woman, and she contemplated the prospect still when the dance ended. As another took form, Georgiana was claimed by Mr Bostwick and went off with him in good spirits while Elizabeth happily accepted Mr Henshaw.

❖❖❖❖❖

Until the musicians put down their instruments for the break, it seemed dancing was the order of the day. The line had formed so consistently long that in excess of twenty minutes was taken up in moving down it completely. But it was readily apparent by the chattering both within the lines and on the sides watching that a fine evening was being passed by all.

As they broke for supper, Lizzy noted Lady Catherine entering the dining room with an air of complacency. She must have done well at the card tables. She was in the company of two older gentlemen, Sir James and another unknown to Lizzy, but who was subsequently proved to be an acquaintance of long standing from the area. The three engaged in lively discourse and remained together for their refreshment.

Others came and went bearing varying selections of food but all, upon encountering Mrs Darcy, offering her laudatory remarks upon the evening. Lizzy sighed; although she knew that this evening had been well planned, still it was her first of such magnitude and a relief to have it underway with no mishaps. Before she followed her nose to the sideboards for some supper of her own, she made a mental note to commend Mrs Reynolds and the staff in the morning.

❖❖❖❖❖

As Kitty stood watching Thomas Reavley make his way through the room, she felt a light hand move around her waist.

"My dear, you are looking very gay tonight. I trust the evening has met your expectations?" said her sister.

"Oh, Jane! Is not this the most perfect ball ever to be held?"

"I dare say every ball receives such acclamation until the next comes along," Jane replied with a laugh. "I do not doubt, however, the attentions of a certain vicar have served to elevate this particular revel in your estimation."

There could be no purpose in denial even had Kitty desired to hide her preference for Mr Reavley; the lie of it would be as quickly uncovered by her countenance when he reappeared a few moments hence. "Still," she replied, in fact ignoring what required no answer, "I cannot believe Lydia has ever seen any thing half so elegant for all her affairs!"

"No, I expect not. But Kitty, must you be so pleased to think so? Do you even now compete with your sister so much?" Jane looked somewhat disquieted at the thought. Given their order and years of birth, it had been natural that Jane and Elizabeth had paired in friendship early on, their well complemented tempers supported their close attachment even as more sisters arrived. Mary had come next after, but despite being barely a year older than Catherine, it was the younger Lydia to whom Kitty had become attached, Mary always something of a force of her own and seemingly quite content in her own interests.

Kitty and Lydia had become inseparable very early on. Though Lydia was younger by two years, she was the more assertive of the pair and had quickly established superintendence of the girls' activities, Kitty following along in both frivolity and trouble. Yet always – though their mutual affection was real enough – there had existed a tacit rivalry between the two, each marking triumphs over the other even as they maintained their closeness: every Assembly declared for the one or other who had danced more often, every compliment to a newly trimmed bonnet tallied, extra marks for which first learnt a new bit of gossip. When Lydia had been invited over her sister to accompany Mrs Forster to Brighton, Kitty had been inconsolable for long weeks. Even Lydia's subsequent elopement had been jealously viewed as a great adventure rather than the danger it had truly been. And the loss of her daily companion to an early marriage and removed to the wilderness of Newcastle had been a punishment to poor Kitty. She felt it sorely for months after, until her elder sisters had taken her into their homes and under some care for her sensibilities.

Jane believed Kitty to have made much progress, despite Lydia's hastily scrawled letters boasting openly of the excitements of life in a regiment. Yet here she was, once more pairing her experiences against those of her sister. "Can you not appreciate your good fortune now without making comparison?" she asked.

"Yes, of course," said Kitty. "I only meant..." She stopped to consider the formulation of her speech, screwing up her face in concentration in the process. "It is only, that tonight has been so full of wonder. I have never before seen such finery, nor felt so... so... singularly happy. And it has crossed my mind to consider, that my sister – for all her haste in marrying Wickham – has not the chance to take pleasure in such things. I want to write to her at once and describe every detail of the ball, even as I feel perhaps I should not."

"Dear Kitty, of course you may write to her of the ball, she will wish to hear it. Only do not attempt to outshine her – simply tell her of your enjoyment, of how you feel tonight, and that will be enough for her to share in your joy."

"I suppose." As they spoke, they could see Mr Reavley beginning to wend his way back towards them with glasses of punch.

"On a happier note, you and Mr Reavley certainly are attentive to one another. Do you well heed that the gentleman's designs may be serious in nature?"

"I do believe they are, Jane." Kitty's voice expressed wonder and trepidation.

"And do you think in like manner?"

"I do not know. I have been trying to form, all this night in odd moments, an image of myself maintaining a parsonage, and I am uncertain I can do so. But I *do* like him, Jane, and I should hate to think of his caring about anyone but *me*."

"My dear, a house is a house, be it a parsonage or a grand manor or a cottage on a farm. It is made a *home* by the strength of feeling that inhabits it. Consider your affections for Mr Reavley, your respect and admiration for him, and his in return for you. If they are such as to warrant uniting with him, the rest will follow. One is not *born* to be a vicar's wife, nor a clerk's nor shopkeeper's wife, nor a soldier's wife for that matter. Only find where your heart resides, and then follow after it." She smiled at her sister before adding to the gentleman who now had nearly reached them. "Mr Reavley, you have great fortitude to brave the throng. My own Mr Bingley went in search of punch ages ago, it seems, and has been lost in the wars."

"Not so, Mrs Bingley," the vicar laughed. "Indeed, I encountered him in a knot of revellers and we wended our way to the punch bowl together; he follows close behind."

Even as Reavley indicated it, Bingley emerged from behind a small party and made his way towards them. Jane, smiling with particular meaning at her sister, took her leave and went to meet her husband.

❖❖❖❖❖

Joining Fitzwilliam and Amelia for her repast, Lizzy said, "I have barely had a moment all evening to engage with a familiar face, I dare say I may be excused doing so now."

"Dear Elizabeth," said the Colonel, "look about you. Your guests hardly appear neglected. You are most welcome to our company for a few moments without grudge."

They spoke amiably of the evening so far, Amelia recounting humorously a dance with an unknown gentleman where she feared for her delicate slippers, looking about her as she spoke in a low voice to ensure neither the offending party nor any but her two friends was within hearing. Fitzwilliam had given up on the dancing after the first four and relegated himself to admiring his friends from the ranks.

"Oh, but you must dance after supper," said Lizzy, "at the very least the Boulanger."

"Only if Mrs Chaney will oblige me for it," he replied with a glance at the lady, who cast her eyes down, but replied that she would be delighted.

On that happy promise, Fitzwilliam then excused himself, indicating that he had espied someone with whom he must have speech. The ladies' sidelong glances as he walked away would leave little doubt in any observer's mind of what topic their own discourse would consist now in his absence.

"Have you any news of note to share?" Lizzy asked lightly, her eyes following her cousin's route to where his aunt rested.

A small pout formed as Amelia said, "No. Indeed, although I should not expect it, yet I confess to some disappointment in his silence on the matter." She smiled then, her face reanimating: "But I find myself most content at the restoration of our friendship. I shall not yet think beyond this pleasure."

"Amelia, do you know..."

❖❖❖❖❖

Georgiana Darcy entered the supper room with Mr Bostwick, a gentleman of some thirty years who stayed on an adjacent estate with his uncle, Mr Grantham. He had somehow contrived to secure the last dance before the break, earning in the act the happy duty to escort Miss Darcy in to supper. One glance at his expression as they made their way through the party would suffice to convince any observer that he would make the most of this exalted responsibility; he intended to cede his position to no one!

He flattered himself that the lively discourse in which he had engaged the lady during their dancing had delighted Miss Darcy even as much as himself. No matter that it was one-sided, she offering little by way of reply to his clever quips. He rather appreciated a timid woman and had no qualms at thought of taking one to wife – it would bode well for a quiet

215

home without discord, no shrill carping after late nights out – and her handsomeness of face and figure would certainly offer him pleasures and the envy of his friends in town. Perhaps a little tall for fashion, but that could be accommodated by encouraging her to remain seated when possible. Surely the maid would have been well schooled also in the art of managing a home; these were all he could desire coupled with an intimate association (hard to come by in town) with Mr Darcy. From the connexion he might even secure a membership to Brooks's.

And of course, Miss Darcy's endowment should be most welcome, give him quite a leg up amongst his cronies. What an opportunity had befallen him when he had grudgingly agreed to spend the Christmas season with his uncle! He could be well on his way with Miss Darcy before she ever arrived in town for the season. Perhaps he should prolong his stay under his uncle's roof to secure greater advantage; it could not hurt to show a dutiful side to the old bore, along with the enticements to be found by calling upon his neighbours at Pemberley.

He believed himself an excellent candidate for the girl. He held a modest house in town, had at present no more debts than any of his acquaintance, and every expectation of inheriting the old pile of bricks a few miles distant from his Uncle Grantham – though it would not be so large as it was now (damned death duties). He was an excellent gentleman of whom no one would speak a word against his character – his friends would never dare if they were to hold any hope of his influence once he was established. He was old enough to have spent his capricious nature – or at least the worst of it – and well up to the task of instructing this young thing to be a proper wife. A thin smile followed on the thought that he could quite fancy that task.

Such were the gentleman's thoughts as the couple established themselves at a place at table. Imagine, then, the blow to his vanity when, not a moment after they had been seated, they were by Miss Darcy's own animated entreaty joined by a group of her friends as they passed: a Miss Bennet who was entirely too giggly for Bostwick's taste but whom he must tolerate with good will as being established to him as sister to Mrs Darcy; a Mrs Annesley, a woman of his own years who appeared without benefit of a Mr Annesley – in short, of little consequence; and two young gentlemen upon whom Miss Darcy immediately proffered (to Mr Bostwick's annoyance) a gay smile of welcome.

The first, the vicar Reavley, offered no consternation to Mr Bostwick; he was of little import as well. Obviously, he was smitten with Miss Bennet and welcome to her. But the other, Mr Hewitt! – there lay trouble. Having little to recommend him to Mr Bostwick's fastidious eye, the pup nevertheless had some small claim upon Miss Darcy's affections, that much was clear. He must discourage this friendship.

While they supped – he with approval noting that Miss Darcy ate little – Mr Bostwick attempted to isolate his lady's attentions through constant discourse, priding himself yet again in his ability to talk much of nothing. But despite his efforts, Miss Darcy took every lull in his speech as leave to turn herself towards the puppy Hewitt across the way with some question or observation. Most unsatisfactory; she would require some tutelage after all in paying proper respect.

"Ahem," said Mr Bostwick after one such desertion; "as I was saying, Miss Darcy..."

"Mr Bostwick! I trust you have found supper to your satisfaction?"

The gentleman rolled his eyes before looking behind him at this latest interruption to see none other than the owner of Pemberley himself. *Ah*, he thought as he smiled to his host, *Miss Darcy cannot fail to notice how her brother singles me out with solicitude.*

"Indeed, Mr Darcy, I am certain there is no finer to be had short of travelling to town."

"And you have supped then enough for your satisfaction?"

"I am well sated, Sir." Mr Bostwick's eyes gleamed at being so graciously regarded.

"Then perhaps, Sir, as you have completed your repast, you will allow me to extract you from your pleasant company to attend your uncle?"

"My... my uncle?"

"Indeed, Sir. He wishes to use profitably the happy assemblage of all parties this evening to discuss the acreage on offer, and cannot imagine doing so absent *your* counsel."

"Oh! er..." Disgruntled at losing his valued place at Miss Darcy's side, still Mr Bostwick could be seen to refuse neither his uncle nor his intended's brother. He, therefore, at once acquiesced and rose with a smarmy apology to the lady and an assurance to atone later for his present desertion to duty. As Mr Bostwick accepted his host's gesture to precede him on their way, Darcy turned to look back at his sister, smiled – and winked.

❖❖❖❖❖

Fitzwilliam approached his aunt as she sat alone in the side dining area, Sir James having that moment left to procure tea for them. It was the first instance the Colonel had espied her unaccompanied this evening. "Lady Catherine." He bowed.

"Fitzwilliam." She looked at him with suspicion, but nodded when he asked permission to join her for a moment.

"Madam," he began. "My conscience prickles me, Aunt, and I find I must go against your wishes once more."

Lady Catherine who had, until this instant, worn an air of contentment, now set her face stubbornly, uncertain as to his purpose but prepared to dislike it nonetheless. Did he mean to refuse yet again the bequest she had outlined that afternoon, even with no obligation on his part? And did he seek to do so here, amongst a crowd, in order to stem any quarrel in the matter? In an instant, she decided that if he was fool enough to reject her latest terms, she would be finished with him; he was no relation of hers, and she would not forbear to apprise him of it, regardless of who might overhear the rebuke.

"Say what you must then, nephew." Her voice was cool.

"I simply, Aunt, cannot accept your generous settlement of this afternoon," he began and, as her lips drew together and her eyes narrowed, he added, "without offering deep and heartfelt gratitude." This stopped her immediately, and she only stared at him. "I know you do not wish for such an outpouring, but I find myself unable to proceed without expressing what your largesse will mean to me."

"I know very well what it will mean to you," she replied, but much of the edge had left her voice. "Your gratitude, however, is misdirected; you have not me to thank, but my daughter. It was Anne who petitioned for such a disposition, and for her sake alone that I acquiesced." She tried to maintain an attitude of indifference, but a glint in her eye belied disinterest.

"I shall convey my appreciation to my cousin as well. Nonetheless," he replied, "please accept my gratitude, on my own behalf and that of any children to come."

She nearly smiled at this before fixing a frown. "If Anne had not become so stubborn in her refusal to marry, you should not have won such a prize from me. Do not believe I understand your own reason, nor that I have fully excused you. I have found very much displeasure in your deportment. It will be long before I might forgive it. But I would have Rosings remain with the family." She did smile now, grudgingly.

Noting this, jovially he said, "You cannot fool me, you old *dragon*!" – drawing a gasp from the lady – "You have a heart in you, and I will not allow you to hide it in this matter."

For one instant, she looked to take him to task for his insolent epithet. But then, smirking – perhaps even enjoying the parallel he had drawn – she relented. "You have salved your conscience and spoken your thanks. I will hear no further of it hereafter. Just get on with it, will you? The *dragon* wishes to see a proper heir to Rosings before she passes from this earth!"

CHAPTER TWENTY

THE ORCHESTRA reconvened after supper as guests began to move yet again into the ballroom. The crowd had decreased by a third or more, a number of people who had danced early now opting for the more sedate atmospheres of the card or social rooms. As dancers began to arrange themselves, Lizzy's gaze moved up the line. There was Edmund Hewitt with Olivia Annesley while Henry Wentworth's partner was a dull lady from a neighbouring estate beside them.

Kitty and Georgiana had circumvented the prohibition against dancing too often with their suitors – they formed a set with Jane and Bingley; Kitty partnering Bingley while Gee obliged Thomas Reavley and Jane graced Nathaniel Hewitt's arm. Lizzy smiled indulgently at the successful contrivance.

Of mild surprise as Lizzy passed them by was the sight of Anne deBourgh awaiting the striking of the music, paired with her cousin Fitzwilliam, while her companion stood next to her and across from Mr Henshaw. Lizzy had never seen Anne so lively; she had danced already with Sir James earlier in the evening. Her lightened spirit apparently did her constitution good as well.

But the biggest surprise of the evening came to Lizzy when her perusal reached the top of the set. The very same Sir James stood elegantly, his attention towards his partner across the line – Lady Catherine deBourgh in haughty splendour. As the music was struck and the lead couple began their steps, a voice at Lizzy's side came. "This season can produce extraordinary surprises, can it not?"

Lizzy threaded her arm through Margaret Gardiner's, squeezing it with affection as she did so. "Indeed," she laughed, "I might have believed myself indulging in fantastical visions, did not you affirm what my eyes tell me!"

"Perhaps these two will renew their former friendship?"

"Mmm, perhaps; though I rather like Sir James too well to wish it for him."

"Lizzy," chided her aunt, "you said yourself Lady Catherine had capitulated to her daughter's wishes and been generous to Colonel Fitzwilliam. Is it not possible Sir James has recalled for the lady a pleasanter time of life?"

"I cannot believe it so. I still must wonder at her submission this afternoon. There was some agency at work there, but I doubt it to have been Sir James." Lizzy glanced now at Anne, screwing up her face in consideration of her delicate cousin as the introductory notes sounded to initiate the country dances. She recalled her earlier conversation with Darcy wherein he had ascribed credit to Anne. This made her realise that she had not seen her husband in her wanderings for some little while.

"Where is Darcy?" Lizzy asked idly to herself as her eyes scanned the room.

"What is that, dear?" asked Aunt Gardiner.

"Oh, it is nothing. I am simply wondering where my husband has hidden himself away."

"Ah. I saw him not long past leaving the supper room with two gentlemen."

Even as Lizzy considered this information, Darcy entered the ballroom with said gentlemen and, a moment later, separated from them and came upon his wife.

"I have just concluded a satisfactory arrangement," Darcy said after Aunt Gardiner had taken herself off, having spotted her friend Mrs Kettering.

"Mr Darcy! Have you been conducting business at your own fete?"

"I confess myself guilty of the charge, Madam," he replied and then, to stave off the rebuke he saw forming in Lizzy's eyes, he hastened to add: "but I have most excellent reason in my defence."

"What reason?"

"That of service to my sister."

"To your sister!" Lizzy's countenance was marked by dubiety. "I have just witnessed you enter with Mr Grantham, Darcy. Surely you do not mean to tell me you bargained yourself his property for Gee's benefit!"

"I most certainly *shall* tell you so and, what is more, it was no bargain." He noted his wife's strained belief. "Do you recall introduction to Mr Grantham's nephew?"

"Mr Bostwick? – I warrant he considers himself quite the dandy."

"So he does. And this dandy was intent upon monopolising Gee's attentions at supper. Mr Grantham kindly called my notice to his nephew's efforts and *more* kindly outlined Mr Bostwick's character to me. He then hinted that as his nephew believes (quite erroneously) he will inherit from Grantham, he might demonstrate personal interest in the business of property transference."

"And you used such business to lure Mr Bostwick away from Georgiana."

"I did." He paused an instant before asking, "Am I to be forgiven?"

"I shall take the matter under advisement." She smiled now. "But why did the business yield no bargain? Did you not tell me Mr Grantham was somewhat desperate to gain any capital?"

"I did and he is. However, the old gentleman had done me a service and I reciprocated. I repaid his kindly meant caveat by allowing him to negotiate a selling price less than asked but higher than I had previously intended to settle. He is a candid and honourable man, which is more than may be said for the sycophantic nephew."

"Mr Darcy, such a spendthrift. What ever shall I do with you?"

"Madam, I can conjure manifold possibilities." He smirked and arched his brows.

"None of which are likely if you do not restore my good graces by going at once to mingle with your guests."

"Then, Madam, I take my leave of you... with anticipation."

Lizzy smiled after him a moment before making her way to the parlour.

❖❖❖❖❖

Sir James bowed to his partner as the last notes receded, their sound replaced by a hum of renewed conversation all about. As he stepped forward then, he said, "You are not so changed as I have thought, Lady Catherine – yet as sharp at your games and as accomplished in your steps."

"To age altered eyes, perhaps," she replied with a hint of smile. "It has been long since I have joined in a dance. One does, of course, reclaim well-interned patterns when warranted; good schooling allows of it. But neither of us moves with the same vigour of youth we once owned. To say else is mere flattery."

Unfazed, Sir James laughed. "And nor should we!" he exclaimed. "I shall leave hopping and skipping to those with the breath for it. But it does my soul well now and again to embark upon the exercise."

"Hmmph," she said.

They began to walk away together from the line as it re-formed.

"When do you return to Kent, Madam?"

"We proceed on Monday. My business here having been concluded, I see no reason to prolong the visit."

"...but for the felicity of family, surely."

This earned him another 'hmmph' by way of reply, and he redirected his comments. "I return Monday as well to Albion House, to conclude my own business of a sort."

Lady Catherine said nothing to suggest further interest in the nature of his business, yet he continued.

"I dare say I shall be established in town by spring if I soon set an agent to seek a modest house there."

At this, Lady Catherine stirred. "You must take caution, Sir, to use a reputable agent. Too many there are who seek to line their own pockets while you are persuaded to lease property of an inferior ilk."

Sir James chuckled. "Perhaps you can recommend a suitable one?"

"Indeed. I will write to him forthwith with an introduction. He will see you well situated in proper rooms and an acceptable location if you call upon him thereon."

"And when I am settled," he replied after proffering an acknowledgment, "perhaps you will dine with me, you and Miss deBourgh, when you journey to town."

"Anne seldom travels," she replied, giving Sir James to believe that the end of it. But as they entered the main parlour and he drew up a chair alongside the one Lady Catherine had selected, she said: "but I travel to town on the odd occasion and would not gainsay an evening of dinner and cards..."

The gentleman bowed and seated himself.

❖❖❖❖❖

Lizzy came upon Anne deBourgh in the music room, listening indifferently to a young woman at the pianoforte.

"You are alone?" Lizzy asked in some surprise, taking a seat adjacent to Anne's fireside chair.

"For the moment," Anne replied. "Fitzwilliam has only just deposited me here and gone to find Frances so that we may retire. I hope I do not offend by withdrawing when she arrives."

"Not at all. I am delighted that you have felt equal to this much of the evening."

"Oh, Elizabeth, I cannot tell you when I last enjoyed myself as much!"

A bit taken aback by her vehemence, nonetheless Lizzy simply smiled in reply before teazing, "I did note you dancing on occasion."

"So I did. But this last with Richard pressed my limits, I own. I was obliged to withdraw before the second, poor man."

"I am certain he was happy to oblige if you were fatigued."

"Yes – he only sought me out, I think, from some misguided debt of gratitude. He need not have done – it is I who am grateful."

"How so?"

Anne smiled in suspicious humour. "You must know my relief at being spared marriage, even with my amiable cousin."

"But it always lay in your power to refuse, Anne; and as I understand, you did so in your way."

"I suppose. But if Fitzwilliam had succumbed to my mother immediately, I doubt I would have had the wherewithal to refuse. I am beholden to his lengthy deliberation, and to *you* of course."

"To *me*! Why ever should you credit *me*?" Lizzy could only imagine her reception by Darcy's aunt in future if she should be blamed for Anne's sudden rebellion, though in truth the thought made her smile.

"For informing me at the start. Had I been surprised by an offer with no previous intelligence, I am certain to have done Mama's bidding; and if Richard had declined her immediately, I may have faced another and more intolerable suitor soon after to accept without a will. But there is more than that for which I owe you credit."

"I cannot imagine it so."

"You are a woman of courage, Elizabeth. I have known this – I have seen you stand well in the face of my mother on several occasions – but I also learnt from your sister Catherine of your bravery in another guise."

Lizzy clearly had no idea to what Anne referred until she added, "*You* turned down a marriage against all prevailing reason, did not you?"

Lizzy was startled before growing miffed at Kitty. Recalling their converse some two days prior concerning her early refusal of Darcy, she was certain she had made herself clear that it was not to be discussed further. How much worse for Darcy if somehow Lady Catherine were to hear of it.

While her thoughts thus formed, Anne said, "When I heard that you refused Mr Collins, against your family's wishes and when marrying him could secure your future, I could only admire such adherence to principle."

Lizzy felt relief to find that *this* was Anne's secret knowledge. Except for care of Charlotte's feelings, she could not concern herself so much as to Mr Collins's vanity as with her husband's sensibilities. Though still she should caution Kitty as to her loose tongue, she forgave her instantly for this lesser indiscretion.

"I did not consider it an act of bravery, Anne, so much as ordinary sense," she chuckled. "I simply found it impossible to imagine that either of us could make the other happy."

"Precisely. When it was to all material advantage to you to accept and urged by your own mother, still you would not. How much more should I have been able to do the same then. And by your example, I had resolved I *would* do so – did, in fact, speak with Richard – and was by that happy fate spared confronting Mama when his own decision was made known."

Lizzy smiled now, placing her hand atop Anne's in sympathy. Only a few seconds on, however, she could not help but say, "Yet surely you did speak up for yourself with your mother. I cannot believe what she divulged to us this afternoon to be wholly of her own devising."

Anne's blush confirmed her hand in Lady Catherine's strange bequests, though she said nothing.

"I must confess at some wonder in how you persuaded such concessions," coaxed Lizzy, little certain of the extent of Anne's design.

The blush deepened, and Anne fidgeted in her seat such that Lizzy withdrew her own hand and sat back. But after a moment, Anne looked at her and smiled timidly. "I am ashamed to say I resorted to trickery," she admitted.

"Trickery!" Lizzy could not imagine anyone less susceptible to such devices than Darcy's aunt, nor one less suited than Anne to employing them.

"Yes. I suppose you know – that my cousin has told you – of the absurd notion my mother held of Frances, Mrs Jenkinson, and myself?" If possible, her colouring underwent yet another darkening. "I may have intimated to Mama that if I were forced into a marriage, such relations were bound to be introduced to society's rumination. I presumed she would rather such speculations be avoided."

Lizzy burst out in laughter at the preposterous notion that Anne had applied extortion to her mother, but then realised from Anne's own quiet laugh that she had not been in jest. "You..." she began; "you truly wrested your bidding from her in this manner?"

Anne only looked down at her lap now, embarrassed at her confession. "You will not tell Mama that you know?"

"I assure you, Anne, I will not. But may I say that my paltry courage pales beside your display." Laughing now, she added, "You most certainly did –"

Whatever Lizzy would have said was surrendered to the approach then of Fitzwilliam and Mrs Jenkinson whereby the latter immediately took charge of her companion and they bid Lizzy a good night. As Anne rose to leave, she pressed Lizzy's hands in complicity, her eyes dancing in a knowing smile.

"Lizzy?" Elizabeth glanced up to see Fitzwilliam with his arm extended to her. "Do you return to the ballroom, my dear?"

Realizing she had been contemplating Anne's revelation, Lizzy stood and took the proffered arm, smiling as she did so and keeping to herself a thought that Fitzwilliam, had he in fact accepted his aunt's initial proposition, may just have gotten more than he could realise in Anne deBourgh. Certainly it was to his cousin largely that he now enjoyed an easier match with Amelia Chaney. Lizzy could hardly await the opportunity to tell Darcy what she had learnt.

❖❖❖❖❖

"Have you been engaged, Madam, for the next dance?"

Amelia Chaney hesitated. Colonel Fitzwilliam had already partnered her earlier in the evening and exacted a promise for the last dance as well; was he now to ask her again for this? It was true that she was little known amongst most of the guests tonight, but still she felt some unease. What would people think of her? She had been persuaded easily to succumb to dancing for its being a private ball and appropriate for the night at hand, and there was no denying she had enjoyed the brief freedom of such activity with several partners for the first sets. But she had considered that following supper she might behave more becoming of her circumstance for the remainder of the night.

Whether it had been his design all along or whether he read something of Amelia's thoughts in her countenance, the Colonel saved her the onus of an awkward decision. "I thought perhaps to take some air," he said, gesturing towards the balcony. "If you are not previously engaged —"

"Oh!" she replied. "Yes, Sir, I should like that. The press of revellers seems to have grown again, has it not?"

"A veritable crush," he agreed as he steered them towards the nearest window opening.

"Mr and Mrs Darcy are well endowed with friends."

"I dare say they are," he said as they stepped out of doors, escaping the crowd. "Most are such as would never presume to call on Pemberley tomorrow, nor will they. They reside in the area, were invited as a seasonal nod, and accepted with alacrity in rabid curiosity to view the house and rub shoulders with its residents. But they will happily retreat along with their hired carriages to virtual anonymity in the early hours."

"I wonder that your own family did not attend."

"Ah, yes. They were invited, it is certain; but my father entertains his own party, notwithstanding which my aunt's presence likely lent the convenience of such excuse an added gravity."

Amelia felt unsure how to respond until she noted the broad smile upon Fitzwilliam's face.

"Have they always been so... at odds, with one another?" she asked.

225

"As long as I have lived," he replied. "I am uncertain what caused their estrangement, though my cousin may well have hit upon a reasonable prospect just of late. But it was not always so – my father and his brother and sisters were very closely aligned in their youth; the Fitzwilliam sense of family has long been held sacrosanct."

They walked slowly as they spoke, passing others who had braved the night air. "There are four siblings?"

"*Were*, yes. Now only my father and Lady Catherine remain."

Enlightenment rose in Amelia's face. "Oh, yes. Mr Darcy's mother was a sister, was not she?"

"She was. Lady Anne died when I was a young man, nearly fourteen years it has been. A blow to the family – Georgiana was in the nursery still, a toddler, and Darcy away at school when his mother took ill. I do not think my uncle ever recovered from her loss. He was very much taken with his wife."

"Was she much like Lady Catherine?"

"Good Lord, no!" he laughed. They had made their way to the end of the balcony now, and stopped near a warming brazier. Fitzwilliam assisted Amelia in arranging her shawl before he leaned upon the stone balustrade and looked out over the park as it lay softly illuminated from lanterns recurrently sprinkled throughout.

"Now as I think on it, perhaps I am too severe in judgment. Certainly they *appeared* as sisters. But Lady Anne was of softer features as well as softer disposition – in fact, Georgiana tonight bears much resemblance to her." He smiled at his memories. "Both Gee and Darcy took after her in many ways, though outwardly Darcy favours his father. But Lady Anne was very well contained within herself, one might say, content to live quietly in understated elegance. She always was more inclined to listen than to lecture, that was one difference from her sister. Then again, she had a stubborn streak when pushed, I recall, and on the occasions it showed itself, the likeness to Lady Catherine was more profound." He laughed.

"And the brother, your uncle?"

"Charles, the youngest of them and best loved universally, I think. I never knew him. He died before I was born, an incident involving runaway horses crossing the path of his curricle, no doubt being driven too fast. Something of an adventurer, as I have heard; never far from trouble as a youth. My father long has avowed that my uncle passed his propensity for trouble on to me! We are by all accounts much alike in temperament."

"Then he must indeed have been very engaging," Amelia said without thought, "and well loved!"

Fitzwilliam looked at her directly now, as she heard her own words and turned violently pink.

❖❖❖❖❖

"Are you acquainted with Castleton, Mrs Annesley – perhaps you passed through it on some occasion?"

"I have not been so fortunate, Mr Wentworth. But Miss Darcy has spoken to me of its charms."

"Ah," he laughed. "Yes! I do believe, however, that for Miss Darcy, the greatest of its charms was young Hewitt there."

"It does appear to have served an auspicious purpose in the course of love," she replied, glancing towards Georgiana who, though she danced at present with a gentleman from a local manor, was never out of view of Nathaniel Hewitt who was standing near the line with his brother.

"So it does!" Something in his tone brought Olivia Annesley's eyes back to Henry Wentworth's to find them smiling warmly at her. "Although, to be precise, Mr Hewitt himself was only stopping at the time from other parts. But the village has still charms of, may I say, more local and long standing a nature."

"I must believe so at your word, Sir, until an opportunity to judge for myself arises."

The smile accompanying her words was enough to spur Mr Wentworth to a bold suggestion. "Perhaps you might make a short call there – as my guest at the inn, of course – before you remove to town... with Miss Darcy." As he noticed her eyes widen at this, though devoid of alarum, he added, "I will of course offer all the protection of my person to two unescorted ladies in such wild country."

Now Olivia laughed delightedly. "But who, Sir, might protect us from *you*?"

"Madam, you injure me!" he cried, but the merry twinkle in his eyes belied his words. "I should be the very soul of gentlemanly propriety, I assure you."

Before Mrs Annesley could respond, the attentions of lady and gentleman alike were drawn to something of a stir making its way in their general direction.

❖❖❖❖❖

Fitzwilliam, displaying an unthinking lack of gentlemanly decorum, laughed at Amelia's discomfort, so high did his heart soar at her ingenuous remarks. This only resulted in the lady's colour being enriched further as she turned from him to divert her gaze to the dim landscape. With her face thus positioned away from his, Fitzwilliam could not see her smile under the blush.

Now cognizant of his lapse in gallantry, the Colonel said, "I seem continually to be seeking your forgiveness, Madam. I assure you my mirth proceeds from enjoyment of your company rather than any desire to make sport of you." He smiled contritely to assuage her embarrassment only to adopt the condition himself.

Amelia glanced away once more but as her colour faded, her smile intensified.

"Surely you know," he continued, glancing about him to note that they were alone on the balcony, all others having gone indoors curious of some slight spectacle playing out there; "you must know, Mrs Chaney... Amelia... the joy I take from our friendship. Indeed, I hope one day I may have leave to call it something more..." As he had spoken he placed his hand without thinking atop Amelia's on the balustrade; removing it again quickly as he realised the action.

She turned again to him and he noted an expression soft but tinged round the edges with anxiety. *Blast!* he thought. *Can I never stem my emotions with this woman? I have mortified her yet again into silence.* Generally an excellent conversationalist, tonight he found it difficult to engage in any safe discourse while his affections threatened at every turn to escape his chest in the attempt to settle their future.

Amelia shivered somewhat, drawing her wrap around her, and Fitzwilliam took advantage now of the moment to extricate himself from a declaration both premature for the lady and that he had promised himself he would not make. "You are chilled, Madam," he said, reverting to her title. "Shall we rejoin the others? I believe another dance has begun while we have taken the air."

"Yes, of course. No, Colonel – wait an instant!"

❖❖❖❖❖

What the stir constituted could not be seen readily by Mr Wentworth and Mrs Annesley. They could only hear a running string of slurred complaints of rough treatment – all in the same strident voice – growing louder and nearer, as groups of revellers separated to allow someone wide passage, then closed in again after its effect. At last the undulate movement of this strange wave culminated at Edmund Hewitt nearby and Mrs Annesley could see it took the form of a woman.

At the curiosity evident in her expression, Wentworth said, "You have not yet the pleasure of acquaintance, I see." When Mrs Annesley nodded he whispered, "This is Mrs Hewitt."

Indeed, Susanna Hewitt it was. She was seated in what could only be great discomfort upon a teetering stack of cushions in a wheeled chair propelled, one could only presume, by a very contrite and silent maid.

"Ah, *Neddy*! *There* you are. Why *ever* did you come *down* without *me*, my dear?"

Wentworth took Mrs Annesley by the elbow and they quietly moved their way over to Mr Hewitt so as to render any assistance as may be wanted. Most of the crowd, after the initial disturbance of the invalid's entry, had resumed their prior activities and attentions; save only some in the immediate area who sensed entertainment to be had in monitoring the strange scene.

Edmund Hewitt had not stood by idly. After a swift, questioning glance at the maid, he leaned down at the chair side so as to present himself at his wife's level. Had her nonsensical commentary to now not alerted him, he could see in her eyes that Susanna had once again cajoled too many a dose of laudanum.

"*Noddy*, dear – Noodly – *Niddy* – oh, *dash* it, Mr Hewitt; I *wish* to dance, Sir!"

"My dear," he replied softly in hope that she also would restrict her tone, "you cannot do so. You must recall your injury."

"*Recall* it? Well, of *course* I *recall* it," she shrieked. Several nearby guests turned deliberately away from the marital encounter even as their ears sharpened to the proceedings.

"I *must* recall it *every* *moment*, as one *does* with a broken *arse!*" Susanna continued incognisant of the tittering around her. "But *this* is a *ball*, is not it? I *must* dance at the *ball!*" She looked from her husband now to his friend, and smiled coyly. "Mr *Wentworth!* *You* will *dance* with me, will *not* you? *You* would not *fail* a suffering *woman?* Now *come* along, and *help* me up! *Show* us your *worth* indeed."

Henry Wentworth managed to forestall such action by regretting that, much as he would be honoured to do so, he felt it incumbent to remind his willing partner that a dance was in progress even now and they could not join the line properly until its conclusion, which excuse the lady appeared to accept. "*Quite* right," she said. "*Quite* right; I am *nothing* if not *always* the very *example* of *propriety.*"

No sooner had he attained her acquiescence, however, than she began to whine to her husband. "But I *wish* to *exhibit* my *gown*, Ned. Is it not *lovely?* I paid *thirty-six* shillings for it, but *worth every penny!* Do you not *think* it? And it shall *move* across the floor so *prettily.*"

Olivia Annesley's first thought was that she could have made better for a tenth the price. The gown, even if one gave consideration that it could not be shown to advantage while the wearer teetered on unstable cushions, little suited the lady; it was far too juvenile for a woman of her years and of little enough taste for any age. All frills and flounces and with an enormous bow of bright blue satin plunked at the waist, it appeared that the lady had read of several new fashion trends and, rather than settle on one, had chosen to unite them all in one garment. Her dress maker should be horse-whipped for producing such a confection. But Olivia's inherent capacity for compassion quickly pushed the thought from her mind, and she too bent down to meet the lady at her chair's level.

"Mrs Hewitt," she began very softly. "I am Mrs Annesley, arrived but yesterday to Pemberley. Allow me, please, the honour to make your acquaintance; and say that, indeed, your gown is singular in its effect. One can see well how it suits you even as you are presently arranged."

Susanna Hewitt checked a moment until she heard the praise of her attire, following which she smiled complacently. She held her hand out in the manner of a queen to a vassal. "*How* do you *do*, Madam?" She started to giggle. "I have *always* wanted to *do* that! '*How do you do?*' So *refined*, do not you *think*?"

"Indeed it is."

"I am *nothing* if not *refined* in the *highest* order. One *cannot* allow one's *guard* to fall, *even* with such *calamity* having visited me. One simply *never* can *know* when one might meet with a *lady of taste*, such as *yourself* – and *myself*, of course." She frowned. "But then, of course I have no *need* to meet with *myself*, have I? *I* am at my disposal *always* –" She began to giggle at the very idea.

Mrs Annesley glanced about her to realise that the present dance was soon to end. She looked to Mr Hewitt and whispered that perhaps they should attempt his wife's extraction before such eventuality. He agreed immediately.

"Susanna," he offered, "I dislike to see you in such pain, my dear. Will you not allow me to return you to the comfort of your chamber?"

"But... but the *dance*! I *wished* to *dance*!"

"And so you did, Madam," replied Mrs Annesley immediately; "do you not recall it?"

Mrs Hewitt looked at her new friend with some confusion. "*Did* I?" When Mrs Annesley only nodded with a bright smile, the invalid suddenly recollected. "I *did*! Despite my *arse*, I *did* dance."

"Yes," agreed Mr Hewitt. "You were splendid, Susanna; and your gown well admired." He cast a grateful eye towards Mrs Annesley.

"Yes," agreed that lady, "you are an exemplar to us all of grace in triumph over pain."

Susanna Hewitt preened at the compliment and, while she was in that happy state, her husband once more offered to relieve her discomfort and restore her to her bed. This time she acquiesced with a sigh. Edmund himself took the chair from the sheepish maid and began to make his way towards the door. Mrs Annesley quite naturally followed him and Mr Wentworth just as naturally followed *her*, the maid bringing up the rear. This odd little procession managed to reach the outer hall just as the next dance was struck.

It had taken three footmen to carry Mrs Hewitt at her insistence down the stairs in her unwieldy chair; but upon facing the return she allowed her husband to lift her from it and carry her on her own. Before he began to mount the steps, however, she had grasped Mrs Annesley's hand tightly in hers and would not relinquish it, murmuring words about her *'dear friend Mrs Angel.'* That lady thus proceeded with them to their rooms, helping to remove the invalid from her ghastly gown and put her to bed, while the two gentlemen waited in the passage. Wentworth had followed behind once more with the chair which remained without so as to preclude its engendering any further misguided notions.

After a time, the maid opened the door to the men to indicate they could enter. Her fearful eyes and faltering voice gave proof of her expectation of rebuke from her employer for the scene just enacted. But Mr Hewitt only glanced at her in resignation, although he cautioned her that no more of the foul pain reliever was to be administered that night. She very contritely assured him it would not – the supply, in fact, had been exhausted.

When the gentlemen entered, Mrs Annesley was seated in a chair next the bed, her hand yet again in the grasp of Susanna, who rambled on in minute description of her triumph in dancing with a *'broken arse.'* "And did you *see* the *astonishment* upon Lady Felloes's *face* as I *skipped* by her without so much as a *grimace* of my *pain?* I should not *doubt* of an invitation *now* to join her *women's league.* No, I should not *doubt* of it at *all.*" Mrs Annesley nodded and smiled in agreement, compassion in her glance.

"*Why* have *we* not *met* before?" asked Susanna suddenly, awaiting no reply before continuing; "And *who* is *your* husband, Madam? *What* is your *name* again? Is he *someone...* of *importance?*"

"My husband, Mrs Hewitt, passed on some four years past."

"Oh! *Oh, dear,*" Susanna laughed with chagrin. "*That* will not do."

Mrs Annesley only smiled once more, and offered to the ailing woman a sip of a calming tisane to aid her sleep.

"My friend," – Hewitt spoke low to Wentworth so as not be overheard – "if you do not marry this 'Mrs Angel', you are a fool of the highest order." With this, he went to relieve the kind lady while his friend – considering that every presumption of her sensible character upon first meeting had been here confirmed – silently formed the seeds of a campaign to ensure that Olivia Annesley would not long remain a lady's companion.

❖❖❖❖❖

Amelia had forestalled Fitzwilliam's suggestion that they return to the ballroom, yet she made no move now to speak. She remained looking up at him as though of several minds about such a simple act.

"Mrs Chaney?"

Amelia lowered her eyes, but then, instead of turning to walk back, she raised them again and, glancing about to ensure they were yet alone, reached out between them to place her hands into his. A shiver raced through Fitzwilliam that had no source in the night air; her touch was searing. The lady as well was affected and, taking a rapid extra breath, she addressed him.

"Before we venture inside, there is a word I am compelled to speak, yet I have no notion if my courage will hold to do so." She smiled tentatively up at him. "Colonel – my dear friend and benefactor – we have, I think, danced something of a courtship these last weeks, if we have spent great effort not to call it such. My position – my mourning, that is – has added complexity to what might, at another time, have been straightforward. No!" she said, as he made to comment. "Will you allow me to finish, Sir, before my will is lost?" He acquiesced and she went on.

"I was never unhappy in my marriage; my husband was a good man and I have mourned his loss. You knew him intimately and can, I think, accept this."

Fitzwilliam mentally chastised himself for his earlier declaration even as he answered. "Of course. Major Cha—" He stopped on seeing an entreaty in her eyes. "Yes, of course," he concluded.

"But I must confess, to you alone, I have never felt for *any* man the *tendresse* that enters unbidden when I am in your company, Sir. Indeed, I have had to remind myself forcibly at times to behave as a widow should; I have failed more often than not, as I do now." She said this while looking down at their hands clasped between them, unable to meet his gaze. But now she did raise her eyes to his.

"You think me too bold, you must, in this confession; it is unseemly. Yet when I thought you entertained a notion of a match with Miss deBourgh, I felt I should never again reconcile my heart to love another. My relief on learning it was not to be was immeasurable! There was hope yet that I might win back your affections."

"Oh, dear lady," said he as he squeezed her hands warmly, "you must know my affections were ever in your trust. I doubt there is any one in all Derbyshire who has not observed my admiration. Indeed, I doubt there was ever a moment of our acquaintance when I did not feel the warmest regard, if the realisation took its time to achieve clarity."

She smiled at him, her very countenance the picture of joy. "It is such expression which emboldens me now. Forgive me, Sir, for I overstep, but I must before my heart should burst from suspended hope." She glanced away and back again, then said, "Looking at you now, I cannot but tell you of the fondest desires of my heart. When I am able to entertain such aspiration once more, some months hence, will you –"

Hesitating again, she closed her eyes and sputtered, "that is, might you be inclined, Sir, to request my hand? Might I depart Pemberley at least with reason to *hope* for such a happy day? I have not a great fortune, but what I have I may offer to your disposal freely —"

Fitzwilliam's jaw dropped nearly to his chest while Amelia now studied his expression, a hesitant smile playing about her lips. In some rational yet humoured corner of his brain he instantly considered the confounded reversal of his role in this business of courtship, between his aunt's proffering of a settlement upon him and now this lady very nearly proposing to him — no, not 'very nearly' at all as it struck him. However, it was not a wholly unpleasant blow to his vanity; rather than feel emasculated, he experienced only exhilaration at being able to throw away caution and plunge into an understanding, even one of necessity to be maintained quietly between them for some months.

Amelia's hands rested still in his; he increased his hold upon them now and composed his expression before saying: "My dearest, sweet Amelia! Your hand, your love, your life — I shall request all! No, I shall *beg* them of you — and offer my own to your service in return! If you have spoken improperly, then let us both be accused of it. There is little in such rebuke can dampen my joy if you will agree to be my wife! Surely you guessed that I was near to addressing you on more than one occasion these past weeks, and would have done gayly but for circumstance."

"I did think it but could not trust my reason, for I wished it perhaps too fervently. But I could no longer sustain the hope — it is too taxing for me — if I judged in error, if my inclinations did not, in fact, find counterpart in yours." Her ease had returned now that she had confessed her feelings and realised that he did not think less of her for so doing. "I have wished to declare my partiality since that night in the garden at Albion Park, if truth be told."

Fitzwilliam recalled the evening with perfect clarity, both the tender moments and his glumness to think he could not provide adequately for the lady. He smiled at her now with gentle intent. "No more so than I, but I confess to believing myself unworthy. I was unable to offer you a garden of your own when I saw the joy you took from that one; how perfectly natural and fitting you looked in its embrace."

"Richard!" she said, incredulous, and she could not know the warmth she engendered in him to hear her utter his given name even in rebuke; he looked forward to vexing her often in the coming years. "Could you truly believe I care so much for such a thing? There is no embrace I could desire more fervently than yours!"

It proved, to be sure, a very short step from joined hands to joined lips as they succumbed to desire, Fitzwilliam only afterward looking about to ensure their delicious impropriety was not witnessed to the lady's detriment. But he could not regret the impulse – the sweet taste of her still clung about his mouth.

"Can you possibly love a foolish old soldier?"

"Indeed, I do believe I could, Sir – had I not set my heart already upon you."

It was only as they made to enter the ballroom again – where revellers' attentions were drawn to the dance while the two composed themselves – that Fitzwilliam realised Amelia had accepted him with no reservations; even unknowing as yet of the mixed blessing of his aunt's and cousin's largesse. He smiled, anticipating a quiet moment to apprise her of their good fortune; and of the day some months hence when he might proclaim aloud his love of this woman.

He was returned from this reverie when he heard his lady chuckle.

"What is it you find amusing?"

Laughing openly now, she said. "Not so amusing had you responded differently to my brash advance." Her features were suffused with delight. "I have only realised that if you had rebuffed me, I should have to remove myself to the Indies with my brother, so great would my mortification have been. I am grateful to have been spared exile!"

"I am most happy to have been of some small service in that regard, Madam," he answered, and none who might have encountered Colonel Fitzwilliam at that moment could have doubted the earnestness of his reply.

❖❖❖❖❖

With a jaunty flourish, Maestro Martinali announced that the Boulanger would be played in a few moments. It was to be the final dance of the evening – or rather the morning now – an announcement that brought happy anticipation along with regret that the ball would soon be over. Guests began to mill around to find their last partners of the night, most long since arranged.

Nathaniel Hewitt reclaimed Georgiana from an older gentleman with whom she had danced the last, and they made their way to Darcy and Lizzy just as Fitzwilliam and Mrs Chaney joined them.

"Why, Cousin," Georgiana teazed, "I believe dancing agrees with you! You look a happy man!"

The eyes of the others moved to Fitzwilliam, who blushed profusely, before noting that Amelia Chaney's countenance was no less altered.

"Richard –" started Lizzy. "Have you some particular intelligence you wish to unburden yourself of?"

The smiles of that gentleman and the lady at his side answered for him, but still he said, "Indeed I do not." Then, at the raised brows all around, he relented. "However, if we should find ourselves gathered together some few months hence – say for a christening or some such occasion" (he said nodding at Elizabeth) – "then I shall have news for you of a most blissful nature, for I have every assurance that I may then announce my intention to wed."

Congratulations were offered by all at this promise of future happiness. The Bingleys and Gardiners came upon them then, curious as to the frivolity amongst the group, and were as well apprised of the forthcoming news. While they congratulated the unofficially happy couple, Nathaniel Hewitt addressed Darcy.

"Sir, I have tonight given great consideration to our present agreement, and I would speak with you of an alteration to it."

Darcy looked from the young man to Georgiana, but found no enlightenment in his sister's bemused expression. Uncertain as to Hewitt's purpose, he glanced around at the others in their group and replied, "Should not we defer this discourse to another time? Perhaps after the ball, in my study?" His quizzical expression gave voice to his ignorance of Nathaniel's purpose.

"I do not believe it necessary. I have but one concern, Sir, and nothing these good people may not know." He looked to Gee briefly, then added. "It is this, Sir. Would you be prepared, Mr Darcy, to move forward the date of my apprenticeship?"

"Move it forward?"

"Yes. I have decided to forego making a tour at the present time, and ask if you are willing to offer me tutelage immediately."

"*No!*"

The others all were drawn by this ejaculation and, as one, turned to the speaker. Georgiana blushed at the attention, but turned to Nathaniel, an earnest frown drawing her mouth into something of a pout. "Mr Hewitt, you cannot do this."

Nathaniel gazed at her an instant, opened his mouth to remonstrate, then stopped. He glanced again at Darcy. It was clear that any assertions he might make to his lady depended first upon his sponsor's willingness to consider his proposal.

"Mr Hewitt, I am prepared to honour my part of the agreement at your convenience. You have only to inform me," Darcy glanced now at his sister and smiled, "when together you have determined your course."

Nathaniel nodded and turned to Georgiana. "Miss Darcy, I assure you I have considered this well –"

His argument was cut off by the warming notes of the orchestra, signalling the last dance. The group took their places, this time husbands and wives partnering with no questions of propriety. At the last moment, Kitty and Thomas Reavley filled in the place that the Gardiners had held for them, as that couple moved out of the line to watch the proceedings quite happily from the side.

It seemed half the card room had come out as well to watch, some taking part as the music was struck now in earnest.

"Mr Hewitt," said Georgiana, stepping in from the line just a little to speak somewhat privately. "I cannot allow you to give up your tour. I *will not* allow of it."

❖❖❖❖❖

"But Georgiana —" Nathaniel Hewitt took up the argument they had been forced to suspend to complete the finishing dance.

All around them people moved to reunite with their wives and husbands, bid farewell to friends, arrange with new acquaintances to meet again, and generally drift to the cloak rooms or to await their carriages. Darcy and Lizzy were fully engaged in bidding a good morning to guests as a steady flow of weary revellers reluctantly dispersed. Little notice was given to the young couple in serious discourse in a shadowed alcove of the entry hall.

"—what can the Italies be to me when my every thought and wish will direct itself towards England, towards *you*!"

Georgiana shook her head once more, stubborn in resistance. "Mr Hewitt, you have avowed you would not deprive me of a season, not only for its pleasures but for the benefits as well — the making of new acquaintances; opportunities to attend concerts, the theatre; an introduction to politics, and education in the wider way of the world. I could no more deprive you of the same benefits of your tour. You *want* this time, and I know well that you have looked forward to it these last months—"

"So I did, but no more! Not since you have declared for me. You must allow me to do this for you... for us."

"No. Nathaniel, if you will not be sensible, then it falls to me to be so. You cannot see it for passion; this notion of yours — it is a sacrifice and one that I will not allow you to make, for it is not necessary. I do not wish it!" As his expression took on a troubling frown, Georgiana smiled sympathetically.

"My brother was right in one judgment, Nathaniel. We are young. How fortunate we were to find each other at such an age, to realise love at such an age. That will not alter, not on my part! My heart is yours and ever shall it be; and despite your beginning with him, Fitz will see it protected for you. But this separation, for all its drawbacks — and I do not discount them — it is good for us; it is necessary to be borne. We will be better for it in the end, in ourselves and for each other. You must go!"

"You at least are not so young as to argue without sense," he replied, chuckling in resignation. "I will go; but not a day will pass that I shall not imagine myself with you."

"I will feel it, here," she said, pressing her hand to her heart, "and return it tenfold. And I *will* wait for you, my love."

❖❖❖❖❖

At last the house was nearly empty but for its residents – several of whom had retired themselves now – and Fitzwilliam escorted Mrs Chaney up the stairs to her chamber before moving on to his own. It would be dawn soon, but thankfully Darcy had arranged for late services; indeed Mr Henshaw himself had been among the last of the party to leave. Fitzwilliam in his state, doubted he would sleep despite his fatigue, but some few hours to rest quietly and come to terms with what the night had brought would be welcome.

As they went they spoke of little things; Fitzwilliam had decided to wait for another day to apprise Amelia of his aunt's legacy. He wished to take joy first in the way circumstances stood between them at this moment. All too soon they arrived at her chambers; he raised her hand and kissed it, wishing her good morning. But he did not leave immediately thereon; rather they stood, her hand still in his, gazing into each others' eyes with new understanding and confidence.

"Richard," said she eventually, her voice low, "I could wish we did not have to remain circumspect, that we were not obliged to remain silent and separate some months before I am free. I am sorry for it –"

Fitzwilliam placed a finger upon her lips to stop her apology. "Madam, you have made me a truly happy man. What are a few months against what we shall form thereafter? My desires can endure this entrenchment. I see in you affection to match what I feel in my own heart, and it is enough for now. I will wait for *you*, my love."

He removed his finger but ensured her continued silence by replacing it with his own lips, stealing yet once more her promise in a kiss of some duration. Only when he realised how closely it threatened all his regulation did he manage to break their sweet contact and bid the equally flustered lady a husky good night.

CHAPTER TWENTY-ONE

Monday, 7 January 1799

❖❖❖❖❖

THE DRIVER GAVE his horses a whistle and, after a snorted reply from them, the Darcy carriage began to pull away from the front entrance, closely following the Hewitt conveyance some yards ahead. These were the last two departures of the morning, and Lizzy and Darcy stood together to wave them off as they had the earlier ones. Since mild temperatures still graced the region, they stayed to watch as the coaches became a speck on the long lane.

"Do you hear that?" asked Darcy when the servants had withdrawn, standing behind his wife and laying his hands on her shoulders affectionately.

"Hear what?"

He smiled as she turned her head towards him. "Silence," he whispered.

She laughed, the sound breaking the unusual quietude for an instant before the stillness fluttered back over them once more as a soft blanket. After a moment, she turned round and put her arm through his. "Must you appear so very pleased at the prospect of being taciturn and unsociable once more?" she asked as they walked back indoors.

"Madam, I am sorely offended. For well over a fortnight, I have been the very soul of affability and society. May I not revel for a few moments in this all-too-brief respite?"

"Mmm, I suppose so. But do not become too accustomed, for it *will* be brief. We shall have half of them back again at week's end!"

"That is five days entire from now. Let us not think on it yet," he shuddered, drawing another laugh from his wife.

❖ ❖ ❖ ❖ ❖

The first departure on the day had been very early indeed as Lady Catherine wished to take advantage of clement weather in such a start in the hope of spending three nights only on the road back to Kent and Rosings. She had called for her carriage before even the special breakfast that had been arranged for the others, barely after first light. She, Anne, and Frances Jenkinson would stop for a morning repast some miles farther on when they changed post horses.

Their leave taking had been a much warmer affair than their sudden arrival had been two weeks earlier. Anne, with newfound spirit was nearly effusive and even Lady Catherine had thawed enough to offer herself to her nephews for embraces. Certainly the words they exchanged were more cordial than formerly. Anne spent some moments with both her cousins while her mother made an amicable parting from Sir James Thornton, and then they were gone.

By the time all the guests had departed the ball early on Sunday morning, Lizzy and Darcy had fallen into their bed and were fast asleep in an instant. As such — and considering they had arisen only in time to prepare for Sunday service — it was the afternoon before they had found a moment to discuss the ball when finally Lizzy related to her husband Anne's diabolical persuasion of her mother. An incredulous but amused Darcy still had shown signs of strained belief as he regarded his cousin and bid her a pleasant journey in the early hour of Monday.

Next to depart after the deBourgh party had been the coaches for Albion Park — the Gardiners with Sir James in his carriage and, following, Bingley and Jane with Kitty. The latter had chosen to accompany her eldest sister upon learning that Thomas Reavley would himself be away from Lambton for some days in taking custody of his new parsonage in Yorkshire. At least in Nottinghamshire, Kitty might find some diversion in assisting the Bingleys and exploring their new home. Absent Sir James, they all planned a return to Pemberley on Friday before setting out for Longbourn the following week.

And lastly, the Hewitt family had departed along with Wentworth and his guests: Colonel Fitzwilliam, Mrs Chaney, Mrs Annesley, and Georgiana in the Darcy carriage. This was a stroke of fortune the Darcys had not looked for, having been resigned to retain custody of the ailing Mrs Hewitt for some weeks yet. But the woman had claimed she could not bear extended separation from her children and had insisted upon taking the painful journey home immediately. Lizzy knew that, more than motherly devotion, it was to do with Mr Grimes refusing Susanna more laudanum — Mrs Hewitt could not too quickly solicit her own physician to call upon her. They would break their journey with Wentworth in Castleton for a few days.

Henry Wentworth's suggestion of entertaining Mrs Annesley and Miss Darcy as his guests had been raised again on Sunday after service. Despite the inclusion of Gee's companion, Darcy had shown reservations for the scheme, aware that Nathaniel Hewitt as well would be of the party for some days. He had warmed considerably to the young man and was coming to terms with the couple's inevitable betrothal – but questioned the level of chaperonage to be expected while his friend Wentworth also courted Mrs Annesley. He was persuaded only when Fitzwilliam readily consented to accompany them; and quite soon the plan was formed. Mrs Chaney would join them as well; and the ladies had rushed off to spend the afternoon in quick preparation.

"*Darcy,*" *Lizzy had asked him when they were alone on Sunday night, "can you truly believe Fitzwilliam an apt reinforcement for Gee's companion given Mrs Chaney's attendance?"*

"*No," he laughed in resignation, "indeed I do not. But... I must trust him, he is Gee's guardian; and I do trust my sister's comportment. Fitzwilliam shall preserve the appearance at least of sufficient decorum."*

She perused his face a moment and saw something more there. "And?"

"*And... I was impressed at Georgiana's sense and skill in keeping young Hewitt to his original plans for his tour. I would allow them a few more days of society."*

"*And?"*

Darcy looked at his wife now, noting her patronizing smirk. "And..." he replied somewhat defiantly, "I was persuaded finally upon realising this proposal will leave Pemberley blessedly free of humanity for several days, but for my own lovely wife and me."

They chuckled together at the admission.

Now, having seen off the last of them, they reached the stairs and Lizzy stopped, in expectation of her husband turning towards his study.

"Have you a great deal of business to attend to?" she asked.

He shrugged. "Nothing of significance. A few letters, and the matter of the magistracy."

"You will take it on then?"

"I have not resigned myself to a decision." He considered his wife a moment as she placed a hand across her abdomen, smiling instinctively.

"On further consideration, however, I have come to *one* decision."

"What is that?"

"My business can wait! I believe I shall take a day of leisure with my wife if she will have me. I warrant we have earned such a one, do not you?"

Holding her hand out to him by way of answer, she smiled more broadly as they made their way up to her sitting room.

"Darcy," she said sweetly, a frown of curiosity lending her expression a mischievous air.

"Yes?" His tone imbued the syllable with distrust.

"Your aunt's business is settled now."

"Mmm."

"Anne's future is happily secured."

"Mmm..."

"Richard and Amelia have settled as well –"

Impatient now to know her intent, Darcy said, "Elizabeth, my dear, have you a point to make?"

She chuckled. "No, no. It is only that I wonder – since the Fitzwilliam family has sorted itself, tell me: beyond Georgiana, you do not possess any Darcy relations, do you?"

He pulled her into an embrace as they laughed, and they enjoyed a moment of quiet ease before finally he replied. "Hmmm. Have I not yet told you about the letter I have had from India of Great Uncle Warren Darcy...?"

Lady Catherine deBourgh, her daughter Anne, and *her* companion Mrs Jenkinson, returned to Kent with something of a fuller understanding and grudging acceptance. Although her Ladyship spoke only as absolutely required to the companion on the three-day journey to Rosings Park, life in general for the three women took on an improved tenor. Lady Catherine's demeanour towards both ladies improving radically – encouraged no doubt as Anne and the companion no longer passed their days in fear of the latter's sudden dismissal, and by Lady Catherine's newfound respect for her daughter. In little time, her manner to Mrs Jenkinson even approached a cordiality no one could have foreseen, though it remained subject to an occasional flash of temper.

But if Lady Catherine's mood in her household improved, her relations without it most decidedly did not. The village and community felt the inevitable effects of a temper which was not being exercised sufficiently within the walls of Rosings. Mr Collins in particular suffered – Lady Catherine found fault in all the sermons he presented for her advance inspection; in his extravagances within the parsonage; his not yet beginning to prepare his garden for spring; his coddling of his flock as she perceived it; the ill behaviour of his child; and all manner of sundry other offenses. Indeed, invitations to dinner and tea at Rosings all but dried up for some months, a source of such befuddled disappointment to the vicar that he took the first opportunity that spring roads would allow to make an extended visit to his in-laws near Meryton, to his wife Charlotte's delight.

✤✤✤✤✤

Lizzy and Darcy enjoyed several days of repose in one another's company before facing guests once more. Jane and Bingley returned from Albion Park on Friday with their relations, but they departed only a few days later, filled with sufficient enthusiasm to see them through breaking their news to Mrs Bennet. As Lizzy had surmised, that group no sooner arrived at Longbourn than Mr Gardiner learnt of 'pressing business' in town, so in the event, he and his wife passed only one night with their sister before taking a post chaise home.

Lizzy had no need to ask Jane how their mother had taken the news of the Bingleys' impending change of residence. Within days, she received letters from all three of her sisters and from Mr Bennet as well, with similar tales of how Mrs Bennet had retired to her bed immediately with a case of nerves, vowing she would never feel strong enough to rise again. In the end it was ten days before she descended from her room, a quite sufficient period for Mr Bennet to have come to terms with the loss to the north of his eldest and second favourite daughter in the blissful quietude of his study, undisturbed but for the occasional wail that penetrated his book-lined walls.

Jane took upon herself the burden of assuaging her mother's lamentations as much as was possible when she was not actively engaged in preparing her own household for an impending move; such that it was with tremendous relief – and no small measure of guilt in consideration of her sisters who remained behind – that Jane climbed into Bingley's carriage a month later for the return, first to Pemberley, then to her new home. She hoped greatly that her mother would recover herself by the time Mrs Bennet travelled to Albion Park for Jane's lying in.

✤✤✤✤✤

Kitty's arrival back at Pemberley from Albion Park was greeted by the disappointing news that Mr Reavley had not yet returned from his new home. This absence, punctuated by Georgiana's still being away in Castleton, caused Kitty to mope about so for a day and a half until, in exasperation, Lizzy and Jane accompanied their sister to call upon Mrs Henshaw. Although that lady's especial relaying of regards to Kitty from her brother gave a short respite from the young woman's unsettled condition, the further news that Thomas Reavley's duties would preclude his return to Lambton before Miss Bennet's own departure brought on a gradual thickening of her unpleasing mood that began as they returned from the vicarage, and continued all the way to Longbourn.

Her spirits did revive upon returning home, as she gained an attentive new audience to regale with all the details of her Christmastide in Derbyshire, and particularly of the Twelfth Night Ball. She never tired of reliving the event to any of her family or the servants who would suffer its recitation.

When Mrs Bennet took to her rooms upon Jane's news, and Mary Bennet had soured finally of hearing any more of her sister's tales revisited, Kitty called upon the Lucas family. Lady Lucas was ever eager to hear news of the Bennets – and seemed peculiarly interested in the Bingleys' planned vacating of Netherfield Hall, having suffered Mrs Bennet's superior airs this twelvemonth and more. But Kitty's best audience was to be found in Maria Lucas – eager to have every detail of the ball repeated at least thrice, of Kitty's gown and the general society of their party. She sighed in all the right spots and was particularly effusive in doing so at every mention (and there were many) of Mr Thomas Reavley.

As the satisfaction of reliving her adventure through discourse waned, Kitty once more grew restless, her attentions more and more drawn north to wonder how Mr Reavley occupied his hours – how often he might return the favour of considering her since they no longer met with regularity. She began to watch the lane every morning as Hill returned with the day's mail, even volunteering to go for it herself when the weather suited the walk. She watched hopeful of a letter from Lizzy bringing news or, yet more to be preferred, the conveyance of a direct greeting from the vicar.

When one such surveillance of the housekeeper yielded Kitty a letter from Mrs Henshaw of Lambton – addressed to her "dear young friend" and fully half taken up in relating in minute insinuating detail how the lady's brother busied himself in making improvements to his parsonage to render it comfortable for a family one day – Kitty rushed off at the first possible moment to Netherfield to petition her sister to take her along to Pemberley when the Bingleys departed the following week. Her request was gently rebuffed owing to Mrs Bennet's continued distress and her need for her remaining daughters, leaving a disappointed Kitty to wish away the days until the entire family would travel north in April. One can only imagine whether she learnt anything of patience or fortitude in the exercise.

❖❖❖❖❖

The party for Castleton arrived there to a cacophony of whining from the ailing Susanna Hewitt, she crying out for an apothecary to relieve her of her constant misery. To the relief of the *remainder* of the party, the medical man was summoned post haste, Wentworth even going so far as to order his own carriage to be sent along for retrieval of the good man. Within an hour, he had arrived, Mrs Hewitt was resting easily with a complaisant smile, and the others began a most pleasant visit, first touring the inn and its environs, then striking out for the little village that lay higgledy-piggledy along the hillside. (It must be here stated that, even before the arrival of the apothecary, Mrs Hewitt somehow managed on arrival to shake off assistance and walk herself to her rooms, change her attire for a dressing robe, and order and consume substantial refreshments, which must leave one to wonder at the true source of her misery.)

The Hewitts remained only two days before Susanna again felt the desire to consult her own familiar physician and the couple struck off for their home on Wednesday morning. Nathaniel Hewitt remained behind a few days more with his friends. Finally, unable to longer delay his preparations for departure to London and following, to his tour, he reluctantly took his leave of Georgiana on Saturday before her own return home on Monday.

The days at Castleton passed quickly and merrily, as one might expect of a company consisting of lovers in their varied stages of courtship. Although proper decorum was maintained at all times, ample opportunities were found for Georgiana and her Mr Hewitt to engage in intimate discourse; to envision their future with the flights of fancy and enthusiasm of youth, and to repeat avowals of faith and constancy during their impending separation. Colonel Fitzwilliam and Mrs Chaney found their share as well of intimacy with as gratifying, if not quite as naive, a view to their own future. And Henry Wentworth made every effort – successfully one must add – to impress Olivia Annesley with the comforts to be found in his chosen home and living. Indeed, that couple made rapid progress to understanding one another, such that when the Pemberley party made to return thither, it had been well settled that Mr Wentworth would spend the upcoming season in town with Hewitt, to the satisfaction of himself, Mrs Annesley – and of Georgiana who considered it all according to design and good fortune.

While they resided in Castleton, Fitzwilliam escorted the party one day to the garrison near Stockport where they called upon Major Soames. Colonel Fitzwilliam had the happy duty to relay to the major a set of new orders for himself and his corporal, transferring them to town with all haste – and further, to relate that the good major's work would require close association with Fitzwilliam himself. The Corporal, upon being called within to hear this news, availed himself of the closest female – in the event Georgiana Darcy – and twirled her around in delight; only afterward, upon realising his precipitous action, apologising profusely for the offense to the escalating laughter of the entire party.

When, some week after the Fitzwilliam party had returned to the Darcys, Nathaniel Hewitt made a last visit to Pemberley en route to London, his friend Wentworth took to accompany the young man. From there, after a bittersweet leave taking of his young lady, Mr Hewitt travelled in the company of Fitzwilliam and Mrs Chaney to town where the latter resumed their lives during their wait for spring.

Young Mr Hewitt visited the Gardiners as had been previously arranged. That couple did their best to lessen Nathaniel's loneliness by entertaining him some days until his ship would sail – indeed, in his short time with them, he became quite a favourite of the Gardiner children for his prowess at spillikins. When the time came for Mr Hewitt to join his travel companions, the Gardiner family entire accompanied the young gentleman at last to see him off for his tour.

EPILOGUE

LADY CATHERINE DeBOURGH and Sir James Thornton, in the end, did not renew any of the intimate feelings that had characterised their youthful acquaintance, each having changed too much to recall such passions. They did, however, see one another from time to time in London, forming a recurring cordial acquaintance, and Sir James even garnered invitations to visit Rosings on more than one occasion where he continued to befriend Miss Anne deBourgh as well.

As it happened, Lady Catherine enjoyed four years of additional irascibility before her heart ailment claimed her – an unfortunate circumstance of its being weakened further by the contraction of an influenza rampant one winter. Upon her passing, Sir James became a source of great comfort to Anne deBourgh, sharing with the young woman some genuinely sorrowful feeling at the lady's demise. As they had long planned to do, Miss deBourgh and Mrs Jenkinson then moved to smaller premises at Tetley Grange and with Darcy's assistance, leasing Rosings Park and all its grandeur for a quite handsome sum to a family which had made its fortune in the West Indies trade. At the grange, the two ladies lived comfortably for nearly three years before Anne followed her mother to Elysium, but though short, they were happy years. Passers-by on late spring or summer evenings often heard the sweet notes of a piano and a pleasant harmonizing of voices, one strong, one weak, accompanying the music drifting out from open windows. Little conjecture ever attached to the circumstance of the ladies' shared domicile.

If Sir James had not reclaimed an intimate relationship with Lady Catherine, nonetheless he established one of warmth with others of his Pemberley introduction. He divided his living arrangements between the gate cottage at Albion Park and a set of comfortable rooms in St James. When in Nottinghamshire, he was often found wandering its gardens and became even more a favourite with Jane and Bingley, such that they all began to think of him as family – a fatherly advisor to Charles Bingley and kindly old uncle to their children. And when he resided in town, his friendship with Edward and Margaret Gardiner grew as well, such that wherever he found himself, it was with no lack of satisfying companionship.

Jane and Charles Bingley found life in Nottinghamshire in general – and Albion Park in particular – well suited to their temperaments, making friends of their neighbours with ease and particularly enjoying the opportunities afforded them by residing within half a day's drive of Pemberley. Mrs Bennet upon her first visit to Albion Park, spent two months proclaiming the disadvantages of a drafty old building – echoing, had any of them realised it, the exact comments of Bingley's sisters upon their introductory visits – even as she made herself at home there. She did not cease in her persuasions to draw Bingley back to Netherfield Park until that property had been lost to them by being leased once more, after which time she passed her complaints in finding fault with the new tenant, whose chief offenses appeared to be three daughters, a lack of marriageable sons, and a preference for the society of Lady Lucas over herself.

Catherine Bennet coughed and fidgeted for two days in the carriage when the date finally arrived to return to Pemberley for Lizzy's lying in. Darcy had sent his coach for the family, all of whom would journey first to Derbyshire before transporting Mrs Bennet and Mary to Albion Park. Kitty had worked herself into such a state of anticipation as to a reunion with Mr Reavley that her face broke out in spots all over, such that she spent the first three days at Pemberley in her room until she was fit to her own satisfaction of being seen once more.

To the delight of Kitty's complexion and a family tiring of her nervous speculation, Mr Reavley called upon the Darcys and their family very shortly after the Bennets had arrived, and showed great enthusiasm in reuniting with the young woman. Thereafter, when the duties of both allowed, he would travel often to visit his sister and call upon his friends at the great house, always being then afforded an invitation to stay and dine.

On a warm early summer's evening while walking in the shrubbery to the side of the house, Thomas Reavley proposed to Catherine Bennet and was promptly and enthusiastically accepted. Mr Bennet, who could not have been surprised by the subsequent petition by the vicar, gave his consent readily with only moderate teazing of the couple. His relief at Kitty's being secured was pleasantly accompanied by finding the young man agreeable enough as a son – sharing with Lizzy his opinion that he found Mr Reavley generally rational but with enough oddity of nature to prevent his being altogether dull.

A September wedding date at Longbourn was proposed and agreed upon by all the family. Mrs Bennet, upon receiving the news by letter at

Albion Park, was so overcome with joy and immediately thereafter with convulsions of anxiety concerning all the planning to be done, that she must journey at once from the Bingley residence to that of the Darcys to meet her new son forthwith. Despite the encounter, Thomas Reavley honoured his promise and made of Kitty a vicar's wife.

Georgiana passed the initial weeks of her separation from Nathaniel Hewitt in being of as much service as possible to Elizabeth, and the two sisters grew closer in their hearts. It was with a fair amount both of anticipation and regret that she took her leave in the spring for town, excited for her season but less so at the prospect of not being at Pemberley for the birth of her nephew or niece. Darcy accompanied the ladies but, once establishing his sister and her companion within society, he returned with haste to Derbyshire.

Darcy had softened before Nathaniel Hewitt took his tour, granting the young man and his sister allowance to correspond through the conveyance of their mutual friends Mrs Annesley and Mr Wentworth. This made the young lovers' separation more tolerable as they shared their discrete experiences freely and often. After a few months, however, no letters arrived to Mr Wentworth for days on end; that gentleman came to dread the look of hopeful expectation on Miss Darcy's face when they met, knowing he had no missive to pass along. Georgiana, unable to believe her Nathaniel would willingly cease their correspondence, began to concern herself that something untoward had happened to the young man.

Then, one evening while attending a ball given by Lady Winterhurst, she was astonished to find herself approached by the very gentleman. Unable longer to remain sanguine in only hearing of the delights of Georgiana's season, young Hewitt had booked himself passage and returned to share in a part of it. His failure to correspond now explained fully by his crossing, the reunited couple passed a joyous evening. Nathaniel resided with his brother in his town house some six weeks before reluctantly returning to his friends and tutor.

Susanna Hewitt recovered fully from her skating injury and insisted upon spending the entire season in London in recompense for her winter seclusion. As early as was socially acceptable, she packed up her husband and her best gowns and they relocated to town, where she determined she would act as a benefactress to Miss Darcy.

But the joys of the season were not to be hers. On the day of their arrival, wearing a new gown which she had with great pride designed herself, Susanna Hewitt caught her toe in the flounce at its hem and tripped upon the stairs, tumbling some seven feet to the bottom. Although her coccyx remained intact, her right leg did not, having suffered serious fracture in two places. The season, barely stirring for all of London, had ended for Susanna Hewitt before it began. She was laid up for several months, during the heat of summer, with little solace beyond access to the most prestigious physicians from whom, one after the other in succession, she could wheedle sufficient doses of pain relief. Edmund Hewitt was as dutiful a husband as his wife would allow, but she soon took to sending him away for attempting to regulate her dependence on her laudanum. As such, he often had leisure time to enjoy his guests – his friend Wentworth and, for a time, his brother – as well as other pursuits.

Henry Wentworth offered to Olivia Annesley midway through the season and, there being no one from whom permission must be obtained, they proposed to publish banns immediately. On a hot August morning, they married at St James church with Edward Hewitt and Georgiana as witnesses. The only guests were Mr and Mrs Gardiner, Sir James Thornton, and Colonel Fitzwilliam with Mrs Chaney, themselves recently engaged.

Richard Fitzwilliam and Amelia Chaney had weathered their obligatory silence well, in no small measure for the fact that they were able to continue a close acquaintance for some months under the guise of escorting Miss Darcy socially. The fact that Mrs Chaney was in light mourning by spring gave her more freedom of activity and she was frequently to be seen joining her friends in walks in Hyde Park, at concerts, or even an occasional ball.

On one particular evening, in the company of Mr Wentworth and Mrs Annesley, she was to meet the Colonel and his niece at Astley's. Fitzwilliam and Georgiana were in their seats, only moments from the start of the evening's programme, when in walked two of their party. But where was Mrs Chaney? It was only then that Georgiana pointed behind Mrs Annesley to a lovely, honey-haired young woman, the glow of her curls set off beautifully by a tawny gold gown and a wide smile. Her mourning officially ended, she and Fitzwilliam announced their understanding that very night.

When Fitzwilliam notified his family – including Lady Catherine – of his impending marriage, his aunt immediately transferred twenty thousand pounds to his keeping with no ill humour. Shortly after, he travelled with his lady to Rosings in order that both might thank her Ladyship properly. To his surprise, his aunt accepted Amelia with every courtesy, going so far as to host a dinner party one evening for the couple, though she did not attend their wedding some weeks later. In subsequent visits, Mrs Fitzwilliam and Anne deBourgh formed a friendship of consequence, and within eleven months of their marriage, Colonel Fitzwilliam and his wife provided Lady Catherine deBourgh "a proper heir for Rosings," a stout son they christened Charles Lewis Fitzwilliam.

Colonel and Mrs Fitzwilliam, after inheriting Rosings's custodianship for their son, never inhabited the property themselves, their preferences running to less ostentatious dwellings. With some of the capital from Lady Catherine's endowment, as well as that from his own father, Fitzwilliam (as he had often imagined doing) purchased a modest property on the Dorset coast as a wedding gesture to his wife. The couple had visited several available ones, but knew at first glance that Broome House was the last they would have to survey. The house was ample in size and well apportioned, the stable kept well, and the small park neat with a view of the bay beyond Charmouth at its southern extremity. But most convincing for its purchase was that, leading out from the back drawing room windows, sat a perfectly groomed garden of gravel walks and roses, colourful and hearty from the distant sea breeze, and bordered by the bright bushes for which the estate had been named.

Rosings continued to be leased for many years until Charles Fitzwilliam inherited the property on his majority. He then resided there for a short while but, having acquired more the tastes of his father and mother, he quickly determined to lease the estate once again, establishing himself from its substantial rents in a Dorset property not far from his boyhood home to the delight of his aging parents.

And therein, on such a contented note, did I purpose to end this narrative.

'But wait!' I hear some of you protest. Is there not yet unfinished business? Can we leave yet unknowing which of Darcy and Bingley won their wager to first produce an heir? Of the state of health of Elizabeth Darcy and Jane Bingley? And what of Georgiana Darcy and Nathaniel Hewitt, and the subsequent events of their courtship?

So, faithful readers, some small titbit more I offer to you. On a glorious morning in May, very near in fact to the birth date of Fitzwilliam Darcy, his wife Elizabeth delivered to him a child. Her confinement was a difficult one, but both mother and infant remained strong and healthy, and Darcy once being admitted to see them, did not leave them for three days but only to write hastily scrawled notes to Mrs Bennet, Georgiana, and to the Bingleys of the fine eyes his son and heir possessed. Unbeknownst to him at the time, on that same morning, Jane Bingley safely produced a daughter who at once became the concentrated pride of a doting father. But as to which child arrived first, I shall leave it to you to believe as you choose, for the descendants of those two fine families debate the point to this day. Suffice it to say that Eliza Bingley and Benedict Darcy were thrown together so often in childhood, along with their subsequent siblings, as to appear to all and sundry as sister and brother rather than mere cousins.

As for Miss Darcy and her young gentleman, the lady spent a season of wonder, being courted with zeal both by gentlemen and by the ladies of society for her favour. Although oftentimes her shy temperament neared to becoming overwhelmed at the invitations she received, for the most part she thrived under the guidance of Mrs Annesley and her cousin Fitzwilliam, as well as Mrs Chaney, Henry Wentworth and Edmund Hewitt. She delighted in the birth of her nephew, and again at the marriages of her dear companion to Mr Wentworth and of her dearer cousin Retched to his Amelia.

Mr Nathaniel Hewitt, excepting of course the two month interruption to temporarily reunite with Miss Darcy, remained in the Italian states some fourteen months before returning to take up his apprenticeship at Pemberley. Once grown accustomed to being away from his love he fell, as so many do, under the enchantments of that warm countryside; returning well broadened in his views, increased in his acquaintance, laden with purchases (to include an exquisite ring of emerald for a delicate finger), and prepared to begin the real work of securing his future.

But more than this I cannot say, dear reader, though I risk your disapprobation. For the subsequent apprenticeship, the residence under one roof of these young lovers, and the eventual resolution of their courtship — well, *that* is yet another story too long to relate with any justice in the small space remaining to this volume.

ABOUT THE AUTHOR

Tess Quinn has been a fan of English author Jane Austen since her first introduction to <u>Pride and Prejudice</u> at age thirteen. Forty years and countless readings later, she began to write stories based on Miss Austen's works, indulging in borrowing some of the author's best loved characters (and occasionally lesser loved ones) to provide new experiences, new narratives and on occasion original new 'friends' for them. The joy – and challenge – in writing these stories lies in retaining these recognizable characters that Jane Austen gave the world, while further exploring the traits and quirks that still enthral her readers two hundred years later.

Tess is at present working on her third novel-length piece after the publication of anthologies of short stories which were released in 2011 and 2013. When not writing to feed her soul, Tess gets equal pleasure from travelling wherever funds will take her; attending Regency events in costume—never lost that little-girl delight in 'dressing up'; photography—though she's running out of wall space; or relaxing in a comfy chair with a good book, her cat Smudge in her lap and a nice cup of Yorkshire Gold tea. She is a U.S. native currently residing in New York, yet her heart often can be found in other places and times, most notably Regency or Medieval England.